The Hidden Children

Robert W. Chambers

Contents

THE HIDDEN CHILDREN

BY

Robert W. Chambers

The Hidden Children by Robert W. Chambers, 1914

TO MY MOTHER Whatever merit may lie in this book is due to her wisdom, her sympathy and her teaching

AUTHOR'S PREFACE

No undue liberties with history have been attempted in this romance. Few characters in the story are purely imaginary. Doubtless the fastidious reader will distinguish these intruders at a glance, and very properly ignore them. For they, and what they never were, and what they never did, merely sugar-coat a dose disguised, and gild the solid pill of fact with tinselled fiction.

But from the flames of Poundridge town ablaze, to the rolling smoke of Catharines-town, Romance but limps along a trail hewed out for her more dainty feet by History, and measured inch by inch across the bloody archives of the nation.

The milestones that once marked that dark and dreadful trail were dead men, red and white. Today a spider-web of highways spreads over that Dark Empire of the League, enmeshing half a thousand towns now all a-buzz by day and all a-glow by night.

Empire, League, forest, are vanished; of the nations which formed the Confederacy only altered fragments now remain. But their memory and their great traditions have not perished; cities, mountains, valleys, rivers, lakes, and ponds are endowed with added beauty from the lovely names they wear--a tragic yet a charming legacy from Kanonsis and Kanonsionni, the brave and mighty people of the Long

House, and those outside its walls who helped to prop or undermine it, Huron and Algonquin.

Perhaps of all national alliances ever formed, the Great Peace, which is called the League of the Iroquois, was as noble as any. For it was a league formed solely to impose peace. Those who took up arms against the Long House were received as allies when conquered--save only the treacherous Cat Nation, or Eries, who were utterly annihilated by the knife and hatchet or by adoption and ultimate absorption in the Seneca Nation.

As for the Lenni-Lenape, when they kept faith with the League they remained undisturbed as one of the "props" of the Long House, and their role in the Confederacy was embassadorial, diplomatic and advisory--in other words, the role of the Iroquois married women. And in the Confederacy the position of women was one of importance and dignity, and they exercised a franchise which no white nation has ever yet accorded to its women.

But when the Delawares broke faith, then the lash fell and the term "women" as applied to them carried a very different meaning when spat out by Canienga lips or snarled by Senecas.

Yet, of the Lenape, certain tribes, offshoots, and clans remained impassive either to Iroquois threats or proffered friendship. They, like certain lithe, proud forest animals to whom restriction means death, were untamable. Their necks could endure no yoke, political or purely ornamental. And so they perished far from the Onondaga firelight, far from the open doors of the Long House, self-exiled, self-sufficient, irreconcilable, and foredoomed. And of these the Mohicans were the noblest.

In the four romances--of which, though written last of all, this is the third, chronologically speaking--the author is very conscious of error and shortcoming. But the theme was surely worth attempting; and if the failure to convince be only partial then is the writer grateful to the Fates, and well content to leave it to the next and better man.

BROADALBIN,

Early Spring, 1913.

NOTE

During the serial publication of "The Hidden Children" the author received the following interesting letters relating to the authorship of the patriotic verses quoted in Chapter X., These letters are published herewith for the general reader as well as for students of American history.

R. W. C.

149 WEST EIGHTY-EIGHTH STREET,

NEW YORK CITY.
MRS. HELEN DODGE KNEELAND:

DEAR MADAM: Some time ago I accidentally came across the verses written by Samuel Dodge and used by R. W. Chambers in story "Hidden Children." I wrote to him, inviting him to come and look at the original manuscript, which has come down to me from my mother, whose maiden name was Helen Dodge Cocks, a great-granddaughter of Samuel Dodge, of Poughkeepsie, the author of them.

So far Mr. Chambers has not come, but he answered my note, inclosing your note to him. I have written to him, suggesting that he insert a footnote giving the authorship of the verses, that it would gratify the descendants of Samuel Dodge, as well as be a tribute to a patriotic citizen.

These verses have been published a number of times. About three years ago by chance I read them in the December National Magazine, p. 247 (Boston), entitled "A Revolutionary Puzzle," and stating that the author was unknown. Considering it my duty to place the honor where it belonged, I wrote to the editor, giving the facts, which he courteously published in the September number, 1911, p. 876.

Should you be in New York any time, I will take pleasure in showing you the original manuscripts.

Very truly yours,

ROBERT S. MORRIS, M.D.
MR. ROBERT CHAMBERS,

New York.

DEAR SIR: I have not replied to your gracious letter, as I relied upon Dr. Morris to prove to you the authorship of the verses you used in your story of "The Hidden Children." I now inclose a letter from him, hoping that you will carry out his suggestion. Is it asking too much for you to insert a footnote in the next magazine or in the story when it comes out in book form? I think with Dr. Morris that this should be done as a "tribute to a patriotic citizen."

Trusting that you will appreciate the interest we have shown in this matter, I am

Sincerely yours,

HELEN DODGE KNEELAND.

May 21st, 1914.

Ann Arbor, Michigan.

MRS. FRANK G. KNEELAND,

727 E. University Avenue.
 THE LONG HOUSE
 "Onenh jatthondek sewarih-wisa-anongh-kwe kaya-renh-kowah!
Onenh wa-karigh-wa-kayon-ne.
Onenh ne okne joska-wayendon.
Yetsi-siwan-enyadanion ne
Sewari-wisa-anonqueh."
 "Now listen, ye who established the Great League!

Now it has become old.
Now there is nothing but wilderness.
Ye are in your graves who established it."
 "At the Wood's Edge."
 NENE KARENNA
 When the West kindles red and low,
Across the sunset's sombre glow,
The black crows fly--the black crows fly!
High pines are swaying to and fro
In evil winds that blow and blow.
The stealthy dusk draws nigh--draws nigh,
Till the sly sun at last goes down,
And shadows fall on Catharines-town.

 Oswaya swaying to and fro.
 By the Dark Empire's Western gate
Eight stately, painted Sachems wait
For Amochol--for Amochol!
Hazel and samphire consecrate
The magic blaze that burns like Hate,
While the deep witch-drums roll--and roll.
Sorceress, shake thy dark hair down!
The Red Priest comes from Catharines-town.

 Ha-ai! Karenna! Fate is Fate.
 Now let the Giants clothed in stone
Stalk from Biskoonah; while, new grown,
The Severed Heads fly high--fly high!
White-throat, White-throat, thy doom is known!
O Blazing Soul that soars alone
Like a Swift Arrow to the sky,
High winging--fling thy Wampum down,
Lest the sky fall on Catharines-town.

White-throat, White-throat, thy course is flown.

R. W. C.

CHAPTER I
THE BEDFORD ROAD

In the middle of the Bedford Road we three drew bridle. Boyd lounged in his reeking saddle, gazing at the tavern and at what remained of the tavern sign, which seemed to have been a new one, yet now dangled mournfully by one hinge, shot to splinters.

The freshly painted house itself, marred with buckshot, bore dignified witness to the violence done it. A few glazed windows still remained unbroken; the remainder had been filled with blue paper such as comes wrapped about a sugar cone, so that the misused house seemed to be watching us out of patched and battered eyes.

It was evident, too, that a fire had been wantonly set at the northeast angle of the house, where sill and siding were deeply charred from baseboard to eaves.

Nor had this same fire happened very long since, for under the eaves white-faced hornets were still hard at work repairing their partly scorched nest. And I silently pointed them out to Lieutenant Boyd.

"Also," he nodded, "I can still smell the smoky wood. The damage is fresh enough. Look at your map."

He pushed his horse straight up to the closed door, continuing to examine the dismantled sign which hung motionless, there being no wind stirring.

"This should be Hays's Tavern," he said, "unless they lied to us at Ossining. Can you make anything of the sign, Mr. Loskiel?"

"Nothing, sir. But we are on the highway to Poundridge, for behind us lies the North Castle Church road. All is drawn on my map as we see it here before us; and this should be the fine dwelling of that great villain Holmes, now used as a tavern by Benjamin Hays."

"Rap on the door," said Boyd; and our rifleman escort rode forward and drove his rifle-butt at the door, "There's a man hiding within and peering at us behind the third window," I whispered.

"I see him," said Boyd coolly.

Through the heated silence around us we could hear the hornets buzzing aloft under the smoke-stained eaves. There was no other sound in the July sunshine.

The solemn tavern stared at us out of its injured eyes, and we three men of the Northland gazed back as solemnly, sobered once more to encounter the trail of the Red Beast so freshly printed here among the pleasant Westchester hills.

And to us the silent house seemed to say: "Gentlemen, gentlemen! Look at the plight I'm in--you who come from the blackened North!" And with never a word of lip our heavy thoughts responded: "We know, old house! We know! But at least you still stand; and in the ashes of our Northland not a roof or a spire remains aloft between the dwelling of Deborah Glenn and the ford at the middle fort."

Boyd broke silence with an effort; and his voice was once more cool and careless, if a little forced:

"So it's this way hereabouts, too," he said with a shrug and a sign to me to dismount. Which I did stiffly; and our rifleman escort scrambled from his sweatty saddle and gathered all three bridles in his mighty, sunburnt fist.

"Either there is a man or a ghost within," I said again, "Whatever it is has moved."

"A man," said Boyd, "or what the inhumanity of man has left of him."

And it was true, for now there came to the door and opened it a thin fellow wearing horn spectacles, who stood silent and cringing before us. Slowly rubbing his workworn hands, he made us a landlord's bow as listless and as perfunctory as ever I have seen in any ordinary. But his welcome was spoken in a whisper.

"God have mercy on this house," said Boyd loudly. "Now, what's amiss, friend? Is there death within these honest walls, that you move about on tiptoe?"

"There is death a-plenty in Westchester, sir," said the man, in a voice as colorless as his drab smalls and faded hair. Yet what he said showed us that he had noted our dress, too, and knew us for strangers.

"Cowboys and skinners, eh?" inquired Boyd, unbuckling his belt.

"And leather-cape, too, sir."

My lieutenant laughed, showing his white teeth; laid belt, hatchet, and heavy knife on a wine-stained table, and placed his rifle against it. Then, slipping cartridge sack, bullet pouch, and powder horn from his shoulders, stood eased, yawning and stretching his fine, powerful frame.

"I take it that you see few of our corps here below," he observed indulgently.

The landlord's lack-lustre eyes rested on me for an instant, then on Boyd:

"Few, sir."

"Do you know the uniform, landlord?"

"Rifles," he said indifferently.

"Yes, but whose, man? Whose?" insisted Boyd impatiently.

The other shook his head.

"Morgan's!" exclaimed Boyd loudly. "Damnation, sir! You should know Morgan's! Sixth Company, sir; Major Parr! And a likelier regiment and a better company never wore green thrums on frock or coon-tail on cap!"

"Yes, sir," said the man vacantly.

Boyd laughed a little:

"And look that you hint as much to the idle young bucks hereabouts--say it to some of your Westchester squirrel hunters----" He laid his hand on the landlord's shoulder. "There's a good fellow," he added, with that youthful and winning smile which so often carried home with it his reckless will--where women were concerned--"we're down from Albany and we wish the Bedford folk to know it. And if the gallant fellows hereabout desire a taste of true glory--the genuine article--why, send them to me, landlord--Thomas Boyd, of Derry, Pennsylvania, lieutenant, 6th company of Morgan's--or to my comrade here, Mr. Loskiel, ensign in the same corps."

He clapped the man heartily on the shoulder and stood looking around at the stripped and dishevelled room, his handsome head a little on one side, as though in frankest admiration. And the worn and pallid landlord gazed back at him with his faded, lack-lustre eyes--eyes that we both understood, alas--eyes made dull with years of fear, made old and hopeless with unshed tears, stupid from sleepless nights, haunted with memories of all they had looked upon since His Excellency marched out of the city to the south of us, where the red rag now fluttered on fort and shipping from King's Bridge to the Hook.

Nothing more was said. Our landlord went away very quietly. An hostler, presently appearing from somewhere, passed the broken windows, and we saw our rifleman go away with him, leading the three tired horses. We were still yawning and drowsing, stretched out in our hickory chairs, and only kept awake by the flies, when our landlord returned and set before us what food he had. The fare was scanty enough, but we ate hungrily, and drank deeply of the fresh small beer which he fetched in a Liverpool jug.

When we two were alone again, Boyd whispered:

"As well let them think we're here with no other object than recruiting. And so we are, after a fashion; but neither this state nor Pennsylvania is like to fill its quota here. Where is your map, once more?"

I drew the coiled linen roll from the breast of my rifle shirt and spread it out. We studied it, heads together.

"Here lies Poundridge," nodded Boyd, placing his finger on the spot so marked. "Roads a-plenty, too. Well, it's odd, Loskiel, but in this cursed, debatable land I feel more ill at ease than I have ever felt in the Iroquois country."

"You are still thinking of our landlord's deathly face," I said. "Lord! What a very shadow of true manhood crawls about this house!"

"Aye--and I am mindful of every other face and countenance I have so far seen in this strange, debatable land. All have in them something of the same expression. And therein lies the horror of it all, Mr. Loskiel God knows we expect to see deathly faces in the North, where little children lie scalped in the ashes of our frontier-- where they even scalp the family hound that guards the cradle. But here in this sleepy, open countryside, with its gentle hills and fertile valleys, broad fields and neat stone walls, its winding roads and orchards, and every pretty farmhouse standing as though no war were in the land, all seems so peaceful, so secure, that the faces of the people sicken me. And ever I am asking myself, where lies this other hell on earth, which only faces such as these could have looked upon?"

"It is sad," I said, under my breath. "Even when a lass smiles on us it seems to start the tears in my throat."

"Sad! Yes, sir, it is. I supposed we had seen sufficient of human degradation in the North not to come here to find the same cringing expression stamped on every countenance. I'm sick of it, I tell you. Why, the British are doing worse than merely filling their prisons with us and scalping us with their savages! They are slowly but surely marking our people, body and face and mind, with the cursed imprint of slavery. They're stamping a nation's very features with the hopeless lineaments of serfdom. It is the ineradicable scars of former slavery that make the New Englander whine through his nose. We of the fighting line bear no such marks, but the peaceful people are beginning to--they who can do nothing except endure and suffer."

"It is not so everywhere," I said, "not yet, anyway."

"It is so in the North. And we have found it so since we entered the 'Neutral Ground.' Like our own people on the frontier, these Westchester folk fear everybody. You yourself know how we have found them. To every question they try to give an answer that may please; or if they despair of pleasing they answer cautiously, in order not to anger. The only sentiment left alive in them seems to be fear; all else of human passion appears to be dead. Why, Loskiel, the very power of will has deserted them; they are not civil to us, but obsequious; not obliging but subservient. They yield with apathy and very quietly what you ask, and what they apparently suppose is impossible for them to retain. If you treat them kindly they receive it coldly, not gratefully, but as though you were compensating them for evil done them by you. Their countenances and motions have lost every trace of animation. It is not serenity but apathy; every emotion, feeling, thought, passion, which is not merely instinctive has fled their minds forever. And this is the greatest crime that Britain has wrought upon us." He struck the table lightly with doubled fist, "Mr. Loskiel," he said, "I ask you--can we find recruits for our regiment in such a place as this? Damme, sir, but I think the entire land has lost its manhood."

We sat staring out into the sunshine through a bullet-shattered window.

"And all this country here seems so fair and peaceful," he murmured half to himself, "so sweet and still and kindly to me after the twilight of endless forests where men are done to death in the dusk. But hell in broad sunshine is the more horrible."

"Look closer at this country," I said. "The highways are deserted and silent, the very wagon ruts overgrown with grass. Not a scythe has swung in those hay fields; the gardens that lie in the sun are but tangles of weeds; no sheep stir on the hills, no cattle stand in these deep meadows, no wagons pass, no wayfarers. It may be that the wild birds are moulting, but save at dawn and for a few moments at sundown they seem deathly silent to me."

He had relapsed again into his moody, brooding attitude, elbows on the table, his handsome head supported by both hands. And it was not like him to be downcast. After a while he smiled.

"Egad," he said, "it is too melancholy for me here in the open; and I begin to long for the dusk of trees and for the honest scalp yell to cheer me up. One knows what to expect in county Tryon--but not here, Loskiel--not here."

"Our business here is like to be ended tomorrow," I remarked.

"Thank God for that," he said heartily, rising and buckling on his war belt. He added: "As for any recruits we have been ordered to pick up en passant, I see small chance of that accomplishment hereabout. Will you summon the landlord, Mr. Loskiel?"

I discovered the man standing at the open door, his warn hands clasped behind him, and staring stupidly at the cloudless sky. He followed me back to the taproom, and we reckoned with him. Somehow, I thought he had not expected to be paid a penny--yet he did not thank us.

"Are you not Benjamin Hays?" inquired Boyd, carelessly retying his purse.

The fellow seemed startled to hear his own name pronounced so loudly, but answered very quietly that he was.

"This house belongs to a great villain, one James Holmes, does it not?" demanded Boyd.

"Yes, sir," he whispered.

"How do you come to keep an ordinary here?"

"The town authorities required an ordinary. I took it in charge, as they desired."

"Oh! Where is this rascal, Holmes?"

"Gone below, sir, some time since."

"I have heard so. Was he not formerly Colonel of the 4th regiment?"

"Yes, sir."

"And deserted his men, eh? And they made him Lieutenant-Colonel below, did they not?"

"Yes, sir."

"Colonel--of what?" snarled Boyd in disgust.

"Of the Westchester Refugee Irregulars."

"Oh! Well, look out for him and his refugees. He'll be back here one of these days, I'm thinking."

"He has been back."

"What did he do?"

The man said listlessly: "It was like other visits. They robbed, tortured, and killed. Some they burnt with hot ashes, some they hung, cut down, and hung again when they revived. Most of the sheep, cattle, and horses were driven off. Last year thousands of bushels of fruit decayed in the orchards; the ripened grain lay rotting where wind and rain had laid it; no hay was cut, no grain milled."

"Was this done by the banditti from the lower party?"

"Yes, sir; and by the leather-caps, too. The leather-caps stood guard while the Tories plundered and killed. It is usually that way, sir. And our own renegades are as bad. We in Westchester have to entertain them all."

"But they burn no houses?"

"Not yet, sir. They have promised to do so next time."

"Are there no troops here?"

"Yes, sir."

"What troops?"

"Colonel Thomas's Regiment and Sheldon's Horse and the Minute Men."

"Well, what the devil are they about to permit this banditti to terrify and ravage a peaceful land?" demanded Boyd.

"The country is of great extent," said the man mildly. "It would require many troops to cover it. And His Excellency has very, very few."

"Yes," said Boyd, "that is true. We know how it is in the North--with hundreds of miles to guard and but a handful of men. And it must be that way." He made no effort to throw off his seriousness and nodded toward me with a forced smile. "I am twenty-two years of age," he said, "and Mr. Loskiel here is no older, and we fully expect that when we both are past forty we will still be fighting in this same old war. Meanwhile," he added laughing, "every patriot should find some lass to wed and breed the soldiers we shall require some sixteen years hence."

The man's smile was painful; he smiled because he thought we expected it; and I turned away disheartened, ashamed, burning with a fierce resentment against the fate that in three years had turned us into what we were--we Americans who had never known the lash--we who had never learned to fear a master.

Boyd said: "There is a gentleman, one Major Ebenezer Lockwood, hereabouts. Do you know him?"

"No, sir."

"What? Why, that seems strange!"

The man's face paled, and he remained silent for a few moments. Then, furtively, his eyes began for the hundredth time to note the details of our forest dress, stealing stealthily from the fringe on legging and hunting shirt to the Indian beadwork on moccasin and baldrick, devouring every detail as though to convince himself. I think our pewter buttons did it for him.

Boyd said gravely: "You seem to doubt us, Mr. Hays," and read in the man's unsteady eyes distrust of everything on earth--and little faith in God.

"I do not blame you," said I gently. "Three years of hell burn deep."

"Yes," he said, "three years. And, as you say, sir, there was fire."

He stood quietly silent for a space, then, looking timidly at me, he rolled back his sleeves, first one, then the other, to the shoulders. Then he undid the bandages.

"What is all that?" asked Boyd harshly.

"The seal of the marauders, sir."

"They burnt you? God, man, you are but one living sore! Did any white man do that to you?"

"With hot horse-shoes. It will never quite heal, they say."

I saw the lieutenant shudder. The only thing he ever feared was fire--if it could be said of him that he feared anything. And he had told me that, were he taken by the Iroquois, he had a pistol always ready to blow out his brains.

Boyd had begun to pace the room, doubling and undoubling his nervous fingers. The landlord replaced the oil-soaked rags, rolled down his sleeves again, and silently awaited our pleasure.

"Why do you hesitate to tell us where we may find Major Lockwood?" I asked gently.

For the first time the man looked me full in the face. And after a moment I saw his expression alter, as though some spark--something already half dead within him was faintly reviving.

"They have set a price on Major Lockwood's head," he said; and Boyd halted to listen--and the man looked him in the eyes for a moment.

My lieutenant carried his commission with him, though contrary to advice and practice among men engaged on such a mission as were we. It was folded in his beaded shot-pouch, and now he drew it out and displayed it.

After a silence, Hays said:

"The old Lockwood Manor House stands on the south side of the village of Poundridge. It is the headquarters and rendezvous of Sheldon's Horse. The Major is there."

"Poundridge lies to the east of Bedford?"

"Yes, sir, about five miles."

"Where is the map, Loskiel?"

Again I drew it from my hunting shirt; we examined it, and Hays pointed out the two routes.

Boyd looked up at Hays absently, and said: "Do you know Luther Kinnicut?"

This time all the colour fled the man's face, and it was some moments before the sudden, unreasoning rush of terror in that bruised mind had subsided sufficiently for him to compose his thoughts. Little by little, however, he came to himself again, dimly conscious that he trusted us--perhaps the first strangers or even neighbours whom he had trusted in years.

"Yes, sir, I know him," he said in a low voice.

"Where is he?"

"Below--on our service."

But it was Luther Kinnicut, the spy, whom we had come to interview, as well as to see Major Lockwood, and Boyd frowned thoughtfully.

I said: "The Indians hereabout are Mohican, are they not, Mr. Hays?"

"They were," he replied; and his very apathy gave the answer a sadder significance.

"Have they all gone off?" asked Boyd, misunderstanding.

"There were very few Mohicans to go. But they have gone."

"Below?"

"Oh, no, sir. They and the Stockbridge Indians, and the Siwanois are friendly to our party."

"There was a Sagamore," I said, "of the Siwanois, named Mayaro. We believe that Luther Kinnicut knows where this Sagamore is to be found. But how are we to first find Kinnicut?"

"Sir," he said, "you must ask Major Lockwood that. I know not one Indian from the next, only that the savages hereabout are said to be favourable to our party."

Clearly there was nothing more to learn from this man. So we thanked him and strapped on our accoutrements, while he went away to the barn to bring up our horses. And presently our giant rifleman appeared leading the horses, and still munching a bough-apple, scarce ripe, which he dropped into the bosom of his hunting shirt when he discovered us watching him.

Boyd laughed: "Munch away, Jack, and welcome," he said, "only mind thy manners when we sight regular troops. I'll have nobody reproaching Morgan's corps that the men lack proper respect--though many people seem to think us but a parcel of militia where officer and man herd cheek by jowl."

On mounting, he turned in his saddle and asked Hays what we had to fear on our road, if indeed we were to apprehend anything.

"There is some talk of the Legion Cavalry, sir--Major Tarleton's command."

"Anything definite?"

"No, sir--only the talk when men of our party meet. And Major Lockwood has a price on his head."

"Oh! Is that all?"

"That is all, sir."

Boyd nodded laughingly, wheeled his horse, and we rode slowly out into the Bedford Road, the mounted rifleman dogging our heels.

From every house in Bedford we knew that we were watched as we rode; and what they thought of us in our flaunting rifle dress, or what they took us to be-- enemy or friend--I cannot imagine, the uniform of our corps being strange in these parts. However, they must have known us for foresters and riflemen of one party or t'other; and, as we advanced, and there being only three of us, and on a highway, too, very near to the rendezvous of an American dragoon regiment, the good folk not only peeped out at us from between partly closed shutters, but even ventured to open their doors and stand gazing after we had ridden by.

Every pretty maid he saw seemed to comfort Boyd prodigiously, which was always the case; and as here and there a woman smiled faintly at him the last vestige of sober humour left him and he was more like the reckless, handsome young man I had come to care for a great deal, if not wholly to esteem.

The difference in rank between us permitted him to relax if he chose; and though His Excellency and our good Baron were ever dinning discipline and careful respect for rank into the army's republican ears, there was among us nothing like the aristocratic and rigid sentiment which ruled the corps of officers in the British service.

Still, we were not as silly and ignorant as we were at Bunker Hill, having learned something of authority and respect in these three years, and how necessary to discipline was a proper maintenance of rank. For once--though it seems incredible--men and officers were practically on a footing of ignorant familiarity; and I have heard, and fully believe, that the majority of our reverses and misfortunes arose because no officer represented authority, nor knew how to enforce discipline because lacking that military respect upon which all real discipline must be founded.

Of all the officers in my corps and in my company, perhaps Lieutenant Boyd was slowest to learn the lesson and most prone to relax, not toward the rank and file--yet, he was often a shade too easy there, also--but with other officers. Those ranking him were not always pleased; those whom he ranked felt vaguely the mistake.

As for me, I liked him greatly; yet, somehow, never could bring myself to a careless comradeship, even in the woods or on lonely scouts where formality and circumstance seemed out of place, even absurd. He was so much of a boy, too--handsome, active, perfectly fearless, and almost always gay--that if at times he seemed a little selfish or ruthless in his pleasures, not sufficiently mindful of others or of consequences, I found it easy to forgive and overlook. Yet, fond as I was of him, I never had become familiar with him--why, I do not know. Perhaps because he ranked me; and perhaps there was no particular reason for that instinct of aloofness which I think was part of me at that age, and, except in a single instance, still remains as the slightest and almost impalpable barrier to a perfect familiarity with any person in the world.

"Loskiel," he said in my ear, "did you see that little maid in the orchard, how shyly she smiled on us?"

"On you," I nodded, laughing.

"Oh, you always say that," he retorted.

And I always did say that, and it always pleased him.

"On this accursed journey south," he complained, "the necessity for speed has spoiled our chances for any roadside sweethearts. Lord! But it's been a long, dull trail," he added frankly. "Why, look you, Loskiel, even in the wilderness somehow I always have contrived to discover a sweetheart of some sort or other--yes, even in the Iroquois country, cleared or bush, somehow or other, sooner or later, I stumble on some pretty maid who flutters up in the very wilderness like a partridge from under my feet!"

"That is your reputation," I remarked.

"Oh, damme, no!" he protested. "Don't say it is my reputation!"

But he had that reputation, whether he realised it or not; though as far as I had seen there was no real harm in the man--only a willingness to make love to any petticoat, if its wearer were pretty. But my own notions had ever inclined me toward quality. Which is not strange, I myself being of unknown parentage and birth, high or low, nobody knew; nor had anybody ever told me how I came by my strange name, Euan Loskiel, save that they found the same stitched in silk upon my shift.

For it is best, perhaps, that I say now how it was with me from the beginning, which, until this memoir is read, only one man knew--and one other. For I was discovered sleeping beside a stranded St. Regis canoe, where the Mohawk River washes Guy Park gardens. And my dead mother lay beside me.

He who cared for me, reared me and educated me, was no other than Guy Johnson of Guy Park. Why he did so I learned only after many days; and at the proper time and place I will tell you who I am and why he was kind to me. For his was not a warm and kindly character, nor a gentle nature, nor was he an educated man himself, nor perhaps even a gentleman, though of that landed gentry which Tryon County knew so well, and also a nephew of the great Sir William, and became his son-in-law.

I say he was not liked in Tryon County, though many feared him more than they feared young Walter Butler later; yet he was always and invariably kind to me. And when with the Butlers, and Sir John, and Colonel Claus, and the other Tories he fled to Canada, there to hatch most hellish reprisals upon the people of Tryon who had driven him forth, he wrote to me where I was at Harvard College in Cambridge to bid me farewell.

He said to me in that letter that he did not ask me to declare for the King in the struggle already beginning; he merely requested, if I could not conscientiously so declare, at least that I remain passive, and attend quietly to my studies at Cambridge until the war blew over, as it quickly must, and these insolent people were taught their lesson.

The lesson, after three years and more, was still in progress; Guy Park had fallen into the hands of the Committee of Sequestration and was already sold; Guy Johnson roamed a refugee in Canada, and I, since the first crack of a British musket, had learned how matters stood between my heart and conscience, and had carried a rifle and at times my regiment's standard ever since.

I had no home except my regiment, no friends except Guy Johnson's, and those I had made at College and in the regiment; and the former would likely now have greeted me with rifle or hatchet, whichever came easier to hand.

So to me my rifle regiment and my company had become my only home; the officers my parents; my comrades the only friends I had.

I wrote to Guy Johnson, acquainting him of my intention before I enlisted, and the letter went to him with other correspondence under a flag.

In time I had a reply from him, and he wrote as though something stronger than hatred for the cause I had embraced was forcing him to speak to me gently.

God knows it was a strange, sad letter, full of bitterness under which smouldered something more terrible, which, as he wrote, he strangled. And so he ended, saying that, through him, no harm should ever menace me; and that in the fullness of time, when this vile rebellion had been ended, he would vouch for the mercy of His Most Christian Majesty as far as I was concerned, even though all others hung in chains.

Thus I had left it all--not then knowing who I was or why Guy Johnson had been kind to me; nor ever expecting to hear from him again.

Thinking of these things as I rode beside Lieutenant Boyd through the calm Westchester sunshine, all that part of my life--which indeed was all of my life except these last three battle years--seemed already so far sway, so dim and unreal, that I could scarce realise I had not been always in the army--had not always lived from day to day, from hour to hour, not knowing one night where I should pillow my head the next.

For at nineteen I shouldered my rifle; and now, at Boyd's age, two and twenty, my shoulder had become so accustomed to its not unpleasant weight that, at moments, thinking, I realised that I would not know what to do in the world had I not my officers, my company, and my rifle to companion me through life.

And herein lies the real danger of all armies and of all soldiering. Only the strong character and exceptional man is ever fitted for any other life after the army becomes a closed career to him.

I now remarked as much to Boyd, who frowned, seeming to consider the matter for the first time.

"Aye," he nodded, "it's true enough, Loskiel. And I for one don't know what use I could make of the blessings of peace for which we are so madly fighting, and which we all protest that we desire."

"The blessings of peace might permit you more leisure with the ladies," I suggested smilingly. And he threw back his handsome head and laughed.

"Lord!" he exclaimed. "What chance have I, a poor rifleman, who may not even wear his hair clubbed and powdered."

Only field and staff now powdered in our corps. I said: "Heaven hasten your advancement, sir."

"Not that I'd care a fig," he protested, "if I had your yellow, curly head, you rogue. But with my dark hair unpowdered and uncurled, and no side locks, I tell you, Loskiel, I earn every kiss that is given me--or forgiven. Heigho! Peace would truly be a blessing if she brought powder and pretty clothing to a crop-head, buckskinned devil like me."

We were now riding through a country which had become uneven and somewhat higher. A vast wooded hill lay on our left; the Bedford highway skirted it. On our right ran a stream, and there was some swampy land which followed. Rock outcrops became more frequent, and the hard-wood growth of oak, hickory and chestnut seemed heavier and more extensive than in Bedford town. But there were orchards; the soil seemed to be fertile and the farms thrifty, and it was a pleasant land save for the ominous stillness over all and the grass-grown highway. Roads and lanes, paths and pastures remained utterly deserted of man and beast.

This, if our map misled us not, should be the edges of the town of Poundridge; and within a mile or so more we began to see a house here and there. These farms became more frequent as we advanced. After a few moments' riding we saw the first cattle that we had seen in many days. And now we began to find this part of the Westchester country very different, as we drew nearer to the village, for here and there we saw sheep feeding in the distance, and men mowing who leaned on their scythes to see us pass, and even saluted us from afar.

It seemed as though a sense of security reigned here, though nobody failed to mark our passing or even to anticipate it from far off. But nobody appeared to be afraid of us, and we concluded that the near vicinity of Colonel Sheldon's Horse accounted for what we saw.

It was pleasant to see women spinning beside windows in which flowers bloomed, and children gazing shyly at us from behind stone walls and palings. Also, in barnyards we saw fowls, which was more than we had seen West of us--and now and again a family cat dozing on some doorstep freshly swept.

"I had forgotten there was such calm and peace in the world," said Boyd. "And the women look not unkindly on us--do you think, Loskiel?"

But I was intent on watching a parcel of white ducks leaving a little pond, all walking a-row and quacking, and wriggling their fat tails. How absurd a thing to suddenly close my throat so that I could not find my voice to answer Boyd; for ever before me grew the almost forgotten vision of Guy Park, and of our white waterfowl on the river behind the house, where I had seen them so often from my chamber window leaving the water's edge at sundown.

A mile outside the town a leather-helmeted dragoon barred our way, but we soon satisfied him.

We passed by the Northwest road, crossed the Stamford highway, and, consulting our map, turned back and entered it, riding south through the village.

Here a few village folk were abroad; half a dozen of Sheldon's dragoons lounged outside the tavern, to the rail of which their horses were tied; and we saw other men with guns, doubtless militia, though few wore any fragment of uniform, save as their hats were cocked or sprigged with green.

Nobody hailed us, not even the soldiers; there was no levity, no jest directed toward our giant rifleman, only a courteous but sober salute as we rode through Poundridge town and out along the New Canaan highway where houses soon became fewer and soldiers both afoot and ahorse more frequent.

We crossed a stream and two roads, then came into a street with many houses which ran south, then, at four corners, turned sharp to the east. And there, across a little brook, we saw a handsome manor house around which some three score cavalry horses were picketed.

Yard, lawn, stables and barns were swarming with people--dragoons of Sheldon's Regiment, men of Colonel Thomas's foot regiment, militia officers, village gentlemen whose carriages stood waiting; and some of these same carriages must have come from a distance, perhaps even from Ridgefield, to judge by the mud and dust that clotted them.

Beyond the house, on a road which I afterward learned ran toward Lewisboro, between the Three Lakes, Cross Pond, and Bouton's, a military convoy was passing, raising a prodigious cloud of dust. I could see, and faintly hear, sheep and cattle; there was a far crack of whips, a shouting of drovers and teamsters, and, through the dust, we caught the sparkle of a bayonet here and there.

Somewhere, doubtless, some half starved brigade of ours was gnawing its nails and awaiting this same convoy; and I silently prayed God to lead it safely to its destination.

"Pretty women everywhere!" whispered Boyd in my ear. "Our friend the Major seems to have a houseful. The devil take me if I leave this town tomorrow!"

As we rode into the yard and dismounted, and our rifleman took the bridles, across the crowded roadway we could see a noble house with its front doors wide open and a group of ladies and children there and many gentlemen saluting them as they entered or left the house.

"A respectable company," I heard Boyd mutter to himself, as he stood slapping the dust from hunting-shirt and leggings and smoothing the fringe. And, "Damme, Loskiel," he said, "we're like to cut a most contemptible figure among such grand folk--what with our leather breeches, and saddle-reek for the only musk we wear. Lord! But yonder stands a handsome girl--and my condition mortifies me so that I could slink off to the mews for shame and lie on straw with the hostlers."

There was, I knew, something genuine in his pretense of hurt vanity, even under the merry mask he wore; but I only laughed.

A great many people moved about, many, I could see, having arrived from the distant country; and there was a great noise of hammering, too, from a meadow below, where, a soldier told us, they were erecting barracks for Sheldon's and for other troops shortly expected.

"There is even talk of a fort for the ridge yonder," he said. "One may see the Sound from there."

We glanced up at the ridge, then gazed curiously around, and finally walked down along the stone wall to a pasture. Here, where they were building the barracks, there had been a camp; and the place was still smelling stale enough. Tents were now being loaded on ox wagons; and a company of Colonel Thomas's regiment was filing out along the road after the convoy which we had seen moving through the dust toward Lewisboro.

People stood about looking on; some poked at the embers of the smoky fires, some moused and prowled about to see what scrap they might pick up.

Boyd's roving gaze had been arrested by a little scene enacting just around the corner of the partly-erected barracks, where half a dozen soldiers had gathered around some camp-women, whose sullen attitude discouraged their gallantries. She was dressed in shabby finery. On her hair, which was powdered, she wore a jaunty chip hat tied under her chin with soiled blue ribbons, and a kerchief of ragged lace hid her bosom, pinned with a withered rose. The scene was sordid enough; and, indifferent, I gazed elsewhere.

"A shilling to a penny they kiss her yet!" he said to me presently, and for the second time I noticed the comedy--if you choose to call it so--for the wench was now struggling fiercely amid the laughing men.

"A pound to a penny!" repeated Boyd; "Do you take me, Loskiel?"

The next moment I had pushed in among them, forcing the hilarious circle to open; and I heard her quick, uneven breathing as I elbowed my way to her, and turned on the men good-humoredly.

"Come, boys, be off!" I said. "Leave rough sport to the lower party. She's sobbing." I glanced at her. "Why, she's but a child, after all! Can't you see, boys? Now, off with you all in a hurry!"

There had evidently been some discipline drilled into Colonel Thomas's regiments the men seemed instantly to know me for an officer, whether by my dress or voice I know not, yet Morgan's rifle frock could be scarcely familiar to them.

A mischievous sergeant saluted me, grinning, saying it was but idle sport and no harm meant; and so, some laughing, others seeming to be ashamed, they made haste to clear out. I followed them, with a nod of reassurance to the wench, who might have been their drab for aught I knew, all camps being full of such poultry.

"Gallantly done!" exclaimed Boyd derisively, as I came slowly back to where he stood. "But had I been fortunate enough to think of intervening, egad, I believe I would have claimed what she refused the rest, Loskiel!"

"From a ruddied camp drab?" I asked scornfully.

"Her cheeks and lips are not painted. I've discovered that," he insisted, staring back at her.

"Lord!" said I. "Would you linger here making sheep's eyes at yonder ragged baggage? Come, sir, if you please."

"I tell you, I would give a half year's pay to see her washed and clothed becomingly!"

"You never will," said I impatiently, and jogged his elbow to make him move. For he was ever a prey to strange and wayward fancies which hitherto I had only smiled at. But now, somehow--perhaps because there might have been some excuse for this one--perhaps because what a man rescues he will not willingly leave to another--even such a poor young thing as this plaything of the camp--for either of these reasons, or for none at all, this ogling of her did not please me.

Most unwillingly he yielded to the steady pressure of my elbow; and we moved on, he turning his handsome head continually. After a while he laughed.

"Nevertheless," said he, "there stands the rarest essence of real beauty I have ever seen, in lady born or beggar; and I am an ass to go my way and leave it for the next who passes."

I said nothing.

He grumbled for a while below his breath, then:

"Yes, sir! Sheer beauty--by the roadside yonder--in ragged ribbons and a withered rose. Only--such Puritans as you perceive it not."

After a silence, and as we entered the gateway to the manor house:

"I swear she wore no paint, Loskiel--whatever she is like enough to be."

"Good heavens!" said I. "Are you brooding on her still?"

Yet, I myself was thinking of her, too; and because of it a strange, slow anger was possessing me.

"Thank God," thought I to myself, "no woman of the common class could win a second glance from me. In which," I added with satisfaction, "I am unlike most other men."

A Philistine thought the same, one day--if I remember right.

CHAPTER II
POUNDRIDGE

We now approached the door of the manor house, where we named ourselves to the sentry, who presently fetched an officer of Minute Men, who looked us over somewhat coldly.

"You wish to see Major Lockwood?" he asked.

"Yes," said Boyd, "and you may say to him that we are come from headquarters express to speak with him on private business."

"From whom in Albany do you come, sir?"

"Well, sir, if you must have it, from General Clinton," returned Boyd in a lower voice. "But we would not wish it gossipped aloud."

The man seemed to be perplexed, but he went away again, leaving us standing in the crowded hall where officers, ladies of the family, and black servants were continually passing and repassing.

Very soon a door opened on our left, and we caught a glimpse of a handsome room full of officers and civilians, where maps were scattered in confusion over tables, chairs, and even on the floor. An officer in buff and blue came out of the room, glanced keenly at us, made a slight though courteous inclination, but instead of coming forward to greet us turned into another room on the right, which was a parlour.

Then the minute officer returned, directed us where to place our rifles, insisted firmly that we also leave under his care our war axes and the pistol which Boyd carried, and then ushered us into the parlour. And it occurred to me that the gentleman on whose head the British had set a price was very considerably inclined toward prudence.

Now this same gentleman, Major Lockwood, who had been seated behind a table when we entered the parlour, rose and received us most blandly, although I noted that he kept the table between himself and us, and also that the table drawer was open, where I could have sworn that the papers so carelessly heaped about covered a brace of pistols.

For to this sorry pass the Westchester folk had come, that they trusted no stranger, nor were like to for many a weary day to come. Nor could I blame this gentleman with a heavy price on his head, and, as I heard later, already the object of numerous and violent attempts in which, at times, entire regiments had been employed to take him.

But after he had carefully read the letter which Boyd bore from our General of Brigade, he asked us to be seated, and shut the table drawer, and came over to the silk-covered sofa on which we had seated ourselves.

"Do you know the contents of this letter?" he asked Boyd bluntly.

"Yes, Major Lockwood."

"And does Mr. Loskiel know, also?"

"Yes, sir," I answered.

The Major sat musing, turning over and over the letter between thumb and forefinger.

He was a man, I should say, of forty or a trifle more, with brown eyes which sometimes twinkled as though secretly amused, even when his face was gravest and most composed; a gentleman of middle height, of good figure and straight, and of manners so simple that the charm of them struck one afterward as a pleasant memory.

"Gentlemen," he said, looking up at us from his momentary abstraction, "for the first part of General Clinton's letter I must be brief with you and very frank. There are no recruits to be had in this vicinity for Colonel Morgan's Rifles. Riflemen are of the elite; and our best characters and best shots are all enlisted--or dead or in prison----" He made a significant gesture toward the south. And we thought of the Prison Ships and the Provost, and sat silent.

"There is," he added, "but one way, and that is to pick riflemen from our regiments here; and I am not sure that the law permits it in the infantry. It would be our loss, if we lose our best shots to your distinguished corps; but of course that is not to be considered if the interests of the land demand it. However, if I am not mistaken, a recruiting party is to follow you."

"Yes, Major."

"Then, sir, you may report accordingly. And now for the other matters. General Clinton, in this letter, recommends that we speak very freely together. So I will be quite frank, gentlemen. The man you seek, Luther Kinnicut, is a spy whom our Committee of Safety maintains within the lines of the lower party. If it be necessary I can communicate with him, but it may take a week. Might I ask why you desire to question him so particularly?"

Boyd said: "There is a Siwanois Indian, one Mayaro, a Sagamore, with whom we have need to speak. General Clinton believes that this man Kinnicut knows his whereabouts."

"I believe so, too," said the Major smiling. "But I ask your pardon, gentlemen; the Sagamore, Mayaro, although a Siwanois, was adopted by the Mohicans, and should be rated one."

"Do you know him, sir?"

"Very well indeed. May I inquire what it is you desire of Mayaro?"

"This," said Boyd slowly; "and this is the real secret with which I am charged--a secret not to be entrusted to paper--a secret which you, sir, and even my comrade, Mr. Loskiel, now learn for the first time. May I speak with safety in this room, Major?"

The Major rose, opened the door into the hall, dismissed the sentry, closed and locked the door, and returned to us.

"I am," he said smiling, "almost ashamed to make so much circumstance over a small matter of which you have doubtless heard. I mean that the lower party has seen fit to distinguish me by placing a price upon my very humble head; and as I am not only Major in Colonel Thomas's regiment, but also a magistrate, and also, with my friend Lewis Morris, a member of the Provincial Assembly, and of the Committee of Safety, I could not humour the lower party by permitting them to capture so many important persons in one net," he added, laughing. "Now, sir, pray proceed. I am honoured by General Clinton's confidence."

"Then, sir," said Boyd very gravely, "this is the present matter as it stands. His Excellency has decided on a daring stroke to be delivered immediately; General Sullivan has been selected to deal it, General Clinton is to assist. A powerful army is gathering at Albany, and another at Easton and Tioga. The enemy know well enough that we are concentrating, and they have guessed where the blow is to be struck. But, sir, they have guessed wrong!"

"Not Canada, then?" inquired the Major quietly.

"No, sir. We demonstrate northward; that is all. Then we wheel west by south and plunge straight into the wilderness, swift as an arrow files, directly at the heart of the Long House!"

"Sir!" he exclaimed, astonished.

"Straight at the heart o! the Iroquois Confederacy, Major! That is what is to be done--clean out, scour out, crush, annihilate those hell-born nations which have so long been terrorizing the Northland. Major Lockwood, you have read in the New England and Pennsylvania papers how we have been threatened, how we have been struck, how we have fought and suffered. But you, sir, have only heard; you have not seen. So I must tell you now that it is far worse with us than we have admitted. The frontier of New York State is already in ashes; the scalp yell rings in our forests day and night; and the red destructives under Brant, and the painted Tories under Walter Butler, spare neither age nor sex--for I myself have seen scalps taken from the tender heads of cradled infants--nay, I have seen them scalp the very hound on guard at the cabin door! And that is how it goes with us, sir. God save you, here, from the blue-eyed Indians!"

He stopped, hesitated, then, softly smiting one fist within the other:

"But now I think their doom is sounding--Seneca, lying Cayuga, traitorous On-ondaga, Mohawk, painted renegade--all are to go down into utter annihilation. Nor is that all. We mean to sweep their empire from end to end, burn every town, every castle, every orchard, every grain field--lay waste, blacken, ravage, leave nothing save wind-blown ashes of that great Confederacy, and of the vast granary which has fed the British northern armies so long. Nothing must remain of the Long House; the Senecas shall die at the Western door; the Keepers of the Eastern door shall die. Only the Oneida may be spared--as many as have remained neutral or loyal to us--they and such of the Tuscaroras and Lenni-Lenape as have not struck us; and the

Stockbridge and White Plains tribes, and the remnants of the Mohicans.

"And that is why we have come here for riflemen, and that is why we are here to find the Sagamore, Mayaro. For our Oneidas have told us that he knows where the castles of the Long House lie, and that he can guide our army unerringly to that dark, obscure and fearsome Catharines-town where the hag, Montour, reigns in her shaggy wilderness."

There was a long silence; and I for one, amazed at what I had heard--for I had made certain that we were to have struck at Canada--was striving to reconcile this astounding news with all my preconceived ideas. Yet, that is ever the way with us in the regiments; we march, not knowing whither; we camp at night not knowing why. Unseen authority moves us, halts us; unseen powers watch us, waking and sleeping, think for us, direct our rising and our lying down, our going forth and our return--nay, the invisible empire envelops us utterly in sickness and in health, ruling when and how much we eat and sleep, controlling every hour and prescribing our occupation for every minute. Only our thoughts remain free; and these, as we are not dumb, unthinking beasts, must rove afield to seek for the why and wherefore, garnering conclusions which seldom if ever are corroborated.

So I; for I had for months now made sure that our two armies in the North were to be flung pell mell on Quebec and on Niagara. Only regarding the latter place had I nearly hit the mark; for it seemed reasonable that our army, having once swept the Long House, could scarcely halt ere we had cleaned out that rat's nest of Indians and painted Tories which is known as Fort Niagara, and from which every dreadful raid of the destructives into Tryon County had been planned and executed.

Thinking of these things, my deep abstraction was broken by the pleasant voice of Major Lockwood.

"Mr. Boyd," he said, "I realise now how great is your need of riflemen to fill the State's quota. If there is anything I or my associates can do, under the law, it shall be done; and when we are able to concentrate, and when your recruiting party arrives, I will do what I can, if permitted, to select from the dragoons of Sheldon and Moylan, and from my own regiment such men as may, by marksmanship and character, qualify for the corps d'elite."

He rose and began to pace the handsome parlour, evidently worried and perplexed; and presently he halted before us, who had of course risen in respect.

"Gentlemen," he said, "I must lay bare to you our military necessity, embarrassment, and mortification in this country of Westchester, so that you may clearly understand the difficulty of furnishing the recruits you ask for.

"South of us, from New York to North Castle, our enemy is in possession. We are attempting to hold this line; but it is a vast country. We can count on very few Continental troops; our militia has its various rendezvous, and it turns out at every call. The few companies of my regiment of foot are widely scattered; one company left here as escort to the military train an hour ago. Sheldon's 2nd Light Dragoons are scattered all over the country. Two troops and headquarters remain now here at my house."

He waved his hand westward: "So desperate is our condition, gentlemen, that Colonel Moylan's Dragoons have been ordered here, and are at this moment, I suppose, on the march to join us. And--I ask you, gentlemen--considering that in New York City, just below us, there are ten thousand British regulars, not counting the partizan corps, the irregulars, the Tory militia, the numberless companies of marauders--I ask you how you can expect to draw recruits from the handful of men who have been holding--or striving to hold--this line for the last three years!"

Boyd shook his head in silence. As for me, it was not my place to speak, nor had I anything to suggest.

After a moment the Major said, more cheerfully:

"Well, well, gentlemen, who knows after all? We may find ways and means. And now, one other matter remains to be settled, and I think I may aid you."

He went to the door and opened it. The sentry who stood across the hall came to him instantly and took his orders; and in a few moments there entered the room four gentlemen to whom we were made known by Major Lockwood. One of these was our Captain of Minute Men. They were, in order, Colonel Sheldon, a fretful gentleman with a face which seemed to me weak, almost stupid; Colonel Thomas, an iron-grey, silent officer, stern but civil; Captain William Fancher, a Justice of the Peace, Judge of the Court of Common Pleas, and holding his commission as Captain of Minute Men; and a Mr. Alsop Hunt, a Quaker, son-in-law of Major Lockwood, and a most quiet and courteous gentleman.

With one accord we drew chairs around the handsome centre table, where silver candlesticks glimmered and a few books lay in their fine, gilded bindings.

It was very evident to us that in the hands of these five gentlemen lay the present safety of Westchester County, military and civil. And to them Major Lockwood made known our needs--not, however, disturbing them in their preconceived notion, so common everywhere, that the blow to be struck from the North was to be aimed at the Canadas.

Colonel Sheldon's weak features turned red and he said almost peevishly that no recruits could be picked up in Westchester, and that we had had our journey for our pains. Anyway, he'd be damned if he'd permit recruiting for riflemen among his dragoons, it being contrary to law and common sense.

"I've a dozen young fellows who might qualify," said Colonel Thomas bluntly, "but if the law permits Mr. Boyd to take them my regiment's volleys wouldn't stop a charge of chipmunks!"

We all laughed a little, and Captain Fancher said:

"Minute Men are Minute Men, Mr. Boyd. You are welcome to any you can enlist from my company."

Alsop Hunt, being a Quaker, and personally opposed to physical violence, offered no suggestion until the second object of our visit was made known. Then he said, very quietly:

"Mayaro, the Mohican Sagamore, is in this vicinity."

"How do you know that, Alsop?" asked Major Lockwood quickly.

"I saw him yesterday."

"Here in Poundridge?"

Mr. Hunt glanced at Colonel Thomas, then with a slight colour mounting to his temples:

"The Sagamore was talking to one of the camp-women last evening--toward sundown on the Rock Hills. We were walking abroad for the air, my wife and I----" he turned to Major Lockwood: "Betsy whispered to me, 'There is a handsome wench talking to an Indian!' And I saw the Sagamore standing in the sunset light, conversing with one of the camp-women who hang about Colonel Thomas's regiment.".

"Would you know the slattern again?" asked Colonel Thomas, scowling.

"I think so, Colonel. And to tell the truth she was scarce a slattern, whatever else she may be--a young thing--and it seemed sad to us--to my wife and me."

"And handsome?" inquired Boyd, smiling at me.

"I may not deny it, sir," said Mr. Hunt primly. "The child possessed considerable comeliness."

"Why," said Boyd to me, laughingly, "she may be the wench you so gallantly rescued an hour since." And he told the story gayly enough, and with no harm meant; but it embarrassed and annoyed me.

"If the wench knows where the Sagamore may be found," said Major Lockwood, "it might be well for Mr. Loskiel to look about and try to find her."

"Would you know her again?" inquired Colonel Thomas.

"No, sir, I----" And I stopped short, because what I was about to say was not true. For, when I had sent the soldiers about their business and had rejoined Boyd-- and when Boyd had bidden me turn again because the girl was handsome, there had been no need to turn. I had seen her; and I knew that when he said she was beautiful he said what was true. And the reason I did not turn, to look again was because beauty in such a woman should inspire no interest in me.

I now corrected myself, saying coolly enough:

"Yes, Colonel Thomas, on second thought I think I might know her if I see her."

"Perhaps," suggested Captain Fancher, "the wench has gone a-gypsying after the convoy."

"These drabs change lovers over night," observed Colonel Thomas grimly. "Doubtless Sheldon's troopers are already consoling her."

Colonel Sheldon, who had been fiddling uneasily with his sword-knot, exclaimed peevishly:

"Good God, sir! Am I also to play chaplain to my command?"

There was a curious look in Colonel Thomas's eyes which seemed to say: "You might play it as well as you play the Colonel;" but Sheldon was too stupid and too vain, I think, to perceive any affront.

And, "Where do you lodge, gentlemen?" inquired our Major, addressing us both; and when he learned that we were roofless he insisted that we remain under his roof, nor would he hear of any excuses touching the present unsuitability of our condition and attire.

"Gentlemen, gentlemen! I will not accept a refusal," he said. "We are plain folk and live plainly, and both bed and board are at your disposal. Lord, sir! And what would Clinton think were I to send two officers of his corps d'elite to a village ordinary!"

We had all risen and were moving toward the door. A black servant came when the Major pulled the bell card, and showed Boyd and myself to two pretty chambers, small, but very neat, where the linen on the beds smelled fresh and sweet, and the westering sun struck golden through chintz curtains drawn aside.

"Gad!" said Boyd, eying the bed. "It's long since my person has been intimately acquainted with sheet and pillow. What a pretty nest, Loskiel. Lord! And here's a vase of posies, too! The touch feminine--who could mistake it in the sweet, fresh whiteness of this little roam!"

Presently came our rifleman, Jack Mount, bearing our saddle-bags; and we stripped and washed us clean, and put on fresh linen and our best uniforms of soft doeskin, which differed from the others only in that they were clean and new, and that the thrums were gayer and the Iroquois beadwork more flamboyant.

"If I but had my hair in a snug club, and well powdered," sighed Boyd, lacing his shirt. "And I tell you, Loskiel, though I would not boast, this accursed rifle-shirt and these gaudy leggings conceal a supple body and a leg as neatly turned as any figure more fortunately clothed in silken coat and stockings!"

I began to laugh, and he laughed, too, vowing he envied me my hair, which was yellow and which curled of itself so that it needed no powder.

I can see him yet, standing there in the sunshine, both hands gripping his dark hair in pretense of grief, and vowing that he had a mind to scalp himself for very vexation. Alas! That I remember now such idle words, spoken in the pride and strength and gayety of youth! And always when I think of him I remember his dread of fire--the only fear he ever knew. These things--his brown eyes and quick, gay smile--his lithe and supple person--and his love of women--these I remember always, even while already much that concerned this man and me begins to fade with the stealthy years.

While the sun still hung high in the west, and ere any hint of evening was heard either in the robin's note or from the high-soaring martins, we had dressed. Boyd went away first, saying carelessly that he meant to look to the horses before paying his respects to the ladies. A little later I descended, a black servant conducting me to the family sitting room.

Here our gallant Major made me known to his lady and to his numerous family--six young children, and still a seventh, the pretty maid whom we had seen on approaching the house, who proved to be a married daughter. Betsy, they called her--and she was only seventeen, but had been two years the wife of Alsop Hunt.

As for the Major's lady, who seemed scarce thirty and was six years older, she so charmed me with her grace, and with the bright courage she so sweetly maintained in a home which every hour of the day and night menaced, that even Mrs. Hunt, with her gay spirits, imperious beauty, and more youthful attractions, no more than shared my admiration for her mother.

In half an hour Lieutenant Boyd came in, was presented, and paid his homage gayly, as he always did. Yet, I thought a slight cloud rested on his brow, but this soon passed, and I forgot it.

So we talked of this and that as lightly as though no danger threatened this house; and Boyd was quickly at his best with the ladies. As for me, I courted the children. And I remember there were two little maids of fourteen and eleven, Ruhannah and Hannah, sweet and fresh as wild June roses, who showed me the tow cloth for our army which they were spinning, and blushed at my praise of their industry. And there was Mary, ten, and Clarissa, eight, and two little boys, one a baby--all save the last two children carding or spinning flax and tow.

It was not easy to understand that this blooming matron could be mother of all of these, so youthful she seemed in her Quaker-cut gown of dove-colour--though it was her handsome, high-spirited daughter who should have worn the sober garb.

"Not I," said she, laughing at Boyd. "I'd sooner don jack-boots and be a dragoon--and we would completely represent a holy cause, my husband with his broad-brim and I with my sword. What do you say, Mr. Boyd?"

"I beg of you first to consider the rifle-frock if you must enlist!" urged Boyd, with such fervour that we all laughed at his gallant effort to recruit such beauty for our corps; for even a mental picture of Betsy Hunt in rifle-frock seemed too adorable. Mr. Hunt, entering, smiled in his quiet, embarrassed way; and I thought that this wise and gentle-mannered man must have more than a handful in his spirited young wife, whose dress was anything but plain.

I had taken the tiny maid, Clarissa, upon my knees and was telling her of the beauty of our Northland, and of that great, dusky green ocean of giant pines, vast as the sea and as silent and uncharted, when Major Lockwood bent over me saying in a quiet voice that it might be well for me to look about in the town for the wench who knew the whereabouts of Mayaro.

"While there is still daylight," he added, as I set Clarissa on the floor and stood up, "and if she be yet here you should find her before supper time. We sup at six, Mr. Loskiel."

I bowed, took leave of the ladies, exchanged an irritated glance for Boyd's significant grin, and went out to the porch, putting on my light round cap of moleskin. I liked neither my present errand, nor Boyd's smile either.

Now, I had not thought to take with me my side-arms, but a slave waited at the door with my belt. And as I buckled it and hung war-axe and heavy hunting blade, I began to comprehend something of the imminent danger which so apparently lurked about this country. For all military men hereabouts went armed; and even in the house I had noticed that Major Lockwood wore his sword, as did the other officers--some even carrying their pistols.

The considerable throng of people whom we had first seen in the neighborhood of the house had scattered or gone off when the infantry had left. Carpenters were still sawing and hammering on the flimsy new barracks down in the meadow, and there seemed to be a few people there. But on strolling thither I saw nothing of the wench; so turned on my heel and walked briskly up the road.

About the village itself there was nothing to be seen of the girl, nor did I know how to make inquiries--perhaps dreading to do so lest my quest be misunderstood or made a jest of by some impertinent fellow.

In the west a wide bank of cloud had pushed up over the horizon and was already halving the low-hanging sun, which presently it entirely swallowed; and the countryside grew luminously grey and that intense green tinged the grass, which is with us the forerunner of an approaching storm.

But I thought it far off, not then knowing the Hudson's midsummer habits, nor the rapid violence of the July storms it hatches and drives roaring among the eastern hills and across the silvery Sound.

So, with a careless glance aloft, I pursued my errand, strolling hither and thither through the pleasant streets and lanes of old Poundridge, always approaching any groups of soldiers that I saw because I thought it likely that the wench might haunt her kind.

I did not find her; and presently I began to believe it likely that she had indeed gone off a-gypsying after the escort companies toward Lewisboro.

There is a road which, skirting the Stone Hills, runs east by north between Cross Pond and the Three Lakes; and, pursuing it, I came on a vidette of Sheldon's regiment, most carelessly set where he could see nothing, and yet be seen a mile away.

Supposing he would halt me, I walked up to him; and he continued to munch the green bough-apple he was eating, making me a most slovenly salute.

Under his leather helmet I saw that my dragoon was but a child of fifteen--scarce strong enough to swing the heavy sabre at his pommel or manage the sawed-off musket which he bore, the butt resting wearily on his thigh. And it made me sober indeed to see to what a pass our country had come, that we enlisted boys and were obliged to trust to their ignorance for our protection.

"It will rain before sundown," he said, munching on his apple; "best seek shelter, sir. When it comes it will come hard."

"Where runs this road?" I asked.

"To Boutonville."

"And what is Boutonville?"

"It's where the Boutons live--a mile or two north, sir. They're a wild parcel."

"Are they of our party?"

"Oh, yes, sir. But they hunt the leather-caps as we hunt quail--scare up a company, fire, and then track down the scattered."

"Oh; irregulars."

"No, sir, not skinners. They farm it until the British plague them beyond endurance. Then," he added significantly, "they go a-hunting with their dogs."

I had already turned to retrace my steps when it occurred to me that perhaps an inquiry of this lad might not be misunderstood.

So I walked up to his horse and stood caressing the sorry animal while I described to him the wench I was seeking.

"Yes, sir," he said seriously, "that's the one the boys are ever plaguing to make her rage."

"Do you know her?"

"By sight, yes, sir."

"She is one of the camp followers, I take it," said I carelessly.

"I don't know. The boys are ever plaguing her. She came from the North they say. All I know is that in April she was first seen here, loitering about the camp where the White Plains Indians were embodied. But she did not go off with the Continentals."

"She was loitering this afternoon by the camp of Colonel Thomas's men," I said.

"Very like, sir. Did the men plague her?"

"Yes."

He bit into his apple, unconcerned:

"They are all after her. But I never saw her kind to any man--whatever she may be."

Why, I did not know, but what he said gave me satisfaction.

"You do not know which way she went?" I asked.

"No, sir. I have been here but the half hour. She knows the Bouton boys yonder. I have seen her coming and going on this road, sometimes with an Indian----"

"With a Sagamore?"

He continued his munching. Having swallowed what he chewed, he said:

"I know nothing of savages or Sagamores. The Indian may have been a Sagamore."

"Do you know where he is to be found?"

"No, sir, I do not."

"Perhaps this young girl knows?"

"Doubtless she does, seeing she journeys about with him on the ridge yonder, which we call the Rock Hills."

"Do you know her name, soldier?"

"They call her Lois, I believe."

And that was all the news I could get of her; and I thanked the boy and slowly started to retrace my steps toward the village.

Already in the air there was something of that stillness which heralds storms; no leaves on bush and tree were now stirring; land and sky had grown sombre all around me; and the grass glimmered intensely green.

Where the road skirted the Stone Hills were no houses, nothing, in fact, of human habitation to be seen save low on the flank of the rocky rampart a ruined sugar house on the edge of a maple ridge, I do not know what made me raise my head to give it a second glance, but I did; and saw among the rocks near it a woman moving.

Nor do I know, even now, how at that distance and in the dusk of a coming storm I could perceive that it was she whom I was now seeking. But so certain was I of this that, without even taking thought to consider, I left the highway, turned to the right, and began to mount the hillside where traces of a path or sheep-walk were faintly visible under foot among the brambles. Once or twice I glanced upward to see whether she observed me, but the scrubby foliage now hid her as well as the sap-house, and I hastened because the light was growing very dim now, and once or twice, far away, I thought I heard the muttering of thunder.

It was not long before I perceived the ramshackle sap-house ahead of me among the maples. Then I caught sight of her whom I was seeking.

It was plain that she had not yet discovered me, though she heard me moving in the thicket. She stood in a half-crouching, listening attitude, then slowly began to retreat, not cowering, but sullenly and with a certain defiance in her lithe movement, like some disturbed and graceful animal which is capable of defending itself but prefers to get away peaceably if permitted.

I stepped out into the clearing and called to her through the increasing gloom; and for a moment thought she had gone. Then I saw her, dimly, watching me from the obscurity of the dark doorway.

"You need have no fear of me," I called to her pleasantly. "You know me now, do you not?"

She made no answer; and I approached the doorway and stood peering into her face through the falling twilight. And for a moment I thought I had been mistaken; but it was she after all.

Yet now she wore neither the shabby chip hat with its soiled blue ribbon tied beneath her chin, nor any trace of hair powder, nor dotted kerchief cross-fastened at her breast and pinned with the withered rose.

And she seemed younger and slimmer and more childish than I had thought her, her bosom without its kerchief meagre or unformed, and her cheeks not painted either, but much burned by the July sun. Nor were her eyes black, as I had supposed, but a dark, clear grey with black lashes; and her unpowdered hair seemed to be a reddish-chestnut and scarce longer than my own, but more curly.

"Child," I said, smiling at her, I know not why, "I have been searching for you ever since I first saw you----"

And: "What do you want of me?" said she, scarce moving her lips.

"A favour."

"Best mount your cobbler's mare and go a-jogging back, my pretty lad."

The calm venom in her voice and her insolent grey eyes took me aback more than her saucy words.

"Doubtless," I said, "you have not recognized in me the officer who was at some slight pains to be of service----"

"What is it you desire?" said she, so rudely that I felt my face burn hot.

"See here, my lass," said I sharply, "you seem to misunderstand my errand here."

"And am like to," said she, "unless you make your errand short and plainer--though I have learned that the errands which bring such men as you to me are not too easily misunderstood."

"Such men as I----"

"You and your friend with the bold, black eyes. Ask him how much change he had of me when he came back."

"I did not know he had seen you again," said I, still redder. And saw that she believed me not.

"Birds sing; men lie," said she. "So if----"

"Be silent! Do you hear!" I cut her short with such contempt that I saw the painful colour whip her cheeks and her eyes quiver.

Small doubt that what she had learned of men had not sweetened her nor taught her confidence. But whatever she had been, and whatever she was, after all concerned not me that I should take pains to silence her so brutally.

"I am sorry I spoke as I did," said I, "--however mistaken you are concerning my seeking you here."

She said nothing.

"Also," I added, with a sudden resurgance of bitterness that surprised myself, "my conduct earlier in your behalf might have led you to a wiser judgment."

"I am wise enough--after my own fashion," she said indifferently.

"Does a man save and then return to destroy?"

"Many a hunter has saved many a spotted fawn from wolf and fox--so he might kill it himself, one day."

"You do yourself much flattery, young woman," I said, so unpleasantly that again the hot colour touched her throat and brow.

"I reason as I have been taught," she said defiantly. "Doubtless you are self-instructed."

"No; men have taught me. You witnessed, I believe, one lesson. And your comrade gave me still another."

"I care to witness nothing," I said, furious; "far less desire to attempt your education. Is all plain now?"

"Your words are," she said, with quiet contempt.

"My words are one with my intention," said I, angrily; far in spite of my own indifference and contempt, hers was somehow arousing me with its separate sting hidden in every word she uttered. "And now," I continued, "all being plain and open between us, let me acquaint you with the sole object of my visit here to you."

She shrugged her shabby shoulders and waited, her eyes, her expression, her very attitude indifferent, yet dully watchful.

"You know the Sagamore, Mayaro?" I asked.

"You say so."

"Where is he to be found?" I continued patiently.

"Why do you desire to know?"

The drab was exasperating me, and I think I looked it, for the slightest curl of her sullen lips hinted a scornful smile.

"Come, come, my lass," said I, with all the patience I could still command, "there is a storm approaching, and I do not wish to get wet. Answer my civil question and I'll thank you and be off about my business. Where is this Sagamore to be found?"

"Why do you wish to know?"

"Because I desire to consult him concerning certain matters."

"What matters?"

"Matters which do not concern you!" I snapped out.

"Are you sure of that, pretty boy?"

"Am I sure?" I repeated, furious. "What do you mean? Will you answer an honest question or not?"

"Why do you desire to see this Sagamore?" she repeated so obstinately that I fairly clenched my teeth.

"Answer me," I said. "Or had you rather I fetched a file of men up here?"

"Fetch a regiment, and I shall tell you nothing unless I choose."

"Good God, what folly!" I exclaimed. "For whom and for what do you take me, then, that you refuse to answer the polite and harmless question of an American officer!"

"You had not so named yourself."

"Very well, then; I am Euan Loskiel, Ensign in Morgan's rifle regiment!"

"You say so."

"Do you doubt it?"

"Birds sing," she said. Suddenly she stepped from the dark doorway, came to where I stood, bent forward and looked me very earnestly in the eyes--so closely that something--her nearness--I know not what--seemed to stop my heart and breath for a second.

Then, far on the western hills lightning glimmered; and after a long while it thundered.

"Do you wish me to find this Sagamore for you?" she asked very quietly.

"Will you do so?"

A drop of rain fell; another, which struck her just where the cheek curved under the long black lashes, fringing them with brilliancy like tears.

"Where do you lodge?" she asked, after a silent scrutiny of me.

"This night I am a guest at Major Lockwood's. Tomorrow I travel north again with my comrade, Lieutenant Boyd."

She was looking steadily at me all the time; finally she said:

"Somehow, I believe you to be a friend to liberty. I know it--somehow."

"It is very likely, in this rifle dress I wear," said I smiling.

"Yet a man may dress as he pleases."

"You mistrust me for a spy?"

"If you are, why, you are but one more among many hereabouts. I think you have not been in Westchester very long. It does not matter. No boy with the face you wear was born to betray anything more important than a woman."

I turned hot and scarlet with chagrin at her cool presumption--and would not for worlds have had her see how the impudence stung and shamed me.

For a full minute she stood there watching me; then:

"I ask pardon," she said very gravely.

And somehow, when she said it I seemed to experience a sense of inferiority--which was absurd and monstrous, considering what she doubtless was.

It had now begun to rain in very earnest; and was like to rain harder ere the storm passed. My clothes being my best, I instinctively stepped into the doorway; and, of a sudden, she was there too, barring my entry, flushed and dangerous, demanding the reason of my intrusion.

"Why," said I astonished, "may I not seek shelter from a storm in a ruined sugar-house, without asking by your leave?"

"This sap-house is my own dwelling!" she said hotly. "It is where I live!"

"Oh, Lord," said I, bewildered, "--if you are like to take offense at everything I say, or look, or do, I'll find a hospitable tree somewhere----"

"One moment, sir----"

"Well?"

She stood looking at me in the doorway, then slowly dropped her eyes, and in the same law voice I had heard once before:

"I ask your pardon once again," she said. "Please to come inside--and close the door. An open door draws lightning."

It was already drawing the rain in violent gusts.

The thunder began to bang with that metallic and fizzling tone which it takes on when the bolts fall very near; flash after flash of violet light illuminated the shack at intervals, and the rafters trembled as the black shadows buried us.

"Have you a light hereabout?" I asked.

"No,"

For ten minutes or more the noise of the storm made it difficult to hear or speak. I could scarce see her now in the gloom. And so we waited there in silence until the roar of the rain began to die away, and it slowly grew lighter outside and the thunder grew more distant.

I went to the door, looked out into the dripping woods, and turned to her.

"When will you bring the Sagamore to me?" I demanded.

"I have not promised."

"But you will?"

She waited a while, then:

"Yes, I will bring him."

"When?"

"Tonight."

"You promise?"

"Yes."

"And if it rains again"

"It will rain all night, but I shall send you the Sagamore. Best go, sir. The real tempest is yet to break. It hangs yonder above the Hudson. But you have time to gain the Lockwood House."

I said to her, with a slight but reassuring smile, most kindly intended:

"Now that I am no longer misunderstood by you, I may inform you that in what you do for me you serve our common country." It did not seem a pompous speech to me.

"If I doubted that," she said, "I had rather pass the knife you wear around my throat than trouble myself to oblige you."

Her words, and the quiet, almost childish voice, seemed so oddly at variance that I almost laughed; but changed my mind.

"I should never ask a service of you for myself alone," I said so curtly that the next moment I was afraid I had angered her, and fearing she might not keep her word to me, smiled and frankly offered her my hand.

Very slowly she put forth her own--a hand stained and roughened, but slim and small. And so I went away through the dripping bush, and down the rocky hill. A slight sense of fatigue invaded me; and I did not then understand that it came from my steady and sustained efforts to ignore what any eyes could not choose but see--this young girl's beauty--yes, despite her sorry mien and her rags--a beauty that was fashioned to trouble men; and which was steadily invading my senses whether I would or no.

Walking along the road and springing over the puddles, I thought to myself that it was small wonder such a wench was pestered in a common soldier's camp. For she had about her everything to allure the grosser class--a something--indescribable perhaps--but which even such a man as I had become unwillingly aware of. And I must have been very conscious of it, for it made me restless and vaguely ashamed that I should condescend so far as even to notice it. More than that, it annoyed me not a little that I should bestow any thought upon this creature at all; but what irritated me most was that Boyd had so demeaned himself as to seek her out behind my back.

When I came to the manor house, it had already begun to rain again; and even as I entered the house, a tempest of rain and wind burst once more over the hills with a violence I had scarcely expected.

Encountering Major Lockwood and Lieutenant Boyd in the hall, I scowled at the latter askance, but remembered my manners, and smoothed my face and told them of my success.

"Rain or no," said I, "she has promised me to send this Sagamore here tonight. And I am confident she will keep her word."

"Which means," said Boyd, with an unfeigned sigh, "that we travel north tomorrow. Lord! How sick am I of saddle and nag and the open road. Your kindly hospitality, Major, has already softened me so that I scarce know how to face the wilderness again."

And at supper, that evening, Boyd frankly bemoaned his lot, and Mrs. Lockwood condoled with him; but Betsy Hunt turned up her pretty nose, declaring that young men were best off in the woods, which kept them out o' mischief. She did not know the woods.

And after supper, as she and my deceitful but handsome lieutenant lingered by the stairs, I heard her repeat it again, utterly refusing to say she was sorry or that she commiserated his desperate lot. But on her lips hovered a slight and provoking smile, and her eyes were very brilliant under her powdered hair.

All women liked Boyd; none was insensible to his charm. Handsome, gay, amusing--and tender, alas!--too often--few remained indifferent to this young man, and many there were who found him difficult to forget after he had gone his careless way. But I was damning him most heartily for the prank he played me.

I sat in the parlour talking to Mrs. Lockwood. The babies were long since in bed; the elder children now came to make their reverences to their mother and father, and so very dutifully to every guest. A fat black woman in turban and gold ear-hoops fetched them away; and the house seemed to lose a trifle of its brightness with the children's going.

Major Lockwood sat writing letters on a card-table, a cluster of tall candles at his elbow; Mr. Hunt was reading; his wife and Boyd still lingered on the stairs, and their light, quick laughter sounded prettily at moments.

Mrs. Lockwood, I remember, had been sewing while she and I conversed together. The French alliance was our topic; and she was still speaking of the pleasure it had given all when Lewis Morris brought to her house young Lafayette. Then, of a sudden, she turned her head sharply, as though listening.

Through the roar of the storm I thought I heard the gallop of a horse. Major Lockwood lifted his eyes from his letters, fixing them on the rain-washed window.

Certainly a horseman had now pulled up at our very porch; Mr. Hunt laid aside his book very deliberately and walked to the parlour door, and a moment later the noise of the metal knocker outside rang loudly through the house.

We were now all rising and moving out into the hall, as though a common instinct of coming trouble impelled us. The black servant opened; a drenched messenger stood there, blinking in the candle light.

Major Lockwood went to him instantly, and drew him in the door; and they spoke together in low and rapid tones.

Mrs. Lockwood murmured in my ear:

"It's one of Luther's men. There is bad news for us from below, I warrant you."

We heard the Major say:

"You will instantly acquaint Colonels Thomas and Sheldon with this news. Tell Captain Fancher, too, in passing."

The messenger turned away into the storm, and Major Lockwood called after him:

"Is there no news of Moylan's regiment?"

"None, sir," came the panting answer; there ensued a second's silence, a clatter of slippery hoofs, then only the loud, dull roar of the rain filled the silence.

The Major, who still stood at the door, turned around and glanced at his wife.

"What is it, dear--if we may know?" asked she, quite calmly.

"Yes," he said, "you should know, Hannah. And it may not be true, but--somehow, I think it is. Tarleton is out."

"Is he headed this way, Ebenezer?" asked Mr. Hunt, after a shocked silence.

"Why--yes, so they say. Luther Kinnicut sends the warning. It seems to be true."

"Tarleton has heard, no doubt, that Sheldon's Horse is concentrating here," said Mr. Hunt. "But I think it better for thee to leave, Ebenezer."

Mrs. Lockwood went over to her husband and laid her hand on his sleeve lightly. The act, and her expression, were heart-breaking, and not to be mistaken. She knew; and we also now surmised that if the Legion Cavalry was out, it was for the purpose of taking the man who stood there before our eyes. Doubtless he was quite aware of it, too, but made no mention of it.

"Alsop," he said, turning to his son-in-law, "best take the more damaging of the papers and conceal them as usual. I shall presently be busied with Thomas and Sheldon, and may have no time for such details."

"Will they make a stand, do you think?" I whispered to Boyd, "or shall we be sent a-packing?"

"If there be not too many of them I make a guess that Sheldon's Horse will stand."

"And what is to be our attitude?"

"Stand with them," said he, laughing, though he knew well that we had been cautioned to do our errand and keep clear of all brawls.

CHAPTER III
VIEW HALLOO!

It rained, rained, rained, and the darkness and wind combined with the uproar of the storm to make venturing abroad well nigh impossible. Yet, an orderly, riding at hazard, managed to come up with a hundred of the Continental foot, convoying the train, and, turning them in their slopping tracks, start back with them through a road running shin-high in mud and water.

Messengers, also, were dispatched to call out the district militia, and they plodded all night with their lanterns, over field and path and lonely country road.

As for Colonel Sheldon, booted, sashed, and helmeted, he sat apathetic and inert in the hall, obstinately refusing to mount his men.

"For," says he, "it will only soak their powder and their skins, and nobody but a fool would ride hither in such a storm. And Tarleton is no fool, nor am I, either; and that's flat!" It was not as flat as his own forehead.

"Do you mean that I am a fool to march my men back here from Lewisboro?" demanded Colonel Thomas sharply, making to rise from his seat by the empty fireplace.

Duels had sprung from less provocation than had been given by Colonel Sheldon. Mr. Hunt very mildly interposed; and a painful scene was narrowly averted because of Colonel Thomas's cold contempt for Sheldon, which I think Captain Fancher shared.

Major Lockwood, coming in at the moment, flung aside his dripping riding cloak.

"Sir," said he to Sheldon, "the rumour that the Legion is abroad has reached your men, and they are saddling in my barns."

"What damned nonsense!" exclaimed Sheldon, in a pet; and, rising, strode heavily to the door, but met there his Major, one Benjamin Tallmadge, coming in, all over mud.

This fiery young dragoon's plume, helmet, and cloak were dripping, and he impatiently dashed the water from feathers and folds.

"Sir!" began Colonel Sheldon loudly, "I have as yet given no order to saddle!"

And, "By God, sir," says Tallmadge, "the orders must have come from somebody, for they're doing it!"

"Sir--sir!" stammered Sheldon, "What d'ye mean by that?"

"Ah!" says Tallmadge coolly, "I mean what I say. Orders must have been given by somebody."

No doubt; for the orders came from himself, the clever trooper that he was-- and so he left Sheldon a-fuming and Major Lockwood and Mr. Hunt most earnestly persuading him to sanction this common and simple precaution.

Why he conducted so stupidly I never knew. It required all the gentle composure of Mr. Hunt and all the vigorous logic of Major Lockwood to prevent him from ordering his men to off-saddle and retire to the straw above the mangers.

Major Tallmadge and a cornet passed through the hall with their regimental standard, but Sheldon pettishly bade them to place it in the parlour and await further orders--for no reason whatever, apparently, save to exhibit a petty tyranny.

And all the while a very forest of candles remained lighted throughout the house; only the little children were asleep; the family servants and slaves remained awake, not daring to go to bed or even to close their eyes to all these rumours and uncertainties.

Colonel Thomas, his iron-grey head sunk on his breast, paced the hall, awaiting the arrival of the two escort companies of his command, yet scarcely hoping for such good fortune, I think, for his keen eyes encountered mine from time to time, and he made me gestures expressive of angry resignation.

As for Sheldon, he pouted and sulked on a sofa, and drank mulled wine, peevishly assuring everybody who cared to listen that no attack was to be apprehended in such a storm, and that Colonel Tarleton and his men now lay snug abed in New York town, a-grinning in their dreams.

A few drenched and woe-begone militia men, the pans of their muskets wrapped in rags, reported, and were taken in charge by Captain Fancher as a cattle guard for Major Lockwood's herd.

None of Major Lockwood's messengers were yet returned. Our rifleman had saddled our own horses, and had brought them up under one of a row of sheds which had recently been erected near the house. A pair of smoky lanterns hung under the dripping rafters; and by their light I perceived the fine horses of Major Lockwood, and of Colonels Sheldon and Thomas also, standing near ours, bridled and saddled and held by slaves.

Mrs. Lockwood sat near the parlour door, quietly sewing, but from time to time I saw her raise her eyes and watch her husband. Doubtless she was thinking of those forty golden guineas which were to be paid for the delivery of his head--perhaps she was thinking of Bloody Cunningham, and the Provost, and the noose that dangled in a painted pagoda betwixt the almshouse and the jail in that accursed

British city south of us.

Mrs. Hunt had far less to fear for her quiet lord and master, who combatted the lower party only with his brains. So she found more leisure to listen to Boyd's whispered fooleries, and to caution him with lifted finger, glancing at him sideways; and I saw her bite her lips at times to hide the smile, and tap her slender foot, and bend closer over her tabouret while her needle flew the faster.

As for me, my Sagamore had not arrived; and I finally cast a cloak about me and went out to the horse-sheds, where our rifleman lolled, chewing a lump of spruce and holding our three horses.

"Well, Jack," said I, "this is rare weather for Colonel Tarleton's fox hunting."

"They say he hunts an ass, sir, too," said Jack Mount under his breath. "And I think it must be so, for there be five score of Colonel Sheldon's dragoons in yonder barns, drawing at jack-straws or conning their thumbs--and not a vidette out--not so much as a militia picket, save for the minute men which Colonel Thomas and Major Lockwood have sent out afoot."

There was a certain freedom in our corps, but it never warranted such impudent presumption as this; and I sharply rebuked the huge fellow for his implied disrespect toward Colonel Sheldon.

"Very well, sir. I will bite off this unmilitary tongue o' mine and feed it to your horse. Then, sir, if you but ask him, he will tell you very plainly that none of his four-footed comrades in the barn have carried a single vidette on their backs even as far as Poundridge village, let alone Mile-Square."

I could scarcely avoid smiling.

"Do you then, for one, believe that Colonel Tarleton will venture abroad on such a night?"

"I believe as you do," said the rifleman coolly, "--being some three years or more a soldier of my country."

"Oh! And what do I believe, Jack?"

"Being an officer who commands as good a soldier as I am, you, sir, believe as I do."

I was obliged to laugh.

"Well, Jack--so you agree with me that the Legion Cavalry is out?"

"It is as sure that nested snake's eggs never hatched out rattlers as it is certain that this wild night will hatch out Tarleton!"

"And why is it so certain in your mind, Jack Mount?"

"Lord, Mr. Loskiel," he said with a lazy laugh, "you know how Mr. Boyd would conduct were he this same Major Tarleton! You know what Major Parr would do-- and what you and I and every officer and every man of Morgan's corps would do on such a night to men of Sheldon's kidney!"

"You mean the unexpected."

"Yes, sir. And this red fox on horseback, Tarleton, has ever done the same, and will continue till we stop his loping with a bit o' lead."

I nodded and looked out into the rain-swept darkness. And I knew that our videttes should long since have been set far out on every road twixt here and Bedford village.

Captain Fancher passed with a lantern, and I ventured to accost him and mention very modestly my present misgivings concerning our present situation.

"Sir," said the Captain, dryly, "I am more concerned in this matter than are you; and I have taken it upon myself to protest to Major Tallmadge, who is at this moment gone once more to Colonel Sheldon with very serious representations."

"Lieutenant Boyd and I have volunteered as a scout of three," I said, "but Colonel Sheldon has declined our services with scant politeness."

Fancher stood far a moment, his rain-smeared lantern hanging motionless at his side.

"Tarleton may not ride tonight," he said, and moved off a step or two; then, turning: "But, damn him, I think he will," said he. And walked away, swinging his light as furiously as a panther thrashes his tail.

By the pointers of my watch it now approached three o'clock in the morning, and the storm was nothing abating. I had entirely despaired of the Sagamore's coming, and was beginning to consider the sorry pickle which this alarm must leave us in if Tarleton's Legion came upon us now; and that with our widely scattered handfuls we could only pull foot and await another day to find our Sagamore; when, of a sudden there came a-creeping through the darkness, out o' the very maw of the storm, a slender shape, wrapped to the eyes in a ragged scarlet cape. I knew her; but I do not know how I knew her.

"It is you!" I exclaimed, hastening forward to draw her under shelter.

She came obediently with me, slipping in between the lanterns and among the horses, moving silently at my elbow to the farther shed, which was empty.

"You use me very kindly," I said, "to venture abroad tonight on my behalf."

"I am abroad," she said, "on behalf of my country."

Only her eyes I could see over the edge of the scarlet cloak, and they regarded me very coldly.

"I meant it so," I said hastily, "What of the Sagamore? Will he come?"

"He will come as I promised you."

"Here?" I said, delighted. "This very night?"

"Yes, here, this night."

"How good--how generous you have been!" I exclaimed with a warmth and sincerity that invaded every fibre of me. "And have you come through this wild storm all the long way afoot?"

"Yes," she said, calmly, "afoot. Since when, sir, have beggars ridden to a tryst except in pretty fables?"

"Had I known it, I would have taken horse and gone for you and brought you here riding pillion behind me."

"Had I desired you to come for me, Mr. Loskiel, I should not have troubled you here."

She loosened the shabby scarlet cloak so that it dropped from below her eyes and left the features exposed. Enough of lantern light from the other shed fell on her face for me to see her smooth, cool cheeks all dewy with the rain, as I had seen them once before in the gloom of the coming storm.

She turned her head, glancing back at the other shed where men and horses stood in grotesque shadow shapes under the windy lantern light; then she looked cautiously around the shed where we stood.

"Come nearer," she motioned.

And once again, as before, my nearness to her seemed for a moment to meddle with my heart and check it; then, as though to gain the beats they lost, every little pulse began to hurry faster.

She said in a low voice:

"The Sagamore is now closeted with Major Lockwood. I left him at the porch and came out here to warn you. Best go to him now, sir. And I will bid you a--good night."

"Has he business also with Major Lockwood?"

"He has indeed. You will learn presently that the Sagamore came by North Castle, and that the roads south of the church are full of riders--hundreds of them--in jack-boots and helmets."

"Were their jackets red?"

"He could not tell. They were too closely cloaked,"

"Colonel Moylan's dragoons?" I said anxiously. "Do you think so?"

"The Sagamore did not think so, and dared not ask, but started instantly cross-country with the information. I had been waiting to intercept him and bring him here to you, as I promised you, but missed him on the Bedford road, where he should have passed. Therefore, I hastened hither to confess to you my failure, and chanced to overtake him but a moment since, as he crossed the dooryard yonder."

Even in my growing anxiety, I was conscious of the faithfulness that this poor girl had displayed--this ragged child who had stood in the storm all night long on the Bedford road to intercept the Indian. Faithful, indeed! For, having missed him, she had made her way here on foot merely to tell me that she could not keep her word to me.

"Has the Sagamore spoken with Colonel Sheldon?" I asked gently.

"I do not know."

"Will you tarry here till I return?"

"Have you further use of me, Mr. Loskiel?"

Her direct simplicity checked me. After all, now that she had done her errand, what further use had I for her? I did not even know why I had asked her to tarry here until my return; and searched my mind seeking the reason. For it must have been that I had some good reason in my mind.

"Why, yes," I said, scarce knowing why, "I have further use for you. Tarry for a moment and I shall return. And," I added mentally, "by that time I shall have discovered the reason."

She said nothing; I hastened back to the house, where even from the outside I could hear the loud voice of Sheldon vowing that if what this Indian said were true, the cavalry he had discovered at North Castle must be Moylan's and no other.

I entered and listened a moment to Major Lockwood, urging this obstinate man to send out his patrols; then I walked over to the window where Boyd stood in whispered consultation with an Indian.

The savage towered at least six feet in his soaking moccasins; he wore neither lock nor plume, nor paint of any kind that I could see, carried neither gun nor blanket, nor even a hatchet. There was only a heavy knife at the beaded girdle, which belted his hunting shirt and breeches of muddy tow-cloth.

As I approached them, the Mohican turned his head and shot a searching glance at me. Boyd said:

"This is the great Sagamore, Mayaro, Mr. Loskiel; and I have attempted to persuade him to come north with us tomorrow. Perhaps your eloquence will succeed where my plain speech has failed." And to the tall Sagamore he said: "My brother, this is Ensign Loskiel, of Colonel Morgan's command--my comrade and good friend. What this man's lips tell you has first been taught them by his heart. Squirrels chatter, brooks babble, and the tongues of the Iroquois are split. But this is a man, Sagamore, such as are few among men. For he lies not even to women." And though his countenance was very grave, I saw his eyes laughing at me.

The Indian made no movement until I held out my hand. Then his sinewy fingers touched mine, warily at first, like the exploring antennae of a nervous butterfly. And presently his steady gaze began to disturb me.

"Does my brother the Sagamore believe he has seen me somewhere heretofore?" I asked, smilingly. "Perhaps it may have been so--at Johnson Hall--or at Guy Park, perhaps, where came many chiefs and sachems and Sagamores in the great days of the great Sir William--the days that are no more, O Sagamore!"

And: "My brother's given name?" inquired the savage bluntly.

"Euan--Euan Loskiel, once of the family of Guy Johnson, but now, for these three long battle years, officer in Colonel Morgan's regiment," I said. "Has the wise Sagamore ever seen me before this moment?"

The savage's eyes wavered, then sought the floor.

"Mayaro has forgotten," he replied very quietly, using the Delaware phrase--a tongue of which I scarcely understood a word. But I knew he had seen me somewhere, and preferred not to admit it. Indian caution, thought I, and I said:

"Is my brother Siwanois or Mohican?"

A cunning expression came into his features:

"If a Siwanois marries a Mohican woman, of what nation are the children, my new brother, Loskiel?"

"Mohican," I said in surprise,--"or so it is among the Iroquois," and the next moment could have bitten off my tongue for vexation that I should have so clumsily reminded a Sagamore of a subject nation of his servitude, by assuming that the Lenni-Lenape had conformed even to the racial customs of their conquerors.

The hot flush now staining my face did not escape him, and what he thought of my stupid answer to him or of my embarrassment, I did not know. His calm countenance had not altered--not even had his eyes changed, which features are quickest to alter when Indians betray emotion.

I said in a mortified voice:

"The Siwanois Sagamore will believe that his new brother, Loskiel, meant no offense." And I saw that the compliment had told.

"Mayaro has heard," he said, without the slightest emphasis of resentment. Then, proudly and delicately yielding me reason, and drawing his superb figure to its full and stately height: "When a Mohican Sagamore listens, all Algonquins listen, and the Siwanois clan grow silent in the still places. When a real man speaks, real men listen with respect. Only the Canienga continue to chirp and chatter; only the Long House is full of squirrel sounds and the noise of jays." His lip curled contemptuously. "Let the echoes of the Long House answer the Kanonsis. Mayaro's ears are open."

Boyd, with a triumphant glance at me, said eagerly:

"Is not this hour the hour for the great Siwanois clan of the Lenni-Lenape to bid defiance to the Iroquois? Is it not time that the Mohawks listen to the reading of those ancient belts, and count their dishonoured dead with brookside pebbles from the headwaters of the Sacandaga to the Delaware Capes?"

"Can squirrels count?" retorted Mayaro disdainfully. "Does my white brother understand what the blue-jays say one to another in the yellowing October woods? Not in the Kanonsis, nor yet in the Kanonsionni may the Mohicans read to the Mohawks the ancient wampum records. The Lenni-Lenape are Algonquin, not Huron-Iroquois. Let those degraded Delawares who still sit in the Long House count their white belts while, from both doors of the Confederacy, Seneca and Mohawk belt-bearers hurl their red wampum to the four corners of the world."

"The Mohicans, while they wait, may read of glory and great deeds," I said, "but the belts in their hands are not white. How can this be, my brother?"

The Sagamore's eyes flashed:

"The belts we remember are red!" he said. "We Mohicans have never understood Iroquois wampum. Let the Lenape of the Kansonsionni bear Iroquois belts!"

"In the Long House," said I, "the light is dim. Perhaps the Canienga's ambassadors can no longer perceive the red belts in the archives of the Lenape."

It had so far been a careful and cautious exchange of subtlest metaphor between this proud and sensitive Mohican and me; I striving to win him to our cause by recalling the ancient greatness and the proud freedom of his tribe, yet most carefully avoiding undue pressure or any direct appeal for an immediate answer to Boyd's request. But already I had so thoroughly prepared the ground; and the Sagamore's responses had been so encouraging, that the time seemed to have come to put the direct and final question. And now, to avoid the traditional twenty-four hours' delay which an Indian invariably believes is due his own dignity before replying to a vitally important demand, I boldly cast precedent and custom to the four winds, and once more seized on allegory to aid me in this hour of instant need.

I began by saluting him with the most insidious and stately compliment I could possibly offer to a Sagamore of a conquered race--a race which already was nearly extinct--investing this Mohican Sagamore with the prerogatives of his very conquerors by the subtlety of my opening phrase:

"O Sagamore! Roya-neh! Noble of the three free clans of a free Mohican people! Our people have need of you. The path is dark to Catharines-town. Terror haunts those frightful shades. Roya-nef! We need you!"

"Brother! Is there occasion for belts between us to confirm a brother's words, when this leathern girth I wear around my body carries a red wampum which all may see and read--my war axe and my knife?"

I raised my right arm slowly, and drew with my forefinger a great circle in the air around us:

"Brother! Listen attentively! Since a Sagamore has read the belt I yesterday delivered, the day-sun has circled us where we now stand. It is another day, O Roya-neh! In yonder fireplace new ashes whiten, new embers redden. We have slept (touching my eyelids and then laying my right hand lightly over his); we have eaten (again touching his lips and then my own); and now--now here--now, in this place and on this day, I have returned to the Mohican fire--the Fire of Tamanund! Now I am seated (touching both knees). Now my ears are open. Let the Sagamore of the Mohicans answer my belt delivered! I have spoken, O Roya-neh!"

For a full five minutes of intense silence I knew that my bold appeal was being balanced in the scales by one of a people to whom tradition is a religion. One scale was weighted with the immemorial customs and usages of a great and proud people; the other with a white man's subtle and flattering recognition of these customs, conveyed in metaphor, which all Indians adore, and appealing to imagination--an appeal to which no Huron, no Iroquois, no Algonquin, is ever deaf.

In the breathless silence of suspense the irritable, high-pitched voice of Colonel Sheldon came to my ears. It seemed that after all he had sent out a few troopers and that one had just returned to report a large body of horsemen which had passed the Bedford road at a gallop, apparently headed for Ridgefield. But I scarcely noted what was being discussed in the further end of the hall, so intent was I on the Sagamore's reply--if, indeed, he meant to answer me at all. I could even feel Boyd's body quivering with suppressed excitement as our elbows chanced to come in contact; as for me, I scarce made out to control myself at all, and any nether lip was nearly bitten through ere the Mohican lifted his symmetrical head and looked me full and honestly in the eyes.

"Brother," he said, in a curiously hushed voice, "on this day I come to you here, at this fire, to acquaint you with my answer; answering my brother's words of yesterday."

I could hear Boyd's deep breath of profound relief. "Thank God!" I thought.

The Sagamore spoke again, very quietly:

"Brother, the road is dark to Catharines-town. There are no stars there, no moon, no sun--only a bloody mist in the forest. For to that dreadful empire of the Iroquois only blind trails lead. And from them ghosts of the Long House arise and stand. Only a thick darkness is there--an endless gloom to which the Mohican hatchets long, long ago dispatched the severed souls they struck! In every trail they stand, these ghosts of the Kanonsi, Seneca, Cayuga, Onondaga--ghosts of the Tuscarora. The Mohawk beasts who wear the guise of men are there. Mayaro spits upon them! And upon their League! And upon their Atotarho the Siwanois spit!"

Suddenly his arm shot out and he grasped the hilt of my knife, drew it from my belt, and then slowly returned it. I drew his knife and rendered it again.

"Brother," he said, "I have this day heard your voice coming to me out of the Northland! I have read the message on the belt you bore and wear; your voice has not lied to my ears; your message is clear as running springs to my eyes. I can see through to their pleasant depths. No snake lies hidden under them. So now--now, I say--if my brother's sight is dimmed on the trail to Catharines-town, Mayaro will teach him how to see under the night-sun as owls see, so that behind us, the steps of many men shall not stumble, and the darkness of the Long House shall become redder than dawn, lighted by the flames of a thousand rifles!

"Brother! A Sagamore never lies. I have drawn my brother's knife! Brother, I have spoken!"

And so it was done in that house and in the dark of dawn. Boyd silently gave him his hands, and so did I; then Boyd led him aside with a slight motion of dismissal to me.

As I walked toward the front door, which was now striding open, I saw Major Tallmadge go out ahead of me, run to the mounting-block, and climb into his saddle. Colonel Sheldon followed him to the doorway, and called after him:

"Take a dozen men with you, and meet Colonel Moylan! A dozen will be sufficient, Major!"

Then he turned back into the house, saying to Major Lockwood and Mr. Hunt he was positive that the large body of dragoons in rapid motion, which had been seen and reported by one of our videttes a few minutes since, could be no other than Moylan's expected regiment; and that he would mount his own men presently and draw them up in front of the Meeting House.

The rain had now nearly ceased; a cloudy, greyish horizon became visible, and the dim light spreading from a watery sky made objects dimly discernible out of doors.

I hastened back to the shed where I had left the strange maid swathed in her scarlet cape; and found her there, slowly pacing the trampled sod before it.

As I came up with her, she said:

"Why are the light dragoons riding on the Bedford road? Is aught amiss?"

"A very large body of horse has passed our videttes, making toward Ridgefield.

Colonel Sheldon thinks it must be Moylan's regiment."

"Do you?"

"It may be so."

"And if it be the leather-caps?"

"Then we must find ourselves in a sorry pickle."

As I spoke, the little bugle-horn of Sheldon's Horse blew boots and saddles, and four score dragoons scrambled into their saddles down by the barns, and came riding up the sloppy road, their horses slipping badly and floundering through the puddles and across the stream, where, led by a captain, the whole troop took the Meeting House road at a stiff canter.

We watched them out of sight, then she said:

"I have awaited your pleasure, Mr. Loskiel. Pray, in what further manner can I be of service to--my country?"

"I have come back to tell you," said I, "that you can be of no further use. Our errand to the Sagamore has now ended, and most happily. You have served your country better than you can ever understand. I have come to say so, and to thank you with--with a heart--very full."

"Have I then done well?" she asked slowly.

"Indeed you have!" I replied, with such a warmth of feeling that it surprised myself.

"Then why may I not understand this thing that I have done--for my country?"

"I wish I might tell you."

"May you not?"

"No, I dare not."

She bit her lip, gazing at nothing over the ragged collar of her cape, and stood so, musing. And after a while she seemed to come to herself, wearily, and she cast a tragic upward glance at me. Then, dropping her eyes, and with the slightest inclination of her head, not looking at me at all, she started across the trampled grass.

"Wait----" I was by her side again in the same breath.

"Well, sir?" And she confronted me with cool mien and lifted brows. Under them her grey eyes hinted of a disdain which I had seen in them more than once.

"May I not suitably express my gratitude to you?" I said.

"You have already done so."

"I have tried to do so properly, but it is not easy for me to say how grateful to you we men of the Northland are--how deeply we must ever remain in your debt. Yet--I will attempt to express our thanks--if you care to listen."

After a pause: "Then--if there is nothing more to say--"

"There is, I tell you. Will you not listen?"

"I have been thanked--suitably.... I will say adieu, sir."

"Would you--would you so far favour me as to make known to me your name?" I said, stammering a little.

"Lois is my name," she said indifferently.

"No more than that?"

"No more than that."

How it was now going with me I did not clearly understand, but it appeared to be my instinct not to let her slip away into the world without something more friendly said--some truer gratitude expressed--some warmth.

"Lois," I said very gravely, "what we Americans give to our country demands no ignoble reward. Therefore, I offer none of any sort. Yet, because you have been a good comrade to me--and because now we are about to go our different ways into the world before us--I ask of you two things. May I do so?"

After a moment, looking away from me across the meadow:

"Ask," she said.

"Then the first is--will you take my hand in adieu--and let us part as good soldiers part?"

Still gazing absently across the meadow, she extended her hand. I retained it for a moment, then released it. Her arm fell inert by her side, but mine tingled to the shoulder.

"And one more thing," I said, while this strange and curious reluctance to let her go was now steadily invading me.

"Yes?"

"Will you wear a comrade's token--in memory of an hour or two with him?"

"What!"

She spoke with a quick intake of breath and her grey eyes were on me now, piercing me to the roots of speech and motive.

I wore a heavy ring beaten out of gold; Guy Johnson gave it. This I took from my trembling finger, scarce knowing why I was doing it at all, and stooping and lifting her little, wind-roughened hand, put it on the first finger I encountered-- blindly, now, and clumsily past all belief, my hand was shaking so absurdly.

If my face were now as red as it was hot, hers, on the contrary, had become very strange and still and white. For a moment I seemed to read distrust, scorn, even hatred, in her level stare, and something of fear, too, in every quickening breath that moved the scarlet mantle on her breast. Then, in a flash, she had turned her back on me and was standing there in the grey dawn, with both hands over her face, straight and still as a young pine. But my ring was shining on her finger.

Emotion of a nature to which I was an utter stranger was meddling with my breath and pulses, now checking, now speeding both so that I stood with mind disconcerted in a silly sort of daze.

At length I gathered sufficient composure to step to her side again.

"Once more, little comrade, good-bye," I said. "This ends it all."

Again she turned her shoulder to me, but I heard her low reply:

"Good-bye--Mr. Loskiel."

And so it ended.

A moment later I found myself walking aimlessly across the grass in no particular direction. Three times I turned in my tracks to watch her. Then she disappeared beyond the brookside willows.

I remember now that I had turned and was walking slowly back to where our horses stood, moving listlessly through the freshly mowed meadow between drenched haystacks--the first I had seen that year--and God alone knows where were my thoughts a-gypsying, when, very far away, I heard a gun-shot.

At first I could perceive nothing, then on the distant Bedford road I saw one of our dragoons running his horse and bending low in his saddle.

Another dragoon appeared, riding a diable--and a dozen more behind these; and on their heels a-galloping, a great body of red-jacketed horsemen--hundreds of them--the foremost shooting from their saddles, the great mass of them swinging their heavy cutlasses and spurring furiously after our flying men.

I had seen far more than was necessary, and I ran for my horse. Other officers came running, too--Sheldon, Thomas, Lockwood, and my Lieutenant Boyd.

As we clutched bridle and stirrup and popped upward into out saddles, it seemed that the red-coats must cut us off, but we spurred out of the meadow into the Meeting House road, and Boyd cried furiously in my ear:

"See what this damned Sheldon has done for us now! God! What disgrace is ours!"

I saw Colonel Sheldon presently, pale as death, and heard him exclaim:

"Oh, Christ! I shall be broke for this! I shall be broke!"

I made out to say to Boyd:

"The enemy are coming in hundreds, sir, and we have scarce four score men mounted by the Meeting House."

"They'll never stand, either," he panted. "But if they do we'll see this matter to an end."

"Our orders?" I asked.

"Damn our orders," said he. "We'll see this matter to an end."

We rode hard, but already some of Tallmadge's terror-stricken patrol were overhauling us, and the clangor of the British cavalry broke louder and louder on our ears as we came in sight of the Meeting House. Sheldon's four score troopers heard the uproar of the coming storm, wavered, broke, and whirled their horses about into a most disorderly flight along the Stamford road. Everybody ran--there was no other choice for officers and men--and close on our heels came pelting the 17th British Dragoons, the Hussars, and Mounted Yagers of the Legion; and behind these galloped their mounted infantry.

A mad anxiety to get away from this terrible and overwhelming force thundering on our heels under full charge possessed us all, I think, and this paramount necessity held shame and fury in abeyance. There was nothing on earth for us to do but to ride and try to keep our horses from falling headlong on the rocky, slippery road; for it was now a very hell of trampling horsemen, riding frantically knee against knee, buffeted, driven, crowded, crushed, slipping; and trooper after trooper went down with a crash under the terrible hoofs, horse and rider battered instantly into eternity.

For full three-quarters of a mile they ran us full speed, and we drove on headlong; then at the junction of the New Canaan road our horsemen separated, and I found myself riding in the rear beside Boyd and Jack Mount once more. Turning to look back, I perceived the Legion Cavalry were slowing to a trot to rest their hard-blown horses; and gradually our men did the same. But the Hussars continued to come on, and we continued our retreat, matching our speed to theirs.

They let drive at us once with their heavy pistols, and we in the rear returned their fire, emptying one saddle and knocking two horses into the roadside bushes.

Then they ran us hard again, and strove to flank us, but the rocky country was too stiff for their riders, and they could not make out to cut us off or attain our flanks.

"What a disgrace! What a disgrace!" was all Boyd found to say; and I knew he meant the shameful surprise, not the retreat of our eighty light horsemen before the thundering charge of their heavy hundreds.

Our troopers did not seem really frightened; they now jogged along doggedly, but coolly enough. We had with us on the New Canaan road some twenty light dragoons, not including Boyd, myself, and Jack Mount--one captain, one cornet and a trumpeter lad, the remainder being rank and file, and several mounted militiamen.

The captain, riding in the rear with us, was ever twisting his hatless head to scowl back at the Hussars; and he talked continually in a loud, confident voice to reassure his men.

"They're dropping off by tens and twenties," he said. "If they keep to that habit we'll give 'em a charge. Wait till the odds lessen. Steady there, boys! This cattle chase is not ended. We'll fetch 'em a crack yet. We'll get a chance at their mounted infantry yet. All in God's time, boys. Never doubt it."

The bugle-horns of the Legion were now sounding their derisive, fox-hunting calls, and behind us we could hear the far laughter and shouting: "Yoicks! Forrard! Stole away--stole away!"

My cheeks began to burn; Boyd gnawed his lips continually, and I saw our dragoons turning angrily in their saddles as they understood the insult of the British trumpets.

Half a mile farther on there ran a sandy, narrow cross road into the woods on either side of us.

The captain drew bridle, stood up in his stirrups, and looked back. For some time, now, the taunting trumpets had not jeered us, and the pursuit seemed to have slackened after nearly three hard miles of running. But they still followed us, though it was some minutes before their red jackets came bobbing up again over the sandy crest of the hill behind us.

All our men who had been looking back were now wheeled; and we divided, half backing into the sandy road to the right, half taking the left-hand road under command of Lieutenant Boyd.

"They are not too many," said the dragoon captain coolly, beckoning to his little bugle-horn.

Willows hid us until their advanced troopers were close to where we sat--so close that one of our excited dragoons, spurring suddenly forward into the main road, beat down a Hussar's guard, flung his arms around him, and tore him from his saddle. Both fell from their horses and began to fight fisticuffs in the sandy ditch.

We charged instantly, and the enemy ran for it, our troopers raising the view halloo in their turn and whipping out their sabres. And all the way back to the Stamford road we ran them, and so excited became our dragoons that we could scarce hold them when we came in sight once more of the British main body now reforming under the rolling smoke of Poundridge village, which they had set on fire.

But further advance was madness, even when the remainder of our light troop came cantering down the Stamford road to rejoin us and watch the burning town, for we could now muster but two score and ten riders, having lost nearly thirty dead or missing.

A dozen of Captain Fancher's militia came up, sober farmers of the village that lay below us buried in smoke; and our dragoons listened to the tales of these men, some of whom had been in the village when the onset came, and had remained there, skulking about to pick off the enemy until their main farces returned.

"Tarleton was in a great rage, I warrant you," said one big, raw-boned militia-man. "He rode up to Major Lockwood's house with his dragoons, and says he: 'Burn me this arch rebel's nest!' And the next minute the Yagers were running in and out, setting fire to the curtains and lighting bundles of hay in every room. And I saw the Major's lady stand there on her doorstep and demand the reason for such barbarity--the house already afire behind her. Mrs. Hunt and the servants came out with the children in their arms. And, 'By God, madam,' says Tarleton, 'when shots are fired at my men from houses by the inhabitants of any town in America, I'll burn the town and hang the men if I can get 'em.' Some Hussars came up, driving before them the Major's fine herd of imported cattle--and a troop of his brood mares--the same he has so often had to hide in the Rock Hills. 'Stand clear, madam!' bawls Tarleton. 'I'll suffer nothing to be removed from that house!' At this the Major's lady gives one long look after her children, which Betsy Hunt and the blacks are carrying through the orchard; then she calmly enters the burning house and comes out again with a big silver platter and a load of linen from the dining-room in her arms. And at that a trooper draws his sabre and strikes her with the flat o' the blade--God, what a blow!--so that the lady falls to her knees and the heavy silver platter rolls out on the grass and the fine linen is in the mud. I saw her blacks lift her and get her off through the orchard. I sneaked out of the brook willows, took a long shot at the beast who struck her, and then pulled foot."

There was a shacked silence among the officers who had gathered to listen. Until this moment our white enemies had offered no violence to ladies. So this brutality toward the Major's lady astounded us.

Somebody said in a low voice:

"They've fired the church, now."

Major Lockwood's house was also burning furiously, as also were his barns and stables, his sheds, and the new, unfinished barracks. We could see it all very plainly from the hilltop where we had gathered.

"Alsop Hunt was taken," said a militiaman. "They robbed him of his watch and purse, damning him for a rebel broad-brim. He's off to the Provost, I fear."

"They took Mr. Reed, too," said another. "They had a dozen neighbours under guard when I left."

Sheldon, looking like death, sat his saddle a little apart. No one spoke to him. For even a deeper disgrace had now befallen the dragoons in the loss of their standard left behind in Lockwood's house.

"What a pitiful mess!" whispered Boyd. "Is there nothing to be done but sit here and see the red beasts yonder sack the town?"

Before I could answer, I caught the sound of distant firing on the Lewisboro road. Colonel Thomas reared stiffly in his saddle, and:

"Those are my own men!" he said loudly, "or I lie like a Tory!"

A hill half a mile north of us suddenly became dark with men; we saw the glitter of their muskets, saw the long belt of white smoke encircle them, saw red-jacketed men run out of a farmhouse, mount, and gallop toward the burning town.

Along the road below us a column of Continental infantry appeared on the run, cheering us with their hats.

A roar from our dragoons answered them; our bugle-horn spoke, and I saw Major Tallmadge, with a trumpeter at his back, rein in while the troopers were re-forming and calling off amid a whirlwind of rearing horses and excited men.

Below in the village, the British had heard and perfectly understood the volley from Thomas's regiment, and the cavalry and mounted infantry of the Legion were assembling in the smoke, and already beginning a rapid retreat by the Bedford road.

As Boyd and I went clattering down the hill, we saw Major Lockwood with Thomas's men, and we rode up to him. He passed his sword to the left hand, and leaning across in his saddle, exchanged a grip with us. His face was ghastly.

"I know--I know," he said hurriedly. "I have seen my wife and children. My wife is not badly injured. All are in safety. Thank you, gentlemen."

We wheeled our horses and fell in beside our infantry, now pressing forward on a heavy run, so that Colonel Thomas and Major Lockwood had to canter their horses.

Firing instantly broke out as we entered the smoky zone where the houses were burning. Into it, an our left, galloped Sheldon's light dragoons, who, having but five muskets in the command, went at the Yagers with naked sabres; and suddenly found themselves in touch with the entire Legion cavalry, who set up a Loud bawling:

"Surrender, you damned rebels! Pull up, there! Halt!"

I saw a trooper, one Jared Hoyt, split the skull of a pursuing British dragoon straight across the mouth with a back-handed stroke, as he escaped from the melee; and another, one John Buckhout, duck his head as a dragoon fired at him, and, still ducking and loudly cursing the fellow, rejoin us as we sheered off from the masses of red-jacketed riders, wheeled, and went at the mounted Yagers, who did not stand our charge.

There was much smoke, and the thick, suffocating gloom was lighted only by streaming sparks, so that in the confusion and explosion of muskets it was difficult to manoeuvre successfully and at the same time keep clear of Tarleton's overwhelming main body.

This body was now in full but orderly retreat, driving with it cattle, horses, and some two dozen prisoners, mostly peaceable inhabitants who had taken no part in the affair. Also, they had a wagon piled with the helmets, weapons, and accoutrements of Sheldon's dead riders; and one of their Hussars bore Sheldon's captured standard in his stirrup.

To charge this mass of men was not possible with the two score horsemen left us; and they retreated faster than our militia and Continentals could travel. So all we could do was to hang on their rear and let drive at them from our saddles.

As far as we rode with them, we saw a dozen of their riders fall either dead or wounded from their horses, and saw their comrades lift them into one of the wagons. Also we saw our dragoons and militia take three prisoners and three horses before we finally turned bridle after our last long shot at their rear guard.

For our business here lay not in this affair, and Boyd had disobeyed his orders in not avoiding all fighting. He knew well enough that the bullets from our three rifles were of little consequence to our country compared to the safe accomplishment of our mission hither, and our safe return with the Siwanois. Fortune had connived at our disobedience, for no one of us bore so much as a scratch, though all three of us might very easily have been done to death in the mad flight from the Meeting House, amid that plunging hell of horsemen.

Fortune, too, hung to our stirrup leathers as we trotted into Poundridge, for, among a throng of village folk who stood gazing at the smoking ashes of the Lockwood house, we saw our Siwanois standing, tall, impassive, wrapped in his blanket.

And late that afternoon we rode out of the half-ruined village, northward. Our saddle-bags were full; our animals rested; and, beside us, strode the Sagamore, fully armed and accoutred, lock braided, body oiled and painted for war--truly a terrific shape in the falling dusk.

On the naked breast of this Mohican warrior of the Siwanois clan, which is called by the Delawares "The Clan of the Magic Wolf," outlined in scarlet, I saw the emblem of his own international clan--as I supposed--a bear.

And of a sudden, within me, vaguely, something stirred--some faint memory, as though I had once before beheld that symbol on a dark and naked breast, out-lined in scarlet. Where had I seen it before? At Guy Park? At Johnson Hall? Fort Johnson? Butlersbury? Somewhere I had seen that symbol, and in that same paint. Yes, it might easily have been. Every nation of the Confederacy possessed a clan that wore the bear. And yet--and yet--this bear seemed somehow different--and yet familiar--strangely familiar to me--but in a manner which awoke within me an unrest as subtle as it was curious.

I drew bridle, and as the Sagamore came up, I said uneasily:

"Brother, and ensign of the great bear clan of many nations, why is the symbol that you wear familiar to me--and yet so strangely unfamiliar?"

He shot a glance of lightning intelligence at me, then instantly his features be-came smoothly composed and blank again.

"Has my brother never before seen the Spirit Bear?" he asked coldly.

"Is that a clan, Mayaro?"

"Among the Siwanois only." "That is strange," I muttered. "I have never before seen a Siwanois. Where could I have seen a Siwanois? Where?"

But he only shook his head.

Boyd and Mount had pricked forward; I still lingered by the Mohican. And presently I said:

"That was a brave little maid who bore our message to you."

He made no answer.

"I have been wondering," I continued carelessly, "whether she has no friends--so poor she seems--so sad and friendless, Have you any knowledge of her?"

The Indian glanced at me warily, "My brother Loskiel should ask these ques-tions of the maid herself."

"But I shall never see her again, Sagamore. How can I ask her, then?"

The Indian remained silent. And, perhaps because I vaguely entertained some future hope of loosening his tongue in her regard, I now said nothing more con-cerning her, deeming that best. But I was still thinking of her as I rode northward through the deepening dusk.

A great weariness possessed me, no doubt fatigue from the day's excitement and anxiety. Also, for some hours, that curious battle-hunger had been gnawing at my belly so that I had liked to starve there in my saddle ere Boyd gave the signal to off-saddle for the night.

CHAPTER IV
A TRYST

Above the White Plains the territory was supposed to be our own. Below, seventeen thousand red-coats held the city of New York; and their partisans, irregulars, militia, refugee-corps, and Legion-horsemen, harried the lines. Yet, except the enemy's cruisers which sometimes strayed far up the Hudson, like impudent hawks circling within the very home-yard, we saw nothing of red-rag or leather-cap north of our lines, save only once, when Lieutenant-Colonel Simcoe nearly caught us.

His Excellency's army lay in position all around us, now, from West Point down the river; and our light-horsemen patrolled as far south as the unhappy country from which we had retired through the smoke of Bedford's burning farms and the blaze of church and manor at Poundridge. That hilly strip was then our southern frontier, bravely defended by Thomas and Lockwood, shamefully neglected by Sheldon, as we had seen. For which he was broke, poor devil, and a better man set there to watch the red fox Tarleton, to harry Emmeriek, and to throw the fear o' God into that headlong blockhead, Simcoe, a brave man, but so possessed by hatred for "Mr." Washington that every move he made was like a goaded bull--his halts merely the bewilderment of baffled fury, his charges blind and bellowing.

I know how he conducted, not from hearsay alone, but because at sunrise on our second day northward, before we struck the river-road, we had like to have had a brush with him, his flankers running afoul of us not far beyond a fortified post heavily held by our Continentals.

It was the glimpse of cannon and levelled bayonets that bewildered him; and his bawling charge sheered wide o' the shabby Continental battle-line, through which we galloped into safety, our Indian sticking to my crupper like a tree-cat with every claw. And I remember still the grim laughter that greeted us from those unshaven, powder-blackened ranks, and how they laughed, too, as they fired by platoons at the far glimmer of Simcoe's helmets through the chestnut trees.

And in the meantime, all the while, even from the very first evening when we off-saddled in the rocky Westchester woods and made our first flying-camp, I had become uneasy concerning the Siwanois--uncertain concerning his loyalty to the very verge of suspicion.

I said nothing of this to Lieutenant Boyd, having nothing definite to communicate. Nor did I even hint my suspicions, because distrust in the mind of such a man as Boyd would be very difficult to eradicate, and the slightest mishandling of our delicate situation might alienate the Sagamore forever.

Yet, of one thing I had become almost convinced: the Siwanois, while we slept, met and held communication with somebody outside our camp.

On the first night this had happened; for, awaking and missing the Sagamore, who had been left on guard, I lay a-watching under my blanket, and when he came in to the fire once more, it seemed to me that far in the woods I heard the faint sound of another person retiring stealthily through the tell-tale bushes that choke all second growth hereabouts.

On the second day we crossed to the other side of the Hudson in flat boats, with our horses. But on that night it was the same, I feigning sleep when it came time for the Siwanois to relieve the man on guard. And once again, after he had silently inspected us all, the Sagamore stole away into leafy depths, but halted as before within earshot still. And once again some nascent sense within me seemed to become aware of another human being somewhere moving in the woods outside our fire.

How I divined it I do not know, because this time I could hear no sound in the starry obscurity of the Western Catskills, save only those familiar forest sounds which never cease by night--unseen stirrings of sleeping birds, the ruffle, of feathers, the sudden rustle of some furry thing alarmed, the scratchings and pickings in rotting windfalls, the whisper of some falling leaf severed by insects or relaxing its brief clasp of the mother stem in the precocity of a maturity premature.

Yet, so strong now had become my suspicions that I was already preparing to unroll my blanket, rise, and creep after the Siwanois, when his light and rapid foot-fall sounded on the leaves close to my head; and, as before, while again I feigned sleep, far in the thicket somebody moved, cautiously retreating into tangled depths. But whether I really heard or only guessed, I do not know down to this very day.

On the third night it rained and we made a bark hut. Perhaps the Siwanois did his talking with this unseen visitor while away in pretense of peeling bark, for he did not creep abroad that night. But, somehow, I knew he had kept some tryst.

Now, on this fourth day, and our journey drawing to its end, I resolved to follow the Siwanois if he stirred from our fire, and discover for myself with what manner of visitor he held these stealthy councils.

During the long day's march I lagged and watched and listened in vain for any follower along our route. Sometimes I even played at flanker, sometimes rode far on ahead, and, at times, stuck to the Indian hour after hour, seeming not to watch him, but with every sense alert to surprise some glance, some significant movement, some cunning and treacherous signal, to convince me that the forest had eyes that marked us, and ears which heard us, and that the Siwanois knew it, and aided and abetted under our very gaze.

But I had seen him do nothing that indicated him to be in secret communication with anybody. He marked neither tree nor stone, nor leaf nor moss, as far as I could see; dropped nothing, made no sound at all save when he gravely answered some observation that we offered. Once, even, I found a pretext to go back on the trail, searching to find some sign he might have left behind him: and had my journey for my pains.

Now, had this same Indian been an Iroquois I might have formed some reasonable judgment concerning his capacity for treachery; but I had seen few Delawares in my life, and had never heard them speak at all, save to boast in their cups of Uncas, Tamanund, and Miontonomoh. As for a Siwanois Mohican, this Sagamore of the Magic Clan was the first of his tribe and ensign that I had ever beheld. And with every motive and every interest and desire in the world to believe him honest--and even in my secret heart believing him to be so--yet I could not close eyes and ears to what so stealthily was passing in the midnight woods around me. And truly it was duty, nor any motive baser, that set me after him that starlit night, when, as before, being on guard, he left the fire about midnight: and I out of my blanket and after him in a trice.

The day was the 7th of July, a Wednesday, I remember, as I had writ it in my journal, my habit being to set down every evening, or as near the date as convenient, a few words which briefly recorded the day's events.

The night before we had camped in the woods along the Catskill road leading toward Cobus-kill; this night, being fine and warm, we made open camp along a stream, within a few miles' journey of the Middle Fort; and, soupaan being eaten, let the coals die and whiten into ashes. This, partly because we needed not the warmth, partly from precaution. For although on the open roads our troops in detachments were now concentrating, moving on Otsego Lake and the upper waters of the Delaware and Susquehanna, this was no friendly country, and we knew it. So the less firelight, the snugger we might lie in case of some stray scalping party from the west or north.

Now, as I say, no sooner did the Siwanois leave his post and go a-roving than I went after him, with infinite precaution; and I flatter myself that I made no more noise on the brookside moss than the moon-cast shadow of a flying cloud. Guy Johnson was no skilful woodsman, but his Indians were; and of them I learned my craft. And scout detail in Morgan's Rifles, too, was a rare school to finish any man and match him with the best who ran the woods.

Too near his heels I dared not venture, as long as his tall form passed like a shadow against the white light that the stars let in through the forest cleft, where ran the noisy stream. But presently he turned off, and for a moment I thought to lose him in the utter blackness of the primeval trees. And surely would have had I not seen close to me a vast and smoothly slanting ledge of rock which the stars shining on made silvery, and on which no tree could grow, scarce even a tuft of fern, so like a floor it lay in a wide oval amid the forest gloom.

Somewhere upon that dim and sparkling esplanade the Siwanois had now seated himself. For a while, straining my eyes where I lay flat among the taller fringing ferns, I could just make out a blot in the greyness where he sat upright, like a watching catamount under the stars.

Then, across the dimness, another blot moved to join him; and I felt my hair stir as chilling certainty shocked from me my lingering hope that I had been mistaken.

Faintly--oh, scarce audible at all--the murmur of two voices came to me there where I lay under the misty lustre of the stars. Nearer, nearer I crept, nearer, nearer, until I lay flat as a shadow there, stark on the shelf of rock. And, as though they had heard me, and as if to spite me, their voices sank to whispers. Yet, I knew of a certainty that I had neither been observed nor heard.

Hushed voices, whispers, undertones as soft as summer night winds--that was all I heard, all I could make of it; and sniffed treason as I lay there, making no question of the foulness of this midnight tryst.

It was an hour, I think, they sat there, two ghostly figures formless against the woods; then one rose, and presently I saw it was the Sagamore.

Noiselessly he retraced his steps across the silvery esplanade of rock; and if my vague, flat outline were even visible to him I passed for a shadow or a cleft beneath his notice--perhaps for a fallen branch or heap of fern and withered leaf--I know not. But I let him go, unstirring, my eyes riveted upon the other shape, seated there like some grey wraith upon a giant's tombstone, under the high stars.

Beyond the ferns I saw the shadow of the Sagamore against the stream pass toward our camp. Then I addressed myself to the business before me; loosened knife and hatchet in their beaded sheaths, stirred, moved forward inch by inch, closer, closer, then to the left to get behind, nearer, ever nearer, till the time had come for me to act. I rose silently to my moccasined feet, softly drew my heavy knife against events, and lightly struck the ringing blade against my hatchet.

Instantly the grey shape bounded upright, and I heard a whispering cry of terror stifled to a sob.

And then a stunning silence fell between us twain.

For I was staring upon the maid who had brought the Sagamore to us, and she was looking back at me, still swaying on her feet and all a-tremble from the dreadful fear that still possessed her.

"Lois?" I made out to whisper.

She placed one hand against her side, fighting for breath; and when she gained it sighed deeply once or twice, with a low sound like the whimpering wings of doves.

At her feet I saw a cup of water shining, a fragment of corn bread and meat. Near these lay a bundle with straps on it.

"In God's name," I said in a ghostly voice, "what does this mean? Why have you followed us these four days past? Are you mad to risk a scalping party, or, on the open road, hazard the rough gallantries of soldiers' bivouacs? If you had business in these parts, and desired to come, why did you not tell me so and travel with us?"

"I did not wish to ask that privilege of----" She hesitated, then bent her head.

"----of any man. What harm have I caused you by following?"

I said, still amazed and wondering:

"I understand it all now. The Sagamore brings you food. Is that true?"

"Yes," she said sullenly.

"And you have kept in touch with us ever since we started?"

"With Mayaro."

"Why?"

"I have told you that I had no wish to travel in your company."

"But for protection----"

"Protection! I have heard that, too, from men. It is ever on men's lips--that word meaning damnation. I thank you, Mr. Loskiel, I require no protection."

"Do you distrust Lieutenant Boyd or me? Or what?"

"Men! And you twain are two of them."

"You fear such men as we are!" I demanded impatiently.

"I know nothing of you," she answered, "save that you are men."

"Do you mean Mr. Boyd--and his thoughtless gallantry----"

"I mean men! All men! And he differs in nothing from the rest that I can see. Which is why I travel without your leave on my own affairs and by myself--spite of the Iroquois." She added bitterly; "And it is known to civilization that the Iroquois are to be trusted where the white man is not!"

Her meaning was plain enough now. What this young girl had seen and suffered and resented amid a world of men I did not know. Boyd's late gallantry, idle, and even ignoble as it had appeared to me, had poisoned her against me also, confirming apparently all she ever had known of men.

If this young, lonely, ragged thing were what her attitude and words made plain, she had long endured her beauty as a punishment. What her business might be in lingering around barracks and soldiers' camps I could not guess; but women who haunted such resorts seldom complained of the rough gallantries offered. And if their charms faded, they painted lip and cheek, and schooled the quivering mouth to smile again.

What her business might now be in following our little detail northward I could not surmise. Here was no barracks wench! But wench or gypsy or what not, it was impossible that I should leave her here alone. Even the thought of it set one cold.

"Come into camp this night," I said.

"I will not."

"You must do so. I may not leave you here alone."

"I can care for myself."

"Yes--as you cared for yourself when I crept up behind you. And if I had been a savage--then what?"

"A quick end," she said coolly.

"Or a wretched captivity--perhaps marriage to some villainous Iroquois----"

"Yes, sir; but nothing worse than marriage!"

"Child!" I exclaimed. "Where have you lived to belie the pitiful youth of you with such a worldly-worn and bitter tongue? I tell you all men are not of that stripe! Do you not believe me?"

"Birds sing, sir."

"Will you come into camp?" I repeated hotly.

"And if I will not?"

"Then, by heaven, I'll carry you in my arms! Will you come?"

She laughed at me, dangerously calm, seated herself, picked up the partly eaten food, and began to consume it with all the insolent leisure in the world.

I stood watching her for a few moments, then sat down cross-legged before her.

"Why do you doubt me, Lois?" I asked.

"Dear sir, I do not doubt you," she answered with faintest malice.

"I tell you I am not of that stripe!" I said angrily.

"Then you are not a man at all. I tell you I have talked with men as good as you, and heard them protest as you do--yes, with all the gentle condescension that you use, all of your confidence and masterful advice. Sooner or later all have proved the same," she shrugged; "----proved themselves men, in plainer words."

She sat eating thoughtfully, looking aloft now and then at the thick splendor of the firmament.

Then, breaking a bit of corn bread, she said gravely:

"I do not mean that you have not been kind, as men mean kindness. I do not even mean that I blame men. God made them different from us. And had He made me one, doubtless I had been as all men are, taking the road through life as gaily, sword on thigh and hat in hand to every pretty baggage that a kindly fate made wayfarer with me. No, I have never blamed a man; only the silly minx who listens."

After a short silence, I said: "Who, in the name of heaven, are you, Lois?"

"Does that concern you?"

"I would have it concern me--if you wish."

"Dear sir," she said very coolly, "I wish nothing of the kind."

"You do not trust me."

"Why, yes, as I trust every man--except a red one."

"Yet, I tell you that all that animates me is a desire to render you a comrade's service----"

"And I thank you, Mr. Loskiel, because, like other men, you mean it generously and well. Yet, you are an officer in the corps d'elite; and you would be ashamed to have the humblest bugler in your regiment see you with such a one as I."

She broke another morsel from her bread:

"You dare not cross a camp-parade beside me. At least the plaything of an officer should walk in silk, whatever clothes a soldier's trull. Sir, do you suppose I do not know?"

She looked up at the stare, and then quietly at me.

"The open comradeship of any man with me but marks us both. Only his taste is criticized, not his morals. But the world's judgment leaves me nothing to cover me except the silk or rags I chance to wear. And if I am brave and fine it would be said of me, 'The hussy's gown is brave and fine!' And if I go in tatters, 'What slattern have we here, flaunting her boldness in the very sun?' So a comradeship with any man is all one to me. And I go my way, neither a burden nor a plaything, a scandal only to myself, involving no man high or low save where their advances wrong us both in the world's eyes--as did those of your friend, yonder by a dead fire asleep."

"All men are not so fashioned. Can you not believe me?"

"You say so, sir."

"Yes; and I say that I am not."

"Birds sing."

"Lois, will you let me aid you?"

"In what? The Sagamore feeds me; and the Middle Fort is not so far."

"And at the Middle Fort how will you live?"

"As I have lived; wash for the soldiers; sew for them--contrive to find a living as I journey."

"Whither?"

"It is my own affair."

"May I not aid?"

"You could not if you would; you would not if you could."

"Ask me, Lois."

"No." She shook her head. Then, slowly: "I do thank you for the wish, Mr. Loskiel. But the Siwanois himself refuses what I ask. And you would, also, did you know my wish."

"What is your wish?"

She shook her head: "It is useless to voice it--useless."

She gathered the scant fragments of her meal, wrapped them in a bit of silver birch-bark, unrolled her bundle, and placed them there. Then she drained the tin cup of its chilly water, and, still sitting there cross-legged on the rock, tied the little cup to her girdle. It seemed to me, there in the dusk, that she smiled very faintly; and if it was so it was the first smile I had had of her when she said:

"I travel light, Mr. Loskiel. But otherwise there is nothing light about me."

"Lois, I pray you, listen. As I am a man, I can not leave you here."

"For that reason, sir, you will presently take your leave."

"No, I shall remain if you will not come into camp with us."

She said impatiently:

"I lie safer here than you around your fire. You mean well; now take your leave of me--with whatever flight of fancy," she added mockingly, "that my present condition invests me with in the eyes of a very young man."

The rudeness of the fling burnt my face, but I answered civilly:

"A scalping party may be anywhere in these woods. It is the season; and neither Oneida Lake nor Fort Niagara itself are so distant that their far-hurled hatchets may not strike us here."

"I will not go with you," said she, making of her bundle a pillow. Then, very coolly, she extended her slim body and laid her head on the bundle.

I made no answer, nor any movement for fully an hour. Then, very stealthily, I leaned forward to see if she truly slept. And found her eyes wide open.

"You waste time mounting sentry over me," she said in a low voice. "Best employ your leisure in the sleep you need."

"I can not sleep."

"Nor I--if you remain here awake beside me."

She raised herself on her elbow, peering through the darkness toward the stream.

"The Siwanois has been standing yonder by the stream watching us this full hour past. Let him mount sentry if he wishes."

"You have a tree-cat's eyes," I said. "I see nothing."

Then I rose and unbuckled my belt. Hatchet and knife dangled from it. I stooped and laid it beside her. Then, stepping backward a pace or two, I unlaced my hunting shirt of doe-skin, drew it off, and, rolling it into a soft pillow, lay down, cradling my cheek among the thrums.

I do not know how long I lay there before I fell asleep from very weariness of the new and deep emotions, as strange to me as they were unwelcome. The restlessness, the misgivings which, since I first had seen this maid, had subtly invaded me, now, grown stronger, assailed me with an apprehension I could neither put from me nor explain. Nor was this vague fear for her alone; for, at moments, it seemed as though it were for myself I feared--fearing myself.

So far in my brief life, I had borne myself cleanly and upright, though the times were loose enough, God knows, and the master of Guy Park had read me no lesson or set me no example above the morals and the customs of his class and of the age.

It may have been pride--I know not what it was, that I could notice the doings of Sir John and of young Walter Butler and remain aloof, even indifferent. Yet, this was so. Never had a woman's beauty stirred me otherwise than blamelessly, never had I entertained any sentiment toward fashionable folly other than aversion and a kind of shamed contempt.

Nor had I been blind at Guy Park and Butlersbury and Tribes Hill, nor in Albany, either. I knew Clarissa Putnam; I also knew Susannah Wormwood and her sister Elizabeth, and all that pretty company; and many another pretty minx and laughing, light-minded lass in county Tryon. And a few in Cambridge, too. So I was no niais, no naive country fool, unless to remain aloof were folly. And I often wondered to myself how this might really be, when Boyd rallied me and messmates laughed.

And now, as I lay there under the clustered stars, my head pillowed on my deer-skin shirt, my mind fell a-groping for reason to bear me out in my strained and strange perplexity.

Why, from the time I first had spoken to her, should thoughts of this strange and ragged maid have so possessed me that each day my memory of her returned, haunting me, puzzling me, plaguing my curiosity till imagination awoke, spurring my revery to the very border of an unknown land where rides Romance, in armour, vizor down.

Until this night I had not crossed that border, nor ever thought to, or dreamed of doing it. No beggar-maiden-seeking king was I by nature, nor ever felt for shabby dress and common folk aught but the mixture of pity and aversion which breeds a kind of charity. And, I once supposed, were the Queen of Sheba herself to pass me in a slattern's rags, only her rags could I ever see, for all her beauty.

But how was it now with me that, from the very first, I had been first conscious of this maid herself, then of her rags. How was it that I felt no charity, nor pity of that sort, only a vague desire that she should understand me better--know that I meant her kindness--God knows what I wished of her, and why her grey eyes haunted me, and why I could not seem to put her from my mind.

That now she fully possessed my mind I convinced myself was due to my very natural curiosity concerning her; forgetting that a week ago I should not have condescended to curiosity.

Who and what was she? She had been schooled; that was plain in voice and manner. And, though she used me with scant courtesy, I was convinced she had been schooled in manners, too, and was no stranger to usages and customs which mark indelibly where birth and breeding do not always.

Why was she here? Why alone? Where were her natural protectors then? What would be her fate a-gypsying through a land blackened with war, or haunting camps and forts, penniless, in rags--and her beauty ever a flaming danger to herself, despite her tatters and because of them.

I slept at last; I do not know how long. The stars still glittered overhead when

I awoke, remembered, and suddenly sat upright.

She was gone. I might have known it. But over me there came a rush of fear and anger and hurt pride; and died, leaving a strange, dull aching.

Over my arm I threw my rifle-frock, looked dully about to find my belt, discovered it at my feet. As I buckled it, from the hatchet-sling something fell; and I stooped to pick it up.

It was a wild-rose stem bearing a bud unclosed. And to a thorn a shred of silver birch-bark clung impaled. On it was scratched with a knife's keen point a message which I could not read until once more I crept in to our fire, which Mount had lighted for our breakfast.

And there I read her message: "A rose for your ring, comrade. And be not angry with me."

I read it again, then curled it to a tiny cylinder and placed it in my pouch, glancing sideways at the reclining Mohican. Boyd began to murmur and stretch in his blanket, then relaxed once more.

So I lay down, leaving Jack Mount a-cooking ashen cakes, and yawning.

CHAPTER V
THE GATHERING

Now, no sooner had we broken camp, covered our fire, packed, saddled, and mounted, than all around us, as we advanced, the wilderness began to wear an aspect very different to that brooding solitude which hitherto had been familiar to us--our shelter and our menace also.

For we had proceeded on our deeply-trodden war trail no more than a mile or two before we encountered the raw evidences of an army's occupation. Everywhere spotted leads, game trails, and runways had been hacked, trimmed, and widened into more open wood-walks; foot-paths enlarged to permit the passage of mounted men; cattle-roads cleared, levelled, made smoother for wagons and artillery; log bridges built across the rapid streams that darkled westward, swamps and swales paved with logs, and windfalls hewn in twain and the huge abattis dragged wide apart or burnt to ashes where it lay. Yet, still the high debris bristling from some fallen forest giant sprawling athwart the highway often delayed us. Our details had not yet cleared out the road entirely.

We were, however, within a wolf-hound's easy run to Cherry Valley, Fort Hunter, and the Mohawk--the outer edges of my own country. Northeast of us lay Schenectady behind its fort; north of us lay my former home, Guy Park, and near it old Fort Johnson and Johnson Hall. Farther still to the northward stretched the Vale and silvery Sacandaga with its pretty Fish House settlement now in ashes; and Summer House Point and Fonda's Bush were but heaps of cinders, too, the brave Broadalbin yeomen prisoners, their women and children fled to Johnstown, save old man Stoner and his boys, and that Tory villain Charlie Cady who went off with Sir John.

Truly I should know something of these hills and brooks and forests that we now traversed, and of the silent, solitary roads that crept into the wilderness, penetrating to distant, lonely farms or grist mills where some hardy fellow had cleared the bush and built his cabin on the very borders of that dark and fearsome empire which we were gathering to enter and destroy.

Here it lay, close on our left flank--so close that its strange gigantic shadow fell upon us, like a vast hand, stealthy and chill.

And it was odd, but on the edges of these trackless shades, here, even with fresh evidences on every side that our own people lately passed this way--yes, even when we began to meet or overtake men of our own color--the stupendous desolation yielded nothing of its brooding mystery and dumb magnificence.

Westward, the green monotony of trees stretched boundless as an ocean, and as trackless and uncharted--gigantic forests in the depths of which twilight had brooded since first the world was made.

Here, save for the puny, man-made trail--save for the tiny scars left by his pygmy hacking at some high forest monument, all this magic shadow-land still bore the imprint of our Lord's own fingers.

The stillness and the infinite majesty, the haunting fragrance clinging to the craftsmanship of hands miraculous; all the sweet odour and untainted beauty which enveloped it in the making, and which had remained after creation's handiwork was done, seemed still to linger in this dim solitude. And it was as though the twilight through the wooded aisles was faintly tinctured still, where the sweet-scented garments of the Lord had passed.

There was no underbrush, no clinging sprays or fairy brambles intertwined under the solemn arches of the trees; only the immemorial strata of dead leaves spread one above another in endless coverlets of crumbling gold; only a green and knee-deep robe of moss clothing the vast bases of the living columns.

And into this enchanted green and golden dusk no sunlight penetrated, save along the thread-like roads, or where stark-naked rocks towered skyward, or where, in profound and velvet depths, crystalline streams and rivers widened between their Indian willow bottoms. And these were always set with wild flowers, every bud and blossom gilded by the sun.

As we journeyed on, the first wayfarer we encountered after passing our outer line of pickets was an express rider from General Sullivan's staff, one James Cook, who told us that the right division of the army, General James Clinton's New York brigade, which was ours, was still slowly concentrating in the vicinity of Otsego Lake; that innumerable and endless difficulties in obtaining forage and provisions had delayed everything; that the main division, Sullivan's, was now arriving at Easton and Wyoming; and that, furthermore, the enemy had become vastly agitated over these ominous preparations of ours, but still believed, from their very magnitude, that we were preparing for an advance into Canada.

"Ha-ha!" said Boyd merrily. "So much the better, for if they continue to believe that, they will keep their cursed scalping parties snug at home."

"No, sir," said the express soberly. "Brant and his Mohawks are out somewhere or other, and so is Walter Butler and his painted crew."

"In this same district?"

"No doubt of it, sir. Indians fired on our pickets last week. It will go hard with the outlying farms and settlements. Small doubt, too, that they will strike heavily and strive to draw this army from whatever plan it meditated."

"Then," said Boyd with a careless laugh, "it is for us to strike more heavily still and draw them with the very wind of our advance into a common vortex of destruction with the Iroquois."

The express rode on, and Boyd, in excellent humour, continued talking to me, saying that he knew our Commander-in-Chief, and that he was an officer not to be lightly swayed or turned from the main purpose, but would hew to the line, no matter what destruction raged and flamed about him.

"No, Loskiel, they may murder and burn to right and left of us, and it may wring his heart and ours to hear the agonized appeals for aid; but if I judge our General, he will not be halted or drawn aside until the monstrous, loathesome body of this foul empire lies chopped to bits, writhing and dying in the flames of Catharines-town."

"He must truly be a man of iron," said I, "if we win through."

"We will win through, Loskiel," he said gaily, "--to Catharines-town or paradise--to hell or heaven. And what a tale to tell our children--we who survive!"

An odd expression came into his handsome face, and he said in a low and dreamy voice:

"I think that almost every man will live to tell that story--yet, I can never hear myself telling the tale in years to come."

On paths and new-made highways we began to encounter people and cattle--now a long line of oxen laden with military stores or with canoes and flatboats, and conducted by batt-men in smock and frock, now a sweating company of military surveyors from headquarters, burdened with compass, chain, and Jacob-staff, already running their lines into the wilderness. Here trudged the frightened family of some settler, making toward the forts; there a company of troops came gaily marching out on some detail, or perhaps, with fixed bayonets, herded sheep and cattle down some rutted road.

It seemed scarce possible that we were already within scouting range of that never-to-be-forgotten region of Wyoming, where just one year ago old John Butler with his Rangers, his hell-born Senecas, and Johnson's Greens, had done their bloody business; where, in "The Shades of Death," a hundred frightened women and little children had perished in that ghastly darkness. Also, we were but a few miles from that scene of terror where, through the wintry dawn at Cherry Valley, young Walter Butler damned his soul for all eternity while men, women, and children, old and young, died horribly amid the dripping knives and bayonets of his painted fiends, or fell under the butchering hatchets of his Senecas.

I could see that Boyd also was thinking of this ghastly business, as I caught his sombre eye. He seemed to shudder, then:

"Patience," he muttered grimly, with a significant nod toward the Siwanois, who strode silently between our horses. "We have our guide at last. A Siwanois hates the Iroquois no more fiercely than do we white-skins. Wait till he leads our van within rifle-range of Catharines-town! And if Walter Butler be there, or that bloodless beast Sir John, or Brant, or any of that hell-brood, and if we let them get away, may God punish us with the prisoner's fire! Amen."

Never before had I heard him speak that way, or with such savage feeling; and his manner of expression, and the uncanny words he used concerning fire caused me to shudder, too--knowing that if he had ever dreaded anything it was the stake, and the lingering death that lasted till the very soul lay burnt to cinders before the tortured body died. We exchanged no further conversation; many people passed and repassed us; the woods opened somewhat; the jolly noise of axes resounded near at hand among the trees.

Just ahead of us the road from Mattisses' Grist Mill and Stoney Kill joined ours, where stood the Low Dutch Church. Above us lay the Middle Fort, and the roads to Cherry Valley and Schenectady forked beyond it by the Lutheran Church and the Lower Fort. We took the Cherry Valley Road.

Here, through this partly cleared and planted valley of the Scoharie Kill, between the river and the lake, was now gathering a great concourse of troops and of people; and all the roads were lively with their comings and goings. Every woodland rang with the racket of their saws and axes; over the log bridges rumbled their loaded transport wagons; road and trail were filled with their crowding cattle; the wheels of Eckerson's and Becker's grist mills clattered and creaked under the splash of icy, limpid waters, and everywhere men were hammering and sawing and splitting, erecting soldiers' huts, huts for settlers, sheds, stables, store-houses, and barracks to shelter this motley congregation assembling here under the cannon of the Upper Fort, the Lower, and the Middle.

As we rode along, many faces we passed were familiar to us; we encountered officers from our own corps and from other regiments, with whom we were acquainted, and who greeted us gaily or otherwise, according to their temper and disposition. But everybody--officers, troops, batt-men--looked curiously at our Siwanois Indian, who returned the compliment not at all, but with stately stride and expressionless visage moved straight ahead of him, as though he noticed nothing.

Twice since we had started at daybreak that morning, I had managed to lag behind and question him concerning the maid who now shared well-nigh every thought of mine--asking if he knew who she was, and where she came from, and why she journeyed, and whither.

He answered--when he replied at all--that he had no knowledge of these things. And I knew he lied, but did not know how I might make him speak.

Nor would he tell me how and when she had slipped away from me the night before, or where she had likely gone, pretending that I had been mistaken when I told him I had seen him watching us beside the star-illumined stream.

"Mayaro slept," he said quite calmly. "The soldier, Mount, stood fire-guard. Of what my brother Loskiel and this strange maiden did under the Oneida Dancers and the Belt of Tamanund, Mayaro has no knowledge."

Why should he lie? I did not know. And even were I to attempt to confound his statement by an appeal to Mount, the rifleman must corroborate him, because doubtless the wily Siwanois had not awakened Mount to do his shift at sentry until the maid had vanished, leaving me sleeping.

"Mayaro," I said, "I ask these things only because I pity her and wish her well. It is for her safety I fear. Could you tell me where she may have gone?"

"Fowls to the home-yard; the wild bird to the wood," he said gravely. "Where do the rosy-throated pigeons go in winter? Does my brother Loskiel know where?"

"Sagamore," I said earnestly, "this maid is no wild gypsy thing--no rose-tinted forest pigeon. She has been bred at home, mannered and schooled. She knows the cote, I tell you, and not the bush, where the wild hawk hangs mewing in the sky. Why has she fled to the wilderness alone?"

The Indian said cunningly:

"Why has my brother Loskiel abandoned roof and fire for a bed on the forest moss?"

"A man must do battle for his own people, Sagamore."

"A white maid may do what pleases her, too, for aught I know," he said indifferently.

"Why does it please her to roam abroad alone?"

"How should I know?"

"You do know!"

"Loskiel," he said, "if I know why, perhaps I know of other matters, too. Ask me some day--before they send you into battle."

"What matters do you know of?"

"Ask me no more, Loskiel--until your conch-horns blowing in the forest summon Morgan's men to battle. Then ask; and a Sagamore will answer--a Siwanois Mohican--of the magic clan. Hiero!"

That ended it; he had spoken, and I was not fool enough to urge him to another word.

And now, as I rode, my mind was still occupied with my growing concern for the poor child I had come to pity so. Within me a furtive tenderness was growing which sometimes shamed, sometimes angered me, or left me self-contemptuous, restless, or dully astonished that my pride permitted it. For in my heart such sentiments for such a maid as this--tenderness, consciousness of some subtlety about her that attracted me--should have no place. There was every reason why I should pity her and offer aid; none why her grey eyes should hold my own; none why the frail body of her in her rags should quicken any pulse of mine; none why my nearness to her should stop my heart and breath.

Yet, all day long her face and slim shape haunted me--a certain sullen sweetness of the lips, too--and I remembered the lithe grace of her little hands as she broke the morsels of that midnight meal and lifted the cup of chilly water in which I saw the star-light dancing. And "Lord!" thought I, amazed at my own folly. "What madness lies in these midsummer solitudes, that I should harbor such fantastic thoughts?"

Seldom, as yet, had dream of woman vexed me--and when I dreamed at all it was but a tinselled figment that I saw--the echo, doubtless, of some tale I read concerning raven hair and rosy lips, and of a vague but wondrous fairness adorned most suitably in silks and jewels.

Dimly I was resigned toward some such goal, first being full of honours won with sword and spur, laden with riches, too, and territories stretching to those sunset hills piled up like sapphires north of Frenchman's Creek.

Out of the castled glory of the dawn, doubtless, I thought, would step one day my vision--to admire my fame and riches. And her I'd marry--after our good King had knighted me.

Alas! For our good King had proved a bloody knave; my visionary lands and riches all had vanished; instead of silk attire and sword, I wore a rifle-shirt and skinning-knife; and out of the dawn-born glory of the hills had stepped no silken damsel of romance to pause and worship me--only a slender, ragged, grey-eyed waif who came indifferent as the chilly wind in spring; who went as April shadows go, leaving no trace behind.

We were riding by the High Dutch Church at last, and beyond, between the roads to Duansboro and Cobus-Kill, we saw the tents and huts of the New York brigade--or as much of it as had arrived--from which we expected soon to be detached.

On a cleared hill beyond the Lower Fort, where the Albany Road runs beside the Fox-Kill, we saw the headquarters flag of the 4th brigade, and Major Nicholas Fish at his tent door, talking to McCrea, our brigade surgeon.

Along the stream were the huts lately tenanted by Colonel Philip Van Cortlandt's Second New York Regiment, which had gone off toward Wyalusing. Schott's riflemen camped there now, and, as we rode by, the soldiers stared at our Indian. Then we passed Gansevoort's Third Regiment, under tents and making ready to march; and the log cantonment of Colonel Lamb's artillery, where the cannoneers saluted, then, for no reason, cheered us. Beyond were camped Alden's Regiment, I think, and in the rear the Fourth and Fifth New York. A fort flew our own regimental flag beside the pretty banner of our new nation.

"Oho!" said Boyd, with an oath. "I'm damned if I care for barracks when a bed in the open is good enough. Why the devil have they moved us indoors, do you think?"

I knew no more than did he, and liked our new quarters no better.

At the fort gate the sentry saluted, and we dismounted. Our junior ensign, Benjamin Chambers, a smart young dandy, met us at the guard-house, directed Boyd to Captain Simpson's log quarters, and then led the Sagamore inside.

"Is this our Moses?" whispered the young ensign in my ear. "Egad, Loskiel, he looks a treacherous devil, in his paint, to lead us to the promised land."

"He is staunch, I think," said I. "But for heaven's sake, Benny, are we to sleep in filthy barracks in July?"

"Not you, I hear," he said, laughing, "----though they're clean enough, by the way! But the Major's orders were to build a hut for you and this pretty and fragrant aborigine down by the river, and lodge him there under your eye and nose and rifle. I admit very freely, Loskiel, no man in Morgan's envies you your bed-fellow!" And he whisked his nose with a scented handkerchief.

"They would envy me if they knew this Sagamore as I think I know him," said I, delighted that I was not to lie in barracks foul or clean. "Where is this same humble hut, my fashionable friend?"

"I'll show you presently. I think that Jimmy Parr desires to see your gentle savage," he added flippantly.

We seated ourselves on the gate-bench to await the Major's summons; the dandified young ensign crossed the parade, mincing toward the quarters of Major Parr. And I saw him take a pinch o' the scented snuff he affected, and whisk his supercilious nose again with his laced hanker. It seemed odd that a man like that should have saved our Captain Simpson's life at Saratoga.

Riflemen, drovers, batt-men, frontier farmers, and some of the dirty flotsam--trappers, forest-runners, and the like--were continually moving about the parade, going and coming on petty, sordid business of their own; and there were women there, too--pallid refugees from distant farms, and now domiciled within the stockade; gaunt wives of neighbouring settlers, bringing baskets of eggs or pails of milk to sell; and here and there some painted camp-wanton lingering by the gateway on mischief bent, or gossiping with some sister trull, their bold eyes ever roving.

Presently our mincing ensign came to us again, saying that the Sagamore and I were to report ourselves to the Major.

"Jimmy Parr is in good humour," he whispered. "Leave him in that temper, for mercy's sake, Loskiel; he's been scarcely amiable since you left to catch this six-foot savage for him."

He was a brave soldier, our Major, a splendid officer, and a kind and Christian man, but in no wise inclined to overlook the delinquencies of youthful ensigns; and he had rapped our knuckles soundly more than once. But we all loved him in our small mess of five--Captain Simpson, Lieutenant Boyd, and we two ensigns; and I think he knew it. Had we disliked him, among ourselves we would have dubbed him James, intending thereby disrespect; but to us he was Jimmy, flippantly, perhaps, but with a sure affection under all our impudence. And I think, too, that he knew we spoke of him among ourselves as Jimmy, and did not mind.

"Well, sir," he said sternly, as I entered with the Sagamore and gave him the officer's salute, "I have a good report of you from Lieutenant Boyd. I am gratified,

Mr. Loskiel, that my confidence in your ability and in your knowledge of the Indians was not misplaced. And you may inform me now, sir, how it is proper for me to address this Indian guide."

I glanced at Captain Simpson and Lieutenant Boyd, hesitating for a moment. Then I said:

"Mayaro is a Sagamore, Major--a noble and an ensign of a unique clan--the Siwanois, or magic clan, of the Mohican tribe of the great Delaware nation. You may address him as an equal. Our General Schuyler would so address him. The corps of officers in this regiment can scarce do less, I think."

Major Parr nodded, quietly offered his hand to the silent Siwanois, and, holding that warrior's sinewy fist in an iron grip that matched it, named him to Captain Simpson. Then, looking at me, he said slowly, in English:

"Mayaro is a great chief among his people--great in war, wise in council and debate. The Sagamore of the Siwanois Mohicans is welcome in this army and at the headquarters of this regiment. He is now one of us; his pay is the pay of a captain in the rifles. By order of General Clinton, commanding the Fourth, or New York, Brigade, I am requested to say to the Mohican Sagamore that valuable presents will be offered him for his services by General Sullivan, commander-in-chief of this army. These will be given when the Mohican successfully conducts this army to the Genessee Castle and to Catharines-town. I have spoken."

And to me he added bluntly:

"Translate, Mr. Loskiel."

"I think the Sagamore has understood, sir," said I. "Is it not so, Sagamore?"

"Mayaro has understood," said the Indian quietly.

"Does the great Mohican Sagamore accept?"

"My elder brother," replied the Sagamore calmly, "Mayaro has pledged his word to his younger brother Loskiel. A Mohican Sagamore never lies. Loskiel is my friend. Why should I lie to him? A Sagamore speaks the truth."

Which was true in a measure, at least as far as wanton or idle lying is concerned, or cowardly lying either, But he had lied to me concerning his knowledge of the strange maid, Lois, which kind of untruth all Indians consider more civil than a direct refusal to answer a question.

Boyd stood by, smiling, as the Major very politely informed me of the disposition he had made of the Sagamore and myself, recommended Mayaro to my most civil attention, and added that, for the present, I was relieved from routine duty with my battalion.

If the Siwanois perceived any undue precaution in the Major's manner of lodging him, he did not betray by the quiver of an eyelash that he comprehended he was practically under guard. He stalked forth and across the parade beside me, head high, bearing dignified and tranquil.

At the outer gate our junior ensign languidly dusted a speck of snuff from his wristband, and indicated the roof of our hut, which was visible above the feathery river willows. So we proceeded thither, I resigning my horse to the soldier, Mount, who had been holding him, and who was now detailed to act as soldier-servant to me still.

"Jack," said I, "if there be fresh-baked bread in the regimental ovens yonder, fetch a loaf, in God's name. I could gnaw black-birch and reindeer moss, so famished am I--and the Sagamore, too, no doubt, could rattle a flam with a wooden spoon."

But our chief baker was a Low-Dutch dog from Albany; and it was not until I had bathed me in the Mohawk, burrowed into my soldier's chest, and put on clean clothing that Jack Mount managed to steal the loaf he had asked for in vain. And this, with a bit of salt beef and a bowl of fresh milk, satisfied the Siwanois and myself.

I had been relieved of all routine duty, and was henceforth detailed to foregather with, amuse, instruct and casually keep an eye on my Mohican. In other words, my only duty, for the present, was to act as mentor to the Sagamore, keep him pleasantly affected toward our cause, see that he was not tampered with, and that he had his bellyful three times a day. Also, I was to extract from him in advance any information concerning the Iroquois country that he might have knowledge of.

It was a warm and pleasant afternoon along the river where the batteaux, loaded with stores and soldiers, were passing up, and Oneida canoes danced across the sparkling water toward Fort Plain.

Many of our soldiers were bathing, sporting like schoolboys in the water; Lamb's artillerymen had their horses out to let them swim; many of the troops were washing their shirts along the gravelly reaches, or, seated cross-legged on the bank, were mending rents with needle and thread. Half a dozen Oneida Indians sat gravely smoking and blinking at the scene--no doubt belonging to our corps of runners, scouts, and guides, for all were shaved, oiled, and painted for war, and, under their loosened blankets, I could see their lean and supple bodies, stark naked, except for clout and ankle moccasin.

I sat in the willow-shade before the door of our hut, cross-legged, too, writing in my journal of what had occurred since last I set down the details of the day. This finished, I pouched quill, ink-horn, and journal, and sat a-thinking for a while of that strange maid, and what mischance might come of her woodland roving all alone--with Indian Butler out, and all that vile and painted, blue-eyed crew under McDonald.

Sombre thoughts assailed me there on that sunny July afternoon; I rested my elbow on my knee, forehead pressed against my palm, pondering. And ever within my breast was I conscious of a faint, dull aching--a steady and perceptible apprehension which kept me restless, giving my mind no peace, my brooding thoughts no rest.

That this shabby, wandering girl had so gained me, spite of the rudeness with which she used me, I could never seem to understand; for she had done nothing to win even my pity, and she was but a ragged gypsy thing, and had conducted with scant courtesy.

Why had I given her my ring? Was it only because I pitied her and desired to offer her a gift she might sell when necessary? Why had I used her as a comrade--who had been but the comrade of an hour? Why had I been so loath to part with her whom I scarce had met? What was it in her that had fixed my attention? What allure? What unusual quality? What grace of mind or person?

A slender, grey-eyed gypsy-thing in rags! And I could no longer rid my mind of her!

What possessed me? To what lesser nature in me was such a woman as this appealing? I would have been ashamed to have any officer or man of my corps see me abroad in company with her. I knew it well enough. I knew that if in this girl anything was truly appealing to my unquiet heart I should silence even the slightest threat of any response--discourage, ignore, exterminate the last unruly trace of sentiment in her regard.

Yet I remained there motionless, thinking, thinking--her faded rosebud lying in my hand, drooping but still fragrant.

Dismiss her from my thoughts I could not. The steady, relentless desire to see her; the continual apprehension that some mischance might overtake her, left me no peace of mind, so that the memory of her, not yet a pleasure even, nagged, nagged, nagged, till every weary nerve in me became unsteady.

I stretched out above the river bank, composing my body to rest--sleep perhaps. But flies and sun kept me awake, even if I could have quieted my mind.

So up again, and walked to the hut door, where within I beheld the Sagamore gravely repainting himself with the terrific emblems of death. He was seated cross-legged on the floor, my camp mirror before him--a superb specimen of manhood, naked save for clout, beaded sporran, and a pair of thigh moccasins, the most wonderful I had ever seen.

I admired his war-girdle and moccasins, speaking somewhat carelessly of the beautiful shell-work designs as "wampum"--an Iroquois term.

"Seawan," he said coldly, correcting me and using the softer Siwanois term. Then, with that true courtesy which ever seeks to ease a merited rebuke, he spoke pleasantly concerning shell-beads, and how they were made and from what, and how it was that the purple beads were the gold, the white beads the silver, and the black beads the copper equivalents in English coinage. And so we conducted very politely and agreeably there in the hut, the while he painted himself like a ghastly death, and brightened the scarlet clan-symbol tatooed on his breast by touching its outlines with his brilliant paint. Also, he rebraided his scalp-lock with great care, doubtless desiring that it should appear a genteel trophy if taken from him, and be an honour to his conqueror and himself.

These matters presently accomplished, he drew from their soft and beaded sheaths hatchet and knife, and fell to shining them up as industriously as a full-fed cat polishes her fur.

"Mayaro," said I, amused, "is a battle then near at hand that you make so complete a preparation for it?"

A half-smile appeared for a moment on his lips:

"It is always well to be prepared for life or death, Loskiel, my younger brother."

"Oho!" said I, smiling. "You understood the express rider when he said that Indians had fired on our pickets a week ago!"

The stern and noble countenance of the Sagamore relaxed into the sunniest of smiles.

"My little brother is very wise. He has discovered that the Siwanois have ears like white men."

"Aye--but, Sagamore, I was not at all certain that you understood in English more than 'yes' and 'no.'"

"Is it because," he inquired with a merry glance at me, "my brother has only heard as yet the answer 'no' from Mayaro?"

I bit my lip, reddened, and then laughed at the slyly taunting reference to my lack of all success in questioning him concerning the little maiden, Lois.

At the same time, I realized on what a friendly footing I already stood with this Mohican. Few white men ever see an Iroquois or a Delaware laugh; few ever witness any relaxation in them or see their coldly dignified features alter, except in scorn, suspicion, pride, and anger. Only in time of peace and amid their own intimates or families do our Eastern forest Indians put off the expressionless and dignified mask they wear, and become what no white man believes them capable of becoming--human, tender, affectionate, gay, witty, talkative, as the moment suits.

At Guy Park, even, I had never seen an Iroquois relax in dignity and hauteur, though, of course, it was also true that Guy Johnson was never a man to inspire personal confidence or any intimacy. Nor was Walter Butler either; and Brant and his Mohawks detested and despised him.

But I had been told that Indians--I mean the forest Indians, not the vile and filthy nomad butchers of the prairies--were like ourselves in our own families; and that, naturally, they were a kindly, warm-hearted, gay, and affectionate people, fond of their wives and children, and loyal to their friends.

Now, I could not but notice how, from the beginning, this Siwanois had conducted, and how, when first we met, his eye and hand met mine. And ever since, also--even when I was watching him so closely--in my heart I really found it well-nigh impossible to doubt him.

He spoke always to me in a manner very different to that of any Indian I had ever known. And now it seemed to me that from the very first I had vaguely realized a sense of unwonted comradeship with this Siwanois.

At all events, it was plain enough now that, for some reason unknown to me, this Mohican not only liked me, but so far trusted me--entertained, in fact, so unusual a confidence in me--that he even permitted himself to relax and speak to me playfully, and with the light familiarity of an elder brother.

"Sagamore," I said, "my heart is very anxious for the safety of this little forest-running maid. If I could find her, speak to her again, I think I might aid her."

Mayaro's features became smooth and blank.

"What maiden is this my younger brother fears for?" he asked mildly.

"Her name is Lois. You know well whom I mean."

"Hai!" he exclaimed, laughing softly. "Is it still the rosy-throated pigeon of the forest for whom my little brother Loskiel is spreading nets?"

My face reddened again, but I said, smilingly:

"If Mayaro laughs at what I say, all must be well with her. My elder brother's heart is charitable to the homeless."

"And to children, also," he said very quietly. And added, with a gleam of humour, "All children, O Loskiel, my littlest brother! Is not my heart open to you?"

"And mine to you, Mayaro, my elder brother."

"Yet, you watched me at the fire, every night," he said, with keenest delight sparkling in his dark eyes.

"And yet I tracked and caught you after all!" I said, smiling through my slight chagrin.

"Is my little brother very sure I did not know he followed me?" he asked, amused.

"Did you know, Mayaro?"

The Siwanois made a movement of slight, but good-humoured, disdain:

"Can my brother who has no wings track and follow the October swallow?"

"Then you were willing that I should see the person to whom you brought food under the midnight stars?"

"My brother has spoken."

"Why were you willing that I should see?"

"Where there are wild pigeons there are hawks, Loskiel. But perhaps the rosy throat could not understand the language of a Siwanois."

"You warned her not to rove alone?"

He inclined his head quietly.

"She refused to heed you! Is that true? She left Westchester in spite of your disapproval?"

"Loskiel does not lie."

"She must be mad!" I said, with some heat. "Had she not managed to keep our camp in view, what had become of her now, Sagamore?" I added, reluctantly admitting by implication yet another defeat for me.

"Of course I know that you must have kept in communication with her--though how you did so I do not know."

The Siwanois smiled slyly.

"Who is she? What is she, Mayaro? Is she, after all, but a camp-gypsy of the better class? I can not believe it--yet--she roves the world in tatters, haunting barracks and camps. Can you not tell me something concerning her?"

The Indian made no reply.

"Has she made you promise not to?"

He did not answer, but I saw very plainly that this was so.

Mystified, perplexed, and more deeply troubled than I cared to admit to myself, I rose from the door-sill, buckled on belt, knife, and hatchet, and stood looking out over the river in silence for a while.

The Siwanois said pleasantly, yet with a hidden hint of malice:

"If my brother desires to walk abroad in the pleasant weather, Mayaro will not run away. Say so to Major Parr."

I blushed furiously at the mocking revelation that he had noted and understood the precautions of Major Parr.

"Mayaro," I said, "I trust you. See! You are confided to me, I am responsible for you. If you leave I shall be disgraced. But--Siwanois are free people! The Sagamore is my elder brother who will not blacken my face or cast contempt upon my uniform. See! I trust my brother Mayaro, I go."

The Sagamore looked me square in the eye with a face which was utterly blank and expressionless. Then he gathered his legs under him, sprang noiselessly to his feet, laid his right hand on the hilt of my knife, and his left one on his own, drew both bright blades with a simultaneous and graceful movement, and drove his knife into my sheath, mine into his own.

My heart stood still; I had never expected even to witness such an act--never dared believe that I should participate in it.

The Siwanois drew my knife from his sheath, touched the skin of his wrist with the keen edge. I followed his example; on our wrists two bright spots of blood beaded the skin.

Then the Sagamore filled a tin cup with clean water and extended his wrist. A single drop of blood fell into it. I did the same.

Then in silence still, he lifted the cup to his lips, tasted it, and passed it to me. I wet my lips, offered it to him again. And very solemnly he sprinkled the scarcely tinted contents over the grass at the door-sill.

So was accomplished between this Mohican and myself the rite of blood brotherhood--an alliance of implicit trust and mutual confidence which only death could end.

CHAPTER VI
THE SPRING WAIONTHA

It happened the following afternoon that, having written in my journal, and dressed me in my best, I left the Mohican in the hut a-painting and shining up his weapons, and walked abroad to watch the remaining troops and the artillery start for Otsego Lake.

A foot regiment--Colonel Gansevoort's--had struck tents and marched with its drums and colours early that morning, carrying also the regimental wagons and batteaux. However, I had been told that this veteran regiment was not to go with the army into the Iroquois country, but was to remain as a protection to Tryon County. But now Colonel Lamb's remaining section of artillery was to march to the lake; and whether this indicated that our army at last was fairly in motion, nobody knew. Yet, it seemed scarcely likely, because Lieutenant Boyd had been ordered out with a scout of twenty men toward the West branch of the Delaware, and he told me that he expected to be absent for several days. Besides, it was no secret that arms had not yet been issued and distributed to all the recruits in the foot regiments; that

Schott's riflemen had not yet drawn their equipment, and that as yet we had not collected half the provisions required for an extensive campaign, although nearly every day the batteaux came up the river with stores from Schenectady and posts below.

Strolling up from the river that afternoon, very fine in my best, and, I confess, content with myself except for the lack of hair powder, queue, and ribbon, which ever disconcerted me, I saw already the two guns of the battalion of artillery moving out of their cantonment, the limbers, chests, and the forge well horsed and bright with polish and paint, the men somewhat patched and ragged, but with queues smartly tied and heads well floured.

Had our cannoneers been properly and newly uniformed, it had been a fine and stirring sight, with the artillery bugle-horn sounding the march, and the camp trumpets answering, and Colonel Lamb riding ahead with his mounted officers, very fine and nobly horsed, the flag flying smartly and most beautiful against the foliage of the terraced woods.

A motley assembly had gathered to see them march out; our General Clinton and his staff, in the blue and buff of the New York Line, had come over, and all the officers and soldiers off duty, too, as well as the people of the vicinity, and a horde of workmen, batteaux-men, and forest runners, including a dozen Oneida Indians of the guides.

Poor Alden's 6th Massachusetts foot regiment, which was just leaving for the lake on its usual road-mending detail, stood in spiritless silence to see the artillery pass; their Major, Whiting, as well as the sullen rank and file, seeming still to feel the disgrace of Cherry Valley, where their former colonel lost his silly life, and Major Stacia was taken, and still remained a prisoner.

As for us of Morgan's, we were very sorry for the mortified New Englanders, yet not at all forgetful of their carping and insolent attitude toward the ragged New York Line--where at least the majority of our officers were gentlemen and where proper and military regard for rank was most decently maintained. Gad! To hear your New Englander talk, a man might think that this same war was being maintained and fought by New England alone. And, damn them, they got Schuyler laid aside after all. But the New York Line went about its grim and patient business, unheeding their New England arrogance as long as His Excellency understood the truth concerning the wretched situation. And I for one marvelled that the sniffling 'prentices of Massachusetts and the Connecticut barbers and tin-peddlers had the effrontery to boast of New England valour while that arch-malcontent, Ethan Allen, and his petty and selfish yokels of Vermont, openly defied New York and Congress, nor scrupled to conduct most treasonably, to their everlasting and black disgrace. No Ticonderoga, no Bennington, could wipe out that outrageous treachery, or efface the villainy of what was done to Schuyler--the man who knew no fear, the officer without reproach.

The artillery jolted and clinked away down the rutty road which their wheels and horses cut into new and deeper furrows; a veil of violet dust hung in their wake, through which harness, cannon, and drawn cutlass glittered and glimmered like sunlit ripples through a mist.

Then came our riflemen marching as escort, smart and gay in their brown forest-dress, the green thrums rippling and flying from sleeve and leggin' and open double-cape, and the raccoon-tails all a-bobbing behind their caps like the tails that April lambkins wriggle.

Always the sight of my own corps thrilled me. I thanked God for those big, sun-masked men with their long, silent, gliding stride, their shirts open to their mighty chests, and the heavy rifles all swinging in glancing unison on their caped shoulders, carried as lightly as so many reeds.

I stood at salute as our Major and Captain Simpson strode by; grinned ever so little as Boyd came swinging along, his naked cutlass drawn, scarlet fringes tossing on his painted cape. He whispered as he passed:

"Murphy and Elerson took two scalps last night. They're drying on hoops in the barracks. Look and see if they be truly Seneca."

At that I was both startled and disgusted; but it was well-nigh impossible to prevent certain of our riflemen who had once been wood-runners from treating the Iroquois as the Iroquois treated them. And they continued to scalp them as naturally as they once had clipped pads and ears from panther and wolf. Mount and the rifleman Renard no longer did it, and I had thought to have persuaded Murphy and Elerson to conduct more becoming. But it seemed that I had failed.

My mind was filled with resentful thoughts as I entered the Lower Fort and started across the swarming parade toward the barracks, meaning to have a look at these ghastly trophies and judge to what nation they belonged.

People of every walk in life were passing and repassing where our regimental wagons were being loaded, and I threaded my way with same difficulty amid a busy throng, noticing nobody, unless it were one of my own corps who saluted my cockade.

Halfway across, a young woman bearing a gunny-sack full of linen garments and blankets to be washed blocked my passage, and being a woman I naturally gave her right of way. And the next instant saw it was Lois.

She had averted her head, and was now hurriedly passing on, and I turned sharply on my heel and came up beside her.

"Lois," I managed to say with a voice that was fairly steady, "have you forgotten me?"

Her head remained resolutely averted; and as I continued beside her, she said, without looking at me:

"Do you not understand that you are disgracing yourself by speaking to me on the parade? Pass on, sir, for your own sake."

"I desire to speak to you," I said obstinately.

"No. Pass on before any officers see you!"

My face, I know, was fiery red, and for an instant all the ridicule, the taunts, the shame which I might well be storing up for myself, burned there for anyone to see. But stronger than fear of ridicule rose a desperate determination not to lose this maid again, and whether what I was doing was worthy, and for her sake, or unworthy, and for my own, I did not understand or even question.

"I wish to talk with you," I said doggedly. "I shall not let you go this time."

"Are you mad to so conduct under the eyes of the whole fort?" she whispered. "Go your way!"

"I'd be madder yet to let you get away again. My way is yours."

She halted, cheeks blazing, and looked at me for the first time.

"I ask you not to persist," she said, "----for my sake if not for yours. What an officer or a soldier says to a girl in this fort makes her a trull in the eyes of any man who sees. Do you so desire to brand me, Mr. Loskiel?"

"No," I said between my teeth, and turned to leave her. And, I think, it was something in my face that made her whisper low and hurriedly:

"Waiontha Spring! If you needs must see me for a moment more, come there!"

I scarcely heard, so tight emotion had me by the throat, and walked on blindly, all a-quiver. Yet, in my ears the strange wards sounded: "Waiontha--Waiontha--come to the Spring Waiontha--if you needs must see me."

On a settle before the green-log barrack, some of Schott's riflemen were idling, and now stood, seeing an officer.

"Boys," I said, "where is this latest foolery of Tim Murphy hung to dry?"

They seemed ashamed, but told me, As I moved on, I said carelessly, partly turning:

"Where is the Spring Waiontha?"

"On the Lake Trail, sir--first branch of the Stoney-Kill."

"Is there a house there?"

"Rannock's."

"A path to find it?"

"A sheep walk only. Rannock is dead. The destructives murdered him when they burned Cherry Valley. Mrs. Rannock brings us eggs and milk."

I walked on and entered the smoky barracks, and the first thing I saw was a pair o' scalps, stretched and hooped, a-dangling from the rafters.

Doubtless, Murphy and Elerson meant to sew them to their bullet pouches when cured and painted. And there was one reckless fellow in my company who wore a baldrick fringed with Shawanese scalps; but as these same Shawanese had murdered his father, mother, grandmother, and three little brothers, no officer rebuked him, although it was a horrid and savage trophy; but if the wearing of it were any comfort to him I do not know.

I looked closely at the ornamented scalps, despite my repugnance. They were not Mohawk, not Cayuga, nor Onondaga. Nor did they seem to me like Seneca, being not oiled and braided clean, but tagged at the root with the claws of a tree-lynx. They were not Oneida, not Lenape. Therefore, they must be Seneca scalps. Which meant that Walter Butler and that spawn of satan, Sayanquarata, were now prowling around our outer pickets. For the ferocious Senecas and their tireless war-chief, Sayanquarata, were Butler's people; the Mohawks and Joseph Brant holding the younger Butler in deep contempt for the cruelty he did practice at Cherry Valley.

Suddenly a shaft of fear struck me like a swift arrow in the breast, as I thought of

Butler and of his Mountain Snakes, and of that mad child, Lois, a-gypsying whither her silly inclination led her; and Death in the forest-dusk watching her with a hundred staring eyes.

"This time," I muttered, "I shall put a stop to all her forest-running!" And, at the thought, I turned and passed swiftly through the doorway, across the thronged parade, out of the gate.

Hastening my pace along the Lake Road, meeting many people at first, then fewer, then nobody at all, I presently crossed the first little brook that feeds the Stoney-Kill, leaping from stone to stone. Here in the woods lay the Oneida camp. I saw some squaws there sewing.

The sheep walk branched a dozen yards beyond, running northward through what had been a stump field. It was already grown head-high in weeds and wild flowers, and saplings of bird-cherry, which spring up wherever fire has passed. A few high corn-stalks showed what had been planted there a year ago.

After a few moments following the path, I found that the field ended abruptly, and the solid walls of the forest rose once more like green cliffs towering on every side. And at their base I saw a house of logs, enclosed within a low brush fence, and before it a field of brush.

Shirts and soldiers' blankets lay here and there a-drying on the bushes; a wretched garden-patch showed intensely green between a waste of fire-blackened stumps. I saw chickens in a coop, and a cow switching forest flies. A cloud of butterflies flew up as I approached, where the running water of a tiny rill made muddy hollows on the path. This doubtless must be the outlet to Waiontha Spring, for there to the left a green lane had been bruised through the elder thicket; and this I followed, shouldering my way amid fragrant blossom and sun-hot foliage, then through an alder run, and suddenly out across a gravelly reach where water glimmered in a still and golden pool.

Lois knelt there on the bank. The soldiers' linen I had seen in her arms was piled beside her. In a willow basket, newly woven, I saw a heap of clean, wet shirts and tow-cloth rifle-frocks.

She heard me behind her--I took care that she should--but she made no sign that she had heard or knew that I was there. Even when I spoke she continued busy with her suds and shirts; and I walked around the gravelly basin and seated myself near her, cross-legged on the sand, both hands clasping my knees.

"Well?" she asked, still scrubbing, and her hair was fallen in curls about her brow--hair thicker and brighter, though scarce longer, than my own. But Lord! The wild-rose beauty that flushed her cheeks as she laboured there! And when she at last looked up at me her eyes seemed like two grey stars, full of reflections from the golden pool.

"I have come," said I, "to speak most seriously."

"What is it you wish?"

"A comrade's privilege."

"And what may that be, sir?"

"The right to be heard; the right to be answered--and a comrade's privilege to offer aid."

"I need no aid."

"None living can truthfully say that," said I pleasantly.

"Oh! Do you then require charity from this pleasant world we live in?"

"I did not offer charity to you."

"You spoke of aid," she said coldly.

"Lois--is there in our brief companionship no memory that may warrant my speaking as honestly as I speak to you?"

"I know of none, Do you?"

I had been looking at her chilled pink fingers. My ring was gone.

"A ring for a rose is my only warrant," I said.

She continued to soap the linen and to scrub in silence. After she had finished the garment and wrung it dry, she straightened her supple figure where she was kneeling, and, turning toward me, searched in her bosom with one little, wet hand, drawing from it a faded ribbon on which my ring hung.

"Do you desire to have it of me again?" she asked, without any expression on her sun-freckled face.

"What? The ring?"

"Aye! Desire it!" I repeated, turning red. "No more than you desire the withered bud you left beside me while I slept."

"What bud, sir?"

"Did you not leave me a rose-bud?"

"I?"

"And a bit of silver birch-bark scratched with a knife point?"

"Now that I think of it, perhaps I may have done so--or some such thing--scarce knowing what I was about--and being sleepy. What was it that I wrote? I can not now remember--being so sleepy when I did it."

"And that is all you thought about it, Lois?"

"How can one think when half asleep"

"Here is your rose," I said angrily. "I will take my ring again."

She opened her grey eyes at that.

"Lord!" she murmured in an innocent and leisurely surprise. "You have it still, my rose? Are roses scarce where you inhabit, sir? For if you find the flower so rare and curious I would not rob you of it--no!" And, bending, soaked and soaped another shirt.

"Why do you mock me, Lois?"

"I! Mock you! La! Sir, you surely jest."

"You do so! You have done so ever since we met. I ask you why?" I repeated, curbing my temper.

"Lord!" she murmured, shaking her head. "The young man is surely going stark! A girl in my condition--such a girl as I mock at an officer and a gentleman? No, it is beyond all bounds; and this young man is suffering from the sun."

"Were it not," said I angrily, "that common humanity brought me here and bids me remain for the moment, I would not endure this."

"Heaven save us all!" she sighed. "How very young is this young man who comes complaining here that he is mocked--when all I ventured was to marvel that he had found a wild rose-bud so rare and precious!"

I said to myself: "Damn! Damn!" in fierce vexation, yet knew not how to take her nor how to save my dignity. And she, with head averted, was laughing silently; I could see that, too; and never in my life had I been so flouted to my face.

"Listen to me!" I broke out bluntly. "I know not who or what you are, why you are here, whither you are bound. But this I do know, that beyond our pickets there is peril in these woods, and it is madness for man or maid to go alone as you do."

The laughter had died out in her face. After a moment it became grave.

"Was it to tell me this that you spoke to me in the fort, Mr. Loskiel?" she asked.

"Yes, Two days ago our pickets were fired on by Indians. Last night two rifle-men of our corps took as many Seneca scalps. Do you suppose that when I heard of these affairs I did not think of you--remembering what was done but yesterday at Cherry Valley?"

"Did you--remember--me?"

"Good God, yes!" I exclaimed, my nerves on edge again at the mere memory of her rashness. "I came here as a comrade--wishing to be of service, and--you have used me----"

"Vilely," she said, looking serenely at me.

"I did not say that, Lois----"

"I say it, Mr. Loskiel. And yet--I told you where to find me. That is much for me to tell to any man. Let that count a little to my damaged credit with you.... And--I still wear the ring you gave.... And left a rose for you, Let these things count a little in my favour. For you can scarcely guess how much of courage it had cost me." She knelt there, her bared arms hanging by her side, the sun bright on her curls, staring at me out of those strange, grey eyes.

"Since I have been alone," she said in a low voice, "no man--unless by a miracle it be you--has offered me a service or a kindness except that he awaited his reward. Soon or late their various songs became the same familiar air. It is the only song I've heard from men--with endless variations, truly, often and cunningly disguised--yet ever the same and sorry theme.... Men are what God made them; God has seemed to fashion me to their liking--I scarce know how--seeing I walk in rags, unkempt, and stained with wind and rain, and leaf and earth and sun."

She made a childish gesture, sweeping the curls aside with both her hands:

"I sheared my hair! Look at me, sir--a wild thing in a ragged shift and tattered gown--all burnt and roughened with the sun and wind--not even clean to look on--yet that I am!--and with no friend to speak to save an Indian.... I ask you, sir, what it is in me--and what lack of pride must lie in men that I can not trust myself to the company of one among them--not one! Be he officer, or common soldier--all are the same."

She dropped her head, and, thoughtfully, her hands again crept up and wandered over her cheeks and hair, the while her grey eyes, fixed and remote, seemed lost in speculation. Then she looked up again:

"Why should I think to find you different?" she asked, "Is any man different from his fellows, humble or great? Is it not man himself, not only men, that I must face as I have faced you--with silence, or with sullen speech, or with a hardness far beyond my years, and a gaiety that means nothing more kind than insolence?"

Again her head fell on her breast, and her hands linked themselves on her knees as she knelt there in silence.

"Lois," I said, trying to think clearly, "I do not know that other men and I are different. Once I believed so. But--lately--I do not know. Yet, I know this: selfish or otherwise, I can not endure the thought of you in peril."

She looked at me very gravely; then dropped her head once more.

"I don't know," I said desperately, "I wish to be honest--tell you no lie--tell none to myself. I--your beauty--has touched me--or whatever it is about you that attracts. And, whatever gown you go in, I scarcely see it--somehow--finding you so--so strangely--lovely--in speech also--and in--every way.... And now that I have not lied to you--or to myself--in spite of what I have said, let me be useful to you. For I can be; and perhaps these other sentiments will pass away----"

She looked up so suddenly that I ceased speaking, fearful of a rebuff; but saw only the grave, grey eyes looking straight into mine, and a sudden, deeper colour waning from her cheeks.

"Whatever I am," said I, "I can be what I will. Else I were no man. If your--beauty--has moved me, that need not concern you--and surely not alarm you. A woman's beauty is her own affair. Men take their chance with it--as I take mine with yours--that it do me no deep damage. And if it do, or do not, our friendship is still another matter; for it means that I wish you well, desire to aid you, ease your burdens, make you secure and safe, vary your solitude with a friendly word--I mean, Lois, to be to you a real comrade, if you will. Will you?"

After a moment she said:

"What was it that you said about my--beauty?"

"I take my chances that it do me no deep damage."

"Oh! Am I to take my chance, too?"

"What chance?"

"That--your kindness do me--no damage?"

"What senseless talk is this you utter?"

She shook her head slowly, then:

"What a strange boy! I do not fear you."

"Fear me?" I repeated, flushing hotly. "What is there to fear? I am neither yokel nor beast."

"They say a gentleman should be more dreaded."

I stared at her, then laughed:

"Ask yourself how far you need have dread of me--when, if you desire it, you can leave me dumb, dismayed, lip-bound by your mocking tongue--which God knows well I fear."

"Is my tongue so bitter then? I did not know it."

"I know it," said I with angry emphasis. "And I tell you very freely that----"

She stole a curious glance at me. Something halted me--an expression I had never yet seen there in her face, twitching at her lips--hovering on them now-- parting them in a smile so sweet and winning that, silenced by the gracious transformation, unexpected, I caught my breath, astonished.

"What is your given name?" she asked, still dimpling at me, and her eyes now but two blue wells of light.

"Euan," I said, foolish as a flattered schoolboy, and as awkward.

"Euan," she said, still smiling at me, "I think that I could be your friend--if you do truly wish it. What is it you desire of me? Ask me once more, and make it very clear and plain."

"Only your confidence; that is all I ask."

"Oh! Is that all you ask of me?" she mimicked mockingly; but so sweet her smile, and soft her voice, that I did not mind her words.

"Remember," said I, "that I am older than you. You are to tell me all that troubles you."

"When?"

"Now."

"No. I have my washing to complete, And you must go. Besides, I have mending, darning, and my knitting yet to do. It all means bed and bait to me."

"Will you not tell me why you are alone here, Lois?"

"Tell you what? Tell you why I loiter by our soldiers' camps like any painted drab? I will tell you this much; I need no longer play that shameless role."

"You need not use those words in the same breath when speaking of yourself," I answered hotly.

"Then--you do not credit ill of me?" she asked, a bright but somewhat fixed and painful smile on her red lips.

"No!" said I bluntly. "Nor did I ever."

"And yet I look the part, and seem to play it, too. And still you believe me honest?"

"I know you are."

"Then why should I be here alone--if I am honest, Euan?"

"I do not know; tell me."

"But--are you quite certain that you do not ask because you doubt me?"

I said impatiently: "I ask, knowing already you are good above reproach. I ask so I may understand how best to aid you."

A lovely colour stole into her cheeks.

"You are kind, Euan. And it is true--though--" and she shrugged her shoulders, "what other man would credit it?" She lifted her head a little and looked at me with clear, proud eyes:

"Well, let them say what they may in fort and barracks twixt this frontier and Philadelphia. The truth remains that I have been no man's mistress and am no trull. Euan, I have starved that I might remain exactly what I am at this moment. I swear to you that I stand here unsullied and unstained under this untainted sky which the same God made who fashioned me. I have known shame and grief and terror; I have lain cold and ill and sleepless; I have wandered roofless, hunted, threatened, mocked, beset by men and vice. Soldiers have used me roughly--you yourself saw, there at the Poundridge barracks! And only you among all men saw truly. Why should I not give to you my friendship, unashamed?"

"Give it," I said, more deeply moved than ever I had been.

"I do! I do! Rightly or wrongly, now, at last, and in the end, I give my honest heart and friendship to a man!" And with a quick and winning gesture she offered me her hand; and I took it firmly in my clasp, and fell a-trembling so I could not find a word to utter.

"Come to me to-night, Euan," she said. "I lodge yonder. There is a poor widow there--a Mrs. Rannock--who took me in. They killed her husband in November. I am striving to repay her for the food and shelter she affords me. I have been given mending and washing at the fort. You see I am no leech to fasten on a body and nourish me for nothing. So I do what I am able. Will you come to me this night?"

"Yes." But I could not yet speak steadily.

"Come then; I--I will tell you something of my miserable condition--if you desire to know.... Truly I think, speaking to no one, this long and unhappy silence has eaten and corroded part of me within--so ill am I at moments with the pain and shame I've borne so long--so long, Euan! Ah--you do not--know.... And it may be that when you do come to-night I have repented of my purposes--locked up my wounded heart again. But I shall try to tell you--something. For I need somebody--need kindly council very sorely, Euan. And even the Sagamore now fails me--on the threshold----"

"What?"

"He means it for the best; he fears for me. I will tell you how it is with me when you come to-night. I truly desire to tell you--I--I need to tell you. Will you come to me?"

"On my honour, Lois."

"Then--if you please, will you leave me now? I must do my washing and mending--and----" she smiled, "if you only knew how desperately I need what money I may earn. My garments, Euan, are like to fall from me if these green cockspur thorns give way."

"But, Lois," I said, "I have brought you money!" And I fished from any hunting shirt a great, thick packet of those poor paper dollars, now in such contempt that scarce five hundred of them counted for a dozen good, hard shillings.

"What are you doing?" she said, so coldly that I ceased counting the little squares of currency and looked up at her surprised.

"I am sharing my pay with you," said I. "I have no silver--only these."

"I can not take--money!"

"What?"

"Did you suppose I could?"

"Comrades have a common purse; Why not?"

For a few moments her face wore the same strange expression, then, of a sudden her eyes filled and closed convulsively, and she turned her head, motioning me to leave her.

"Will you not share with me?" I asked, very hot about the ears.

She shook her head and I saw her shoulders heave once or twice.

"Lois," I said gravely, "did you fear I hoped for some--reward? Child--little comrade--only the happiness of aiding you is what I ask for. Share with me then, I beg you. I am not poor."

"No--I can not, Euan," she answered in a stifled voice. "Is there any shame to you in sharing with me?"

"Wait," she whispered. "Wait till you hear. And--thank you--for--your kindness."

"I will be here to-night," I said. "And when we know each other better we will share a common purse."

She did not answer me.

I lingered for a moment, desiring to reassure and comfort her, but knew not how. And so, as she did not turn, I finally went away through the sunlit willows, leaving her kneeling there alone beside the golden pool, her bright head drooping and her hands still covering her face.

As I walked back slowly to the fort, I pondered how to be of aid to her; and knew not how. Had there been the ladies of any officers with the army now, I should have laid her desperate case before them; but all had gone back to Albany before our scout of three returned from Westchester.

Here on the river, within our lines, while the army remained, she would be safe enough from forest peril. Yet I burned and raged to think of the baser peril ever threatening her among men of her own speech and colour. I suppose, considering her condition, they had a right to think her that which she was not and never had been. For honesty and maiden virtue never haunted camps. Only two kinds of women tramped with regiments--the wives of soldiers, and their mistresses.

Yet, somehow her safety must be now arranged, her worth and virtue clearly understood, her needs and dire necessities made known, so that when our army moved she might find a shelter, kind and respectable, within the Middle Fort, or at Schenectady, or anywhere inside our lines.

My pay was small; yet, having no soul dependent on my bounty and needing little myself, I had saved these pitiable dollars that our Congress paid us. Besides, I had a snug account with my solicitor in Albany. She might live on that. I did not need it; seldom drew a penny; my pay more than sufficing. And, after the war had ended--ended----

Just here my heart beat out o' step, and thought was halted for a moment. But with the warm thought and warmer blood tingling me once again, I knew and never doubted that we had not done with one another yet, nor were like to, war or no war. For in all the world, and through all the years of youth, I had never before encountered any woman who had shared with me my waking thoughts and the last and conscious moment ere I slept. But from the time I lost this woman out of my life, something seemed also missing from the world. And when again I found her, life and the world seemed balanced and well rounded once again. And in my breast a strange calm rested me.

As I walked along the rutty lake road, all hatched and gashed by the artillery, I made up my mind to one matter. "She must have clothes!" thought I, "and that's flat!" Perhaps not such as befitted her, but something immediate, and not in tatters--something stout that threatened not to part and leave her naked. For the brier-torn rags she wore scarce seemed to hold together; and her small, shy feet peeped through her gaping shoon in snowy hide-and-seek.

Now, coming hither from the fort, I had already noticed on the Stoney-Kill where our Oneidas lay encamped. So when I sighted the first painted tree and saw the stone pipe hanging, I made for it, and found there the Indians smoking pipes and not in war paint; and their women and children were busy with their gossip, near at hand.

As I had guessed, there by the fire lay a soft and heavy pack of doeskins, open, and a pretty Oneida matron sewing Dutch wampum on a painted sporran for her warrior lord.

The lean and silent warriors came up as I approached, sullenly at first, not knowing what treatment to expect--more shame to the skin we take our pride in!

One after another took the hand I offered in self-respecting silence.

"Brothers," I said, "I come to buy. Sooner or later your young men will put on red paint and oil their bodies. Even now I see your rifles and your hatchets have been polished. Sooner or later the army will move four hundred miles through a wilderness so dark that neither sun nor moon nor stars can penetrate. The old men, the women, the children, and the littlest ones still strapped to the cradle-board, must then remain behind. Is it the truth I speak, my brothers?"

"It is the truth," they answered very quietly, "Then," said I, "they will require food and money to buy with. Is it not true, Oneidas?"

"It is true, brother."

I smiled and turned toward the women who were listening, and who now looked up at me with merry faces.

"I have," said I, "four hundred dollars. It is for the Oneida maid or matron who will sell to me her pretty bridal dress of doeskin--the dress which she has made and laid aside and never worn. I buy her marriage dress. And she will make another for herself against the hour of need."

Two or three girls leaped laughing to their feet; but, "Wait!" said I. "This is for my little sister; and I must judge you where you stand, Oneida forest flowers, so I may know which one among you is most like my little sister in height and girth and narrow feet."

"Is our elder brother's little sister fat and comely?" inquired one giggling and over-plump Oneida maid.

"Not plump," I said; and they all giggled.

Another short one stood on tip-toe, asking bashfully if she were not the proper height to suit me.

But there was a third, graceful and slender, who had risen with the rest, and who seemed to me nearer a match to Lois. Also, her naked, dusky feet were small and shapely.

At a smiling nod from me she hastened into the family lodge and presently re-appeared with the cherished clothing. Fresh and soft and new, she cast the garments on the moss and spread them daintily and proudly to my view for me to mark her wondrous handiwork. And it was truly pretty--from the soft, wampum-broidered shirt with its hanging thrums, to the clinging skirt and delicate thigh-moccasins, wonderfully fringed with purple and inset in most curious designs with painted quills and beads and blue diamond-fronds from feathers of a little jay-bird's wing.

Bit by bit I counted out the currency; and it took some little time. But when it was done she took it eagerly enough, laughing her thanks and dancing away toward her lodge. And if her dusky sisters envied her they smiled on me no less merrily as I took my leave of them. And very courteously a stately chief escorted me to the campfire's edge. The Oneidas were ever gentlemen; and their women gently bred.

Once more at my own hut door, I entered, with a nod to Mayaro, who sat smoking there in freshened war paint. One quick and penetrating glance he darted at the Oneida garment on my arm, but except for that betrayed no curiosity.

"Well, Mayaro," said I, in excellent spirits, "you still wear war paint hopefully, I see. But this army will never start within the week."

The Siwanois smiled to himself and smoked. Then he passed the pipe to me. I drew it twice, rendered it.

"Come," said I, "have you then news that we take the war-trail soon?"

"The war-trail is always open for those who seek it. When my younger brother makes ready for a trail, does he summon it to come to him by magic, or does he seek it on his two legs?"

"Are you hoping to go out with the scout to-night?" I asked. "That would not do."

"I go to-night with my brother Loskiel--to take the air," he said slyly.

"That may not be," I protested, disconcerted. "I have business abroad to-night."

"And I," he said very seriously; but he glanced again at the pretty garments on my arm and gave me a merry look.

"Yes," said I, smilingly, "they are for her. The little lady hath no shoon, no skirt that holds together, save by the grace of cockspur thorns that bind the tatters. Those I have bought of an Oneida girl. And if they do not please her, yet these at least will hold together. And I shall presently write a letter to Albany and send it by the next batteau to my solicitor, who will purchase for her garments far more suitable, and send them to the fort where soon, I trust, she will be lodged in fashion more befitting."

The Sagamore's face had become smooth and expressionless. I laid aside the garments, fished out quill and inkhorn, and, lying flat on the ground, wrote my letter to Albany, describing carefully the maid who was to be fitted, her height, the smallness of her waist and foot as well as I remembered. I wrote, too, that she was thin, but not too thin. Also I bespoke a box of French hair-powder for her, and buckled shoes of Paddington, and stockings, and a kerchief.

"You know better than do I," I wrote, "having a sister to care for, how women dress. They should have shifts, and hair-pegs, and a scarf, and fan, and stays, and scent, and hankers, and a small laced hat, not gilded; cloak, foot-mantle, sun-mask, and a chip hat to tie beneath the chin, and one such as they call after the pretty Mistress Gunning. If women wear banyans, I know not, but whatever they do wear in their own privacy at morning chocolate, in the French fashion, and whatever they do sleep in, buy and box and send to me. And all the money banked with you, put it in her name as well as mine, so that her draughts on it may all be honoured. And this is her name----"

I stopped, dismayed, I did not know her name! And I was about to sign for her full power to share my every penny! Yet, my amazing madness did not strike me as amazing or grotesque, that, within the hour, a maid in a condition such as hers was to divide my tidy fortune with me. Nay, more--for when I signed this letter she would be free to take what she desired and even leave me destitute.

I laughed at the thought--so midsummer mad was I upon that sunny July afternoon; and within me, like a hidden thicket full of birds, my heart was singing wondrous tunes I never knew one note of.

"O Sagamore," I said, lifting my head, "tell me her surname now, because I need it for this business. And I forgot to ask her at the Spring Waiontha."

For a full minute the Indian's countenance turned full on me remained moon-blank. Then, like lightning, flashed his smile.

"Loskiel, my friend, and now my own blood-brother, what magic singing birds have so enchanted your two ears. She is but a child, lonely and ragged--a tattered leaf still green, torn from the stem by storm and stress, blown through the woodlands and whirled here and yonder by every breath of wind. Is it fit that my brother Loskiel should notice such a woman?"

"She is in need, my brother."

"Give, and pass on, Loskiel."

"That is not giving, O my brother."

"Is it to give alone, Loskiel? Or is it to give--that she may render all?"

"Yes, honestly to give. Not to take."

"And yet you know her not, Loskiel."

"But I shall know her yet! She has so promised. If she is friendless, she shall be our friend. For you and I are one, O Sagamore! If she is cold, naked, or hungry, we will build for her a fire, and cover her, and give her meat. Our lodge shall be her lodge; our friends hers, her enemies ours. I know not how this all has come to me, Mayaro, my friend--even as I know not how your friendship came to me, or how now our honour is lodged forever in each other's keeping. But it is true. Our blood has made us of one race and parentage."

"It is the truth," he said.

"Then tell me her name, that I may write it to my friend in Albany."

"I do not know it," he said quietly.

"She never told you?"

"Never," he said. "Listen, Loskiel. What I now tell to you with heart all open and my tongue unloosened, is all I know of her. It was in winter that she came to Philipsburgh, all wrapped in her red cloak. The White Plains Indians were there, and she was ever at their camp asking the same and endless question."

"What question, Mayaro?"

"That I shall also tell you, for I overheard it. But none among the White Plains company could answer her; no, nor no Congress soldier that she asked.

"The soldiers were not unkind; they offered food and fire--as soldiers do, Loskiel," he added, with a flash of Contempt for men who sought what no Siwanois, no Iroquois, ever did seek of any maiden or any chaste and decent woman, white or red.

"I know," I said. "Continue."

"I offered shelter," he said simply. "I am a Siwanois. No women need to dread Mohicans. She learned this truth from me for the first time, I think. Afterward, pitying her, I watched her how she went from camp to camp. Some gave her mending to do, some washing, enabling her to live. I drew clothing and arms and rations as a Hudson guide enrolled, and together she and I made out to live. Then, in the spring, Major Lockwood summoned me to carry intelligence between the lines. And she came with me, asking at every camp the same strange question; and ever the soldiers laughed and plagued and courted her, offering food and fire and shelter--but not the answer to her question. And one day--the day you came to Poundridge-town--and she had sought for me through that wild storm--I met her by the house as I came from North Castle with news of horsemen riding in the rain."

He leaned forward, looking at me steadily.

"Loskiel," he said, "when first I heard your name from her, and that it was you who wanted Mayaro, suddenly it seemed to me that magic was being made. And--I myself gave her her answer--the answer to the question she had asked at every camp."

"Good God!" said I, "did you, then know the answer all the while? And never told her?" But at the same moment I understood how perfectly characteristic of an Indian had been his conduct.

"I knew," he said tranquilly, "but I did not know why this maiden wished to know. Therefore was I silent."

"Why did you not ask her?" But before he spake I knew why too.

"Does a Sagamore ask idle questions of a woman?" he said coldly. "Do the Siwanois babble?"

"No. And yet--and yet----"

"Birds sing, maidens chatter. A Mohican considers ere his tongue is loosed."

"Aye--it is your nature, Sagamore.... But tell me--what was it in the mention of my name that made you think of magic?"

"Loskiel, you came two hundred miles to ask of me the question that this maid had asked in every camp."

"What question?"

"Where lay the trail to Catharines-town," he said.

"Did she ask that?" I demanded in astonishment.

"It was ever the burden of her piping--this rosy-throated pigeon of the woods."

"That is most strange," said I.

"It is doubtless sorcery that she should ask of me an interview with you who came two hundred miles to ask of me the very question."

"But, Mayaro, she did not then know why I had come to seek you."

"I knew as quickly as I heard your name."

"How could you know before you saw me and I had once made plain my business?"

"Birds come and go; but eagles see their natal nest once more before they die."

"I do not understand you, Mayaro."

He made no answer.

"Merely to hear my name from this child's lips, you say you guessed my business with you?"

"Surely, Loskiel--surely. It was all done by magic. And, at once, I knew that I should also speak to her, there in the storm, and answer her her question."

"And did you do so?"

"Yes, Loskiel. I said to her: 'Little sad rosy-throated pigeon of the woods, the vale Yndaia lies by a hidden river in the West. Some call it Catharines-town.'"

I shook my head, perplexed, and understanding nothing.

"Yndaia? Did you say Yndaia, Mayaro?"

Then, as he looked me steadily in the eye, my gaze became uneasy, shifted, fell by an accident upon the blood-red bear reared on his hind legs, pictured upon his breast. And through and through me passed a shock, like the dull thrill of some forgotten thing clutched suddenly by memory--yet clutched in vain.

Vain was the struggle, too, for the faint gleam passed from my mind as it had come; and if the name Yndaia had disturbed me, or seeing the scarlet ensign on his breast, or perhaps both coupled, had seemed to stir some distant memory, I did not know. Only it seemed as though, in mental darkness, I had felt the presence of some living and familiar thing--been conscious of its nearness for an instant ere it had vanished utterly.

The Sagamore's face had become a smooth, blank mask again.

"What has this maid, Lois, to do with Catharines-town?" I asked. "Devils live there in darkness."

"She did not say."

"You do not know?"

"No, Loskiel."

"But," said I, troubled, "why did she journey hither?"

"Because she now believes that only I in all the world could guide her to the vale Yndaia; and that one day I will pity her and take her there."

"Doubtless," I said anxiously, "she has heard at the forts or hereabouts that we are to march on Catharines-town."

"She knows it now, Loskiel"

"And means to follow?" I exclaimed in horror.

"My brother speaks the truth."

"God! What urges the child thither?"

"I do not know, Loskiel. It seems as though a madness were upon her that she must go to Catharines-town. I tell you there is sorcery in all this. I say it--I, a Sagamore of the Enchanted Wolf. Who should know magic when it stirs but I, of the Siwanois--the Magic Clan? Say what you will, my comrade and blood-brother, there is sorcery abroad; and well I know who wrought it, spinning with spiders' webs there by the lost Lake of Kendaia----" He shuddered slightly. "There by the black waters of the lake--that hag--and all her spawn!"

"Catharine Montour!"

"The Toad-woman herself--and all her spawn."

"The Senecas?"

"And the others," he said in a low voice.

A sudden and terrible misgiving assailed me. I swallowed, and then said slowly:

"Two scalps were taken late last night by Murphy and Elerson. And the scalps were not of the Mohawk. Not Oneida, nor Onondaga, nor Cayuga. Mayaro!" I gasped. "So help me God, those scalps are never Seneca!"

"Erie!" he exclaimed with a mixture of rage and horror. And I saw his sinewy hand quivering on his knife-hilt. "Listen, Loskiel! I knew it! No one has told me. I have sat here all the day alone, making my steel bright and my paint fresher, and singing to myself my people's songs. And ever as I sat at the lodge door, something in the summer wind mocked at me and whispered to me of demons. And when I rose and stood at gaze, troubled, and minding every river-breeze, faintly I seemed to scent the taint of evil. If those two scalps be Erie, then where the Cat-People creep their Sorcerer will be found."

"Amochol," I repeated under my breath. And shivered.

For, deep in the secret shadows of that dreadful place where this vile hag, Catharine Montour, ruled it in Catharines-town, dwelt also all that now remained of the Cat-Nation--Eries--People of the Cat--a dozen, it was rumoured, scarcely more--and demons all, serving that horrid warlock, Amochol, the Sorcerer of the Senecas.

What dreadful rites this red priest and his Eries practiced there, none knew, unless it were true that the False Faces knew. But rumour whispered with a thousand tongues of horrors viewless, nameless, inconceivable; and that far to the westward Biskoonah yawned, so close indeed to the world's surface that the waters boiling deep in hell burst into burning fountains in the magic garden where the red priest made his sorcery, alone.

These things I had heard, but vaguely, here and there--a word perhaps at Johnson Hall, a whisper at Fort Johnson, rumours discussed at Guy Park and Schenectady when I was young. But ever the same horror of it filled me, though I believed it not, knowing full well there were no witches, sorcerers, or warlocks in the world; yet, in my soul disturbed concerning what might pass deep in the shadows of that viewless Empire.

"Mayaro," I said seriously, "do you go instantly to the fort and view those scalps."

"Were the braids fastened at the roots with tree-cat claws?"

"Aye!"

"No need to view them, then, Loskiel."

"Are they truly Erie?"

"Cats!" He spat the word from his lips and his eyes blazed.

"And--Amochol!" I asked unsteadily.

"The Cat People creep with the Seneca high priest, mewing under the moon."

"Then--he is surely here?"

"Aye, Loskiel."

"God!" said I, now all a-quiver; "only to slay him! Only to end this demon-thing, this poison spawn of the Woman-Toad! Only to glimpse his scarlet rags fairly along my rifle sight!"

"No bullets touch him."

"That is nonsense, Mayaro----"

"No, Loskiel."

"I tell you he is human! There are no sorcerers on earth. There never were-- except the Witch of Endor----"

"I never heard of her. But the Witch of Catharines-town is living. And her warlock offspring, Amochol!" He squared his broad shoulders, shaking them. "What do

I care?" he said. "I am a Sagamore of the Enchanted Clan!" He struck the painted symbol on his chest. "What do I care for this red priest's sorcery--I, who wear the great Witch Bear rearing in scarlet here across my breast!

"Let the Cat People make their magic! Let Amochol sacrifice to Leshi in Biskoo-nah! Let their accursed Atensi watch the Mohicans from behind the moon. Mayaro is a Sagamore and his clan are Sachems; and the clan was old--old--old, O little brother, before their Hiawatha came to them and made their League for them, and returned again to The Master of Life in his silver cloud-canoe!

"And I say to you, O my blood-brother, that between this sorcerer and me is now a war such as no Mohican ever waged and no man living, white or red, has ever seen. His magic will I fight with magic; his knife and hatchet shall be turned on mine! And I shall deceive and trick and mock him--him and his Erie Cats, till one by one their scalps shall swing above a clean Mohican fire. O Loskiel, my brother, and my other self, a warrior and a Sagamore has spoken. Go, now, to your evening tryst in peace and leave me. For in my ears the Seven Chiefs are whispering--The Thunderers. And Tamanund must hear my speech and read my heart. And the long roll of our Mohican dead must be recited--here and alone by me--the only one who has that right since Uncas died and the Mohican priesthood ended, save for the Sagamores of the Magic Clan.

"Go, now, my brother. Go in peace."

CHAPTER VII
LOIS

When I came to the log house by the Spring Waiontha, lantern in hand and my packet tucked beneath my arm, it was twilight, and the starless skies threatened rain. Road and field and forest were foggy and silent; and I thought of the first time I had ever set eyes on Lois, in the late afternoon stillness which heralded a coming storm.

I had with me, as I say, a camp lantern which enabled me to make my way through the thicket to the Spring Waiontha. Not finding her there, I retraced my steps and crossed the charred and dreary clearing to the house of logs.

No light burned within; doubtless this widow woman was far too poor to afford a light of any sort. But my lantern still glimmered, and I went up to the splintered door and rapped.

Lois opened it, her knitting gathered in her hand, and stood aside for me to enter.

At first, so dusky was the room that I perceived no other occupant beside ourselves. Then Lois said: "Mrs. Rannock, Mr. Loskiel, of whom I spoke at supper, is to be made known to you."

Then first I saw a slight and ghostly figure rise, take shape in the shadows, and move slowly into my lantern's feeble beams----a frail and pallid woman, who made her reverence as though dazed, and uttered not a word.

Lois whispered in my ear:

"She scarcely seems to know she is alive, since Cherry Valley. A Tory slew her little sister with a hatchet; then her husband fell; and then, before her eyes, a blue-eyed Indian pinned her baby to its cradle with a bayonet."

I crossed the room to where she stood, offering my hand; and she laid her thin and work-worn fingers listlessly in mine.

"Madam," I said gently, "there are today two thousand widows such as you betwixt Oriska and Schenectady. And, to our cause, each one of you is worth a regiment of men, your sorrows sacred to us all, strengthening our vows, steeling us to a fierce endeavour. No innocent death in this long war has been in vain; no mother's agony. Yet, only God can comfort such as you."

She shook her head slowly.

"No God can comfort me," she said, in a voice so lifeless that it sounded flat as the words that sleepers utter, dreaming of trouble.

"Shall we be seated outside on the door-sill?" whispered Lois. "The only seat within is on the settle, where she sits."

"Is this the only room?"

"Yes--save for the mouse-loft, where I sleep on last year's corn-husks. Shall we sit outside? We can speak very low. She will not heed us."

Pity for all this stark and naked wretchedness left me silent; then, as the lantern's rays fell on this young girl's rags, I remembered my packet.

"Yes, we will sit outside. But first, I bring you a little gift----"

She looked up quickly and drew back a step, "Oh, but such a little gift, Lois--a nothing--a mere jest of mine which we shall enjoy between us. Take it as I offer it, lightly, and without constraint."

Reluctantly she permitted me to lay the packet in her arms, displeasure still darkening her brow. Then I set my lantern on the puncheon floor and stepped outside, closing the hatchet-battered door behind me.

How long I paced the foggy strip of clearing I do not know. The mist had thickened to rain when I heard the door creak; and, turning in my tracks, caught the lantern's sparkle on the threshold, and the dull gleam of her Oneida finery.

I picked up the lantern and held it high above us.

Smiling and bashful she stood there in her clinging skirt and wampum-broidered vest, her slender, rounded limbs moulded into soft knee-moccasins of fawn-skin, and the Virgin's Girdle knotted across her thighs in silver-tasselled seawan.

And, "Lord!" said I, surprised by the lovely revelation. "What a miracle are you in your forest masquerade!"

"Am I truly fine to please you, Euan?"

I said, disturbed, but striving to speak lightly:

"Little Oneida goddess in your bridal dress, the Seven Dancers are laughing at me from your eyes; and the Day-Sun and the Night-Sun hang from your sacred girdle, making it flash like silvery showers of seawan. Salute, O Watcher at the Gates of Dawn! Onwa oyah! Na-i! A-i! Lois!" And I drew my light war-hatchet from its sheath and raised it sparkling, in salute.

She laughed a little, blushed a little, and bent her dainty head to view her finery once more, examining it gravely to the last red quill sewed to the beaded toe-point.

Then, still serious, she lifted her grey eyes to me:

"I seem to find no words to thank you, Euan. But my heart is--very--full----" She hesitated, then stretched forth her hand to me, smiling; and as I touched it ceremoniously with finger-tip and lip:

"Ai-me!" she exclaimed, withdrawing under shelter. "It is raining, Euan! Your rifle-shirt is wet already, and you are like to take a chill! Come under shelter instantly!"

"Fancy a man of Morgan's with a chill!" I said, but nevertheless obeyed her, set the lantern on the puncheon floor, brushed the fine drops from thrums and hatchet-sheath, rubbed the bright-edged little axe with buck-skinned elbow, and wiped my heavy knife from hilt to blade.

As I looked up, busy with my side-arms, I caught her eye. We smiled at each other; then, as though a common instinct stirred us to caution, we turned and looked silently toward the settle in the corner, where the widow sat brooding alone.

"May we speak freely here, Lois?" I whispered.

She cast a cautious glance at the shadowy figure, then, lowering her voice and leaning nearer:

"I scarcely know whether she truly heeds and hears. She may not--yet--she may. And I do not care to share my confidences with anyone--save you. I promised to tell you something about myself.... I mean to, some day."

"Then you will not tell me now?"

"How can I, Euan?"

We stood silent, thinking. Presently my eyes fell on the rough ladder leading to the loft above. She followed my gaze, hesitated, shot a keen and almost hostile glance at me, softened and coloured, then stole across the room to the ladder's foot.

I lifted the lantern, followed her, and mounted, lighting the way for her along low-hanging eaves among the rustling husks. She dropped the trap-door silently, above the ladder, took the lantern from my hand, set it on the floor, and seated herself beside it on the husks, her cheeks still brightly flushed.

"Is this then your intimate abode?" I asked, half-smiling.

"Could I desire a snugger one?" she answered gaily. "Here is both warmth and shelter; and a clean bed of husks; and if I am lonely, there be friendly little mice to bear me company o' nights. And here my mice and I lie close and listen to the owls."

"And you were reared in comfort!" I said with sudden bitterness.

She looked up quickly, then, shrugging her shoulders:

"There is still some comfort for those who can remember their brief day of ease--none for those who never knew it. I have had days of comfort."

"What age are you, Lois?"

"Twenty, I think."

"Scarce that!" I insisted.

"Do I not seem so?" she asked, smiling.

"Eighteen at most--save for the--sadness--in your eyes that now and then surprises me--if it be sadness that I read there."

"Perhaps it is the wisdom I have learned--a knowledge that means sadness, Euan. Do my eyes betray it, then, so plainly?"

"Sometimes," I said, A faint sound from below arrested our attention.

Lois whispered:

"It is Mrs. Rannock weeping. She often weeps like that at night. And so would I, Euan, had I beheld the horrors which this poor thing was born to look upon--God comfort her! Have you never heard how the destructives slew her husband, her baby, and her little sister eight years old? The baby lay in its cradle smiling up at its murderers. Even the cruel Senecas turned aside, forbearing to harm it. But one of Walter Butler's painted Tories spies it and bawls out: 'This also will grow to be a rebel!' And with that he speared the little smiling creature on his bayonet, tossed it, and caught it--Oh, Euan--Euan!" Shuddering, she flung her arm across her face as though to shut out the vision.

"That villainy," said I, "was done by Newberry or Chrysler, if I remember. And Newberry we caught and hung before we went to Westchester. I saw him hang with that wretched Lieutenant Hare. God! how we cheered by regiments marching back to camp!"

Through the intense stillness I could still hear the woman sobbing in the dark below.

"Lois--little Lois," I whispered, touching her trembling arm with a hand quite as unsteady.

She dropped her arm from her face, looking up at me with eyes widened still in horror.

I said: "Do you then wonder that the thought of you, roaming these woods alone, is become a living dread to me, so that I think of nothing else?"

She smiled wanly, and sat thinking for a while, her pale face pressed between her hands. Presently she looked up.

"Are we so truly friends then, Euan? At the Spring Waiontha it almost seemed as though it could come true."

"You know it has come true."

"Do I?"

"Do you not know it, little Lois?"

"I seem to know it, somehow.... Tell me, Euan, does a true and deathless friend-ship with a man--with you--mean that I am to strip my heart of every secret, hiding nothing from you?"

"Dare you do it, Lois?" I said laughingly, yet thrilled with the candour of her words.

"I could not let you think me better than I am. That would be stealing friend-ship from you. But if you give it when you really know me--that will be dear and wonderful----" She drew a swift breath and smiled.

Surprised, then touched, I met the winning honesty of her gaze in silence.

"Unless you truly know me--unless you know to whom you give your friend-ship--you can not give it rightly. Can you, Euan? You must learn all that I am and have been, Is not this necessary?"

"I--I ask you nothing," I stammered. "All that I know of you is wonderful enough----" Suddenly the danger of the moment opened out before me, checking my very thoughts.

She laid both hands against her temple, pressing them there till her cheeks cooled. So she pondered for a while, her gaze remote. Then, looking fearlessly at me:

"Euan, I am of that sad company of children born without name. I have lately dared to guess who was my father. Presently I will tell you who he was." Her grey and troubled eyes gazed into space now, dreamily. "He died long since. But my mother is living. And I believe she lives near Catharines-town to-day!"

"What! Why do you think so?" I exclaimed, astounded.

"Is not the Vale Yndaia there, near Catharines-town?"

"Yes. But why----"

"Then listen, Euan. Every year upon a certain day--the twelfth of May--no matter where I chance to be, always outside my door I find two little beaded moc-casins. I have had them thirteen times in thirteen years. And every year--save the last two--the moccasins have been made a little larger, as though to fit my grow-ing years. Now, for the last two years, they have remained the same in size, fitting me perfectly. And--I never yet have worn them more than to fit them on and take them off."

"Why?" I asked vaguely.

"I save them for my journey."

"What journey?"

"The long trail through the Long House--straight through it, Euan, to the Western Door. That is the trail I dream of."

"Who leaves these strange moccasins at your threshold every year?"

"I do not know."

"From where do you suppose they come?" I asked, amazed.

"From Catharines-town."

"Do you believe your mother sends them?"

"Oh, Euan, I know it now! Until two years ago I did not understand. But now I know it!"

"Why are you so certain Lois? Is any written message sent with them?"

"Always within one of each pair of moccasins is sewed a strip of silver birch. Always the message written is the same; and this is what is always written:

"Swift moccasins for little feet as swift against the day that the long trail is safe. Then, in the Vale Yndaia, little Lois, seek her who bore you, saved you, lost you, but who love you always.

"Pray every day for him who died in the Regiment de la Reine.

"Pray too for her who waits for you, in far Yndaia."

"What a strange message!" I exclaimed.

"I must heed it," she said under her breath. "The trail is open, and my hour is come."

"But, Lois, that trail means death!"

"Your army makes it safe at last. And now the time is come when I must follow it."

"Is that why you have followed us?"

"Yes, that is why. Until that night in the storm at Poundridge-town I had never learned where the Vale Yndaia lay. Month after month I haunted camps, asking for information concerning Yndaia and the Regiment de la Reine. But of Yndaia I learned nothing, until the Sagamore informed me that Yndaia lay near Catharines-town. And, learning you were of the army, and that the army was bound thither, I followed you."

"Why did you not tell me this at Poundridge? You should have camped with us," I said.

"Because of my fear of men--except red men. And I had already quite enough of your Lieutenant Boyd."

I looked at her seriously; and she comprehended the unasked questions that were troubling me.

"Shall I tell you more? Shall I tell you how I have learned my dread of men--how it has been with me since my foster parents found me lying at their door strapped to a painted cradle-board?"

"You!"

"Aye; that was my shameful beginning, so they told me afterward--long afterward. For I supposed they were my parents--till two years ago. Now shall I tell you all, Euan? And risk losing a friendship you might have given in your ignorance of me?"

Quick, hot, unconsidered words flew to my lips--so sweet and fearless were her eyes. But I only muttered:

"Tell me all."

"From the beginning, then--to scour my heart out for you! So, first and earliest my consciousness awoke to the sound of drums. I am sure of this because when I hear them it seems as though they were the first sounds that I ever heard.... And once, lately, they were like to be the last.... And next I can remember playing with a painted mask of wood, and how the paint tasted, and its odour.... Then, nothing more can I remember until I was a little child with--him I thought to be my father. I may not name him. You will understand presently why I do not."

She looked down, pulling idly at the thrums along her beaded leggins.

"I told you I was near your age--twenty. But I do not really know how old I am, I guess that I am twenty--thereabouts."

"You look sixteen; not more--except the haunting sorrow----"

"I can remember full that length of time.... I must be twenty, Euan. When I was perhaps seven years old--or thereabout--I went to school--first in Schenectady to a Mistress Lydon; where were a dozen children near my age. And pretty Mistress Lydon taught us A--B--C and manners--and nothing else that I remember now. Then for a long while I was at home--which meant a hundred different lodgings--for we were ever moving on from place to place, where his employment led him, from one house to another, staying at one tavern only while his task remained unfinished, then to the road again, north, south, west, or east, wherever his fancy sped before to beckon him.... He was a strange man, Euan."

"Your foster father?"

"Aye. And my foster mother, too, was a strange woman."

"Were they not kind to you?"

"Y-es, after their own fashion. They both were vastly different to other folk. I was fed and clothed when anyone remembered to do it, And when they had been fortunate, they sent me to the nearest school to be rid of me, I think. I have attended many schools, Euan--in Germantown, in Philadelphia, in Boston, in New York. I stayed not long in school at New York because there our affairs went badly. And no one invited us in that city--as often we were asked to stay as guests while the work lasted--not very welcome guests, yet tolerated."

"What was your foster father's business?"

"He painted portraits.... I do not know how well he painted. But he cared for nothing else, except his wife. When he spoke at all it was to her of Raphael, and of Titian, and particularly of our Benjamin West, who had his first three colours of the Indians, they say."

"I have heard so, too."

She nodded absently, fingering her leggin-fringe; then, with a sudden, indrawn breath:

"We were no more than roving gypsies, you see, living from hand to mouth, and moving on, always moving from town to town, remaining in one place while there were portraits to paint--or tavern-signs, or wagons--anything to keep us clothed and fed. Then there came a day in Albany when matters mended over night, and the Patroon most kindly commanded portraits of himself and family. It started our brief prosperity.

"Other and thrifty Dutchmen now began to bargain for their portraits. We took an old house on Pearl Street, and I was sent to school at Mrs. Pardee's Academy for young ladies as a day pupil, returning home at evening. About that time my foster mother became ill. I remember that she lay on a couch all day, watching her husband paint. He and his art were all she cared for. Me she seldom seemed to see--scarcely noticed when she saw me--almost never spake to me, and there were days and weeks, when I saw nobody in that silent house, and sat at meat alone--when, indeed, anyone remembered I was a hungry, growing child, and made provision for me.

"Schoolmates, at first, asked me to their homes. I would not go because I could not ask them to my home in turn. And so grew up to womanhood alone, and shy, and silent among my fellows; alone at home among the shadows of that old Dutch house; ever alone. Always a haunted twilight seemed to veil the living world from me, save when I walked abroad along the river, thinking, thinking.

"Yet, in one sense I was not alone, Euan, for I was fanciful; and roamed accompanied by those bright visions that unawakened souls conjure for company; companioned by all creatures of the mind, from saint to devil. Ai-me! For there were moments when I would have welcomed devils, so that they rid me of my solitude, at hell's own price!"

She drew a long, light breath, smiled at me; then:

"My foster mother died. And when she died the end also began for him. I was taken from my school. So dreadfully was he broken that for months he lay abed never speaking, scarcely eating. And all day long during those dreary months I sat alone in that hushed house of death.

"Debt came first; then sheriffs; then suddenly came this war upon us. But nothing aroused him from his lethargy; and all day long he brooded there in silence, day after day, until our creditors would endure no longer, and the bailiff menaced him. Confused and frightened, I implored him to leave the city--jails seeming to me far more terrible than death--and at last persuaded him to the old life once more.

"So, to avoid a debtor's prison, we took the open road again. But war was ravishing the land; there was no work for him to do. We starved slowly southward, day by day, shivered and starved from town to town across the counter.

"Near to a camp of Continental troops there was a farm house. They took me there as maid-at-all-work, out of charity, I think. My father wandered over to the camp, and there, God alone knows why, enlisted--I shall not tell you in what regiment. But it was Continental Line--a gaunt, fierce, powder-blackened company, disciplined with iron. And presently a dreadful thing befell us. For one morning before sunrise, as I stood scouring the milk-pans by the flare of a tallow-dip, came to me a yawning sergeant of this same regiment to tell me that, as my foster father was to be shot at sunrise, therefore, he desired to see me. And I remember how he yawned and yawned, this lank and bony sergeant, showing within his mouth his yellow fangs!

"Oh, Euan! When I arrived, my foster father--who I then supposed was my own father--lay in a tent a condemned deserter, seeming not even to care, or to comprehend his dreadful plight. All the defence he ever made, they say was that he had tired of dirty camps and foolish drums, and wished to paint again. Euan, it was terrible. He did not understand. He was a visionary--a man of endless silences, dreamy of eye, gentle and vague of mind--no soldier, nor fitted to understand a military life at all.

"I remember the smoky lantern burning red within the tent, and the vast shadows it cast; and how he stood there, looking tranquilly at nothing while I, frightened, sobbed on his breast. 'Lois,' he said, smiling, 'there is a bright company aloft, and watching me. Raphael and Titian are of them. And West will come some day.' And, 'God!' he murmured, wonderingly, 'What fellowship will be there! What knowledge to be acquired a half hour hence--and leave this petty sphere to its own vexed and petty wrangling, its kings and congresses, and its foolish noise of drums.'

"For a while he paid me no attention, save in an absent-minded way to pat my arm and say, 'There, there, child! There's nothing to it--no, not anything to weep for. In less than half an hour my wife and I will be together, listening while Raphael speaks--or Christ, perhaps, or Leonardo.'

"Twice the brigade chaplain came to the tent, but seeing me retired. The third time he appeared my foster father said: 'He's come to talk to me of Christ and Raphael. It is pleasant to hear his kind assurance that the journey to them is a swift one, done in the twinkling of an eye.... So--I will say good-bye. Now go, my child.'

"Locked in my desperate embrace, his wandering gaze came back and met my terror-stricken eyes. And after another moment a slow colour came into his wasted face. 'Lois,' he said, 'before I go to join that matchless company, I think you ought to know that which will cause you to grieve less for me.... And so I tell you that I am not your father.... We found you at our door in Caughnwagha, strapped to a

Seneca cradle-board. Nor had you any name. We did not seek you, but, having you so, bowed to God's will and suffered you to remain with us. We strove to do our duty by you----' His vague gaze wandered toward the tent door where the armed guard stood, terrible and grim and ragged. Then he unloosened my suddenly limp arms about him, muttering to himself of something he'd forgotten; and, rummaging in his pockets found it presently--a packet laced in deerskin. 'This,' he said, 'is all we ever knew of you. It should be yours. Good-bye.'

"I strove to speak, but he no longer heard me, and asked the guard impatiently why the Chaplain tarried. And so I crept forth into the dark of dawn, more dead than living. And presently the rising sun blinded my tear-drowned eyes, where I was kneeling in a field under a tall tree.... I heard the dead-march rolling from the drums, and saw them passing, black against the sunrise.... Then, filing slowly as the seconds dragged, a thousand years passed in processional during the next half hour--ending in a far rattle of musketry and a light smoke blowing east across the fields----"

She passed her fingers across her brow, clearing it of the clinging curls.

"They played a noisy march--afterward. I saw the ragged ranks wheel and manoeuvre, stepping out Briskly to the jolly drums and fifes.... I stood by the grave while the detail filled it cheerily.... Then I went back to the farm house, through the morning dew and sunshine.

"When I had opened my packet and had understood its contents, I made of my clothes a bundle and took the highway to ask of all the world where lay the road to the vale Yndaia, and where might be found the Regiment de la Reine. Wherever was a camp of soldiers, there I loitered, asking the same question, day after day, month after month. I asked of Indians--our Hudson guides, and the brigaded White Plains Indians. None seemed to know--or if they did they made no answer. And the soldiers did not know, and only laughed, taking me for some camp wanton----"

Again she passed her slender hand slowly across her eyes, shaking her head.

"That I am not wholly bad amazes me at times.... I wonder if you know how hunger tampers with the will? I mean more than mere hunger; I mean that dreadful craving never completely satisfied--so that the ceaseless famine gnaws and gnaws while the sick mind still sickens, brooding over what the body seems to need of meat and drink and warmth--day after day, night after night, endless and terrible."

She flushed, but continued calmly: "I had nigh sold myself to some young officer--some gay and heedless boy--a dozen times that winter--for a bit of bread--and so I might lie warm.... The army starved at Valley Forge.... God knows where and how I lived and famished through all that bitter blackness.... An artillery horse had trodden on my hip where I lay huddled in a cow-barn under the straw close to the horses, for the sake of warmth. I hobbled for a month.... And so ill was I become in mind as well as body that had any man been kind--God knows what had happened! And once I even crept abroad meaning to take what offered. Do you deem me vile, Euan?"

"No--no--" I could not utter another word.

She sighed, gazing at space.

"And the cold! Well--this is July, and I must try to put it from my mind. But at times it seems to be still in my bones--deep bitten to the very marrow. Ai-me! I have seen two years of centuries. Their scars remain."

She rocked slightly forward and backward where she sat, her fingers interlaced, twisting and clenching with her memories.

"Ai-me! Hunger and cold and men! Hunger and--men. But it was solitude that nigh undid me. That was the worst of all--the endless silence."

The rain now swept the roof of bark above us, gust after gust swishing across the eaves. Beyond the outer circle of the lantern light a mouse moved, venturing no nearer.

"Lois?"

She lifted her head. "All that is ended now. Strive to forget."

She made no response.

"Ended," I said firmly. "And this is how it ends. I have with my solicitor, Mr. Simon Hake, of Albany, two thousand pounds hard sterling. How I first came by it I do not know. But Guy Johnson placed it there for me, saying that it was mine by right. Now, today, I have written to Mr. Hake a letter. In this letter I have commanded some few trifles to be bought for you, such as all women naturally require."

"Euan!" she exclaimed sharply.

"I will not listen!" said I excitedly. "Do you listen now to me, for I mean to have my way with you--say what you may----"

"I know--I know--but you have done too much already----"

"I have done nothing! Listen! I have bespoken trifles of no value--nothing more--stockings, and shifts, and stays, and powder-puffs, and other articles----"

"I will not suffer this!" she said, an angry colour in her cheeks.

"You suffer now--for lack even of handkerchiefs! I must insist----"

"Euan! My shifts and stays and stockings are none of your affair!" she answered hotly.

"I make them mine!"

"No--nor is it your privilege to offer them!"

"My--what?"

"Privilege!" she said haughtily, flushing clear to her curly hair; and left me checked. She added: "What you offer is impertinence--however kindly meant. No friendship warrants it, and I refuse."

I know not what it was--perhaps my hurt and burning silence under the sudden lash of her rebuff--but presently I felt her hand steal over mine and tighten. And looked up, scowling, to see her eyes brimming with tears and merriment.

"How much of me must you have, Euan? Even my privacy and pride? You have given me friendship; you have clothed me to your fancy. You have had scant payment in exchange--only a poor girl's gratitude. What have I left to offer in return if you bestow more gifts? Give me no more--so that you take from me no more than--gratitude."

"Comrades neither give nor take, Lois. What they possess belongs to both in common."

"I know--it is so said--but--you have had of me for all your bounty only my thanks--and----" she smiled tremulously, "----a wild rose-bud. And you have given so much--so much--and I am far too poor to render----"

"What have I asked of you!" I said impatiently.

"Nothing. And so I am the more inclined to give--I know not what."

"Shall I tell you what to offer me? Then offer me the privilege of giving. It is the rarest gift within your power."

She sat looking at me while the soft colour waned and deepened in her cheeks.

"I--give," she said in a voice scarce audible.

"Then," said I, very happily, "I am free to tell you that I have commanded for your comfort a host of pretty things, and a big box of wood and brass, with a stout hide outside, to keep your clothing in! The lady of Captain Cresson, of the levies, has a noble one. Yours is its mate. And into yours will fit your gowns and shoon, patches and powder, and the hundred articles which every woman needs by day and night. Also I've named you to Mr. Hake, so that, first writing for me upon a slip of paper that I may send it to him--then writing your request to him, you may make draughts for what you need upon our money, which now lies with him. Do you understand me, Lois? You will need money when the army leaves."

Her head moved slightly, acquiescent.

"So far so good, then. Now, when this army moves into the wilderness, and when I go, and you remain, you will have clothing that befits you; you will have means to properly maintain you; and I shall send you by batteau to Mr. Hake, who will find lodging suitable for you--and be your friend, and recommend you to his friends not only for my sake, but, when he sets his eyes on you, for your own sake." I smiled, and added:

"Hiero! Little rosy-throated pigeon of the woods! Loskiel has spoken!"

Now, as I ended, this same and silly wild-thing fell silently a-crying; and never had I dreamed that any maid could be so full o' tears, when by all rights she should have sat dimpling there, happy and gay, and eager as I.

Out o' countenance again, and vexed in my mind, I sat silent, fidgeting, made strange and cold and awkward by her tears. The warm flush of self-approval chilled in my heart; and by and by a vague resentment grew there.

"Euan?" she ventured, lifting her wet eyes.

"What?" said I ungraciously.

"H--have you a hanker? Else I use my scandalous skirt again----"

And the next instant we both were laughing there, she still in tears, I with blithe heart to see her now surrender at discretion, with her grey eyes smiling at me through a starry mist of tears, and the sweet mouth tremulous with her low-voiced thanks.

"Ai-me!" she said. "What manner of boy is this, to hector me and have his will? And now he sits there laughing, and convinced that when the army marches I shall wear his finery and do his bidding. And so I shall--if I remain behind."

"Lois! You can not go to Catharines-town! That's flat!"

"I've wandered hungry and ragged for two years, asking the way. Do you suppose I have endured in vain? Do you suppose I shall give up now?"

"Lois!" I said seriously, "if it is true that the Senecas hold any white captives, their liberation is at hand. But that business concerns the army. And I promise you that if your mother be truly there among those unhappy prisoners she shall be brought back safely from the Vale Yndaia. I will tell Major Parr of this; he shall inform the General. Have no fear or doubt, dear maid. If she is there, and human power can save her, then is she saved already, by God's grace."

She said in a quiet voice:

"I must go with you. And that is why--or partly why--I asked you here tonight. Find me some way to go to Catharines-town. For I must go!"

"Why not inquire of me the road to hell?" I asked impatiently. She said between her teeth:

"Oh, any man might show me that. And guide me, too. Many have offered, Euan."

"What!"

"I ask your pardon. Two years of camps blunts any woman's speech."

"Lois," said I uneasily, "why do you wish to go to Catharines-town, when an armed force is going?"

She sat considering, then, in a low, firm voice:

"To tell you why, is why I asked you here.... And first I must show you what my packet held.... Shall I show you, Euan?"

"Surely, little comrade."

She drew the packet from her bosom, unlaced the thong, unrolled the deer-hide covering.

"Here is a roll of bark," she said. "This I have never had interpreted. Can you read it for me, Euan?"

And there in the lantern light I read it, while she looked down over my shoulder.

"KADON!
"Aesa-yat-yen-enghdon, Lois!

"Etho!

[And here was painted a white dog lying dead, its tongue hanging
out sideways.]

"Hen-skerigh-watonte.

"Jatthon-ten-yonk, Lois!

"Jin-isaya-dawen-ken-wed-e-wayen.

[Here was drawn in outline the foot and claws of a forest lynx.]

"Niyi-eskah-haghs, na-yegh-nyasa-kenra-dake, niya-wennonh!" [Then a
white symbol.]

For a long time I gazed at the writing in shocked silence. Then I asked her if she
suspected what was written there in the Canienga dialect.

"I never have had it read. Indians refuse, shake their heads, and look askance
at me, and tell me nothing; interpreters laugh at me, saying there is no meaning in
the lines. Is there, Euan?"

"Yes," I said.

"You can interpret?"

"Yes."

"Will you?"

I was silent, pondering the fearful meaning which had been rendered plainer
and more hideous by the painted symbols.

"It has to do with the magic of the Seneca priesthood," I muttered. "Here is a
foul screed--and yet a message, too, to you."

Then, with an effort I found courage to read, as it was written:

"I speak! Thou, Lois, mightest have been destroyed! Thus! (Here the white
dog.) But I will frustrate their purpose. Keep listening to me, Lois. That which has
befallen you we place it here (or, 'we draw it here'--i. e., the severed foot and claws
of a lynx). Being born white (literally, 'being born having a white neck'), this happened." And the ghastly sign of Leshi ended it.

"But what does it all signify?" she asked, bewildered.

And even as she spoke, out of the dull and menacing horror of the symbols,
into my mind, leaped terrible comprehension.

I said coolly: "It must have been Amochol--and his Erie sorcerers! How came you in Catharines-town?"

"I? In Catharines-town!" she faltered. "Was I, then, ever there?"

I pointed at the drawing of the dead white dog.

"Somebody saved you from that hellish sacrifice. I tell you it is plain enough to read. The rite is practiced only by the red sorcerers of the Senecas.... Look! It was because your 'neck' was 'white'! Look again! Here is the symbol of the Cat-People-- the Eries--the acolytes of Amochol--here! This spread lynx-pad with every separate claw extended! Yet, it is drawn severed--in symbol of your escape. Lois! Lois! It is plain enough. I follow it all--almost all--nearly--but not quite----"

I hesitated, studying the bark intently, pausing to look at her with a new and keenly searching question in my gaze.

"You have not shown me all," I said.

"All that is written in the Iroquois tongue. But there were other things in the packet with this bark letter." She opened it again upon her lap.

"Here is a soldier's belt-buckle," she said, offering it to me for my inspection.

It was made of silver and there were still traces of French gilt upon the device.

"Regiment de la Reine," I read. "What regiment is that, Lois? I'm sure I've heard of it somewhere. Oh! Now I remember. It was a very celebrated French regiment--cut all to pieces at Lake George by Sir William Johnson in '55. This is an officer's belt-buckle."

"Was the regiment, then, totally destroyed?"

"Utterly. In France they made the regiment again with new men and new officers, and call it still by the same celebrated name."

"You say Sir William Johnson's men cut it to pieces--the Regiment de la Reine?" she asked.

"His Indians, British and Provincials, left nothing of it after that bloody day."

She sat thoughtful for a while, then, bestirring herself, drew from the deerhide packet a miniature on ivory, cracked across, and held together only by the narrow oval frame of gold.

There was no need to look twice. This man, whoever he might be, was this girl's father; and nobody who had ever seen her and this miniature could ever doubt it.

She did not speak, nor did I, conscious that her eyes had never left my face and must have read my startled mind with perfect ease.

Presently I turned the portrait over. There was a lock of hair there under the glass--bright, curly hair exactly like her own. And at first I saw nothing else. Then, as the glass-backed locket glanced in the lantern-light, I saw that on the glass something had been inscribed with a diamond. This is what I read, written across the glass:

"Jean Coeur a son coeur cheri."

I looked up at her.

"Jean Coeur," I repeated. "That is no name for a man----" Suddenly I remembered, years ago--years and years since--hearing Guy Johnson cursing some such man. Then in an instant all came back to me; and she seemed to divine it, for her small hand clutched my arm and her eyes were widening as I turned to meet them.

"Lois," I said unsteadily, "there was a man called Jean Coeur, deputy to the adventurer, Joncaire. Joncaire was the great captain who all but saved this Western Continent to France. Captain Joncaire was feared, detested, but respected by Sir William Johnson because he held all Canada and the Hurons and Algonquins in the hollow of his hand, and had even gained part of the Long House--the Senecas. His clever deputy was called Jean Coeur. Never did two men know the Indians as these two did."

I thought a moment, then: "Somewhere I heard that Captain Joncaire had a daughter. But she married another man--one Louis de Contrecoeur----" I hesitated, glanced again at the name scratched on the glass over the lock of hair, and shook my head.

"Jean Coeur--Louis de Contrecoeur. The names scarce hang together--yet----"

"Look at this!" she whispered in a low, tense voice, and laid a bit of printing in my hand.

It was a stained and engraved sheet of paper--a fly-leaf detached from a book of Voltaire. And above the scroll-encompassed title was written in faded ink: "Le Capitaine Vicomte Louis Jean de Contrecoeur du Regiment de la Reine." And under that, in a woman's fine handwriting: "Mon coeur, malgre; mon coeur, se rendre a Contrecoeur, dit Jean Coeur; coeur contre coeur."

"That," she said, "is the same writing that the birch bark bears, sewed in my moccasins."

"Then," I said excitedly, "your mother was born Mademoiselle Joncaire, and you are Lois de Contrecoeur!"

She sat with eyes lowered, fingering the stained and faded page. After a moment she said:

"I wrote to France--to the Headquarters of the Regiment de la Reine--asking about my--father."

"You had an answer?"

"Aye, the answer came.... Merely a word or two.... The Vicomte Louis Jean de Contrecoeur fell at Lake George in '55----" She lifted her clear eyes to mine. "And died--unmarried."

A chill passed through me, then the reaction came, taking me by the throat, setting my veins afire.

"Then--by God!" I stammered. "If de Contrecoeur died unmarried, his child shall not!"

"Euan! I do not credit what they wrote. If my father married here perhaps they had not heard."

"Lois! Dearest of maids--whichever is the truth I wish to marry you!"

But she stopped her ears with both palms, giving me a frightened look; and checked, but burning still, I stared at her.

"Is that then all you are?" she asked. "A wisp of tow to catch the first spark that flies? A brand ever smouldering, which the first breath o' woman stirs to flame?"

"Never have I loved before----"

"Love! Euan, are you mad?"

We both were breathing fast and brokenly.

"What is it then, if it be not love!" I asked angrily.

"What is it?" she repeated slowly. Yet I seemed to feel in her very voice a faint, cool current of contempt. "Why, it is what always urges men to speak, I fancy-- their natural fire--their easily provoked emotions.... I had believed you different."

"Did you not desire my friendship?" I asked in hot chagrin.

"Not if it be of this kind, Euan."

"You would not have me love you?"

"Love!" And the fine edge of her contempt cut clean. "Love!" she repeated coolly. "And we scarcely know each other; have never passed a day together; have never
broken bread; know nothing, nothing of each other's minds and finer qualities; have
awakened nothing in each other yet except emotions. Friendships have their deeps
and shallows, but are deathless only while they endure. Love hath no shallows,
Euan, and endures often when friendship dies.... I speak, having no knowledge. But
I believe it. And, believing nobly of true love--in ignorance of it, but still in awe--
and having been assailed by clamours of a shameful passion calling itself love--and
having builded in my heart and mind a very lofty altar for the truth, how can I feel
otherwise than sorry that you spoke--hotly, unthinkingly, as you did to me?"

I was silent.

She rose, lifted the lantern, laid open the trap-door.

"Come," she whispered, beckoning.

I followed her as she descended, took the lantern from her hand, glanced at the
shadowy heap, asleep perhaps, on the corner settle, then walked to the door and
opened it. A thousand, thousand stars were sparkling overhead.

On the sill she whispered:

"When will you come again?"

"Do you want me?" I said sullenly.

She made no answer for a moment; suddenly she caught my hand and pressed
it, crushing it between both of hers; and turning I saw her almost helpless with her
laughter.

"Oh, what an infant have I found in this tall gentleman of Morgan's corps!" said
she. "A boy one moment and a man the next--silly and wise in the same breath--
headlong, headstrong, tender, and generous, petty and childish, grave and kind--
the sacred and wondrous being, in point of fact, known to the world as man! And
now he asks, with solemn mien and sadly ruffled and reproachful dignity whether
a poor, friendless, homeless, nameless girl desires his company again!"

She dropped my hand, caught at her skirt's edge, and made me a mocking reverence.

"Dear sir," she said, "I pray you come again to visit me tomorrow, while I am
mending regimental shirts at tuppence each----"

"Lois!" I said sadly. "How can you use me so!"

She began to laugh again.

"Oh, Euan, I can not endure it if you're solemn and sorry for yourself----"

"That is too much!" I exclaimed, furious, and marched out, boiling, under the high stars. And every star o' them, I think, was laughing at the sorriest ass who ever fell in love.

Nevertheless, that night I wrote her name in my letter to Mr. Hake; and the ink on it was scarce sanded when an Oneida runner had it and was driving his canoe down the Mohawk River at a speed that promised to win for him the bonus in hard money which I had promised for a swift journey and a swift return.

And far into the July morning I talked with the Sagamore of Amochol and of Catharines-town; and he listened while he sat tirelessly polishing his scalping-knife and hatchet.

CHAPTER VIII
OLD FRIENDS

The sunrise gun awoke me. I rolled out of my blanket, saw the white cannon-smoke floating above the trees, ran down to the river, and plunged in.

When I returned, the Sagamore had already broken his fast, and once more was engaged in painting himself--this time in a most ghastly combination of black and white, the startling parti-coloured decorations splitting his visage into two equal sections, so that his eyes gleamed from a black and sticky mask, and his mouth and chin and jaw were like the features of a weather-bleached skull.

"More war, O Mayaro, my brother?" I asked in a bantering voice. "Every day you prepare for battle with a confidence forever new; every night the army snores in peace. Yet, at dawn, when you have greeted the sun, you renew your war-paint. Such praiseworthy perseverance ought to be rewarded."

"It has already been rewarded," remarked the Indian, with quiet humour.

"In what manner?" I asked, puzzled.

"In the manner that all warriors desire to be rewarded," he replied, secretly amused.

"I thought," said I, "that the reward all warriors desire is a scalp taken in battle."

He cast a sly glance at me and went on painting.

"Mayaro," said I, disturbed, "is it possible that you have been out forest-running while I've slept?"

He shot a quick look at me, full of delighted malice.

And "Ho!" said he. "My brother sleeps sounder than a winter bear. Three Erie scalps hang stretched, hooped, and curing in the morning sun, behind the bush-hut. Little brother, has the Sagamore done well?"

Straightway I whirled on my heel and walked out and around the hut. Strung like drying fish on a willow wand three scalps hung in the sunshine, the soft July breeze stirring the dead hair. And as soon as I saw them I knew they were indeed Erie scalps.

Repressing my resentment and disgust, I lingered a moment to examine them, then returned to the hut, where the Siwanois, grave as a catamount at his toilet, squatted in a patch of sunshine, polishing his features.

"So you've done this business every night as soon as I slept," said I. "You've crept beyond our outer pickets, risking your life, imperilling the success of this army, merely to satisfy your vanity. This is not well, Mayaro."

He said proudly: "Mayaro is safe. What warrior of the Cat-People need a Sagamore of the Siwanois dread?"

"Do you count them warriors then, or wizards?"

"Demons have teeth and claws. Look upon their scalp-locks, Loskiel!"

I strove to subdue my rising anger.

"You are the only reliable guide in the army today who can take us straight to Catharines-town," I said. "If we lose you we must trust to Hanierri and his praying Oneidas, who do not know the way even to Wyalusing as well as you do. Is this just to the army? Is it just to me, O Sagamore? My formal orders are that you shall rest and run no risk until this army starts from Lake Otsego. My brother Mayaro knew this. I trusted him and set no sentry at the hut door. Is this well, brother?"

The Sagamore looked at me with eyes utterly void of expression.

"Is Mayaro a prisoner, then?" he asked quietly.

Instantly I knew that he was not to be dealt with that way. The slightest suspicion of any personal restraint or of any military pressure brought to bear on him might alienate him from our cause, if not, perhaps, from me personally.

I said: "The Siwanois are free people. No lodge door is locked on them, not even in the Long House. They are at liberty to come and go as the eight winds rise and wane--to sleep when they choose, to wake when it pleases them, to go forth by day or night, to follow the war-trail, to strike their enemies where they find them.

"But now, to one of them--to the Mohican Mayaro, Sagamore of the Siwanois, Sachem of the Enchanted Clan, is given the greatest mission ever offered to any Delaware since Tamenund put on his snowy panoply of feathers and flew through the forest and upward into the air-ocean of eternal light.

"A great army of his embattled brothers trusts in him to guide them so that the Iroquois Confederacy shall be pierced from Gate to Gate, and the Long House go roaring up in flames.

"There are many valiant deeds to be accomplished on this coming march-- deeds worthy of a war-chief of the Lenni-Lenape--deeds fitted to do honour to a Sagamore of the Magic Wolf.

"I only ask of my friend and blood-brother that he reserve himself for these great deeds and not risk a chance bullet in ambush for the sake of an Erie scalp or two--for the sake of a patch of mangy fur which grows on these Devil-Cats of Amochol."

At first his countenance was smooth and blank; as I proceeded, he became gravely attentive; then, as I ended, he gave me a quick, unembarrassed, and merry look.

"Loskiel," he said laughingly, "Mayaro plays with the Cat-People. A child's skill only is needed to take their half-shed fur and dash them squalling and spitting and kicking into Biskoonah!"

He resumed his painting with a shrug of contempt, adding:

"Amochol rages in vain. Upon this wizard a Mohican spits! One by one his scalped acolytes tumble and thump among the dead and bloody forest leaves. The Siwanois laugh at them. Let the red sorcerer of the Senecas make strong magic so that his cats return to life, and the vile fur grows once more where a Mohican has ripped it out!"

"Each night you go forth and scalp. Each morning you paint. Is this to continue, Sagamore?"

"My brother sees," he said proudly. "Cats were made for skinning."

There was nothing to do about it; no more to be said. I now comprehended this, as I stood lacing my rifle-shirt and watching him at his weird self-embellishment.

"The war-paint you have worn each day has seemed to me somewhat unusual," I said curiously.

He glanced sharply up at me, scowled, then said gravely:

"When a Sagamore of the Mohicans paints for a war against warriors, the paint is different. But," he added, and his eyes blazed, and the very scalp-lock seemed to bristle on his shaven head, "when a Lenape Sachem of the Enchanted Clan paints for war with Seneca sorcerers, he wears also the clean symbols of his sacred priesthood, so that he may fight bad magic with good magic, sorcery with sorcery, and defy this scarlet priest--this vile, sly Warlock Amochol!"

Truly there was no more for me to say. I dared not let him believe that his movements were either watched or under the slightest shadow of restraint. I knew it was useless to urge on him the desirability of inaction until the army moved. Be might perhaps have understood me and listened to me, were the warfare he was now engaged in only the red knight-errantry of an Indian seeking glory. But he had long since won his spurs.

And this feud with Amochol was something far more deadly than mere warfare; it was the clash of a Mohican Sagamore of the Sacred Clan with the dreadful and abhorred priesthood of the Senecas--the hatred and infuriated contempt of a noble and ordained priest for the black-magic of a sorcerer--orthodoxy, militant and terrible, scourging blasphemy and crushing its perverted acolytes at the very feet of their Antichrist.

I began to understand this strange, stealthy slaughter in the dark, which only the eyes of the midnight sky looked down on, while I lay soundly sleeping. I knew that nothing I could say would now keep this Siwanois at my side at night. Yet, he had been given me to guard. What should I do? Major Parr might not understand--might even order the Sagamore confined to barracks under guard. The slightest mistake in dealing with the Siwanois might prove fatal to all our hopes of him.

All the responsibility, therefore, must rest on me; and I must use my judgment and abide by the consequences.

Had it been, as I have said, any other nation but the Senecas, I am certain that

I could have restrained the Indian. But the combination of Seneca, Erie, and Amochol prowling around our picket-line was too much for the outraged Sagamore of the Spirit Wolf. And I now comprehended it thoroughly.

As I sat thinking at our bush-hut door, the endless lines of wagons were still passing toward Otsego Lake, piled high with stores, and I saw Schott's riflemen filing along in escort, their tow-cloth rifle-frocks wide open to their sweating chests.

Almost all the troops had already marched to the lake and had pitched tents there, while Alden's chastened regiment was damming the waters so that when our boats were ready the dam might be broken and the high water carry our batteaux over miles of shallow water to Tioga Point, where our main army now was concentrating.

When were the Rifles to march? I did not know. Sitting there in the sun, moodily stripping a daisy of its petals, I thought of Lois, troubled, wondering how her security and well-being might be established.

The hour could not be very distant now before our corps marched to the lake. What would she do? What would become of her if she still refused to be advised by me?

As for her silly desire to go to Catharines-town, the more I thought about it the less serious consideration did I give it. The thing was, of course, impossible. No soldiers' wives were to be permitted to go as far as Wyalusing or Wyoming. Even here, at this encampment, the officers' ladies had left, although perhaps many of them might have remained longer with their husbands had it been known that the departure of the troops for Otsego Lake was to be delayed by the slow arrival of cattle and provisions.

In the meantime, the two companies of my regiment attached to this brigade were still out on scout with Major Parr; and when they returned I made no doubt that we would shoulder packs, harness our wagons, and take the lake road next morning.

And what would become of Lois? Perplexed and dejected, I wandered about the willow-run, pondering the situation; sat for a while on the river-bank to watch the batteaux and the Oneida canoes; then, ever restless with my deepening solicitude for Lois, I walked over to the fort. And the first man I laid eyes on was Lieutenant Boyd, conversing with some ladies on the parade.

He did not see me. He had evidently returned from the main body with a small scout the night before, and now was up and dressed in his best, spick and span and gay, fairly shining in the sunlight as he stood leaning against a log prop, talking with these ladies where they were seated on one of the rustic settles lately made by Alden's men.

Venturing nearer, I found that I knew all of the ladies, for one was the handsome wife of Captain Bleecker, of the 3rd New York, and another proved to be Angelina Lansing, wife of Gerrit Lansing, Ensign in the same regiment.

The third lady was a complete surprise to me, she being that pretty and vivacious Magdalene Helmer--called Lana--the confidante of Clarissa Putnam--a bright-eyed, laughing beauty from Tribes Hill, whom I had known very well at Guy Park, where she often stayed with her friend, Miss Putnam, when Sir John Johnson was there.

As I recognised them, Boyd chanced to glance around, and saw me. He smiled and spoke to the ladies; all lifted their heads and looked in my direction; and Lana Helmer waved her handkerchief and coolly blew me a kiss from her finger-tips.

So, cap in hand, I crossed the parade, made my best bow and respects to each in turn, replaced my cap, and saluted Lieutenant Boyd, who returned my salute with pretended hauteur, then grinned and offered his hand.

"See what a bower of beauty is blossomed over night in these dreary barracks, Loskiel. There seems to be some happiness left in the world for the poor rifleman."

"Do you remain?" I asked of Mrs. Bleecker.

"Indeed we do," she said, laughing, "provided that my husband's regiment remains. As soon as we understood that they had not been ordered into the Indian country we packed our boxes and came up by batteau last night. The news about my husband's regiment is true, is it not?"

"Colonel Gansevoort's regiment is not to join General Sullivan, but is to be held to guard the Valley. I had the news yesterday for certain."

"What luck!" said Boyd, his handsome eyes fixed on Lana Helmer, who shot at him a glance as daring. And it made me uneasy to see she meant to play coquette with such a man as Boyd; and I remembered her high spirits and bright daring at the somewhat loose gatherings at Guy Park, where every evening too much wine was drunk, and Sir John and Clarissa made no secret of the flame that burned between them.

Yet, of Lana Helmer never a suspicious word had been breathed that ever I had heard--for it seemed she could dare where others dared not; say and do and be what another woman might not, as though her wit and beauty licensed what had utterly damned another. Nor did her devotion and close companionship with Clarissa ever seem to raise a question as to her own personal behaviour. And well I remember a gay company being at cards and wine one day in the summer house on the river hew she answered a disrespect of Sir John with a contemptuous rebuke which sent the muddy blood into his face and left him ashamed--the only time I ever saw him so.

Ensign Chambers came a-mincing up, was presented to the ladies, languidly made preparations for taking Mrs. Lansing by storm; and the first deadly grace he pictured for her was his macaroni manner of taking snuff--with which fascinating ceremony he had turned many a silly head in New York ere we marched out and the British marched in.

I talked for a while with Mrs. Bleecker of this and that, striving the while to catch Lana Helmer's eye. For not only did her coquetry with Boyd make me uneasy, knowing them both as I did, but on my own account I desired to speak to her in private when opportunity afforded. Alone and singly either of these people stood in no danger from the outer world. Pitted against each other, what their recklessness might lead to I did not know. For since Boyd's attempted gallantries toward Lois--he believing her to be as youthful and depraved as seemed the case--a deep and growing distrust for this man which I had never before felt had steadily invaded my friendship for him. Also, he had already an affair with a handsome wench at the Middle Fort, one Dolly Glenn, and the poor young thing was plainly mad about him.

I heard Mrs. Lansing propose a stroll to the river before dinner, on the chance of meeting her husband's regiment returning, which suggestion seemed to suit all; and in the confusion of chatter and laughter and the tying of a sun-mask by Mrs. Bleecker, aided by Boyd and by the exquisite courtier, I cleverly contrived to supplant Boyd with Lana Helmer, and not only stuck to her side, but managed to secure the rear of the strolling column.

All this manoeuvre did not escape her, and as we fell a few paces behind, she looked up at me with a most deadly challenge in her violet eyes.

"Now," she said, "that you have driven off your rival, I am resigned to be court-ed.... Heaven knows you wasted opportunities enough at Guy Park."

I laughed.

"How strange it is, Lana," I said, "to be here with you; I in rifle dress and thrums, hatchet, and knife at my Mohawk girdle; you in chip hat and ribbons and dainty gown, lifting your French petticoat over the muddy ruts cut on the King's Highway by rebel artillery!"

"Who would have dreamed it three years ago?" she said, her face now sober enough.

"I thought your people were Tory," said I.

"Not mine, Euan; Clarissa's."

"Where is that child?" I asked pityingly.

"Clarissa? Poor lamb--she's in Albany still."

I did not speak, but it was as though she divined my unasked question.

"Aye, she is in love with him yet. I never could understand how that could be after he married Polly Watts. But she has not changed.... And that beast, Sir John, installed her in the Albany house."

I said: "He's somewhere out yonder with the marauders against whom we are to march. They're all awaiting us, it is said; the whole crew--Johnson's Greens, But-ler's Rangers, McDonald's painted Tories, Brant's Mohawks--and the Senecas with their war-chiefs and their sorcerer, Amochol--truly a motley devil's brood, Lana; and I pray only that one of Morgan's men may sight Walter Butler or Sir John over his rifle's end."

"To think," she murmured, "that you and I have dined and wined with these same gentlemen you now so ardently desire to slay.... And young Walter Butler, too! I saw his mother and his sister in Albany a week ago--two sad and pitiable women, Euan, for every furtive glance cast after them seemed to shout aloud the infamy of their son and brother, the Murderer of Cherry Valley."

"To my mind," said I, "he is not sane at all, but gone stark blood-mad. Heaven! How impossible it seems that this young man with his handsome face and figure, his dreamy melancholy, his charming voice and manners, his skill in verse and music, can be this same Walter Butler whose name is cursed wherever righteousness and honour exist in human breasts. Why, even Joseph Brant has spurned him, they say, since Cherry Valley! Even his own father stood aghast before such infamy. Old John Butler, when he heard the news, dashed his hands to his temples, groaning out: 'I would have crawled from this place to Cherry Valley on my hands and knees to save those people; and why my son did not spare them, God only knows.'"

Lana shook her pretty head.

"I can not seem to believe it of him even yet. I try to think of Walter as a murderer of little children, and it is not possible. Why, it seems but yesterday that I stood plaguing him on the stone doorstep at Guy Park--calling him Walter Ninny and Walter Noodle to vex him. You remember, Euan, that his full name is Walter N. Butler, and that he never would tell us what the N. stands for, but we guessed it stood for Nellis, in honour of Nellis Fonda.... Lord! What a world o' trouble for us all in these three years!"

"I had supposed you married long ago, Lana. The young Patroon was very ardent."

"I? The sorry supposition! I marry--in the face of the sad and miserable examples all my friends afford me! Not I, Euan, unless----" She smiled at me with pretty malice. "----you enter the lists. Do you then enter?" I reddened and laughed, and she, always enchanted to plague and provoke me, began her art forthwith, first innocently slipping her arm through mine, as though to support her flagging steps, then, as if by accident, letting one light finger slip along my sleeve to touch my hand and linger lightly.

Years ago, when we were but seventeen, she had delighted to tease and embarrass me with her sweetly malicious coquetry, ever on the watch to observe my features redden. I remember she sometimes offered to exchange kisses with me; but I was a ninny, and a serious and hopeless one at that, and would have none of her.

I believe we were thinking of the same thing now, and when I caught her eye the gay malice of it was not to be mistaken.

"Lanette," said I, "take care! I am a soldier since you had your saucy way with me. You know that the military are not to be dealt with lightly. And I am grown up in these three years."

"Grown soberer, perhaps. You always did conduct like a pious Broad-brim, Euan."

"I've a mind to kiss you now," said I, vexed.

"Kiss away, kind sir. You have me in the rear o! them. Now's your opportunity!"

"Doubtless you'd cry out."

"Doubtless I wouldn't."

"Wait for some moonlit evening when we're unobserved----"

"Broad-brim!"

I laughed, and so did she, saying:

"I warrant you that your pretty Lieutenant Boyd had never waited for my challenge twice!"

"Best look out for Boyd," said I. "He's of your own careless, reckless kind, Lanette. Sparks fly when flint and steel encounter."

"Cold sparks, friend Broad-brim!"

"Not too cold to set tinder afire."

"Am I then tinder? You should know me better."

"In every one of us," said I, "there is an element which, when it meets its fellow in another, unites with it, turning instantly to fire and burning to the very soul."

"How wise have you become in alchemy and metaphysics!" she exclaimed in mock admiration.

"Oh, I am not wise in anything, and you know it, Lana."

"I don't know it. You've been wise enough to keep clear of me, if that be truly wisdom. Come, Euan, what do you think? Do you and I contain these fellow elements, that you seem to dread our mutual conflagration if you kiss me?"

"You know me better."

"Do I? No, I don't. Young sir, caper not too confidently in your coat of many colours! If you flout me once too often I may go after you, as a Mohawk follows a scalp too often flaunted by the head that wears it!"

I tried to sustain her delighted gaze and reddened, and the impudent little beauty laughed and clung to my arm in a very ecstasy of malice, made breathless by her own mirth.

"Come, court me prettily, Euan. It is my due after all these grey and Quaker years when I made eyes at you from the age of twelve, and won only a scowl or two for my condescension."

But we had reached the river bank, and there the group came once more together, the ladies curious to see the batteaux arriving, loaded with valley sheep, we officers pointing out to them the canoes of our corps of Oneida guides, and Hanierri and the Reverend Mr. Kirkland reading their Testaments under the shade of the trees, gravely absorbed in God.

"A good man," said I, "and brave. But his honest Stockbridge Indians know no more of Catharines-town than do the converted Oneidas yonder."

Boyd nodded: "I prophesy they quit us one and all within an arrow-flight of Wyalusing. Do you take me, Loskiel?"

"No, you are right," I said. "The fear of the Long House chains them, and their long servitude has worn like fetters to their very bones. Redcoats they can face, and have done so gallantly. But there is in them a fear of the Five Nations past all understanding of a white man."

I spoke to a diminished audience, for already Boyd and Lana Helmer had strolled a little way together, clearly much interested in each other's conversation. Presently our precious senior Consign sauntered the other way with pretty Mistress Lansing on his arm. As for me, I was contented to see them go--had been only waiting for it. And what I had thought I might venture to say to Lana Helmer by warrant of old acquaintance, I was now glad that I had not said at all--the years having in no wise subdued the mischief in her, nor her custom of plaguing me. And how much she had ever really meant I could not truly guess. No, it had been anything but wise to speak to her of Lois. But now I meant to mention Lois to Mrs. Bleecker.

We had seated ourselves on the sun-crisped Indian grass, and for a while I let her chatter of Guy Park and our pleasant acquaintance there, and of Albany, too, where we had met sometimes at the Ten Broecks, the Schuylers, and the Patroons. And all the while I was debating within my mind how this proud and handsome, newly-married girl might receive my halting story. For it would not do to conceal anything vital to the case. Her clear, wise eyes would see instantly through any evasion, not to say deception--even a harmless deception. No; if she were to be of any aid in this deeply-perplexing business, I must tell her the story of Lois--not betraying anything that the girl might shrink from having others know, but stating her case and her condition as briefly and as honestly as I might.

And no sooner did I come to this conclusion than I spoke; and after the first word or two Mrs. Bleecker put off her sun-mask and turned, looking me directly in the eyes.

I said that the young lady's name was Lois de Contrecoeur--and if it were not that it was nothing, and human creatures require a name! But this I did not say to her, nor thought it necessary to mention any doubt as to the girl's parentage, only to say she was the child of captives taken by the Senecas after the Lake George rout.

I told of her dreary girlhood, saying merely that her foster parents were now dead and that the child had conceived the senseless project of penetrating to Catharines-town, where she believed her mother, at least, was still held captive.

The tall, handsome girl beside me listened without a word, her intent gaze never leaving me; and when I had done, and the last word in my brief for Lois had been uttered, she bent her head in thought, and so continued minute after minute while I sat there waiting.

At last she looked up at me again, suddenly, as though to surprise my secret reflections; and if she did so I do not know, for she smiled and held out her hand to me with so pretty a confidence that my lips trembled as I pressed them to her fingers. And now something within her seemed to have been reassured, for her eyes and her lips became faintly humorous.

"And where is this most forlorn and errant damsel, Sir Euan?" she inquired. "For if I doubt her when I see her, no more than I doubt you when I look at you, something should be done in her behalf without delay.... The poor, unhappy child! And what a little fool! The Lord looks after his lambs, surely, surely--drat the little hussy! It mads me to even think of her danger. Did a body ever hear the like of it! A-gypsying all alone--loitering around this army's camp! Mercy! And what a little minx it is to so conduct--what with our godless, cursing headlong soldiery, and the loud, swaggering forest-runners! Lord! But it chills me to the bone! The silly, saucy baggage!"

She shuddered there in the hot sunshine, then shot at me a look so keen and penetrating that I felt my ears go red. Which sudden distress on my part again curved her lips into an indulgent smile.

"I always thought I knew you, Euan Loskiel," she said. "I think so still.... As for your fairy damsel in distress--h'm--when may I see her?"

In a low voice I confessed the late raggedness of Lois, and how she now wore an

Oneida dress until the boxes, which I had commanded, might arrive from Albany. I had to tell her this, had to explain how I had won from Lois this privilege of giving, spite of her pride.

"If I could bring her to you," said I, "fittingly equipped and clothed, the pride in her would suffer less. Were you to go with me now in your pretty silk and scarf, and patch and powder, and stand before her in the wretched hut which shelters her--the taint of charity would poison everything. For she is like you, Mrs. Bleecker, lacking only what does not make, but merely and prettily confirms your quality and breeding--clothing and shelter, and the means to live fittingly.... For it is not condescension, not the lesser charity I ask, or she could receive; it is the countenance that birth lends to its equal in dire adversity."

Curious and various were the emotions which passed in rapid succession over her pretty features; and not all seemed agreeable. Then suddenly her eyes reflected a hidden laughter, and presently it came forth, a merry peal, and sweet withal.

"Oh, Euan, what a boy you are! Had I been any other woman--but let it go. You are as translucent as a woodland brook, and--at times you babble like one, confident that your music pleases everyone who hears it.... I pray you let me judge whether the errant lady be what a poet's soul would have her.... I am not speaking with any unkind thought or doubt.... But woman must judge woman. It is the one thing no man can ever do for her. And the less he interferes during the judgment the better."

"Then I'll say no more," said I, forcing a smile.

"Oh, say all you please, as long as you do not tell me what you think about her. Tell me facts, not what your romantic heart surmises. And if she were the queen of Sheba in disguise, or if she were a titled Saint James drab, no honest woman but who would see through and through her, and, ere she rose from her low reverence, would know her truly for exactly what she is."

"Lord!" said I. "Is that the way you read us, also?"

"No. Women may read women. But never one who lived has read truly any man, humble or high. Say that to the next pretty baggage who vows she reads you like a book! And in her secret heart she will know you say the truth--and know it, raging even while her smile remains unaltered. For it is true, Euan; true concerning you men, also. Not one among you all has ever really read us right. The difference is this; we know we can not read you, but scorn to admit it; you honestly believe that you can read us, and often boast of doing it. Which sex is the greater fool, judge you? I have my own opinion."

We both laughed; after a moment she put on her sun-mask and I tied it.

"Where do you and Mrs. Lansing lodge until your husband's regiment returns?" I asked.

"They have given us the old Croghan house. What it lacks in elegance of appointment it gains in hospitality. If we had a dish of tea to brew for you gentlemen we would do it; but Indian willow makes a vile and bitter tea, and I had as lief go tealess, as I do and expect to continue until our husbands teach the Tory King his manners."

She rose, giving me her pretty hand to aid her, shook out her dainty skirts, put up her quizzing glass, and inspected me, smilingly.

"Bring her when you think it time," she said. "Somehow I already believe that she may be something of what your fancy paints her. And that would be a miracle."

"Truly she is a miracle," I said earnestly.

"Then remember not to say it to Angelina Lansing--and above all never hint as much to Lana Helmer. Women are human; and pretty women perhaps a little less than human. Leave them to me. For if this romantic damsel be truly what you picture her, I'll have to tell a pretty fib or two concerning her and you, I warrant you. Leave that saucy baggage, Lanette, to me, Euan. And you keep clear of her, too. She's murderous to men's peace of mind--more fatal than ever since Clarissa played the fool."

"I was assassinated by Lana long ago," said I, smiling. "I am proof."

"Nevertheless, beware!" she whispered, as Boyd and Lana came sauntering up. And there seemed to me to be now about them both a careless indifference, almost studied, and in noticeable contrast to their bright animation when they had left us half an hour ago.

"Such a professional heart-breaker as your Mr. Boyd is," observed Lana coolly to us both. "I never before encountered such assurance. What he must be in queue and powder, silk and small-sword, I dare not surmise. A pitying heaven has protected me so far, and," she added, looking deliberately at Boyd, "I ought to be grateful, ought I not, sir?"

Boyd made her a too low and over-courtly bow.

"Always the gallant and victorious adversary salutes the vanquished as you, fair lady, have saluted me--imputing to my insignificant prowess the very skill and address which has overthrown me."

"Are you overthrown?"

"Prone in the dust, mademoiselle! Draw Mr. Loskiel's knife and end me now in mercy."

"Then I will strike.... Who is the handsome wench who passed us but a moment since, and who looked at you with her very heart trembling in her eyes?"

"How should I know?"

They stood looking smilingly at each other; and their smile did not seem quite genuine to me, but too clear, and a trifle hard, as though somehow it was a sort of mask for some subtler defiance. I reflected uneasily that no real understanding could be possible between these two in such a brief acquaintance; and, reassured, turned to greet our macaroni Ensign and Mistress Angelina Lansing, now approaching us.

That our regimental fop had sufficient diverted her was patent, she being over-flushed and smiling, and at gay swords' points already with him, while he whisked his nose with his laced hanker and scattered the perfume of his snuff to the four winds.

So, two and two, we walked along the road to Croghan's house, where was a negro wench to aid them and a soldier-servant to serve them. And the odd bits of furniture that had been used at our General's headquarters had been taken there to eke out with rough make-shifts, fashioned by Alden's men, a very scanty establishment for these three ladies.

Lana Helmer, to my surprise, motioned me to walk beside her; and all the way to Croghan's house she continued close to me, seeming to purposely avoid Boyd. And he the same, save that once or twice he looked at her, which was more than she did to him, I swear.

She was now very serious and sweet with me on our way to Croghan's, not jeering at me or at any of her teasing tricks, but conversing reasonably and prettily, and with that careless confidence which to a man is always pleasant and sometimes touching.

Of the old days we spoke much; the past was our theme--which is not an un-usual topic for the young, although they live, generally, only in the future. And it was "Do you recall this?" and "Do you remember that?" and "Do you mind the day" when this and that occurred? Incidents we both had nigh forgotten were recalled gravely or smilingly, but there was no laughter--none, somehow, seemed to be left either in her heart or mine.

Twice I spoke of Clarissa, wishing, with kindliest intention, to hear more of the unhappy child; but in neither instance did Lana appear to notice what I had said, continuing silent until I, too, grew reticent, feeling vaguely that something had somehow snapped our mutual thread of sympathy.

At the door of Croghan's house we gathered to make our adieux, then first went mincing our Ensign about his precious business; and then Boyd took himself off, as though with an effort; and Lana and Angelina Lansing went indoors.

"Bring her to me when I am alone," whispered Betty Bleecker, with a very friendly smile. "And let the others believe that you stand for nothing in this af-fair."

And so I went away, thinking of many things--too many and too perplexing, perhaps, for the intellect of a very young man deeply in love--a man who knows he is in love, and yet remains incredulous that it is indeed love which so utterly bewilders and afflicts him.

CHAPTER IX
MID-SUMMER

Since our arrival from Westchester the weather had been more or less unset-tled--fog, rain, chilling winds alternating with days of midsummer heat. But now the exhausting temperature of July remained constant; fiery days of sunshine were succeeded by nights so hot and suffocating that life seemed well-nigh insupportable under tents or in barracks, and officers and men, almost naked, lay panting along the river bank through the dreadful hours of darkness which brought no relief from the fiery furnace of the day.

Schott's riflemen mounted guard stripped to the waist; the Oneidas and Stockbridge scouts strode about unclothed save for the narrow clout and sporran; and all day and all night our soldiers splashed in the river where our horses also stood belly deep, heads hanging, under the willows.

During that brief but scorching period I went to Mrs. Rannock's every evening after dark, and usually found Lois lying in the open under the stars, the garret being like an oven, so she said.

Here we had made up our quarrel, and here, on the patch of uncut English grass, we lay listlessly, speaking only at intervals, gasping for air and coolness, which neither darkness nor stars had brought to this sun-cursed forest-land.

But for the last two nights I had not found Lois waiting for me, nor did Mrs. Rannock seem to know whither she had gone, which caused me much uneasiness.

The third evening I went to find her at Mrs. Rannock's before the after-glow had died from the coppery zenith, and I encountered her moving toward the Spring path, just entering the massed elder bloom. Her face was dewy with perspiration, pale, and somewhat haggard.

"Lois, why have you avoided me?" I exclaimed. "All manner of vague forebodings have assailed me these two days past."

"Listen to this silly lad!" she said impatiently. "As though a few hours' absence lessen loyalty and devotion!"

"But where have you been?"

"Where I may not take you, Euan."

"And where is that?" I asked bluntly.

"Lord! What a catechism is this for a free girl to answer willy-nilly! If you must know, I have played the maid of ancient Greece these two nights past. Otherwise, I had died, I think."

And seeing my perplexed mien, she began to laugh.

"Euan, you are stupid! Did not the Grecian maids spend half their lives in the bath?"

The slight flush of laughter faded from her face; the white fatigue came back; and she passed the back of one hand wearily across her brow, clearing it of the damp curls.

"The deadly sultriness of these nights," she sighed. "I was no longer able to endure the heat under the eaves among my dusty husks. So lately I have stolen at night to the Spring Waiontha to bathe in the still, cold pools. Oh, Euan, it is most delicious! I have slept there until dawn, lying up to my throat in the crystal flood." She laughed again. "And once, lying so, asleep, my body slipped and in I slid, deep, deep in, and awoke in a dreadful fright half drowned."

"Is it wise to sleep so in the Water?" I asked uneasily.

"Oh! Am I ever wise?" she said wearily. "And the blood beats in my veins these heated nights so that I am like to suffocate. I made a bed for me by Mrs. Rannock, but she sobbed in her sleep all night and I could not close my eyes, So I thought of the Spring Waiontha, and the next instant was on my way there, feeling the path with naked feet through the starlight, and dropped my clothing from me in the darkness and sank into the cool, sweet pool. Oh, it was heaven, Euan! I would you might come also."

"I can walk as far as the pool with you, at all events," said I.

"Wonderful! And will you?"

"Do I ever await asking to follow you anywhere?" said I sentimentally.

But she only laughed at me and led the way across the dreary strip of clearing, moving with a swift confidence in her knowledge of the place, which imitating, I ran foul of a charred stump, and she heard what I said.

"Poor lad!" she exclaimed contritely, slipping her hand into mine. "I should have guided you. Does it pain you?"

"Not much."

Our hands were clasped, and she pressed mine with all the sweet freedom of a comradeship which means nothing deeper. For I now had learned from her own lips, sadly enough, how it was with her--how she regarded our friendship. It was to her a deep and living thing--a noble emotion, not a passion--a belief founded on gratitude and reason, not a confused, blind longing and delight possessing every waking moment, ever creating for itself a thousand tender dreams or fanciful and grotesque apprehensions.

Clear-headed so far, reasonable in her affection, gay or tender as the mood happened, convinced that what I declared to be my love for her was but a boy's exaggeration for the same sentiments she entertained toward me, how could she have rightly understood the symptoms of this amazing malady that possessed me--these reasonless extremes of ardour, of dejection, of a happiness so keen and thrilling that it pained sometimes, and even at moments seemed to make me almost drunk.

Nor did I myself entirely comprehend what ailed me, never having been able to imagine myself in love, or ever dreamed that I possessed the capacity for such a violent devotion to any woman. I think now, at that period, somewhere under all the very real excitement and emotion of an adolescent encountering for the first time the sweet appeal of youthful mind and body, that I seemed to feel there might be in it all something not imperishable. And caught myself looking furtively and a little fearfully at her, at times, striving to conceive myself indifferent.

When we came to the Spring Waiontha I had walked straight into the water except for her, so dark it was around us. And:

"How can you ever get back alone?" said she.

"Oho!" said I, laughing, "I left the willow-tips a-dangle, breaking them with my left hand. I am woodsman enough to feel my way out."

"But not woodsman enough to spare your shins in the clearing," she said saucily.

"Shall we sit and talk?" I said.

"Oh, Euan! And my bath! I am fairly melting as I stand here."

"But I have not seen you for two entire nights, Lois."

"I know, poor boy, but you seem to have survived."

"When I do not see you every day I am most miserable."

"So am I--but I am reasonable, too. I say to myself, if I don't see Euan today I will nevertheless see him to-morrow, or the day after, or the next, God willing----"

"Lois!"

"What?"

"How can you reason so coldly?"

"I--reason coldly? There is nothing cold in me where you are concerned. But I have to console myself for not seeing you----"

"I am inconsolable," said I fervently.

"No more than am I," she retorted hotly, as though jealous that I should arrogate to myself a warmer feeling concerning her than she entertained for me.

"I care so much for you, Lois," said I.

"And I for you."

"Not as I care for you."

"Exactly as you care for me. Do you think me insensible to gratitude and affection?"

"I do not desire your gratitude for a few articles----"

"It isn't for them--though I'm grateful for those things too! It's gratitude to God for giving me you, Euan Loskiel! And you ought to take shame to yourself for doubting it!"

I said nothing, being unable to see her in the darkness, much less perceive what expression she wore for her rebuke to me. Then as I stood silent, I felt her little hands groping on my arm; and my own closed on them and I laid my lips to them.

"Ai-me!" she said softly. "Why do we fight and fret each other? Why do I, who adore you so, let you vex me and stir me to say what I do not mean at all. Always remember, Euan--always, always--that whatever I am unkind enough to say or do to vex you, in my secret mind I know that no other man on earth is comparable to you--and that you reign first in my heart--first, and all by yourself, alone."

"And will you try to love me some day, Lois?"

"I do."

"I mean----"

"Oh, Euan, I do--I do! Only--you know--not in the manner you once spoke of----"

"But I love you in that manner."

"No, you do not! If you did, doubtless I would respond; no doubt at all that I also would confess such sentiments in your regard. But it isn't true for either of us. You're a man. All men are prone to harp on those strings.... But--there is no harmony in them to me.... I know my own mind, although you say I don't--and--I do know yours, too. And if a day ever comes that neither you nor I are longer able to think clearly and calmly with our minds, but begin to reason with our emotions, then I shall consider that we are really entering into a state of love--such as you sometimes have mentioned to me--and will honestly admit as much to you.... And if you then desire to wed me, no doubt that I shall desire it, too. And I promise in that event to love you--oh, to death, Euan!" she said, pressing my hands convulsively. "If ever I love--that way--it truly will be love! Are you content with what I say?"

"I must be."

"What an ungracious answer! I could beat you soundly for it! Euan, you some-times vex me so that I could presently push you into that pool.... I do not mean it, dearest lad. You know you already have my heart--perhaps only a child's heart yet, though I have seen ages pass away.... And my eyes have known tears.... Perhaps for that reason I am come out into this new sunshine which you have made for me, to play as children play--having never done so in my youth. Bear with me, Euan. You would not want me if there were nothing in me to respond to you. If there ever is, it will not remain silent. But first I want my play-day in the sunshine you have promised me--the sunlight of a comrade's kindness. Be not too blunt with me. You have my heart, I tell you. Let it lie quiet and safe in your keeping, like some strange, frail chrysalis. I myself know there is a miracle within it; but what that miracle may be, I may not guess till it reveals itself."

"I am a fool," I said. "God never before sent any man such a comrade as He has sent in you to me."

"That was said sweetly and loyally. Thank you. If hearts are to be awakened and won, I think it might be done that way--with such pleasant phrases--given always time."

Presently she withdrew her hands and slipped away from me in the dark.

"Be careful," said I, "or you will slip overboard."

"I mean to presently."

"Then--must I go so soon?"

She did not answer. Once I thought I heard her moving softly, but the sound came from the wrong direction.

"Lois!"

No reply.

"Lois!" I repeated uneasily.

There was a ripple in the pool, silence, then somewhere in the darkness a faint splash.

"Good Lord!" said I. "Have you fallen in?"

"Not fallen in. But I am truly in, Euan. I couldn't endure it any longer; and you didn't seem to want to go.... So please remain where you now are."

"Do you mean to say----" I began incredulously.

And, "Yes, I do!" she said, defiant. "And I think this ought to teach you what a comrade's perfect confidence can be. Never complain to me of my want of trust in you again."

In astonished and uneasy silence, I stood listening. The unseen pool rippled in the darkness with a silvery sound, as though a great fish were swirling there in the pallid lustre of the stars.

After a while she laughed outright--the light, mischievous laughter of a child.

"I feel like one of those smooth and lurking naiads which haunt lost pools-- or like some ambushed water-sprite meditating malice, and slyly alert to do you a harm. Have a care, else I transform you into a fish and chase you under the water, and pinch and torment you!"

And presently her voice came again from the more distant darkness some- where:

"Has the box which you commanded arrived yet, Euan?"

"It is at my hut. A wagon will bring it to you in the morning."

I could hear her clap her wet little hands; and she cried out softly:

"Oh!" and "Oh!" Then she said: "I did not understand at first how much I wished for everything you offered. Only when I saw the ladies at Croghan's house, as I was coming with my mending from the fort--then I knew I wanted everything you have bespoken for me.... Everything, dear lad! Oh, you don't know how truly grate- ful I shall be. No, you don't, Euan! And if the box is really come, when am I going with you to be made known to Mistress Bleecker?"

"I think it is better that I first bring her to you."

"Would she condescend to come?"

"I think so."

There was a pause. I seated myself. Then the soft and indecisive sound of rip- ples stirred by an idle hand broke the heated silence.

"You say they all are your good friends?" she remarked thoughtfully.

"I know them all. Lana Helmer I have known intimately since we were chil- dren."

"Then why is it not better to present me to her first--if you know her so very well?"

"Mrs. Bleecker is older."

"Oh! Is this Miss Helmer then so young?"

"Your age."

"Oh! My age.... And pretty?"

"The world thinks so."

"Oh! And what do you think, Euan?"

"Yes, she is pretty," said I carelessly.

There was a long silence. I sat there, my knees gathered in my arms, staring up at the stars.

Then, faintly came her voice:

"Good-night, Euan."

I rose, laid hold of the willow bush that scraped my shoulders, felt over it until I found the dangling broken branch; stepped forward, groping, until I touched the next broken branch. Then, knowing I was on my trail, I turned around and called back softly through the darkness:

"Good-night, little Lois!"

"Good-night, and sweet dreams, Euan. I will be dressed and waiting for you in the morning to go to Mrs. Bleecker, or to receive her as you and she think fitting.... Is there a looking glass in that same wonder-box?"

"Two, Lois."

"You dear and generous lad!... And are there hair-pegs? Heaven knows if my clipped poll will hold them. Anyway, I can powder and patch, and--oh, Euan! Is there lip-red and curd-lily lotion for the skin? Not that I shall love you any less if there be none----"

"I bespoke of Mr. Hake," said I, laughing, "a full beauty battery, such as I once saw Betty Schuyler show to Walter Butler, having but then received it from New York. And all I know, Lois, is that it was full of boxes, jars, and flasks, and smelled like a garden in late June. And if Mr. Hake has not chosen with discretion I shall go South and scalp him!"

"Euan, I adore you!"

"You adore your battery," said I, not convinced.

"That, too. But you more than my mirrors, and my lip-red, and the lily lotion--more than my darling shifts and stays and shoon and gowns!... I had never dreamed I could accept them from you. But you had become so dear to me--and I could read you through and through--and found you so like myself--and it gave me a new pleasure to humble my pride to your desires. That is how it came about. Also, I saw those ladies.... And I do not think I shall be great friends with your Lana Helmer--even when I am fine and brave in gown and powder to face her on equal terms----"

"Lois, what in the world are you babbling?"

"Let me babble, Euan. Never have I been so happy, so content, so excited yet so confident.... Listen; do you dread tomorrow?"

"I?"

"Yes--that I might not do you honour before your fashionable friends?... And I say to you, have no fear. If my gowns are truly what I think they are, I shall conduct without a tremour--particularly if your Lana be there, and that careless, rakish friend of yours, Lieutenant Boyd."

"Do you remember what you are to say to Boyd if he seems in any wise to think he has met you elsewhere?"

"I can avoid a lie and deal with him," she said with calm contempt. "But there is not a chance he'd know me in my powder."

There was a silence. Then the unseen water rippled and splashed.

"Poor Euan!" she said. "I wish you might dare swim here in this heavenly place with me. But we are not god and goddess, and the fabled age is vanished.... Good-night, dear lad.... And one thing more.... All you are to me--all you have done for me--don't you understand that I could not take it from you unless, in my secret heart, I knew that one day I must be to you all you desire--and all I, too, shall learn to wish for?"

"It is written," I said unsteadily. "It must come to pass."

"It must come," she said, in the hushed voice of a child who dreams, wide-eyed awake, murmuring of wonders.

I slept on the river-sand, not soundly, for all night long men and horses splashed in the water all around me, and I was conscious of many people stirring, of voices, the dip of paddles, and of the slow batteaux passing with the wavelets slapping on their bows. Then, the next I knew--bang! And the morning gun jarred me awake.

I had bathed and dressed, but had not yet breakfasted when one of our regimental wagons came to take the box to Lois--a fine and noble box indeed, in its parti-coloured cowhide cover, and a pretty pattern of brass nails all over it, making here a star and there a sunburst, around the brass plate engraven with her name: "Lois de Contrecoeur."

Then the wagon drove away, and the Sagamore and I broke bread together, seated in the willow shade, the heat in our bush-hut being insupportable.

"No more scalps, Mayaro?" I taunted him, having already inspected the unpleasant trophies behind the hut. "How is this, then? Are the Cats all skinned?"

He smiled serenely. "They have crept westward to lick their scars, Loskiel. A child may safely play in the forest now from the upper castle and Torloch to the Minnisink."

"Has Amochol gone?"

"To make strong magic for his dead Cats, little brother. The Siwanois hatchets are still sticking in the heads of Hiokatoo's Senecas. Let their eight Sachems try to pull them out."

"So you have managed to wound a Seneca or two?"

"Three, Loskiel--but the rifle was one of Sir William's, and carried to the left, and only a half-ounce ball. My brother Loskiel will make proper requisition of the Commissary of Issues and draw a weapon fit for a Mohican warrior."

"Indeed I will," said I, smilingly, knowing well enough that the four-foot, Indian-trade, smooth bore was no weapon for this warrior; nor was it any kindness in such times as these to so arm our corps of Oneida scouts.

After breakfast I went to the fort and found that Major Parr and his command had come in the night before from their long and very arduous scout beyond the Canajoharrie Castle.

The Major received me, inquiring particularly whether I had contrived to keep the Sagamore well affected toward our cause; and seemed much pleased when I told him that this Siwanois and I had practiced the rite of blood-brotherhood.

"Excellent," said he. "And I don't mind admitting to you that I place very little reliance on the mission Indians as guides--neither on the Stockbridge runners nor on the Oneidas, who have come to us more in fear of the Long House than out of any particular loyalty or desire to aid us."

"That is true, sir. They had as soon enter hell as Catharines-town."

The Major nodded and continued to open and read the letters which had arrived during his absence.

"May I draw one of our rifles for my Mohican, sir?" I asked.

"We have very few. Schott's men have not yet all drawn their arms."

"Nevertheless----"

"You think it necessary?"

"I think it best to properly arm the only reliable guide this army has in its service, Major."

"Very well, Mr. Loskiel.... And see that you keep this fellow in good humour. Use your own wit and knowledge; do as you deem best. All I ask of you is to keep this wild beast full fed and properly flattered until we march."

"Yes, sir," I said gravely, thinking to myself in a sad sort of wonder how utterly the majority of white men mistook their red brethren of the forest, and how blind they were not to impute to them the same humanity that they arrogated to themselves.

So much could have been done had men of my blood and colour dealt nobly with a noble people. Yet, even Major Parr, who was no fool and who was far more enlightened than many, spoke of a Mohican Sagamore as "this wild beast," and seriously advised me to keep him "full fed and properly flattered!"

"Yes, sir," I repeated, saluting, and almost inclined to laugh in his face.

So I first made requisition for the lang rifle, then reported to my captain, although being on special detail under Major Parr's personal orders, this was nothing more than a mere courtesy.

The parade already swarmed with our men mustering for inspection; I met Lieutenant Boyd, and we conversed for a while, he lamenting the impossibility of making a boating party with the ladies, being on duty until three o'clock. And:

"Who is this new guest of Mrs. Bleecker?" he asked curiously. "I understand that you are acquainted with her. What is her name? A Miss de Contrecoeur?"

I had not been prepared for that, never expecting that Mrs. Bleecker had already started to prepare the way; but I kept my countenance and answered coolly enough that I had the honour of knowing Miss de Contrecoeur.

"She came by batteau from Albany?"

"Her box," said I, "has just arrived from Albany by batteau."

"Is the lady young and handsome?" he asked, smiling.

"Both, Mr. Boyd."

"Well," he said, with a polite oath, "she must be something more, too, if she hopes to rival Lana Helmer."

So it had already come to such terms of intimacy that he now spoke of her as Lana. For the last few days I had not been to Croghan's house to pay my respects, the heat leaving me disinclined to stir from the shade of the river trees. Evidently it had not debarred Boyd from presenting himself, or her from receiving him, although a note brought to me from Mrs. Bleecker by her black wench said that both she and Angelina Lansing were ill with the heat and kept their rooms.

"We are bidden to cake and wine at five," said I. "Are you going?"

He said he would be present, and so I left him buckling on his belt, and the conch-horn's blast echoing over the parade, sounding the assembly.

At the gate I encountered Lana and Mrs. Lansing and our precious Ensign, come to view the inspection, and exchanged a gay greeting with them.

Then, mending my pace, I hastened to Croghan's house, and found Mrs. Bleecker pacing the foot-path and nibbling fennel.

"How agreeably cool it is growing," she said as I bent over her fingers. "I truly believe we are to have an endurable day at last." She smiled at me as I straightened up, and continued to regard me very intently, still slightly smiling.

"What has disturbed your usual equanimity, Euan? You seem as flushed and impatient as--as a lover at a tryst, for example."

At that I coloured so hotly that she laughed and took my arm, saying:

"There is no sport in plaguing so honest a heart as yours, dear lad. Come; shall we walk over to call upon your fairy princess? Or had you rather bring her here to me?"

"She also leaves it to your pleasure," I said; "Naturally," said Mrs. Bleecker, with a touch of hauteur; then, softening, smiled as much at herself as at me, I think.

"Come," she said gaily. "Sans ceremonie, n'est-ce pas?"

And we sauntered down the road.

"Her box arrived last evening," said I. "God send that Mr. Hake has chosen to please her."

"Is he married?"

"No."

"Lord!" said she gravely. "Then it is well enough that you pray.... Perhaps, however," and she gave me a mischievous look, "you have entrusted such commissions to Mr. Hake before."

"I never have!" I said earnestly, then was obliged to join in her delighted laughter.

"I knew you had not, Euan. But had I asked that question of your friend, Mr. Boyd, and had he answered me as you did, I might have thought he lied."

I said nothing.

"He is at our house every day, and every moment when he is not on duty," she remarked.

"What gallant man would not do the like, if privileged?" I said lightly.

"Lana talks with him too much. Angelina and I have kept our rooms, as I wrote you, truly dreading a stroke of the sun. But Lana! Lord! She was up and out and about with her lieutenant; and he had an Oneida to take them both boating--and then he had the canoe only, and paddled it himself.... They were gone too long to suit me," she added curtly.

"When?"

"Every night. I wish I knew where they go in their canoe. But I can do nothing with Lana.... You, perhaps, might say a friendly word to Mr. Boyd--if you are on that footing with him--to consider Lana's reputation a little more, and his own amusement a little less."

I said slowly: "Whatever footing I am on with him, I will say that to him, if you wish."

"I don't wish you to provoke him."

"I shall take pains not to."

She said impatiently: "There are far too many army duels now. It sickens me to hear of them. Besides, Lana did ever raise the devil beyond bounds with any man she could ensnare--and no harm done."

"No harm," I said. "Walter Butler had a hurt of her bright eyes, and sulked for months. And many another, Mrs. Bleecker. But somehow, Mr. Boyd--"

She nodded: "Yes--he's too much like her--but, being a man, scarcely as innocent of intention, I've said as much to her, and left her pouting--the silly little jade."

We said nothing more, having come in sight of the low house of logs where

Lois dwelt.

"The poor child," said Mrs. Bleecker softly. "Lord! What a kennel for a human being!"

As we approached we saw Mrs. Rannock crossing the clearing in the distance, laden with wash from the fort; and I briefly acquainted my handsome companion with her tragic history. Then, coming to the door, I knocked. A lovely figure opened for us.

So astonished was I--it having somehow gone from my mind that Lois could be so changed, that for a moment I failed to recognise her in this flushed and radiant young creature advancing in willowy beauty from the threshold.

As she sank very low in her pretty reverence, I saw her curly hair all dusted with French powder, under the chip hat with its lilac ribbons tied beneath her chin--and the beauty-patch on her cheek I saw, and how snowy her hands were, where her fingers held her flowered gown spread.

Then, recovering, she rose gracefully from her reverence, and I saw her clear grey eyes star-brilliant as I had never seen them, and a breathless little smile edging her lips.

On Mrs. Bleecker the effect she produced was odd, for that proud and handsome young matron had flushed brightly at first, lips compressed and almost stern; and her courtesy had been none too supple either.

Then in a stupid way I went forward to make my compliments and bend low over the little hand; and as I recovered myself I found her eyes on me for the first time--and for a brief second they lingered, soft and wonderful, sweet, tender, wistful. But the next moment they were clear and brilliant again with controlled excitement, as Mrs. Bleecker stepped forward, putting out both hands impulsively. Afterward she said to me:

"It was her eyes, and the look she gave you, Euan, that convinced me."

But now, to Lois, she said very sweetly:

"I am certain that we are to become friends if you wish it as much as I do."

Lois laid her hands in hers.

"I do wish it," she said.

"Then the happy accomplishment is easy," said Mrs. Bleecker, smiling. "I had expected to yield to you very readily my interest and sympathy, but I had scarce expected to yield my heart to you at our first meeting."

Lois stood mute, the smile still stamped on her lips. Suddenly the tears sprang to her eyes, and she turned away hastily; and Mrs. Bleecker's arm went 'round her waist.

They walked into the house together, and I, still dazed and mazed with the enchanted revelation of her new loveliness, wandered about among the charred stumps, my thoughts a heavenly chaos, as though a million angels were singing in my ears. I could even have seen them, save for a wondrous rosy mist that rolled around them.

How long I wandered I do not know, but presently the door opened, and Lois beckoned me, and I went in to find Mrs. Bleecker down on her knees on the puncheon floor, among the mass of pretty finery overflowing from the box.

"Did Mr. Hake's selection please you?" I asked, "Oh, Euan, how can I make you understand! Everything is too beautiful to be real, and I am certain that a dreadful Cinderella awakening is in store for me."

"Yes--but she wore the slipper in the end."

Lois gave me a shy, sweet look, then, suddenly animated, turned eagerly once more to discuss her wardrobe with her new friend.

"Your Mr. Hake has excellent taste, Euan," observed Mrs. Bleecker. "Or," she added laughingly, "perhaps your late prayer helped." And to Lois she said mischievously: "You know, my dear, that Mr. Loskiel was accustomed to petition God very earnestly that your wardrobe should please you."

Lois looked at me, the smile curving her lips into a happy tenderness.

"He is so wonderful," she said, with no embarrassment. And I saw Mrs. Bleecker look up at her, then smilingly at me, with the slightest possible nod of approbation.

For two hours and more that pair of women remained happy among the ribbons and laces; and every separate article Lois brought to me naively, for me to share her pleasure. And once or twice I saw Mrs. Bleecker watching us intently; and when discovered she only laughed, but with such sweetness and good will that it left me happy and reassured.

"We have arranged that Miss de Contrecoeur is to share my room with me at Croghan's," said Mrs. Bleecker. "And, Euan, I think you should send a wagon for her box at once. The distance is short; we will stroll home together."

I took my leave of them, contented, and walked back to the fort alone, my heart full of thankfulness for what God had done for her that day.

CHAPTER X
IN GARRISON

The end of the month was approaching, and as yet we had received no marching orders, although every evening the heavy-laden batteaux continued to arrive from Albany, and every morning the slow wagon train left for the lake, escorted by details from Schott's irregulars, and Franklin's Wyoming militia.

But our veteran rifle battalion did not stir, although all the other regular regiments had marched to Otsego; and Colonel Gansevoort's 3rd N. Y. Regiment of the Line, which was now under orders to remain and guard the Valley, had not yet returned, although early in the week an Oneida runner had come in with letters for Mrs. Bleecker and Mrs. Lansing from their husbands, saying that the regiment was on its way to the fort, and that they, the ladies, should continue at Croghan's as long as Morgan's Rifles were remaining there in garrison.

Cooler weather had set in with an occasional day of heavy summer rain; and now our garrison life became exceedingly comfortable, especially agreeable because of the ladies' hospitality at Croghan's new house.

Except for Lois and for them my duties on special detail would have become most irksome to me, shut off from the regiment as I was, with only the Mohican to keep an eye on, and nothing else whatever to do except to write at sundown every evening in my daily journal.

Not that I had not come to care a great deal for the Siwanois; indeed, I was gradually becoming conscious of a very genuine affection for this tall Mohican, who, in the calm confidence of our blood-brotherhood, was daily revealing his personality to me in a hundred naive and different ways, and with a simplicity that alternately touched and amused me.

For, after his own beliefs and his own customs, he was every inch a man--courteous, considerate, proud, generous, loyal, and brave. Which seem to me to be the general qualifications for a gentleman.

Except the Seneca Mountain Snakes, the nations of the Long House, considering their beliefs, customs, and limited opportunities, were not a whit inferior to us as men. And the Mohicans have always been their peers.

For, contrary to the general and ignorant belief, except for the Senecas, the Iroquois were civilised people; their Empire had more moral reasons for its existence than any other empire I ever heard of; because the League which bound these nations into a confederacy, and which was called by them "The Great Peace," had been established, not for the purpose of waging war, but to prevent it.

Until men of my own blood and colour had taught them treachery and ferocity and deceit, they had been, as a confederacy, guiltless of these things. Before the advent of the white man, a lie among the Iroquois was punished by death; also, among them, unchastity was scarcely known so rare was it. Even now, that brutal form of violence toward women, white or red, either in time of war or peace, was absolutely non-existent. No captive woman needed to fear that. Only the painted Tories--the blue-eyed Indians--remained to teach the Iroquois that such wickedness existed. For, as they said of themselves, the People of the Morning were "real men."

They had a federal constitution; they had civil and political ceremonies as wisely conceived and as dignified as they were impressive, romantic, and beautiful. Their literature, historical and imaginative, was handed down from generation to generation; and if memory were at fault, there were the wampum belts in their archives to corroborate tradition.

Their federal, national, tribal, sept, and clan systems were devised solely to prevent international decadence and fraternal strife; their secret societies were not sinister; their festivals and dances not immodest; their priesthood not ignoble. They were sedentary and metropolitan people--dwellers in towns--not nomads; they had cattle and fowls, orchards and grain-fields, gardens for vegetables, corrals for breeding stock. They had many towns--some even of two hundred houses, of which dwellings many were cellared, framed, and glazed.

They had their well-built and heavily stockaded forts which, because the first Frenchmen called them chateaux, were still known to us as "castles."

Their family life was, typically, irreproachable; they were tender and indulgent husbands and fathers, charitable neighbours, gay and good-humoured among their friends; and their women were deferred to, respected, and honoured, and had a distinct and important role to play in the social and political practices of the Confederacy.

If they, by necessity, were compelled to decimate the Eries, crush the Hurons, and subdue the Lenape and "make women of them," the latter term meant only that the Lenape could not be trusted to bear arms as allies.

Yet, with truest consideration and courtesy toward these conquered ones, and with a kindly desire to disguise and mitigate a necessary and humiliating restriction, the Iroquois had recognised their priesthood and their clans; had invested the Lenape with the fire-rights at Federal Councils; and had even devised for them a diplomatic role. They were henceforward the ambassadors of the Confederacy, the diplomats and political envoys of the Long House.

And if the Delawares never forgot or forgave their position as a subject nation, yet had the Iroquois done all they dared to soften a nominal servitude which they believed was vitally necessary to the peace and well-being of the entire Iroquois Confederacy.

Of this kind of people, then, were the Iroquois, naturally--not, alas, wholly so after the white man had drugged them with rum, cheated them, massacred them, taught them every vice, inoculated them with every disease.

For I must bear witness to the truth of this, spite of the incredulity of my own countrymen; and, moreover, it is true that the Mohicans were, in all virtuous and noble things, the peers of the civilised people of the Long House.

Those vile, horse-riding, murdering, thieving nomad Indians of the plains-- those homeless, wandering, plundering violators of women and butchers of children, had nothing whatever in common with our forest Indians of the East--were a totally different race of people, mentally, spiritually, and physically. And these two species must ever remain distinct--the Gens des Prairies and the Gens du Bois.

Only the Senecas resembled the degraded robbers of the Western plains in having naturally evil and debased propensities, and entertaining similar gross and monstrous customs and most wicked superstitions. But in the Long House the Senecas were really aliens; every nation felt this, from the Canienga and Oneida peoples, whose skin was almost as white as our own, to the dusky Onondaga, Tuscarora, and

Cayuga--darker people, but no less civilised than the tall, stalwart, and handsome keepers of the Eastern Gate.

I have ventured to say this much concerning the Iroquois so that it may better be understood among my own countrymen how it was possible for me, a white man of unmixed blood, to love and respect a red man of blood as pure and unmixed as mine. A dog-trader learns many things about dogs by dealing in them; an interpreter who deals with men never, ultimately, mistakes a real man, white or red.

My isolation from the regiment, as I say, was now more than compensated by the presence of the ladies at Croghan's house. And Lois had now been lodged with them for more than a week. How much of her sad history Mrs. Bleecker had seen fit to impart to Lana Helmer and Angelina Lansing I did not know. But it seemed to be generally understood in the garrison that Lois had arrived from Albany on Mrs. Bleecker's invitation, and that the girl was to remain permanently under her protection.

The romantic fact that Lois was the orphan of white captives to the Senecas, and had living neither kith nor kin, impressed Angelina sentimentally, and Lana with an insatiable curiosity, if not with suspicion.

As for Boyd, he had not recognised her at all, in her powder, patches, and pretty gowns. That was perfectly plain to Lois and to me. And I could understand it, too, for I hardly recognised her myself. And after the novelty of meeting her had worn off he paid her no particular attention--no doubt because of his headlong, impatient, and undisguised infatuation for Lana, which, with her own propensity for daring indiscretion, embarrassed us all more or less.

No warrant had been given me to interfere; I was on no such intimate terms with Boyd; and as for Lana, she heeded Mrs. Bleecker's cautious sermons as lightly as a bluebird, drifting, heeds the soft air that thrills with his careless flight-song.

What officers there were, regular and militia, who had not yet gone to Otsego Lake, came frequently to Croghan's to pay their respects; and every afternoon there were most agreeable parties at Croghan's; nor was our merriment any less restrained for our lack of chairs and tables and crockery to contain the cakes and nougats, syllabubs and custards, that the black wench, Gusta, contrived for us. Neither were there glasses sufficient to hold the sweet native wines, or enough cups to give each a dish of the rare tea which had come from France, and which Mr. Hake had sent to me from Albany, the thoughtful soul!

If I did not entirely realise it at the time, nevertheless it was a very happy week for me. To see Lois at last where she belonged; to see her welcomed, respected, and admired by the ladies and gentlemen at Croghan's--courted, flattered, sought after in a company so respectable, and so naturally and sweetly holding her own among them without timidity or effort, was to me a pleasure so wonderful that even the quick, light shafts of jealousy--which ignoble but fiery darts were ever buzzing about my ass's ears, sometimes stinging me--could not fatally wound my satisfaction or my deep thankfulness that her dreadful and wretched trials were ended at last, after so many years.

What seemed to Angelina and Lana an exceedingly quick intimacy between Lois and me sentimentally interested the former, and, as I have said, aroused the mischievous, yet not unkindly, curiosity of the latter. Like all people who are deep in intrigue themselves, any hint of it in others excited her sophisticated curiosity. So when we concluded it might be safe to call each other Lois and Euan, Lana's curiosity leaped over all bounds to the barriers of impertinence.

There was, as usual, a respectable company gathered at Croghan's that afternoon; and a floating-island and tea and a punch. Lois, in her usual corner by the northern window, was so beset and surrounded by officers of ours, and Schott's, Franklin's, and Spalding's, and staff-officers halted for the day, that I had quite despaired of a word with her for the present; and had somewhat sulkily seated myself on the stairs to bide my time. What between love, jealousy, and hurt pride that she had not instantly left her irksome poppinjays at the mere sight of me, and flown to me under the noses of them all, I was in two minds whether I would remain in the house or no--so absurd and horridly unbalanced is a young man's mind when love begins meddling with and readjusting its accustomed mechanism. Long, long were my ears in those first days of my heart's undoing!

Solemnly brooding on woman's coldness, fickleness, and general ingratitude, and silently hating every gallant who crowded about her to hold her cup, her fan, her plate, pick up her handkerchief or a bud fallen from her corsage, I could not, however, for the life of me keep my eyes from the cold-blooded little jilt.

She had evidently been out walking before I arrived, for she still wore her coquette garden-hat--the chipstraw affair, with the lilac ribbons tied in a bow under her rounded chin; and a white, thin gown, most ravishing, and all bestrewn with sprigs and posies, which displayed her smooth and delicately moulded throat above the low-pinned kerchief, and her lovely arms from the creamy elbow lace down to her finger tips.

The French hair-powder she wore was not sprinkled in any vulgar profusion; it merely frosted the rich curls, making her pink checks pinker and her grey eyes a darker and purpler grey, and rendering her lips fresh and dewy in vivid contrast. And she wore a patch on her smooth left cheek-bone. And it was a most deadly thing to do, causing me a sentimental anguish unspeakable.

As I sat there worshipping, enchanted, resentful, martyred, alternately aching with loneliness and devotion, and at the same time heartily detesting every man on whom she chanced to smile, comes a sly and fragrant breath in my ear. And, turning, I discover Lana perched on a step of the stairs above me, her mocking eyes brilliant with unkind delight.

"Poor swain a-sighing!" said she. "Love is sure a thorny way, Euan."

"Have a care for your own skirts then," said I ungraciously.

"My skirts!"

"Yours, Lanette. Your petticoat needs mending now."

"If love no more than rend my petticoat I ought to be content," she said cool-ly.

Silenced by her effrontery, which truly passed all bounds, I merely glared at her, and presently she laughed outright.

"Broad-brim," said she, "I was not born yesterday. Have no worries concerning me, but look to yourself, for I think you have been sorely hit at last. And God knows such wounds go hard with a truly worthy and good young man."

"I make nothing of your nonsense," said I coldly.

"What? Nothing? And yonder sits its pretty and romantic inspiration? I am glad I have lived to see the maid who dealt you your first wound!"

"Do you fancy that I am in love?" said I defiantly.

"Why not admit what your lop-ears and moony mien yell aloud to the world entire?"

"Have you no common sense, Lana? Do you imagine a man can fall in love in a brief week?"

"I have been wondering," said she coolly, "whether you have ever before seen her."

"Continue to wonder," said I bluntly.

"I do.... Because you call her 'Lois' so readily--and you came near it the first day you had apparently set eyes on her. Also, she calls you 'Euan' with a tripping lack of hesitation--even with a certain natural tenderness--"

I turned on her, exasperated:

"Come," said I, controlling my temper with difficulty, "I am tired of playing butt to your silly arrows."

"Oh, how you squirm, Euan! Cupid and I are shooting you full as a porcu-pine!"

"If Cupid is truly shooting," said I with malice, "you had best hunt cover, Lana. For I think already a spent shaft or two has bruised you, flying at hazard from his bow."

She smilingly ignored what I had said.

"Tell me," she persisted, "are you not at her pretty feet already? Is not your very soul down on its worthy marrow-bones before this girl?"

"Is not every gallant gentleman who comes to Croghan's at the feet of Miss de Contrecoeur?"

"One or two are in the neighbourhood of my feet," she remarked.

"Aye, and too near to please me," said I.

"Who, for example?"

"Boyd--for example," I replied, giving her a hearty scowl.

"Oh!" she drawled airily. "He is not yet near enough my ankles to please me."

"You little fool," said I between my teeth, "do you think you can play alley-taw and cat's-cradle with a man like that?"

Then a cold temper flashed in her eyes.

"A man like that," she repeated. "And pray, dear friend, what manner of man may be 'a man like that?'"

"One who can over-match you at your own silly sport--and carry the game to its sinister finish! I warn you, have a care of yourself, Lanette. Sir John is a tyro to this man."

She said hotly: "If I should say to him what you have but now said to me, he would have you out for your impertinence!"

"If he continues to conduct as he has begun," said I, "the chances are that I may have him out for his effrontery."

"What! Who gave you the privilege of interfering in my affairs, you silly ninny?"

"So that you display ordinary prudence, I have no desire to interfere," I retorted angrily.

"And if I do not! If I am imprudent! If I choose to be audacious, reckless, shameless! Is it your affair?"

"Suppose I make it mine?"

"You are both silly and insulting; do you know it?"

Flushed, breathing rapidly, we sat facing each other; and I could have shaken the little vixen, so furious was I at myself as well as at her.

"Very well," said I, "continue to play with hell-fire if you like. I'm done with you and with him, too."

"And I with you," she said between her teeth. "And if you were not the honest-meaning marplot that you are, Mr. Boyd should teach you a lesson!"

"I'll teach him one now," said I, springing to my feet and gone quite blind with rage so that I was obliged to stand still a moment before I could discover Boyd where he stood by the open door, trying to converse with Mrs. Lansing, but watching us both with unfeigned amazement.

"Euan!"

Lana's voice arrested me, and I halted and turned, striving to remember decency and that I was conducting like a very boor. This was neither the time nor place to force a quarrel on any man.... And Lana was right. I had no earthly warrant to interfere if she gave me none; perhaps no spiritual warrant either.

Still shaken and confused by the sudden fury which had invaded me, and now sullenly mortified by my own violence and bad manners, I stood with one hand resting on the banisters, forcing myself to look at Lana and take the punishment that her scornful eyes were dealing me.

"Are you coming to your senses?" she asked coldly.

"Yes," I said. "I ask your pardon."

A moment more we gazed at each other, then suddenly her under lip trembled and her eyes filled.

"Forgive me," she stammered. "You are a better friend to me than--many.... I am not angry, Euan."

At that I could scarce control my own voice:

"Lanette--little Lana! Find it in your generous heart to offer me my pardon, for I have conducted like a yokel and a fool! But--but I really do love you."

"I know it, Euan. I did not know it was in me to use you so cruelly. Let us be friends again. Will you?"

"Will you, Lana?"

"Willingly--oh, with all my heart! And--I am not very happy, Euan. Bear with me a little.... There is a letter come from Clarissa; perhaps it is that which edges my tongue and temper--the poor child is so sad and lonely, so wretchedly unhappy-- and Sir John riding the West with all his hellish crew! And she has no news of him--and asks it of me----"

She descended a step and stood on the stair beside me, looking up at me very sweetly, and resting her hand lightly on my shoulder--a caress so frank and uncon-cealed that it meant no more then its innocent significance implied. But at that mo-ment, by chance, I encountered Lois's eyes fixed on me in cold surprise. And, being a fool, and already unnerved, I turned red as a pippin, as though I were guilty, and looked elsewhere till the heat cooled from my cheeks.

"You dear boy," said Lana gently. "If there were more men like you and fewer like--Sir John, there'd be no Clarissas in the world." She hesitated, then smiled audaciously. "Perhaps no Lanas either.... There! Go and court your sweetheart. For she gave me a look but now which boded ill for me or for any other maid or matron who dares lay finger on a single thrum of your rifle-shirt."

"You are wrong," said I. "She cares nothing for me in that manner."

"What? How do you know, you astounding boy?"

"I know it well enough."

Lana shot a swift and curious look straight across the room at Lois, who now did not seem to be aware of her.

"She is beautiful... and--not made of marble," said Lana softly to herself. "Good God, no! Scarcely made of marble.... And some man will awaken her one day.... And when he does he will unchain Aphrodite herself--or I guess wrong." She turned to me smiling. "That girl yonder has never loved."

"Why do you think so?"

"I know it; but I can not tell you why I know it. Women divine where men reason; and we are oftener right than you.... Are you truly in love with her?"

"I can not speak of such things to you," I muttered.

"Lord! Is it as serious as that already? Is it arrived at the holy and sacred stage?"

"Lana! For heaven's sake----"

"I am not jeering; I am realising the solemn fact that you have progressed a certain distance in love and are arrived at a definite and well-known milestone.... And I am merely wondering how far she has progressed--or if she has as yet journeyed any particular distance at all--or any more than set out upon the road. For the look she shot at me convinces me that she has started--in fact, has reached that turn in the thorny path where she is less inclined to defend herself than her own possessions. You seem to be one of them."

Boyd, who had awaited the termination of our tete-a-tete with an impatience perfectly apparent to anybody who chanced to observe him, now seemed able to endure it no longer; and as he approached us I felt Lana's hand on my arm tremble slightly; but the cool smile still curved her lips.

She received him with a shaft of light raillery, and he laughed and retorted in kind, and then we three sauntered over to the table where was the floating island in a huge stone bowl of Indian ware.

Around this, and the tea and punch, everybody was now gathering, and there was much talking and laughing and offering of refreshment to the ladies, and drinking of humourous or gallant toasts.

I remember that Boyd, being called upon, instantly contrived some impromptu verses amid general approbation--for his intelligence was as lithe and graceful as his body was agile. And our foppish Ensign, who was no dolt by a long shot either, made a most deft rondeau in flattery of the ladies, turning it so neatly and unexpectedly that we all drew our side-arms and, thrusting them aloft, cheered both him and the fair subjects of his nimble verses.

I would have been glad to shine in that lively and amusing competition, but possessed no such desirable talents, and so when called upon contrived merely a commonplace toast which all applauded as in duty bound.

And I saw Lois looking at me with an odd, smiling expression, not one thing or another, yet scarcely cordial.

"And now," says Boyd, "each lady in turn should offer an impromptu toast in verse."

Whereupon they all protested that the thing was impossible. But he was already somewhat flushed with the punch and with his own success; and says he, with that occasional and over-flourishing bow of his:

"To divinity nothing is impossible; therefore, the ladies, ever divine, may venture all things."

"Which is why I venture to decline," remarked Lana. But he was set upon it, and would not be denied; and he began a most flowery little speech with the ladies as his inspiration:

"Poetry and grace in mind and body is theirs by nature," said he, "and they have but to open the rosy petals of their lips to enthrall us all with gems of----"

"Lord!" said Mrs. Bleecker, laughing, "I have never writ a verse in my life save on my sampler; and if I were to open the rosy petals of my lips, I should never have done a-giggling. But I'll do it, Mr. Boyd, if you think it will enthrall you."

"As for me," quoth Angelina Lansing, "I require a workshop to manufacture my gems. It follows that they are no true gems at all, but shop-made paste. Ask Lana Helmer; she is far more adept in sugaring refusals."

All turned smilingly toward Lana, who shrugged her shoulders, saying carelessly:

"I must decline! The Muses nine   No sisters are of mine.   Must I repine   Because I'm not divine,   And may not versify some pretty story   To prove to you my own immortal glory?   Make no mistake. Accept; don't offer verses. Kisses received are mercies--given, curses!"

Said Boyd instantly:

"A thousand poems for your couplets! Do you trade with me, Miss Helmer?"

"Let me hear your thousand first," retorted the coquette disdainfully, "ere I make up my mind to be damned."

Major Parr said grimly:

"With what are we others to trade, who can make no verses? Is there not some more common form of wampum that you might consider?"

"A kind and unselfish heart is sound currency," said Lana smiling and turning her back on Boyd; which brought her to face Lois.

"Do make a toast in verse for these importunate gentlemen," she said, "and bring the last laggard to your feet."

"I?" exclaimed Lois in laughing surprise. Then her face altered subtly. "I may not dream to rival you in beauty. Why should I challenge you in wit?"

"Why not? Your very name implies a nationality in which elegance, graceful wit, and taste are all inherent." And she curtsied very low to Lois.

For a moment the girl stood motionless, her slender forefinger crook'd in thought across her lips. Then she glanced at me; the pink spots on her cheeks deepened, and her lips parted in a breathless smile.

"It will give me a pleasure to do honour to any wish expressed by anybody," she said. "Am I to compose a toast, Euan?"

I gazed at her in surprise; Major Parr said loudly: "That's the proper spirit!"

And, "Write for us a toast to love!" cried Boyd.

But Lana coolly proposed a toast to please all, which, she explained, a toast to love would not by any means.

"And surely that is easy for you," she added sweetly, "who of your proper self please all who ever knew you."

"Write us a patriotic toast!" suggested Captain Simpson, "----A jolly toast that all true Americans can drink under the nose of the British King himself."

"That's it!" cried Captain Franklin. "A toast so cunningly devised that our poor fellows in the Provost below, and on that floating hell, the 'Jersey,' may offer it boldly and unrebuked in the very teeth of their jailors! Lord! But that would be a rare bit o' verse--if it could be accomplished," he added dubiously.

Lois stood there smiling, thinking, the tint of excitement still brilliant in her cheeks.

"No, I could not hope to contrive such a verse----" she mused aloud. "Yet--I might try----" She lifted her grey eyes to mine as though awaiting my decision.

"Try," said I--I don't know why, because I never dreamed she had a talent for such trifles.

For a second, as her eyes met mine, I had the sensation of standing there entirely alone with her. Then the clamour around us grew on my ears, and the figures of the others again took shape on every side.

And "Try!" they cried. "Try! Try!"

"Yes," she said slowly. "I will try----" She looked up at me. "----If you wish it."

"Try," I said.

Very quietly she turned and passed behind the punch bowl and into the next room, but did not close the door. And anybody could see her there, seated at the rough pine table, quill in hand, and sometimes motionless, absorbed in her own thoughts, sometimes scratching away at the sheet of paper under her nose with all the proper frenzy of a very poet.

We had emptied the punch bowl before she reappeared, holding out to me the paper which was still wet with ink. And they welcomed her lustily, glasses aloft, but I was in a cold fright for fear she had writ nothing extraordinary, and they might think meanly of her mind, which, after all, I myself knew little of save that it was sweet and generous.

But she seemed in no manner perturbed, waiting smilingly for the noise to quiet. Then she said:

"This is a toast that our poor tyrant-ridden countrymen may dare to offer at any banquet under any flag, and under the very cannon of New York."

She stood still, absent-eyed, thinking for a moment; then, looking up at us:

"It is really two poems in one. If you read it straight across the page as it is written, then does it seem to be a boastful, hateful Tory verse, vilifying all patriots, even His Excellency--God forgive the thought!

"But in the middle of every line there is a comma, splitting the line into two parts. And if you draw a line down through every one of these commas, dividing the written verse into two halves, each separate half will be a poem of itself, and the secret and concealed meaning of the whole will then be apparent."

She laid the paper in my hands; instantly everybody, a-tiptoe with curiosity, clustered around to see. And this is what we all read--the prettiest and most cunningly devised and disguised verse that ever was writ--or so it seems to me:

"Hark--hark the trumpet sounds, the din of war's alarms

O'er seas and solid grounds, doth call us all to arms,
Who for King George doth stand, their honour soon shall shine,
Their ruin is at hand, who with the Congress join.
The acts of Parliament, in them I much delight,
I hate their cursed intent, who for the Congress fight.
The Tories of the day, they are my daily toast,
They soon will sneak away, who independence boast,
Who non-resistant hold, they have my hand and heart,
May they for slaves be sold, who act the Whiggish part.
On Mansfield, North and Bute, may daily blessings pour
Confusions and dispute, on Congress evermore,
To North and British lord, may honours still be done,
I wish a block and cord, to General Washington."

Then Major Parr took the paper, and raising one hand, and with a strange solemnity on his war-scarred visage, he pronounced aloud the lines of the two halves, reading first a couplet from the left hand side of the dividing commas, then a couplet from the right, and so down the double column, revealing the hidden and patriotic poem:

"Hark--hark the trumpet sounds
O'er seas and solid grounds!
The din of war's alarms
Doth call us all to arms!
Who for King George doth stand
Their ruin is at hand:
Their honour soon shall shine
Who with the Congress join:
The acts of Parliament
I hate their cursed intent!
In them I much delight
Who for the Congress fight.
The Tories of the day

They soon will sneak away:
They are my daily toast
Who independence boast.
Who non-resistant hold
May they for slaves be sold.
They have my hand and heart
Who act the Whiggish part.
On Mansfield, North, and Bute,
Confusion and dispute.
May daily blessings pour
On Congress evermore.
To North and British lord,
I wish a block and cord!
May honours still be done
To General Washington!"

As his ringing voice subsided, there fell a perfect silence, then a very roar of cheering filled it, and the hemlock rafters rang. And I saw the colour fly to Lois's face like a bright ensign breaking from its staff and opening in flower-like beauty.

Then every one must needs drink her health and praise her skill and wit and address--save I alone, who seemed to have no words for her, or even to tell myself of my astonishment at her accomplishment, somehow so unexpected.

Yet, why might I not have expected accomplishments from such a pliant intelligence--from a young and flexible mind that had not lacked schooling, irregular as it was? Far by her own confession to me, her education had been obtained, while it lasted, in schools as good as any in the land, if, indeed, all were as excellent as Mrs. Pardee's Young Ladies' Seminary in Albany, or the school kept by the Misses Primrose.

And Major Parr, the senior officer present, must have a glass of wine with her all alone, and offer her his arm to the threshold, where Lana and Boyd were busily plaiting a wreath of green maple-leaves for her, which they presently placed around her chip-straw hat. And we all acclaimed her.

As for Major Parr, that campaign-battered veteran had out his tablets and was painfully copying the verses--he being no scholar--while Boyd read them aloud to us all again in most excellent taste, and Lois laughed and blushed, protesting that her modest effort was not worthy such consideration.

"Egad!" said Major Parr loudly. "I maintain that verses such as these are worth a veteran battalion to any army on earth! You are an aid, an honour, and an inspiration to your country, Miss de Contrecoeur, and I shall take care that His Excellency receives a copy of these same verses----"

"Oh, Major Parr!" she protested in dismay. "I should perish with shame if His Excellency were to be so beset by every sorry scribbler."

"A copy for His Excellency! Hurrah!" cried Captain Simpson. "Who volunteers?"

"I will make it," said I, with jealous authority.

"And I will aid you with quill, sand, and paper," said Lana. "Come with me, Euan."

Lois, who had at first smiled at me, now looked at us both, while the smile stiffened on her flushed face as Lana caught me by the hand and drew me toward the other room where the pine camp-table stood.

While I was writing in my clear and painstaking chirography, which I try not to take a too great pride in because of its fine shading and skillful flourishes, the guests of the afternoon were making their adieux and taking their departure, some afoot, others on horseback.

When I had finished my copy and had returned to the main room, nothing remained of the afternoon party save Boyd and Lana, whispering together by a window, and the black wench, Gusta, clearing away the debris of the afternoon.

Outside in the late sunshine, I could see Mrs. Bleecker and Mrs. Lansing strolling to and fro, arm in arm, but I looked around in vain for Lois.

"She is doubtless gone a-boating with her elegant senior Ensign," said Lana sweetly, from the window. "If you run fast you may kill him yet, Euan."

"I was looking for nobody," said I stiffly, and marched out, ridding them of my company--which I think was what they both desired.

Now, among other and importunate young fops, the senior Ensign and his frippery and his marked attention to Lois, and his mincing but unfeigned devotion to her, had irritated me to the very verge of madness.

Twice, to my proper knowledge, this fellow had had her in an Oneida canoe, and with a guitar at that; and, damn him, he sang with taste and discretion. Also, when not on duty, he was ever to be found lisping compliments into her ear, or, in cool possession of her arm, promenading her to flaunt her beauty--and his good fortune--before the entire fort. And I had had enough of it.

So when I learned that she was off again with him, such a rage and wretchedness possessed me that I knew not what to do. Common sense yelled in my ear that no man of that stripe could seriously impress her; but where is the understanding in a very young man so violently sick with love as was I? All men who approached her I instantly suspected and mentally damned--even honest old Simpson--aye, even Major Parr himself. And I wonder now I had not done something to invite court-martial. For my common sense had been abruptly and completely upset, and I was at that period in a truly unhappy and contemptible plight.

I could not seem to steer my footsteps clear of the river bank, nor deny myself the fierce and melancholy pleasure of gazing at their canoe from afar, so I finally walked in that direction, cursing my own weakness and meditating quarrels and fatal duels.

But when I arrived on the river bank, I could not discover her in any of the canoes that danced in the rosy ripples of the declining sun. So, mooning and miserable, I lagged along the bank toward my bush-hut; and presently, to my sudden surprise, discovered the very lady of whom I had been thinking so intently--not dogged as usual by that insufferable Ensign, but in earnest conversation with the Sagamore.

And, as I gazed at them outlined against the evening sky, I remembered what Betsy Hunt had said at Poundridge--how she had encountered them together on the hill which overlooked the Sound.

Long before I reached them or they had discovered me, the Sagamore turned and took his departure, with a dignified gesture of refusal; and Lois looked after him for a moment, her hand to her cheek, then turned and gazed straight into the smouldering West, where, stretching away under its million giant pines, the vast empire of the Long House lay, slowly darkening against the crimson sunset.

She did not notice me as I came toward her through the waving Indian grass, and even when I spoke her name she did not seem startled, but turned very deliberately, her eyes still reflecting the brooding thoughts that immersed her.

"What is it that you and this Mohican have still to say to each other?" I asked apprehensively.

The vague expression of her features changed; she answered with heightened colour:

"The Sagamore is my friend as well as yours. Is it strange that I should speak with him when it pleases me to do so?"

There was an indirectness in her gaze, as well as in her reply, that troubled me, but I said amiably:

"What has become of your mincing escort? Is he gone to secure a canoe?"

"He is on duty and gone to the fort."

"Where he belongs," I growled, "and not eternally at your heels."

She raised her eyes and looked at me curiously.

"Are you jealous?" she demanded, beginning to smile; then, suddenly the smile vanished and she shot at me a darker look, and stood considering me with lips slightly compressed, hostile and beautiful.

"As for that fop of an Ensign----" I began--but she took the word from my mouth:

"A fiddle-stick! It is I who have cause to complain of you, not you of me! You throw dust in my eyes by accusing where you should stand otherwise accused. And you know it!"

"I? Accused of what?"

"If you don't know, then I need not humiliate myself to inform you. But I think you do know, for you looked guilty enough----"

"Guilty of what?"

"Of what? I don't know what you may be guilty of. But you sat on the stairs with your simpering inamorata--and your courtship quarrels and your tender reconciliations were plain enough to--to sicken anybody----"

"Lois! That is no proper way to speak of----"

"It is your own affair--and hers! I ask your pardon--but she flaunted her intimacy with you so openly and indiscreetly----"

"There is no common sense in what you say!" I exclaimed angrily. "If I----"

"Was she not ever drowning her very soul in your sheep's eyes? And even not scrupling to shamelessly caress you in the face of all----"

"Caress me!"

"Did she not stand for ten full minutes with her hand upon your shoulder, and a-sighing and simpering----"

"That was no caress! It was full innocent and----"

"Is she so innocent? Indeed! I had scarcely thought it of her," she said disdainfully.

"She is a true, good girl, innocent of any evil intention whatsoever----"

"I pray you, Euan, spare me your excited rhapsodies. If you prefer this most bewitching--minx----"

"She is no minx!" I retorted hotly; and Lois as hotly faced me, pink to her ears with exasperation.

"You do favour her! You do! You do! Say what you will, you are ever listening for the flutter of her petticoats on the stairs, ever at her French heels, ever at moony gaze with her--and a scant inch betwixt your noses! So that you come not again to me vowing what you have vowed to me--I care not how you and she conduct----"

"I do prefer you!" I cried, furious to be so misconstrued. "I love only one, and that one is you!"

"Oh, Euan, yours is a most broad and catholic heart; and any pretty penitent can find her refuge there; and any petticoat can flutter it!"

"Yours can. Even your fluttering rags did that!"

She flushed: "Oh, if I were truly weak and silly enough to listen to you----"

"You never do. You give me no hope."

"I do give you hope! I am ever ladling it out to you as they ladle soupaan to the militia! I say to you continually that never have I so devotedly loved any man----"

"That is not love!" I said, furious.

"I do not pretend it to be that same boiling and sputtering sentiment which men call love----"

"Then if it be not true love, why do you care what I whisper to any woman?"

"I do not care," she said, biting the rose-leaf lower lip. "You may whisper any treason you please to any h-heartless woman who snares your f-fancy."

"You do not truly care?"

"I have said it. No, I do not care! Court whom you please! But if you do, my faith in man is dead, and that's flat!"

"What!"

"Certainly.... After your burning vows so lately made to me. But men have no shame. I know that much."

"But," said I, bewildered, "you say that you care nothing for my vows!"

"Did I say so?"

"Yes--you----"

"No, I did not say so!... I--I love your vows."

"How can you love my vows and not me?" I demanded angrily.

"I don't know I can do it, but I do.... But I will love them no longer if you make the selfsame vows to her."

"Now," said I, perplexed and exasperated, "what does it profit a man when a maid confesses that she loves to hear his vows, but loves not him who makes them?"

"For me to love even your vows," said she, looking at me sideways, "is something gained for you--or so it seems to me. And were I minded to play the coquette--as some do----"

"You play it every minute!"

"I? When, pray?"

"When I came to Croghan's this afternoon there were you the centre of 'em all; and one ass in boots and spurs to wave your fan for you--oh, la! And another of Franklin's, in his Wyandotte finery, to fetch and carry; and a dozen more young fools all ogling and sighing at your feet----"

Her lips parted in a quick, nervous laugh:

"Was that the way I seemed? Truly, Euan? Were you jealous? And I scarce heeding one o' them, but my eyes on the doorway, watching for you!"

"Oh, Lois! How can you say that to me----"

"Because it was so! Why did you not come to me at once? I was waiting!"

"There were so many--and you seemed so gay with them--so careless--not even glancing at me----"

"I saw you none the less. I never let you escape the range of my vision."

"I never dreamed you noticed me. And every time you smiled on one of them I grew the gloomier----"

"And what does my gaiety mean--save that the source of happiness lies rooted in you? What do other men count, only that in their admiration I read some recompense for you, who made me admirable. These gowns I wear are yours--these shoon and buckles and silken stockings--these bows of lace and furbelows--this little patch making my rose cheeks rosier--this frost of powder on my hair! All these I wear, Euan, so that man's delight in me may do you honour. All I am to please them--my gaiety, my small wit, which makes for them crude verses, my modesty, my decorum, my mind and person, which seem not unacceptable to a respectable society-- all these are but dormant qualities that you have awakened and inspired----"

She broke off short, tears filling her eyes:

"Of what am I made, then, if my first and dearest and deepest thought be not for you? And such a man as this is jealous!"

I caught her hands, but she bent swiftly and laid her hot cheek for an instant against my hand which held them.

"If there is in me a Cinderella," she said unsteadily, "it is you who have discovered it--liberated it--and who have willed that it shall live. Did you suppose that it was in me to make those verses unless you told me that I could do it? You said, 'Try,' and instantly I dared try.... Is that not something to stir your pride? A girl as absolutely yours as that? And do not the lesser and commonplace emotions seem trivial in comparison--all the heats and passions and sentimental vapours--the sighs and vows and languishing all the inevitable trappings and masqueradings which bedizen what men know as love--do they not all seem mean and petty compared to our deep, sweet knowledge of each other?"

"You are wonderful," I said humbly. "But love is no unreal, unworthy thing, either; no sham, no trite cut-and-dried convention, made silly by sighs and vapours.

"Oh, Euan, it is! I am so much more to you in my soul than if I merely loved you. You are so much more to me--the very well-spring of my desire and pride--my reason for pleasing, my happy consolation and my gratitude.... Seat yourself here on the pleasant, scented grasses and let me endeavour to explain it once and for all time. Will you?

"It is this," she continued, taking my hand between hers, when we were seated, and examining it very intently, as though the screed she recited were written there on my palm. "We are so marvelously matched in every measurement and feature, mental and bodily almost--and I am so truly becoming a vital part of you and you of me, that the miracle is too perfect, too lofty, too serenely complete to vex it with the lesser magic--the passions and the various petty vexations they entail.

"For I would become--to honour you--all that your pride would have me. I would please the world for your sake, conquer it both with mind and person. And you must endeavour to better yourself, day by day, nobly and with high aim, so that the source of my inspiration remain ever pure and fresh, and I attain to heights unthinkable save for your faith in me and mine in you."

She smiled at me, and I said:

"Aye; but to what end?"

"To what end, Euan? Why, for our spiritual and worldly profit."

"Yes, but I love you----"

"No, no! Not in that manner----"

"But it is so."

"No, it is not! We are to be above mere sentiment. Reason rules us."

"Are we not to wed?"

"Oh--as for that----" She thought for a while, closely considering my palm. "Yes--that might some day be a part of it.... When we have attained to every honour and consideration, and our thoughts and desires are purged and lifted to serene and lofty heights of contemplation. Then it would be natural for us to marry, I suppose."

"Meanwhile," said I, "youth flies; and I may not lay a finger on you to caress you."

"Not to caress me--as that woman did to you----"

"Lois!"

"I can not help it. There is in her--in all such women--a sly, smooth, sleek and graceful beast, ever seeming to invite or offer a caress----"

"She is sweet and womanly; a warm friend of many years."

"Oh! And am I not--womanly?"

"Are you, entirely?"

She looked at me troubled:

"How would you have me be more womanly?"

"Be less a comrade, more a sweetheart."

"Familiar?"

My heart was beating fast:

"Familiar to my arms. I love you."

"I--do not permit myself to desire your arms. Can I help saying so--if you ask me?"

"When I love you so----"

"No. Why are you, after all, like other men, when I once hoped----"

"Other men love. All men love. How can I be different----"

"You are more finely made. You comprehend higher thoughts. You can command your lesser passions."

"You say that very lightly, who have no need to command yours!"

"How do you know?" she said in a low voice.

"Because you have none to curb--else you could better understand the greater ones."

She sat with head lowered, playing with a blade of grass. After a while she looked up at me, a trifle confused.

"Until I knew you, I entertained but one living passion--to find my mother and hold her in my arms--and have of her all that I had ached for through many empty and loveless years. Since I have known you that desire has never changed. She is my living passion, and my need."

She bent her head again and sat playing with the scented grasses. Then, half to herself, she said:

"I think I am still loyal to her if I have placed you beside her in my heart. For I have not yet invested you with a passion less innocent than that which burns for her."

She lifted her head slowly, propping herself up on one arm, and looked intently at me.

"What do you know about me, that you say I am unwomanly and cold?" Her voice was low, but the words rang a little.

"Do not deceive yourself," she said. "I am fashioned for love as thoroughly as are you--for love sacred or profane. But who am I to dare put on my crown of womanhood? Let me first know myself--let me know what I am, and if I truly have even a right to the very name I wear. Let me see my own mother face to face--hold her first of all in my embrace--give my lips first to her, yield to her my first caresses.... Else," and her face paled, "I do not know what I might become--I do not know, I tell you--having been all my life deprived of intimacy--never having known familiar kindness or its lightest caress--and half dead sometimes of the need of it!"

She straightened up, clenching her hands, then smiled her breathless little smile.

"Think of it, Euan! For twenty years I have wanted her caresses--or such harmless kindness of somebody--almost of anybody! My foster-mother never kissed me, never put her arm about me--or even laid her hand lightly upon my shoulder--as did that girl do to you on the stairs.... I tell you, to see her do it went through me like a Shawanese arrow----"

She forced a mirthless smile, and clasped her fingers across her knee:

"So bitterly have I missed affection all my life," she added calmly. "...And now you come into my life! Why, Euan--and my sentiments were truly pure and blameless when you were there that night with me on the rock under the clustered stars--and I left for you a rose--and my heart with it!--so dear and welcome was your sudden presence that I could have let you fold me in your arms, and so fallen asleep beside you, I was that deathly weary of my solitude and ragged isolation."

She made a listless gesture:

"It is too late for us to yield to demonstration of your affection now, anyway--not until I find myself safe in the arms that bore me first. God knows how deeply it would affect me if you conquered me, or what I would do for very gratitude and happiness under the first close caress.... Stir not anything of that in me, Euan. Let me not even dream of it. It were not well for me--not well for me. For whether I love you as I do, or--otherwise and less purely--it would be all the same--and I should become--something--which I am not--wedded or otherwise--not my free self, but to my lesser self a slave, without ambition, pride--wavering in that fixed resolve which has brought me hither.... And I should live and die your lesser satellite, unhappy to the very end."

After a silence, I said heavily:

"Then you have not renounced your purpose?"

"No."

"You still desire to go to Catharines-town?"

"I must go."

"That was the burden of your conversation with the Sagamore but now?"

"Yes."

"He refused to aid you?"

"He refused."

"Why, then, are you not content to wait here--or at Albany?"

She sat for a long while with head lowered, then, looking up quietly:

"Another pair of moccasins was left outside my door last night."

"What! At Croghan's? Inside our line!" I exclaimed incredulously.

"Aye. But this time the message sewed within them differed from all the others. And on the shred of bark was written: 'Swift moccasins for little feet as swift. The long trail opens. Come!'"

"You think your mother wrote it?" I asked, astounded.

"Yes.... She wrote the others."

"Well?"

"This writing is the same."

"The same hand that wrote the other messages throughout the years?"

"The same."

"Have you told the Sagamore of this?"

"I told him but now--and for the first time."

"You told him everything?"

"Yes--concerning my first finding--and the messages that came every year with the moccasins."

"And did you show him the Indian writing also?"

"Yes."

"What did he say?"

"Nothing. But there flashed up suddenly in his eyes a reddish light that frightened me, and his face became so hideous and terrible that I could have cried out. But I contrived to maintain my composure, and I said: 'What do you make of it, O Sagamore?' And he spat out a word I did not clearly understand----"

"Amochol?"

"Yes--it sounded like that. What did he mean, Euan?"

"I will presently ask him," said I, thoroughly alarmed. "And in the meanwhile, you must now be persuaded to remain at this post. You are contented and happy here. When we march, you will go back to Schenectady or to Albany with the ladies of the garrison, and wait there some word of our fate.

"If we win through, I swear to you that if your mother be there in Catharinestown I will bring news of her, or, God willing, bring her herself to you."

I rose and aided her to stand; and her hands remained limply in mine.

"I had rather take you from her arms," I said in a low voice, "----if you ever deign to give yourself to me."

"That is sweetly said.... Such giving leaves the giver unashamed."

"Could you promise yourself to me?"

She stood with head averted, watching the last faint stain of color fade from the west.

"Would you have me at any cost, Euan?"

"Any cost."

"Suppose that when I find my mother--I find no name for myself--save hers?"

"You shall have mine then."

"Dear lad!... But--suppose, even then I do not love you--as men mean love."

"So that you love no other man, I should still want you."

"Am I then so vital to you?"

"Utterly."

"To how many other women have you spoken thus?" she asked gravely.

"To none."

"Truly?"

"Truly, Lois."

She said in a low voice:

"Other men have said it to me.... I have heard them swear it with tears in their eyes and calling God to witness. And I knew all the while that they were lying--perjuring their souls for the sake of a ragged, unripe jade, and a wild night's frolic.... Well--God made men.... I know myself, too.... To love you as you wish is to care less for you than I already do. I would not willingly.... Yet, I may try if you wish it.... So that is all the promise I dare make you. Come--take me home now--if you care to walk as far with me."

"And I who am asking you to walk through life with me?" I said, forcing a laugh.

We turned; she took my arm, and together we moved slowly back through the falling dusk.

And, as we approached her door, came a sudden and furious sound of galloping behind us, and we sprang to the side of the road as the express thundered by in a storm of dust and driving pebbles.

"News," she whispered. "Do they bring good news as fast as bad?"

"It may mean our marching orders," I said, dejected.

We had now arrived at Croghan's, and she was withdrawing her arm from mine, when the hollow sound of a conch-horn went echoing and booming through the dusk.

"It does mean your marching orders!" she exclaimed, startled.

"It most certainly means something," said I. "Good-night--I must run for the fort----"

"Are you going to----to leave me?"

"That horn is calling out Morgan's men----"

"Am I not to see you again?"

"Why, yes--I expect so--but if----"

"Oh! Is there an 'if'? Euan, are you going away forever?"

"Dear maid, I don't know yet what has happened----"

"I do! You are going!... To your death, perhaps--for all I know----"

"Hush! And good-night----"

She held to my offered hand tightly:

"Don't go--don't go----"

"I will return and tell you if----"

"'If!' That means you will not return! I shall never see you again!"

I had flung one arm around her, and she stood with one hand clenched against her lips, looking blankly into my face.

"Good-bye," I said, and kissed her clenched hand so violently that it slipped sideways on her cheek, bruising her lips.

She gave a faint gasp and swayed where she stood, very white in the face.

"I have hurt you," I stammered; but my words were lost in a frightful uproar bursting from the fort; and:

"God!" she whispered, cowering against me, as the horrid howling swelled on the affrighted air.

"It is only the Oneidas' scalp-yell," said I. "They know the news. Their death-halloo means that the corps of guides is ordered out. Good-bye! You have means to support you now till I return. Wait for me; love me if it is in you to love such a man. Whatever the event, my devotion will not alter. I leave you in God's keeping, dear. Good-bye."

Her hand was still at her bruised lips; I bent forward; she moved it aside. But I kissed only her hand.

Then I turned and ran toward the fort; and in the torch-light at the gate encountered Boyd, who said to me gleefully:

"It's you and your corps of guides! The express is from Clinton. Hanierri remains; the Sagamore goes with you; but the regiment is not marching yet awhile. Lord help us! Listen to those beastly Oneidas in their paint! Did you ever hear such a wolf-pack howling! Well, Loskiel, a safe and pleasant scout to you." He offered his hand. "I'll be strolling back to Croghan's. Fare you safely!"

"And you," I said, not thinking, however, of him. But I thought of Lana, and wished to God that Boyd were with us on this midnight march, and Lana safe in Albany once more.

As I entered the fort, through the smoky flare of torches, I saw Dolly Glenn waiting there; and as I passed she gave a frightened exclamation.

"Did you wish to speak to me?" I asked.

"Is--is Lieutenant Boyd going with you?" she stammered.

"No, child."

She thanked me with a pitiful sort of smile, and shrank back into the darkness.

I remained but a few moments with Major Parr and Captain Simpson; a rifleman of my own company, Harry Kent, brought me my pack and rifle--merely sufficient ammunition and a few necessaries--for we were to travel lightly. Then Captain Simpson went away to inspect the Oneida scouts.

"I wish you well," said the Major quietly. "Guard the Mohican as you would the apple of your eye, and--God go with you, Euan Loskiel."

I saluted, turned squarely, and walked out across the parade to the postern.

Here I saw Captain Simpson inspecting the four guides, one of whom, to me, seemed unnecessarily burdened with hunting shirt and blanket.

Running my eye along their file, where they stood in the uncertain torchlight, I saw at once that the guides selected by Major Parr were not all Oneidas. Two of them seemed to be; a third was a Stockbridge Indian; but the fourth--he with the hunting-shirt and double blanket, wore unfamiliar paint.

"What are you?" said I in the Oneida dialect, trying to gain a square look at him in the shifty light.

"Wyandotte," he said quietly.

"Hell!" said I, turning to Captain Simpson. "Who sends me a Wyandotte?"

"General Clinton," replied Simpson in surprise. "The Wyandotte came from Fortress Pitt. Colonel Broadhead, commanding our left wing, sent him, most highly recommending him for his knowledge of the Susquehanna and Tioga."

I took another hard look at the Wyandotte.

"You should travel lighter," said I. "Split that Niagara blanket and roll your hunting-shirt."

The savage looked at me a moment, then his sinewy arms flew up and he snatched the deerskin shirt from his naked body. The next instant his knife fairly leaped from its beaded sheath; there was a flash of steel, a ripping sound, and his blue and scarlet blanket lay divided. Half of it he flung to a rifleman, and the other half, with his shirt, he rolled and tied to his pack.

Such zeal and obedience pleased me, and I smiled and nodded to him. He showed his teeth at me, which I fancied was his mode of smiling. But it was somewhat hideous, as his nose had been broken, and the unpleasant dent in it made horridly conspicuous by a gash of blood-red paint.

I buckled my belt and pack and picked up my rifle. Captain Simpson shook hands with me. At the same moment, the rifleman sent to our bush-hut to summon the Mohican returned with him. And a finer sight I never saw; for the tall and magnificently formed Siwanois was in scarlet war-paint from crown to toe, oiled, shaven save for the lock, and crested with a single scarlet plume--and heaven knows where he got it, for it was not dyed, but natural.

His scarlet and white beaded sporran swung to his knees; his ankle moccasins were quilled and feathered in red and white; the Erie scalps hung from his girdle, hooped in red, and he bore only a light pack-slung, besides his rifle and short red blanket.

"Salute, O Sagamore! Roya-neh!" I said in a low voice, passing him.

He smiled, then his features became utterly blank, as one by one the eyes of the other Indians flashed on his for a moment, then shifted warily elsewhere.

I made a quick gesture, turned, and started, heading the file out into the darkness.

And as we advanced noiselessly and swung west into the Otsego road, I was aware of a shadow on my right--soft hands outstretched--a faint whisper as I kissed her tightening fingers. Then I ran on to head that painted file once more, and for a time continued to lead at hazard, blinded with tears.

And it was some minutes before I was conscious of the Mohican's hand upon my arm, guiding my uncertain feet through the star-shot dark.

CHAPTER XI
A SCOUT OF SIX

We were now penetrating that sad and devastated region laid waste so recently by Brant, Butler, and McDonald, from Cobus-Kill on the pleasant river Askalege, to Minnisink on the silvery Delaware--a vast and mournful territory which had been populous and prosperous a twelvemonth since, and was now the very abomination of desolation.

Cherry Valley lay a sunken mass of blood-wet cinders; Wyoming had gone up in a whirlwind of smoke, and the wretched Connecticut inhabitants were dead or fled; Andrustown was now no more, Springfield, Handsome Brook, Bowmans, Newtown-Martin--all these pretty English villages were vanished; the forest seedlings already sprouted in the blackened cellars, and the spotted tree-cats squalled from the girdled orchards under the July moon.

Where horses, cows, sheep, men, women, and children had lain dead all over the trampled fields, the tall English grass now waved, yellowing to fragrant hay; horses, barns, sheds--nay, even fences, wagons, ploughs, and haycocks had been laid in cinders. There remained not one thing that could burn which had not been burned. Only breeze-stirred ashes marked these silent places, with here and there a bit of iron from wagon or plough, rusting in the dew, or a steel button from some dead man's coat, or a bone gone chalky white--dumb witnesses that the wrath of England had passed wrapped in the lightning of Divine Right.

But Great Britain's flaming glory had swept still farther westward, for German Flatts was gone except for its church and one house, which were too near the forts for the destructives to burn. But they had laid in ashes more than a hundred humble homes, barns, and mills, and driven off more than a thousand cattle, horses, sheep, and oxen, leaving the barnyard creatures dead or dying, and ten thousand skipples of grain afire.

So it was no wonder that the provisioning of our forces at Otsego had been slow, and that we now had five hundred wagons flying steadily between Canajoharie and the lake, to move our stores as they arrived by batteaux from below. And there were some foolish and impatient folk in Congress, so I heard, who cried out at our delay; and one more sinister jackass, who had said that our army would never move until a few generals had been court-martialed and shot. And our Major Parr said that he wished to God we had the Congress with us so that for once they might have their bellyful of stratagem and parched corn.

But it is ever so with those home-loving and unsurpassed butcher-generals, baker-brigadiers, candlestick-colonels, who, yawning in bed, win for us victories while we are merely planning them--and, rolling over, go to sleep with a consciousness of work well done, the candle snuffed, and the cat locked out for the night.

About eleven o'clock on the first night out, I halted my scout of six and lay so, fireless, until sun-up. We were not far, then, from the head of the lake; and when we marched at dawn next morning we encountered a company of Alden's men mending roads as usual; and later came upon an entire Continental regiment and a company of Irregular Rifles, who were marching down to the lake to try out their guns. Long after we quitted them we heard their heavy firing, and could distinguish between the loud and solid "Bang!" of the muskets and the sharper, whip-lash crack of the long rifles.

The territory that now lay before us was a dense and sunless wilderness, save for the forest openings made by rivers, lakes, and streams. And it was truly the enemy's own country, where he roamed unchecked except for the pickets of General Sullivan's army, which was still slowly concentrating at Tioga Point whither my scout of six was now addressed. And the last of our people that we saw was a detail of Alden's regiment demolishing beaver dams near the lake's outlet which, they informed us, the beavers rebuilt as fast as they were destroyed, to the rage and confusion of our engineers. We saw nothing of the industrious little animals, who are accustomed to labor while human beings sleep, but we saw their felled logs and cunningly devised dams, which a number of our men were attacking with pick and bar, standing in the water to their arm-pits.

Beyond them, at the Burris Farm, we passed our outlying pickets--Irregular Riflemen from the Scoharie and Sacandaga, tall, lean, wiry men, whose leaf-brown rifle-dress so perfectly blended with the tree-trunks that we were aware of them only when they halted us. And, Lord! To see them scowl at my Indians as they let us through, so that I almost expected a volley in our backs, and was relieved when we were rid o' them.

When, later, we passed Yokam's Place, we were fairly facing that vast solitude of twilight which lay between us and the main army's outposts at the mouth of the Tioga. Except for a very few places on the Ouleout, and the Iroquois towns, the region was uninhabited. But the forest was beautiful after its own somewhat appalling fashion, which was stupendous, majestic, and awe-inspiring to the verge of apprehension.

Under these limitless lanes of enormous trees no sunlight fell, no underbrush grew. All was still and vague and dusky as in pillared aisles. There were no birds, no animals, nothing living except the giant columns which bore a woven canopy of leaves so dense that no glimmer of blue shone through. Centuries had spread the soundless carpet that we trod; eons had laid up the high-sprung arches which vanished far above us where vault and column were dimly merged, losing all form in depthless shadow.

There was an Indian path all the way from the lake, good in places, in others invisible. We did not use it, fearing an ambush.

The Mohican led us; I followed him; the last Oneida marked the trees for a new and better trail, and a straighter one not following every bend in the river. And so, in silence we moved southward over gently sloping ground which our wagons and artillery might easily follow while the batteaux fell down the river and our infantry marched on either bank, using the path where it existed.

Toward ten o'clock we came within sound of the river again, its softly rushing roar filling the woods; and after a while, far through the forest dusk, we saw the thin, golden streak of sunlight marking its lonely course.

The trail that the Mohican now selected swung ever nearer to the river, and at last, we could see low willows gilded by the sun, and a patch of blue above, and a bird flying.

Treading in file, rifles at trail, and knife and hatchet loosened, we moved on swiftly just within that strip of dusk that divides the forest from the river shrub; and I saw the silver water flowing deep and smooth, where batteaux as well as canoes might pass with unvexed keels; and, over my right shoulder, above the trees, a baby peak, azure and amethyst in a cobalt sky; and a high eagle soaring all alone.

The Mohican had halted; an Oneida ran down to the sandy shore and waded out into mid-stream; another Oneida was peeling a square of bark from a towering pine. I rubbed the white square dry with my sleeve, and with a wood-coal from my pouch I wrote on it:

"Ford, three feet at low water."

The Stockbridge Indian who had stepped behind a river boulder and laid his rifle in rest across the top, still stood there watching the young Oneida in midstream who, in turn, was intently examining the river bank opposite.

Nothing stirred there, save some butterflies whirling around each other over a bed of purple milkweed, but we all watched the crossing, rifles at a ready, as the youthful Oneida waded slowly out into the full sunshine, the spray glittering like beaded topazes on his yellow paint.

Presently he came to a halt, nosing the farther shore like a lean and suspicious hound at gaze; and stood so minute after minute.

Mayaro, crouching beside me, slowly nodded.

"He has seen something," I whispered.

"And I, too," returned the Mohican quietly.

I looked in vain until the Sagamore, laying his naked arm along my cheek, sighted for me a patch of sand and water close inshore--a tiny bay where the current clutched what floated, and spun it slowly around in the sunshine.

A dead fish, lying partly on the shore, partly in the water, was floating there.

I saw it, and for a moment paid it no heed; then in a flash I comprehended. For the silvery river-trout lying there carried a forked willow-twig between gill and gill-cover. Nor was this all; the fish was fresh-caught, for the gills had not puffed out, nor the supple body stiffened. Every little wavelet rippled its slim and limber length; and a thread of blood trailed from the throat-latch out over the surface of the water.

Suddenly the young Oneida in mid-stream shrank aside, flattening his yellow painted body against a boulder, and almost at the same instant a rifle spoke.

I heard the bullet smack against the boulder; then the Mohican leaped past me. For an instant the ford boiled under the silent rush of the Oneidas, the Stockbridge Indian, and the Mohican; then they were across; and I saw the willows sway and toss where they were chasing something human that bounded away through the thicket. I could even mark, without seeing a living soul, where they caught it and where it was fighting madly but in utter silence while they were doing it to death-- so eloquent were the feathery willow-tops of the tragedy that agitated each separate slender stem to frenzy.

Suddenly I turned and looked at the Wyandotte, squatting motionless beside me. Why he had remained when the red pack started, I could not understand, and with that confused thought in mind I rose, ran down to the water's edge, the Wyandotte following without a word.

A few yards below the ford a giant walnut tree had fallen, spanning the stream to a gravel-spit; I crossed like a squirrel on this, the burly Wyandotte padding over at my heels, sprang to the bottom sand, and ran up the willow-gully.

They were already dragging out what they had killed; and I came up to them and looked down on the slain man who had so rashly brought destruction upon his own head.

He wore no paint; he was not a warrior but a hunter. "St. Regis," said the Mohican briefly.

"The poor fool," I said sadly.

The young Oneida in yellow clapped the scalp against a tree-trunk carelessly, as though we could not easily see by his blazing eyes and quivering nostrils that this was his first scalp taken in war. Then he washed the blade of his knife in the river, wiped it dry and sheathed it, and squatted down to braid the dead hair into the hunters-lock.

We found his still smouldering fire and some split fish baking in green leaves; nets, hooks, spears, and a bark shoulder-basket. And he had been a King's savage truly enough, foraging, no doubt, for Brant or Butler, who had great difficulty in maintaining themselves in a territory which they had so utterly laid waste--for we found in his tobacco pouch a few shillings and pennies, and some pewter buttons stamped, "Butler's Rangers." Also I discovered a line of writing signed by old John Butler himself, recommending the St. Regis to one Captain Service, an uncle of Sir John Johnson, and a great villain who recently had been shot dead by David Elerson, one of my own riflemen, while attempting to brain Tim Murphy with an axe.

"The poor fool," I repeated, turning away, "Had he not meddled with war when his business lay only in hunting, he had gone free or, if we had caught him, only as a prisoner to headquarters."

Mayaro shrugged his contempt of the St. Regis hunter; the Oneida youth sat industriously braiding his first trophy; the others had rekindled the embers of the dead man's fire and were now parching his raw corn and dividing the baked river-trout into six portions.

Mayaro and I ate apart, seated together upon a knoll whence we could look down upon the river and upon the fire, which I now ordered to be covered.

From where I sat I could see the burly Wyandotte, squatting with the others at his feed, and from time to time my glance returned to him. Somehow, though I knew not why, there was about this Indian an indefinable something not entirely reassuring to me; yet, just what it might be I was not able to say.

Truly enough he had a most villainous countenance, what with his native swarthiness and his broken and dented nose, so horridly embellished with a gash of red paint. He was broad and squat and fearfully powerful, being but a bulk of gristly muscle; and when he leaped a gully or a brook, he seemed to strike the earth like a ball of rubber and slightly rebound an the light impact. I have seen a sinewy panther so rebound when hurled from a high tree-top.

The Oneida youth had now braided and oiled his scalp and was stretching it on a willow hoop, very busy with the pride and importance of his work. I glanced at Mayaro and caught a gleam of faint amusement in his eyes; but his features remained expressionless enough, and it seemed to me that his covert glance rested on the Wyandotte more often than on anybody.

The Mohican, as was customary among all Indians when painted for war, had also repainted his clan ensign, although it was tatooed on his breast; and the great Ghost Bear rearing on its hind quarters was now brilliantly outlined in scarlet. But he also wore what I had never seen any other Indian wear when painted for any ceremony in North America. For, just below the scarlet bear, was drawn in sapphire blue the ensign of his strange clan-nation--the Spirit Wolf, or Were-Wolf. And a double ensign worn by any priest, hunter, or warrior I had never before beheld. No Delaware wore it unless belonging to the Wolf Clan of the Lenni-Lenape, or unless he was a Siwanois Mohican and a Sagamore. For there existed nowhere at that time any social and political society among any Indian nation which combined clan and tribal, and, in a measure, national identity, except only among the Siwanois people, who were all three at the same time.

As I salted my parched corn and ate it, sitting cross-legged on my hillock, my eyes wandered from one Indian to another, reading their clan insignia; and I saw that my Oneida youth wore the little turtle, as did his comrade; that the Stock-bridge Indian had painted a Christian Cross over his tattooed clan-totem--no doubt the work of the Reverend Mr. Kirkland--and that the squatting Wyandotte wore the Hawk in brilliant yellow.

"What is yonder fellow's name?" I asked Mayaro, dropping my voice.

"Black-Snake," replied the Mohican quietly.

"Oh! He seems to wear the Hawk."

The Sagamore's face grew smooth and blank, and he made no comment.

"It's a Western clan, is it not, Mayaro?"

"It is Western, Loskiel."

"That clan does not exist among the Eastern nations?"

"Clans die out, clans are born, clans are altered with the years, Loskiel."

"I never heard of the Hawk Clan at Guy Park," said I.

He said, with elaborate carelessness:

"It exists among the Senecas."

"And apparently among the Wyandottes."

"Apparently."

I said in a low voice:

"Yonder Huron differs from any Indian I ever knew. Yet, in what he differs I can not say. I have seen Senecas like him physically. But Senecas and Hurons not only fought but interbred. This Wyandotte may have Seneca blood in him."

The Sagamore made no answer, and after a moment I said:

"Why not confess, Mayaro, that you also have been perplexed concerning this stranger from Fort Pitt? Why not admit that from the moment he joined us you have had your eye on him--have been furtively studying him?"

"Mayaro has two eyes. For what are they unless to observe?"

"And what has my brother observed?"

"That no two people are perfectly similar," he said blandly.

"Very well," I said, vexed, but quite aware that no questions of mine could force the Sagamore to speak unless he was entirely ready. "I suppose that there exist no real grounds on which to suspect this Wyandotte. But you know as well as do I that he crossed not the river with the others when they did to death that wretched St. Regis hunter. Also, that there are Wyandottes in our service at Fortress Pitt, I did not know before."

I waited a moment, but the Mohican said nothing, and I saw his eyes, veiled like a dreaming bird of prey, so immersed did he seem to be in his own and secret reflections.

Presently I rose, went down to the fire, felt with my fingers among the ashes to be certain no living spark remained, chatted a moment with the Oneida youth, praising him till under all his modesty I saw he was like to burst with pride; then gave the signal for departure.

"Nevertheless," I added, addressing them all, "this is not a scalping party; it is the six eyes of an army spying out a way through this wilderness, so that our wagons, artillery, horses, and cattle may pass in safety to Tioga Point.

"Let the Sagamore strike each tree to be marked, as he leads forward. Let the Mole repeat the blow unless otherwise checked. Then shall the Oneida, Grey-Feather, mark clearly the tree so doubly designated. The Oneida, Tahoontowhee, covers our right flank, marching abreast of the Mohican; the Wyandotte, Black-Snake, covers our left flank, keeping the river bank in view. March!"

All that afternoon we moved along south and west, keeping in touch with the Susquehanna, which here is called Oak Creek, though it is the self-same stream.

And we scouted the river region thoroughly, routing out nothing save startled deer that bounded from their balsam beds and went off crashing through the osiers, or a band of wild turkeys that, bewildered, ran headlong among us so that Tahoonto-whee knocked over two with his rifle butt, and, slinging them to his shoulders, went forward buried in plumage like same monstrous feathered goblin of the forest.

The sun was now dropping into the West; the woods on our right had darkened; on our left a pink light netted the river ripples. Filing in perfect silence, save for the light sound of a hatchet and the slithering of sappy bark, I had noticed, or thought I noticed, that the progress of the Wyandotte was less quiet than ours, where he ranged our left flank, supposedly keeping within the forest shadow.

Once or twice I thought I heard a small stone fall to the willow gully, as though accidentally dislodged by his swiftly passing moccasins. Once, at any rate, I caught the glimmer of the sun striking some bit of metal on him, where he had incautiously ranged outside the protecting shadow belt.

That these things were purely accidental I felt sure, yet I did not care to have them repeated. And for a long while there was neither sound nor sun-glitter from him. Then, without even a glance or a word for me, the Mohican quietly dropped back from the lead, waited until the last Oneida had passed, and moved swiftly on a diagonal course to the left, which brought him in the tracks of the Wyandotte.

He continued on that course for a while, I taking his place in the lead, and the Wyandotte unconscious that he was followed. Then the Sagamore came gliding into our file again, and as he passed me to resume his lead, he whispered:

"Halt, and return along the bank. The Black-Snake has overrun a ford where there are signs for my brother to read and consider."

I turned sharply and lifted my hand; and as the file halted I caught a glimpse of the Oneida, Tahoontowhee, on our right, and motioned him to cross, head the Wyandotte, and return with him. And when in a few moments he came toward us, followed by the Huron, I said, addressing them all:

"There should be a ford hereabouts, if I am not badly mistaken, and I think we have accidentally overrun it. Did you see nothing that might indicate it, Black-Snake, my brother?"

There was a furtive flicker of the Wyandotte's eyes which seemed to include everybody before him, then he said very coolly that he had seen no riffle that might indicate shallow water, but that there was a ford not far below, and we ought to strike it before sunset.

"Halt here," said I, pretending to remain still unconvinced. "Sagamore, do you come with me a rod or so upstream."

"There is no ford within a rod or two," said the Wyandotte stolidly.

And, after we had left the others, the Mohican murmured, as we hastened on:

"No, not with one rod or two, but the third rod marks it."

Presently, speeding under the outer fringe of trees, I caught sight of a thin line across the water, slanting from shore to shore--not a ripple, but as though the edge of an invisible reef slightly affected the smooth-flowing, glassy surface of the stream.

"He might have overlooked that," said I.

The Sagamore's visage became very smooth; and we climbed down among the willows toward the sand below, and there the Mohican dropped on his hands and knees.

Directly under his eyes I saw the faint print of a moccasin. Startled, I said nothing; the Mohican studied the print for a few moments, then, crouching, crept forward among the sand-willows. I followed; and at long intervals I could make out the string of moccasin tracks, still visible in the loose, dry sand.

"Could it be the St. Regis?" I whispered. "He may have been here spearing fish. These tracks are not new.... And the Wyandotte might have overlooked these, too."

"Maybe St. Regis," he said.

We had now crept nearly to the edge of the water, the dry and scarcely discernible tracks leading us. But they were no fresher in the damp sand. However, the Mohican did not seem satisfied, so we pulled off our thigh-moccasins and waded out.

Although the water looked deep enough along the unseen reef, yet we found nowhere more than four feet, and so crossed to the other side. But before I could set foot on the shelving sand the Mohican pulled me back into the water and pointed. There was no doubting the sign we looked upon. A canoe had landed here within an hour, had been pushed off again with a paddle without anybody landing. It was as plain as the nose on your face.

Which way had it gone, upstream or down? If it had gone upstream, the Wyandotte must have seen it and passed it without reporting it. In other words, he was a traitor. But if the canoe had gone downstream from this spot, or from some spot on the left bank a little above it, there was nothing to prove that the Wyandotte had seen it. In fact, there was every probability that he had not seen it at all. And I said as much to the Sagamore.

"Maybe," he replied calmly.

We now cautiously recrossed the stream, scarcely liking our exposed position, but there was no help for it. After we had dressed, I marked the trees from the ford across the old path, which was visible here, and so through to our main, spotted trail; the Mohican peeled a square of bark, I wiped the white spot dry, and wrote with my wood-coal the depth of water at the crossing; then we moved swiftly forward to join the halted scouts.

Mayaro said to me: "We have discovered old moccasin tracks, but no ford and no canoe marks. It is not necessary for the Black-Snake to know."

"Very well," said I calmly. "Do you suspect him!"

"Maybe. Maybe not. But--he once wore his hair in a ridge."

"What!"

"I looked down on him while he ate fish at the St. Regis fire. He has not shaved his head since two weeks. There is a thin line dividing his head, where the hairs at their roots are bent backward. Much oil and brushing make hairs grow that way."

"But--what Indians wear their hair that way--like the curved ridge on a dragoon's helmet?"

"The Eries."

I stared at him without comprehension, for I knew an Erie scalp when I saw one.

"Not the warriors," he added quietly.

"What in heaven's name do you mean?" I demanded. But we were already within sight of the others, and I heeded the cautioning touch of his hand on my arm, and was silent.

When we came up to them I said:

"There are no riffles to indicate a ford"--which was true enough--"and on the sand were only moccasin tracks a week old."

"The Black-Snake saw them," said the Wyandotte, so frankly and calmly that my growing but indefinite suspicions of his loyalty were arrested for the moment.

"Why did not the Black-Snake report them?" I asked.

"They were St. Regis, and a week old, as my brother says." And he smiled at us all so confidingly that I could no longer believe ill of him.

"Nevertheless," said I, "we will range out on either flank as far as the ford which should be less than a mile down stream." And I placed the Wyandotte between both Oneidas and on the forest side; and as the valley was dry and open under its huge standing timber, I myself led, notching the trail and keeping a lively eye to the left, wherever I caught a glimpse of water sparkling.

Presently the Mohican halted in view of the river-bank, making a sign for me to join him, which I did, briefly bidding the Stockbridge Mole to notch the trees in my stead.

"A canoe has passed," said the Sagamore calmly.

"What! You saw it?"

"No, Loskiel. But there was spray on a boulder in a calm pool."

"Perhaps a deer crossed, or a mink or otter crawled across the stone."

"No; the drops were many, but they lay like the first drops of a rain, separate and distinct."

"A great fish leaping might have spattered it."

"There was no wash against the rock from any fish-swirl."

"Then you believe that there is a canoe ahead of us going with the current?"

"An hour ahead--less, I think."

"Why an hour?"

"The sun is low; the river boulders are not hot. Water might dry on them in an hour or less. These drops were nearly dry, save one or two where the sun made them shine."

"A careless paddle-stroke did it," I said in a low voice.

"No Indian is careless."

"What do you mean by that?"

"I mean, Loskiel, that the boulder was splashed purposely, or that there are white men in that canoe."

"Splashed purposely?" I said, bewildered.

"Perhaps. The Black-Snake had the river watch--until you changed our stations."

"You think it might have been a sign for him from possible confederates."

"Maybe. Maybe clumsy white men."

"What white men? No forest runners dare range these woods at such a time as this. Do you mean a scalping party of Butler's men?"

"Maybe."

We had been walking swiftly while we spoke together in low and guarded tones; now I nodded my comprehension, sheered off to the right, took the trail-lead, replacing the Stockbridge Mole, and signalled the nearest Oneida, Grey-Feather, to join Mayaro on the left flank. This made it necessary for me to call the Wyandotte into touch, which I did; and the other Oneida, the "Night-Hawk," or Tahoonto-whee, closed in from the extreme outer flank.

The presence of that canoe worried me, nor could I find any explanation for it. None of our surveyors was out--no scouts had gone in that direction. Of course I knew that we were likely to run across scouts or scalping parties of the enemy almost anywhere between the outlet to Otsego Lake and Tioga Point, yet somehow had not expected to encounter them until we had at least reached the Ouleout.

Another thing; if this phantom canoe was now within an hour of us, and going with the current, it must at one time have been very, very close to us--in fact, just ahead and within sight of the Wyandotte, if, indeed, it had not come silently downstream from behind us and shot past us in plain view of the Black-Snake.

Was the Wyandotte a traitor? For only he could have seen this. And I own that I felt more comfortable having him on our right flank in the forest, and away from the river; and as I notched my trees I kept him in view, sideways, and pondered an the little that I knew of him, but came to no conclusion. For of all things in the world I know less of treachery and its wiles than of any other stratagem; and so utterly do I misunderstand it, and so profound is my horror of it, that I never can credit it to anybody until I see them hanged by the neck for it or shot in hollow square, a-sitting upon their coffins.

Presently I saw the Sagamore stop and make signs to me that the ford was in sight. Immediately I signalled the Wyandotte and the farther Oneida to close in; and a few moments later we were gathered in the forest shadow above the river, lying on our bellies and gazing far down stream at the distant line of ripples running blood-red under the sunset light.

Was there an ambush there, prepared for us? God knew. Yet, we must approach and examine that ford, and pass it, too, and resume our march on the right bank of the river to avoid the hemlock swamps and rocky hills ahead, which no wagons or artillery could hope to pass.

My first and naturally cautious thought was to creep nearer and then send the Wyandotte out under cover of our clustered rifles. But if he were truly in any collusion with an unseen enemy they would never fire on him, and so it would be useless to despatch him on such a mission.

"Wait for the moon," said the Sagamore very quietly.

His low, melodious voice startled me from my thoughts, and I looked around at him inquiringly.

"I will go," said the Wyandotte, smiling.

"One man will never draw fire from an ambush," said the Grey-Feather cunningly. "The wild drake swims first into the net; the flock follows."

"Why does my younger brother of the Oneida believe that we need fear any ambush at yonder ford?" asked the Wyandotte so frankly that again I felt that I could credit no ill of any man who spoke so fairly.

"Listen to the crows," returned the Oneida. "Their evening call to council is long and deliberate--Kaah! Kaah! Kaah--h! What are they saying now, Black-Snake, my elder brother?"

I glanced at the Mohican in startled silence, for we all were listening very intently to the distant crows.

"They have discovered an owl, perhaps," said the Wyandotte, smiling, "and are tormenting him."

"Or a Mountain Snake," said the Sagamore blandly.

Now, what the Sagamore said so innocently had two meanings. He might have meant that the cawing of the crows indicated that they were objecting to a rattlesnake sunning on some rock. Also he might have meant to say that their short, querulous cawing betrayed the presence of Seneca Indians in ambush.

"Or a Mountain Snake," repeated the Siwanois, with a perfectly blank face. "The red door of the West is still open."

"Or a bear," said the Grey-Feather, cunningly slurring the Canienga word and swallowing the last syllable so that it might possibly have meant "Mohawk."

The Wyandotte turned good-humouredly to the Mohican, not pretending to misunderstand this subtle double entendre and play upon words.

"You, Sagamore of the Loups," he said, carrying out the metaphor, "are closer to the four-footed people than are we Wyandottes."

"That is true," said the Grey-Feather. "My elder brother, the Black-Snake, wears the two-legged hawk."

Which, again, if it was meant that way, hinted that the Hawk was an alien clan, and neither recognized nor understood by the Oneida. Also, by addressing the Wyandotte as "elder" brother, the Oneida conveyed a broad hint of blood relationship between Huron and Seneca. Yet, there need have been nothing definitely offensive in that hint, because among all the nations a certain amalgamation always took place after an international conflict.

The Wyandotte did not lose his temper, nor even, apparently, perceive how slyly he was being baited by all except myself.

"What is the opinion of the Loup, O Sagamore?" he asked lightly.

"Does my brother the Black-Snake desire to know the Sagamore's opinion concerning the cawing of yonder crows?"

The Wyandotte inclined his ugly head.

"I think," said the Mohican deliberately, "that there may be a tree-cat in their vicinity."

A dead silence followed. The Wyandotte's countenance was still smiling, but I thought the smile had stiffened and become fixed, though not a tremour moved him. Yet, what the Mohican had said--always with two meanings, and one quite natural and innocent--meant, if taken in its sinister sense, that not only might there be Senecas lying in ambush at the ford, but also emissaries from the Red Priest Amochol himself. For the forest lynx, or tree-cat, was the emblem of these people; and every Indian present knew it.

Still, also, every man there had seen crows gather around and scold a lynx lying flattened out on some arching limb.

Whether now there was any particular suspicion of this Wyandotte among the other Indians; whether it was merely their unquenchable and native distrust of any Huron whatever; whether the subtle chaff were playful or partly serious, I could not determine from their manner or expression. All spoke pleasantly and quietly, and with open or expressionless countenances. And the Wyandotte still smiled, although what was going on under that urbane mask of his I had no notion whatsoever.

I turned cautiously, and looked behind us. We were gathered in a kind of natural and moss-grown rocky pulpit, some thirty feet above the stream, and with an open view down its course to the distant riffles. Beyond them the river swung southward, walling our view with its flanking palisade of living green.

"We camp here," I said quietly. "No fire, of course. Two sentinels--the Night Hawk and the Black-Snake. The guard will be relieved every two hours. Wake me at the first change of watch."

I laid my watch on a rock where all could see it, and, opening my sack, fished out a bit of dried beef and a handful of parched corn.

Mayaro shared with me on my motioned invitation; the others fell to in their respective and characteristic manners, the Oneidas eating like gentlemen and talking together in their low and musical voices; the Wyandotte gobbling and stuffing his cheeks like a chipmunk. The Stockbridge Mole, noiseless and mum as the occult and furry animal which gave to him his name, nibbled sparingly all alone by himself, and read in his Algonquin Testament between bites.

The last level sun rays stripped with crimson gold the outer edges of the woods; the stream ran purple and fire, and the ceaseless sighing of its waters sounded soft as foliage stirring on high pines.

I said to the Mole in a low voice:

"Brother in Christ, do you find consolation and peace in your Testament when the whole land lies writhing under the talons and bloody beak of war?"

The Stockbridge warrior looked up quietly:

"I read the promise of the Prince of Peace, brother, who came to the world not bearing a sword."

"He came to fulfill, not to destroy," I said.

"So it is written, brother."

"And yet you and I, His followers, go forth armed to slay."

"To prepare a place for Him--His humble instruments--lest His hands be soiled with the justice of God's wrath. What is it that we wade in blood, so that He pass with feet unsoiled?"

"My brother has spoken."

The burning eyes of the calm fanatic were fastened on me, then they serenely reverted to the printed page on his knees; and he continued reading and nibbling at his parched and salted corn. If ever a convert broke bread with the Lord, this red disciple now sat supping in His presence, under the immemorial eaves of His leafy temple.

The Grey-Feather, who had been listening, said quietly:

"We Iroquois alone, among all Indians, have always acknowledged one Spirit. We call Him the Master of Life; you Christians call Him God. And does it truly avail anything with Tharon, O my brother Loskiel, if I wear the Turtle, or if my brother the Mole paints out the Beaver on his breast with a Christian cross?"

"So that your religion be good and you live up to it, sign and symbol avail nothing with God or with Tharon," said I.

"Men wear what they love best," said the Mole, lightly touching his cross.

"But under cross and clan ensign," said I, "lies a man's secret heart. Does the Master of Life judge any man by the colour of his skin or the paint he wears, or the clothing? Christ's friends were often beggars. Did Tharon ever ask of any man what moccasins he wore?"

The Sagamore said gravely:

"Uncas went naked to the Holder of the Heavens."

It was a wonderful speech for a Sagamore and an Algonquin, for he used the Iroquois term to designate the Holder of Heaven. The perfect courtesy of a Christian gentleman could go no further. And I thought of our trivial and petty and warring sects, and was silent and ashamed.

The Wyandotte wiped his powerful jaw with a handful of dead leaves, and looked coldly around at the little circle of men who differed with one another so profoundly in their religious beliefs.

"Is this then the hour and the place to discuss such matters, and irritate the Unseen?"

All eyes were instantly turned on the pagan; the Oneidas seemed troubled; the Sagamore serious. Only the Christian Indian remained placid and indifferent, his

Testament suspended in his hand. But he also was listening.

As for me, I knew as well as did the others what the pagan and burly Wyandotte meant.

To every Indian--even to many who had been supposedly converted--air, earth, and water still remained thronged with demons. The vast and sunless wilderness was peopled with goblins and fairies. No natural phenomenon occurred except by their agency. Where the sun went after it had set, where the moon hid, the stars, the four great winds, the eight thunders--all remained mysteries to these red children of the forest. And to these mysteries demons held the keys. For no star fell, showering the night with incandescence, no comet blazed aloft, its streaming hair sweeping from zenith to horizon, no eclipse devoured sun or moon, no sunrise painted the Long House golden, no sunset stained its lodge-poles crimson, no waters ran, no winds blew, no clouds piled up quivering with lightning, no thunder rumbled, except that it was done by demons.

Fur, feather, and silver-scale also had souls, and slyly took council together when alone; the great trees talked to one another in forest depths; moonlit rocks conversed in secret; and peak whispered to peak above the flowing currents of the mist.

It was useless to dispute such matters with them, while every phenomenon of nature remained to them a mystery. For they had brains and a matchless imagination, and they were obliged to solve these things for themselves as best they knew how, each people according to its personal characteristics.

So, among the Onondagas, Oneidas, and Mohawks, evil demons were few, and good fairies many; among the Cayugas good and bad seemed fairly balanced; but among the sullen, brutal, and bestial Senecas, devils, witches, demons, and goblins were in the vast majority. And their perverted Erie priesthood, which had debauched some of their own Sachems, was a stench in the nostrils of any orthodox Sachem, and, to an ordained Sagamore, an offense and sacrilege unspeakable.

I sat looking hard at the Wyandotte, inclined to speak, yet unwilling to meddle where intervention must be useless.

His small, unwinking eyes met mine.

"There are demons," he said in a low voice.

"Demons in human form," I nodded. "Some were at Cherry Valley a year ago."

"There are witches," he said.

I shook my head: "None."

"And Giants of Stone, and Flying Heads, and the Dead Hunter, and the Lake Serpent," he persisted sullenly.

"There never were either giants or witches," I replied.

The Mole looked up from his Testament in surprise, but said nothing. Yet, by his expression I knew he was thinking of the Witch of Endor, and the Dukes of Edom, and the giants of the scriptures. But it seemed hopeless to modify his religious teachings by any self-developed theories of mine.

All I desired to do was to keep this pagan Huron from tampering with my warriors' nerves. And it required but little of the supernatural to accomplish this.

No Indian, however brave and faithful and wise in battle, however cunning and tireless and unerring on forest trail or on uncharted waters, could remain entirely undisturbed by any menace of invisible evil. For they were an impulsive race, ever curbing their impulses and blindly seeking for reason. But what appealed to their emotions and their imagination still affected them most profoundly, and hampered the slow, gradual, but steady development of a noble race emerging by its own efforts from absolute and utter ignorance.

I said quietly: "After all, the Master of Life stands sentry while the guiltless sleep!"

"Amen," said the Mole, lifting his calm eyes to the roof of leaves above.

An owl began to hoot--one of those great, fierce cat-owls of the North. Every Indian listened.

The Sagamore said pleasantly to the Wyandotte:

"It is as though he were calling the lynxes together--as Amochol the Accursed summons his Cat-People to the sacrifice."

"I know nothing of Amochol and his sacrifices," said the Wyandotte carelessly.

"Yet you Wyandottes border the Western Gate."

The Huron shrugged.

"Hear the Eared One squall," said Grey-Feather, as the great owl yelled through the darkening forest.

"One would think to hear an Erie speaking," said the Sagamore, looking steadily at the Black-Snake. But the latter seemed totally unaware of what amounted now to a persistent baiting.

"They say," continued the Sagamore, "that the Erie priesthood learned from the Nez Perces a strange and barbarous fashion."

"What fashion?" asked Grey-Feather, so innocently that I could not determine whether he was playing into the Sagamore's hands.

"The fashion of wearing the hair in a short, stiff ridge," said the Mohican. "Has the Black-Snake ever seen it worn that way?"

"Never," said the Huron. And there was neither in his voice nor on his features the slightest tremour that we could discover in the fading light of the afterglow.

I rose to put an end to this, for my own nerves were now on edge; and I directed the two sentinels to their posts, the Wyandotte and the Oneida, Tahoontowhee.

Then I lay down beside the Mohican. All the Indians had unrolled and put on their hunting shirts; I spread my light blanket and pillowed my head on my pack.

In range of my vision the Mole had dropped to his knees and was praying with clasped hands. Shamed, I arose and knelt also, to say in silence my evening prayer, so often slurred over while I lay prone, or even entirely neglected.

Then I returned to my blanket to lie awake and think of Lois, until at last I dreamed of her. But the dream was terrible, and I awoke, sweating, and found the Sagamore seated upright in the darkness beside me.

"Is it time to change the guard?" I asked, still shivering from the horror of my dream.

"You have scarce yet closed your eyes, Loskiel."

"Why are you seated upright wide awake, my brother?"

"There is evil in the wind."

"There is no wind stirring."

"A witch-wind came slyly while you slept. Did you not dream, Loskiel?" In spite of me I shivered again.

"That is foolishness," said I. "The Wyandotte's silly talk has made us wakeful. Our sentinels watch. Sleep, Mayaro."

"Have you need of sleep, Loskiel?"

"I? No. Sleep you, then, and I will sit awake if it reassures you."

The Sagamore set his mouth close to my ear:

"The Wyandotte is not posted where you placed him."

"What? How do you know?"

"I went out to see. He sits on a rock close to the water."

"Damn him," I muttered angrily. "I'll teach him----"

"No!"

The Mohican's iron grip held me in my place.

"The Night-Hawk understands. Let the Wyandotte remain unrebuked and undisturbed while I creep down to yonder ford."

"I do not intend to reconnoitre the ford until dawn," I whispered.

"Let me go, Loskiel."

"Alone?"

"Secretly and alone. The Siwanois is a magic clan. Their Sagamores see and hear where others perceive nothing. Let me go, Loskiel."

"Then I go, also."

"No."

"What of our blood-brotherhood, then?"

There was a silence; then the Mohican rose, and taking my hand in his drew me noiselessly to my feet beside him.

By sense of touch alone we lifted our rifles from our blankets, blew the powder from the pans, reprimed. Then, laying my left arm lightly on his shoulder, I followed his silent figure over the moss and down among the huge and phantom trees faintly outlined against the starlit water.

CHAPTER XII
AT THE FORD

When at length from the forest's edge we saw star-beams splintering over broken water, cutting the flat, translucent darkness of the river with necklaces of light, we halted; for this was the ford foaming there in obscurity with its silvery, mellow voice, unheeded in the wilderness, yet calling ever as that far voice called through the shadows of ages dead.

Now, from where we stood the faint line of sparkles seemed to run a little way into the darkness and vanish. But the indications were sufficient to mark the spot where we should enter the water; and, stepping with infinite precaution, we descended to the gravel. Here we stripped to the clout and laid our rifles on our moccasins, covering the pans with our hunting shirts. Then we strapped on our war-belts, loosening knife and hatchet, pulled over our feet our spare ankle-moccasins of oiled moose-hide soled with the coarse hair of the great, blundering beast himself.

I led, setting foot in the icy water, and moving out into the shadow with no more noise than a chub's swirl or a minnow's spatter-leap when a great chain-pike snaps at him.

Feeling my way over bed stones and bottom gravel with my feet, striving in vain to pierce the dense obscurity, I moved forward with infinite caution, balancing as best I might against the current. Ankle-deep, shin-deep, knee-deep we waded out. Presently the icy current chilled my thighs, rising to my waistline. But it grew no deeper.

Yet, here so swift was the current that I scarcely dared move, and was peering around to find the Sagamore, when a shape loomed up on my left. And I reached out and rested my hand on the shadowy shoulder, and stood so, swaying against the stream.

Suddenly a voice said, in the Seneca dialect:

"Is it thou, Butler?"

And every drop of blood froze in my body.

God knows how I found voice to answer "Yes," and how I found courage to let my hand remain upon my enemy's shoulder.

"It is I, Hiokatoo," said the low voice.

"Move forward," I said; and dropped my hand from his shoulder.

Somehow, although I could see nothing, all around me in the water I felt the presence of living creatures. At the same moment somebody came close to me from behind, and the Sagamore breathed his name in my ear.

I managed to retain my presence of mind, and, laying my mouth against his ear in the darkness, I whispered:

"The Seneca Hiokatoo and his warriors--all around us in the water. He mistakes me for Walter Butler, They have been reconnoitring our camp."

I felt the body of the Mohican stiffen under my grasp, Then he said quietly:

"Stand still till all have passed us."

"Yes; but let no Seneca hear your Algonquin speech. If any speak I will answer for you."

"It is well," said the Sagamore quietly. And I heard him cautiously loosening his hatchet.

Presently a dark form took shape in the gloom and passed us without speaking; then another, and another, and another, all wading forward with scarce a ripple sounding against their painted bodies. Then one came up who spoke also in Seneca dialect, saying to the Mohican that the canoe was to be sent up stream on observation, and asking the whereabouts of McDonald.

So they were all there, the bloody crew! But once more I found voice to order the Seneca across, saying that I would attend to the canoe when the time came to employ it.

This Indian seemed to understand very little English, and he hesitated; but I laid my hand flat on his naked back, and gave him a slight shove toward the farther shore. And he went on, muttering.

Two more passed. We waited in nervous silence for the next, not knowing how many had been sent to prowl around our camp. And as no more came, I whispered to the Sagamore:

"Let us go back. If more are to come, and if there be among them Butler or McDonald or any white man, he will never mistake me for any of his fellows after he hears me speak."

The Sagamore turned, the water swirling to his waist. I followed. We encountered nobody until the water began to shoal. Then, in mid-stream, a dark figure loomed out of the night, confronting us, and I heard him say in the Seneca language:

"Halt and turn. You travel the wrong way!"

"Go forward and mind your business!" I said in English.

The shadowy figure seemed astounded, remaining motionless there in the ford. Suddenly he bent forward as though to see my features, and at the same instant the Sagamore seized him and jerked his head under water.

But he could not hold him, for the fellow was oiled, and floundered up in the same instant. No doubt the water he had swallowed kept the yell safe in his throat, but his hatchet was out and high-swung as the Sagamore grasped his wrist, holding his arm in the air. Then, holding him so, the Mohican passed his knife through the man's heart, striking with swiftness incredible again and again; and as his victim collapsed, he eased him down into the water, turned him over, and took his shoulders between his knees.

"God!" I whispered. "Don't wait for that!"

But the Siwanois warrior was not to be denied; and in a second or two the wet scalp flapped at his belt.

Rolling over and over with the current, the limp body slipped down stream and disappeared into deeper shadows. We waded swiftly toward our own shore, crawled across the gravel, drew on our clothing, and stole up into the woods above.

"They'll know it by sunrise," I said. "How many did you count?"

"Thirteen in that war-party, Loskiel. And if Butler and McDonald be with them, that makes fifteen--and doubtless other renegades besides."

"Then we had best pull foot," said I. And I drew my knife and blazed the ford; and, as well as I might without seeing, wrote the depth of water on the scar.

I heard the Mohican's low laughter.

"The Senecas will see it and destroy it. But it will drive them frantic," he said.

"Whatever they do to this tree will but mark the ford more plainly," said I.

And the Mohican laughed and laughed and patted my shoulder, as we moved fast on our back trail. I think he was excited, veteran though he was, at his taking of a Seneca warrior's scalp. "Had you not jerked him under water when he leaned forward over your shoulder to see what manner of man was speaking English," said I, "doubtless he had awakened the forest with his warning yell in another moment."

"Let him yell at the fishes, now," said the Mohican, laughing. "No doubt the eels will understand him; they are no more slippery than he."

Save for the vague forms of the trees dimly discerned against the water, the darkness was impenetrable; and except for these guides, even an Indian could scarcely have moved at all. We followed the bank, keeping just within the shadows; and I was ever scanning the spots of starlit water for that same canoe which I had learned was to go upstream to watch us.

Presently the Siwanois checked me and whispered:

"Yonder squats your Wyandotte sentinel."

"Where? I can not see him."

"On that flat rock by the deep water, seeming a part of it."

"Are you certain?"

"Yes, Loskiel."

"You saw him move?"

"No. But a Siwanois of the Magic Clan makes nothing of darkness. He sees where he chooses to see.

"Mayaro," said I, "what do you make of this Wyandotte?"

"He has quitted his post without orders for a spot by the deep water. A canoe could come there, and he could speak to those within it."

"That might damn a white soldier, but an Indian is different."

"He is a Wyandotte--or says he is."

"Yes, but he came with credentials from Fortress Pitt."

"Once," said the Sagamore, "he wore his hair in a ridge."

"If the Eries learned that from the Nez Perces, why might not the Wyandottes also learn it?"

"He wears the Hawk."

"Yes, I know it."

"He saw the moccasin tracks in the sand at the other ford, Loskiel, and remained silent."

"I know it."

"And I believe, also, that he saw the canoe."

"Then," said I, "you mean that this Wyandotte is a traitor."

"If he be a Wyandotte at all."

"What?"

"He may be Huron; he may be a Seneca-Huron. But we Indians think differently, Loskiel."

"What do you think?"

"We do not know for certain. But"--and the Mohican's voice became quietly ferocious--"if a war-arrow ever struck this Wyandotte between the shoulders I think every tree-cat in the Long House would squall at the condoling council."

"You think this Wyandotte an Erie in disguise?" I asked incredulously.

"We Indians of different nations are asking that question of each other, Loskiel."

"What is the mind of the Grey-Feather concerning this?" I asked, horrified.

"Oneida and Stockbridge begin to believe as I believe."

"That this creature is a spy engaged to lead us to our deaths? Do they believe that this self-styled Wyandotte is an infamous Erie?"

"We so believe, Loskiel. We are not yet certain."

"But you who have taken Erie scalps should know----"

"We know an Erie by his paint and lock; by his arms and moccasins. But when an Erie wears none of these it is not easy to determine exactly what he might be. There is, in the Western nation, much impure blood, much mixing of captive and adopted prisoners with the Seneca conquerors. If an Erie wear cats' claws at the root of his scalp-lock, even a blind Quaker might know him. If one of their vile priests wear his hair in a ridge, then, unless he be a Nez Perce, there need be no doubt. But this man dresses and paints and conducts like no Erie I have ever seen. And yet I believe him one, and a Sachem at that!"

"Then, by God!" said I in a cold fury. "I will go down to the stream and put him under arrest until such time as his true colours may be properly determined!"

"Loskiel, if yonder Indian once saw in your eye that you meant to take him, he would slip between your hands like a spotted trout and be off down stream to his comrades. Go not toward him angry, or with anything in your manner and voice that he might distrust."

"I never learned to smile in the face of a traitor!"

"Learn now, then. Brother, you are young; and war is long. And of many aspects are they who take arms in their hands to slay. Strength is good; quickness and a true eye to the rifle-sight are good. But best of all in war are the calmness and patience of wisdom. A Sagamore has spoken."

"What would you have me do?"

"Nothing, yet."

"But we must make a night march of it, and I could not endure that infamous creature's company, even if it were safe for us to take him with us."

"My brother may remain tranquil. The Grey-Feather and I are watching him.

The praying Indian and Tahoontowhee understand also. When we once are certain, the Erie dies."

"When you are certain," said I in a fury, "I will have him properly tried by military court and hung as high as Amherst hung two of his fellow devils. I wish to God he had executed the entire nation while he was about it. For once Sir William Johnson was wrong to interfere."

The Sagamore laughed and laid one hand on my shoulder:

"Is it a custom for an Ensign to pass judgment on a Major-General, O Loskiel, my dear but much younger brother?"

I blushed hot with annoyance and shame. Of all things on earth, self-control was the most necessary quality to any officer commanding Indians.

"The Sagamore is right," I said in a mortified voice.

"The Sagamore has lived longer than his younger brother," he rejoined gently.

"And is far wiser," said I.

"A little wiser in some few things concerning human life, Loskiel.... Does my brother desire that Mayaro shall bring in the Wyandotte?"

"Bring him," I said; and walked forward toward our camp.

Tahoontowhee stopped me with his challenge, then sprang forward at the sound of my voice.

"Men in the woods," he whispered, "creeping up from the South. They saw no fire and prowled no nearer than panthers prowl when they know a camp is awake."

"Senecas," I said briefly. "We make a night march of it. Remain on guard here. The Grey-Feather will bring your pack to you when we pick you up."

As I ascended the rocky pulpit, both the Grey-Feather and the Stockbridge were standing erect and wide awake, packs strapped and slung, rifles in hand.

"Senecas," I said. "Too many for us."

"Are we not to strike?" asked the Oneida wistfully, as the Mohican came swiftly up the rock followed by the Wyandotte, who seemed inclined to lag.

"Why did you quit your post?" I asked him bluntly.

"There was a better post and more to see on the rock," he said simply.

"You made a mistake. Your business is to obey your commanding officer. Do you understand?"

"The Black-Snake understands."

"Did you discover nothing from your rock?"

"Nothing. Deer moved in the woods."

"Red deer," I said coolly.

"A July deer is in the red coat always."

"The deer you heard are red the whole year round."

"Eho! The Black-Snake understands."

"Very well. Tie your pack, sling it, and shoulder your rifle. We march immediately."

He seemed to be willing enough, and tied his points with alacrity. Nor could I, watching him as well I might in so dark a spot, see anything suspicious in any movement he made.

"The Sagamore leads," I said; "the Black-Snake follows; I follow him; after me the Mole; and the Oneidas close the rear.... Attention!... Trail arms! File!"

And as we climbed out of our pulpit and descended over the moss to the soundless carpet of moist leaves:

"Silence," I said. "A sound may mean the death of us all. Cover your rifle-pans with your blankets. No matter what happens, no man is to fire without orders----"

I stopped abruptly and laid my hand on the Black-Snake's hatchet-sheath, feeling it all over with my finger-tips in the dark.

"Damnation!" I said. "There are tin points on the fringe! You might better wear a cow-bell! Where did you get it?"

"It was in my pack."

"You have not worn it before. Why do you wear it now?"

"It is looser in time of need."

"Very well. Stand still." I whipped out my knife and, bunching the faintly tinkling thrums in my fingers, severed the tin points and tossed them into the darkness.

"I can understand," said I, "a horse-riding Indian of the plains galloping into battle all over cow-bells, but never before have I heard of any forest Indian wearing such a fringe in time of war."

The rebuke seemed to stun the Wyandotte. He kept his face averted while I spoke, then at my brief word stepped forward into his place between myself and the Mohican.

"March!" I said in a low voice.

The Sagamore led us in a wide arc north, then west; and there was no hope of concealing or covering our trail, for in the darkness no man could see exactly where the man in front of him set foot, nor hope to avoid the wet sand of rivulets or the soft moss which took the imprint of every moccasin as warm wax yields to the seal.

That there was in the primeval woods no underbrush, save along streams or where the windfall had crashed earthward, made travelling in silence possible.

The forest giants branched high; no limbs threatened us; or, if there were any, the Sagamore truly had the sight of all night-creatures, for not once did a crested head brush the frailest twig; not once did a moccasined foot crash softly through dead and fallen wood.

The slope toward the river valley became steeper; we travelled along a heavily-wooded hillside at an angle that steadily increased. After an hour of this, we began to feel rock under foot, and our moccasins crushed patches of reindeer moss, dry as powder.

It was in such a place as this, or by wading through running water, that there could be any hope of hiding our trail; and as we began to traverse a vast, flat shoulder of naked rock, I saw that the Mohican meant to check and perplex any pursuit next morning.

What was my disgust, then, to observe that the Wyandotte's moccasins were soaking wet, and that he left at every step his mark for the morning sun to dry at leisure.

Stooping stealthily, I laid my hand flat in his wet tracks, and felt the grit of sand. Accidentally or otherwise, he had stepped into some spring brook which we had crossed in the darkness. Clearly the man was a fool, or something else.

And I was obliged to halt the file and wait until the Wyandotte had changed to spare moccasins; which I am bound to say he seemed to do willingly enough. And my belief in his crass stupidity grew, relieving me of fiercer sentiments which I had begun to harbour as I thought of all we knew or suspected concerning this man.

So it was forward once more across the naked, star-lit rock, where blueberry bushes grew from crevices, and here and there some tall evergreen, the roots of which were slowly sundering the rock into soil.

Rattlesnakes were unpleasantly numerous here--this country being notorious for them, especially where rocks abound. But so that they sprung their goblin rattles in the dark to warn us, we had less fear of them than of that slyer and no less deadly cousin of theirs, which moved abroad at night as they did, but was often too lazy or too vicious to warn us.

The Mohican sprang aside for one, and ere I could prevent him, the Wyandotte had crushed it. And how to rebuke him I scarcely knew, for what he had done seemed natural enough. Yet, though the Mohican seized the twisting thing and flung it far into the blueberry scrub, the marks of a bloody heel were now somewhere on the rocks for the rising sun to dry but not to obliterate. God alone knew whether such repeated evidence of stupidity meant anything worse. But now I was resolved to have done with this Indian at the first opportunity, and risk the chance of clearing myself of any charge concerning disobedience of orders as soon as I could report to General Sullivan with my command.

The travelling now, save for the dread of snakes, was pleasant and open. We had been gradually ascending during the last two hours, and now we found ourselves traversing the lengthening crest of a rocky and treeless ridge, with valleys on either side of us, choked with motionless lakes of mist, which seemed like vast snow fields under the splendour of the stars.

I think we all were weary enough to drop in our tracks and sleep as we fell. But I gave no order to halt, nor did I dream of interfering with the Sagamore, or even ask him a single question. It was promising to give me a ruder schooling than my regiment could offer me--this travelling with men who could outrun and outmarch the vast majority of white men.

Yet, I had been trained under Major Parr, and with such men in my command as Elerson, Mount, and Murphy; and I had run with Oneidas before and scouted far and wide with the best of them.

It was the rock-running that tired us, and I for one was grateful when we left the starlit obscurity of the ridge and began to swing downward, first through berry scrub and ground-hemlock, then through a thin belt of birches into the dense blackness of the towering forest.

Down, ever down we moved on a wide-slanting and easy circle, such as the high hawk swings when he is but a speck in the midsummer sky.

Presently the ground under our feet became level. A low, murmuring sound stole out of the darkness, pleasantly filling our ears as we advanced. A moment later, the Mohican halted; and we caught a faint gleam in the darkness.

"Sisquehanne," he said.

If, was the Susquehanna. Tired as I was I could not forbear a smile when this Mohican saluted the noble river by its Algonquin name in the presence of those haughty Iroquois who owned it. And it seemed to me as though I could hear the feathered crests stiffen on the two Oneida heads; for this was Oneida country, and they had been maliciously reminded that the Lenape had once named for them their river under circumstances in which no Iroquois took any pride. Little evidences of the subtle but ever-living friction between my Mohican and the two Oneidas were plenty, but never more maliciously playful than this. And presently I heard the Sagamore politely mention the Ouleout by its Iroquois name, Aulyoulet, which means "a voice that continues"; and while I sent the Night-Hawk down to the water to try for a crossing, Mohican and Oneida conversed very amiably, the topic being our enemies, and how it was that on the Ouleout and in Pennsylvania they had so often spared the people of that state and had directed their full fury toward New York.

The Oneida said it was because the Iroquois had no quarrel with Penn's people, who themselves disliked the intruding Yankee and New Yorker; but they were infuriated against us because we had driven the Iroquois from their New York lands and had punished them so dreadfully at Oriskany. And he further said that Cherry Valley would not have been made such a shambles except that Colonel Clyde and Colonel Campbell lived there, who had done them so much injury at Oriskany.

I myself thought that this was the truth, for no Iroquois ever forgave us Oriskany; and what we were now about to do to them must forever leave an implacable and unquenchable hatred between the Long House and the people of New York.

For on this river which we now followed, and between us and Tioga, where our main army lay, were the pretty Iroquois towns, Ingaren, Owaga, Chenang, and Owega, with their well-built and well-cellared houses, their tanneries, mills, fields of corn and potatoes, orchards, and pleasant gardens full of watermelons, muskmelons, peas, beans, squashes--in fact, everything growing that might ornament the estate of a proud man of my own colour. Thus had the Mohican described these towns to me. And now, as I sat weary, thinking, I knew that even before our army at Otsego joined the Tioga army, it would utterly destroy these towns on its way down; ruin the fields, and burn and girdle the orchards.

And this was not even the beginning of our destined march of destruction and death from one end of the Long House to the other!

Now our Oneida crept back to us, saying that the river was so low we could cross up to our arm-pits; and stood there naked, a slender and perfect statue, all adrip, and balancing pack and rifle on his head.

Wearily we picked our way down to the willows, stripped, hoisted rifles and packs, and went into the icy water. It seemed almost impossible for me to find courage and energy to dress, even after that chilling and invigorating plunge; but at last I was into my moccasins and shirt again. The Sagamore strode lightly to the lead; the Wyandotte started for the rear, but I shoved him next to the Mohican and in front of me, hating him suddenly, so abrupt and profound was my conviction that his stupidity was a studied treachery and not the consequences of a loutish mind.

"That is your place," I said sharply.

"You gave no orders."

"Nor did I rescind my last order, which was that you march behind the Sagamore."

"Is that to be the order of march?" he asked.

"What do you mean by questioning your officer?" I demanded.

"I am no soldier, but an Indian!" he said sullenly.

"You are employed and paid as a guide by General Sullivan, are you not? Very well. Then obey my orders to the letter, or I'll put you under arrest!"

That was not the way to talk to any Indian; but such a great loathing and contempt far this Wyandotte had seized me, so certain in my mind was I that he was disloyal and that every stupid act of his had been done a-purpose, that I could scarce control my desire to take him by that thick, bull-throat of his and kick him into the river.

For every stupid act or omission of his--or any single one of them--might yet send us all to our deaths. And their aggregate now incensed me; for I could not see how we were entirely to escape their consequences.

Again and again I was on the point of ordering a halt and having the fellow tried; but I dreaded the effect of such summary proceedings on the Oneidas and the Stockbridge, whose sense of justice was keen, and who might view with alarm such punishment meted out to mere stupidity.

It was very evident that neither they nor my Mohican had come to any definite conclusion concerning the Wyandotte. And until they did so, and until I had the unerring authority of my Indians' opinions, I did not care to go on record as either a brutal or a hasty officer. Indians entertain profound contempt for the man who arrives hastily and lightly at conclusions, without permitting himself leisure for deep and dignified reflection.

And I was well aware that with these Indians the success of any enterprise depended entirely upon their opinion of me, upon my personal influence with them.

Dawn was breaking before the Sagamore turned his head toward me. I gave the signal to halt.

"The Ouleout," whispered Tahoontowhee in my ear. "Here is its confluence with the Susquehanna."

The Mohican nodded, saying that we now stood on a peninsula.

I tried to make out the character of the hillock where we stood, but it was not yet light enough to see whether the place was capable of defence, although it would seem to be, having two streams to flank it.

"Sagamore," said I, "you and I will stand guard for the first two hours. Sleep, you others."

One after another unrolled his blanket and dropped where he stood. The Mohican came quietly toward me and sat down to watch the Susquehanna, his rifle across his knees. As for me, I dared not sit, much less lie flat, for fear sleep would overpower me. So I leaned against a rock, resting heavily on my rifle, and strained my sleepy eyes toward the invisible Ouleout. A level stream of mist, slowly whitening, marked its course; and "The Voice that Continues" sounded dreamily among the trees that bordered its shallow flood of crystal.

Toward sunrise I caught the first glimmer of water; in fact, so near was I that I could hear the feeding trout splashing along the reaches, and the deer, one by one, retreating from the shore.

Birds that haunt woodland edges were singing, spite of their moulting fever;

and I heard the Scarlet Tanager, the sweet call of the Crimson Cardinal, the peeping of the Recollet chasing gnats above the water, the lovely, linked notes of the White-throat trailing to a minor infinitely prolonged.

Greyer, greyer grew the woods; louder sang the birds; suddenly a dazzling shaft of pink struck the forest; the first shred of mist curled, detached itself, and floated slowly upward. The sun had risen.

Against the blinding glory, looming gigantic in the mist, I saw the Sagamore, an awful apparition in his paint, turn to salute the rising sun. Then, the mysterious office of his priesthood done, he lifted his rifle, tossed the heavy piece lightly to his shoulder, and strode toward me.

I shook the sleeping Oneidas, and, as they sprang to their feet, I pointed out their posts to them, laid my rifle on my sack, and dropped where I stood like a lump of lead.

I was aroused toward nine by the Mohican, and sat up as wide awake as a disturbed tree-cat, instantly ready for trouble.

"An Oneida on the Ouleout," he said.

"Where?"

"Yonder--just across."

"Friendly?"

"He has made the sign."

"An ambassador?"

"A runner, not a belt-bearer."

"Bring him to me."

Strung along the banks of the Ouleout, each behind a tree, I saw my Indians crouching, rifles ready. Then, on the farther bank, at the water's shallow edge, I saw the strange Indian--a tall, spare young fellow, absolutely naked except clout, ankle moccasins, hatchet-girdle, and pouch; and wearing no paint except a white disc on his forehead the size of a shilling. A single ragged frond hung from his scalp lock.

Answering the signal of the Mohican, he sprang lightly into the stream and crossed the shallow water. My Oneidas seemed to know him, for they accosted him smilingly, and Tahoontowhee turned and accompanied him back toward the spot where I was standing, naively exhibiting to the stranger his first scalp. Which seemed to please the dusty and brier-torn runner, for he was all smiles and animation until he caught sight of me. Then instantly the mask of blankness smoothed his features, so that when I confronted him he was utterly without expression.

I held out my hand, saying quietly:

"Welcome, brother."

"I thank my brother for his welcome," he said, taking my offered hand.

"My brother is hungry," I said. "He shall eat. He is weary because he has came a long distance. He shall rest unquestioned." I seated myself and motioned him to follow my example.

The tall, lank fellow looked earnestly at me; Tahoontowhee lighted a pipe, drew a deep, full inhalation from it, passed it to me. I drew twice, passed it to the runner. Then Tahoontowhee laid a square of bark on the stranger's knees; I poured on it from my sack a little parched corn, well salted, and laid beside it a bit of dry and twisted meat. Tahoontowhee did the same. Then, very gravely and in silence we ate our morning meal with this stranger, as though he had been a friend of many years.

"The birds sing sweetly," observed Tahoontowhee politely.

"The weather is fine," said I urbanely.

"The Master of Life pities the world He fashioned. All should give thanks to Him at sunrise," said the runner quietly.

The brief meal ended, Tahoontowhee laid his sack for a pillow; the strange Oneida stretched out on the ground, laid his dusty head on it, and closed his eyes. The next moment he opened them and rose to his feet. The ceremony and hospitality devolving upon me had been formally and perfectly accomplished.

As I rose, free now to question him without losing dignity in his eyes, he slipped the pouch he wore around in front, where his heavy knife and hatchet hung, and drew from it some letters.

Holding these unopened in my hand, I asked him who he was and from whom and whence he came.

"I am Red Wings, a Thaowethon Oneida of Ironderoga, runner for General Clinton--and my credentials are this wampum string, so that you shall know that I speak the truth!" And he whipped a string of red and black wampum from his pouch and handed it to me.

Holding the shining coil in my hands, I looked at him searchingly.

"By what path did you come?"

"By no path. I left Otsego as you left, crossed the river where you had crossed, recrossed where you did not recross, but where a canoe had landed."

"And then?"

"I saw the Mengwe," he said politely, as the Sagamore came up beside him.

Mayaro smiled his appreciation of the Algonquin term, then he spat, saying:

"The Mengwe were Sinako and Mowawak. One has joined the Eel Clan."

"The Red Wings saw him. The Cat-People of the Sinako sat in a circle around that scalpless thing and sang like catamounts over their dead!"

It is impossible to convey the scorn, contempt, insult, and loathing expressed by the Mohican and the Oneida, unless one truly understand the subtlety of the words they used in speaking of their common enemies.

"The Red Wings came by the Charlotte River?" I asked.

"By the Cherry, Quenevas, and Charlotte to the Ouleout. The Mengwe fired on me as I stood on a high cliff and mocked them."

"Did they follow you?"

"Can my brother Loskiel trail feathered wings through the high air paths? A little way I let them follow, then took wing, leaving them to whine and squall on the Susquehanna."

"And Butler and McDonald?" I demanded, smiling.

"I do not know. I saw white men's tracks on the Charlotte, not two hours old. They pointed toward the Delaware. The Minisink lies there."

I nodded. "Now let the Red Wings fold his feathers and go to rest," I said, "until I have read my letters and considered them."

The Oneida immediately threw himself on the ground and drew his pouch under his head. Before I could open my first letter, he was asleep and breathing quietly as a child. And, on his naked shoulder, I saw a smear of balsam plastered over with a hazel leaf, where a bullet had left its furrow. He had not even mentioned that he had been hit.

The first letter was from my General Clinton:

"Have a care," he wrote, "that your Indians prove faithful. The Wyandotte I assigned to your command made a poor impression among our Oneida guides. This I hear from Major Parr, who came to tell me so after you had left. Remember, too, that you and your Mohican are most necessary to General Sullivan. Interpreters trained by Guy Johnson are anything but plenty; and another Mohican who knows the truest route to Catharines-town is not to be had for whistling."

This letter decided me to rid myself of the Wyandotte. Here was sufficient authority; time enough had elapsed since he had joined us for me to come to a decision. Even my Indians could not consider my judgment hasty now.

I cast a cold glance at him, where he stood in the distance leaning against a huge walnut tree and apparently keeping watch across the Ouleout. The Grey-Feather was watching there, too, and I had no doubt that his wary eyes were fixed as often on the Wyandotte as on the wooded shore across the stream.

A second letter was from Major Parr, and said:

"An Oneida girl called Drooping Wings, of whom you bought some trumpery or other, came to the fort after you had left, and told me that among the party in their camp was an adopted Seneca who had seen and recognized your Wyandotte as a Seneca and not as a Huron.

"Not that this information necessarily means that the Indian called Black-Snake is a traitor. He brought proper credentials from the officer commanding at Pitt. But it is best that you know of this, and that you feel free to use your judgment accordingly."

"Yes," said I to myself, "I'll use it."

I took another long look at the suspect, then opened my third and last letter. It was from Lois; and my heart beat the "general" so violently that for a moment it stopped my breath:

"Euan Loskiel, my comrade, and my dear friend: Since you have gone, news has come that our General Wayne, with twelve hundred light infantry, stormed and took Stony Point on the Hudson on the 15th of this past month. All the stores, arms, ammunition, and guns are ours, with more than five hundred prisoners. The joy at this post is wonderful to behold; our soldiers are mad with delight and cheer all day long.

"Lieutenant Beatty tells me that we have taken fourteen pieces of good ordnance, seven hundred stand of arms, tents, rum, cheese, wine, and a number of other articles most agreeable to recount.

"On Wednesday morning last a sad affair; at Troop Beating three men were brought out to be shot, all found guilty of desertion, one from the 4th Pennsylvania, one from the 6th Massachusetts, and one from the 3rd New York. The troops were drawn up on the grand parade. Two of the men were reprieved by the General; the third was shot.... It meant more to me, kneeling in my room with both hands over my ears to shut out the volley, than it meant to those who witnessed the awful scene. Marching back, the fifes and drums played 'Soldiers' Joy.' I had forgotten to stop my ears, and heard them.

"On Tuesday rain fell. News came at noon that Indians had surprised and killed thirty-six haymakers near Fort Schuyler; and that other Indians had taken fifteen or seventeen of our men who were gathering blueberries at Sabbath Day Point. Whereupon Colonel Gansevoort immediately marched for Canajoharie with his regiment, which had but just arrived; and in consequence Betty Bleecker and Angelina are desolate.

"As you see from this letter, we have left Croghan's new house, and are living at Otsego in a fine Bush House, and near to the place where Croghan's old house stood before it was destroyed.

"Sunday, after an all night rain, clear skies; and all the officers were being schooled in saluting with the sword, the General looking on. In the afternoon the Chaplain, 'Parson' Gano, as the soldiers call him, gave us a sermon. I went with Betty and Angelina. Miss Helmer went on the lake in a batteau with Mr. Boyd. The Rifles tried their guns on the lake, shooting at marks. Murphy and Elerson made no misses.

"On Monday the officers had a punch, most respectable and gay. We ladies went with Major Parr, Lieutenant Boyd, and the Ensign you so detest, to view the hilarity, but not to join, it being a sociable occasion for officers only, the kegs of rum being offered by General Clinton--a gentleman not famed for his generosity in such matters.

"This, Euan, is all the general news I have to offer, save that the army expects its marching orders at any moment now.

"Euan, I am troubled in my heart. First, I must acquaint you that Lana Helmer and I have become friends. The night you left I was sitting in my room, thinking; and Lana came in and drew my head on her shoulder. We said nothing to each other all that night, but slept together in my room. And since then we have come

to know each other very well in the way women understand each other. I love her
dearly.

"Euan, she will not admit it, but she is mad about Lieutenant Boyd--and it is
as though she had never before loved and knows not how to conduct. Which is
strange, as she has been so courted and is deeply versed in experience, and has lived
more free of restraint than most women I ever heard of. Yet, it has taken her like
a pernicious fever; and I do neither like nor trust that man, for all his good looks,
and his wit and manners, and the exceedingly great courage and military sagacity
which none denies him.

"Yesterday Lana came to my little room in our Bush House, where I sleep on
a bed of balsam, and we sat there, the others being out, and she told me about Clarissa, and wept in the telling. What folly will not a woman commit for love! And
Sir John riding the wilderness with his murdering crew! May the Lord protect and
aid all women from such birds o' passage and of prey! And I thought I had seen the
pin-feathers of some such plumage on this man Boyd. But he may moult to a pret-
tier colour. I hope so--but in my heart I dare not believe it. For he is of that tribe of
men who would have their will of every pretty petticoat they notice. Some are less
unscrupulous than others, that is the only difference. And he seems still to harbour
a few scruples, judging from what I see of him and her, and what I know of her.

"Yet, if a man bear not his good intention plainly written on his face, and yet
protests he dies unless you love him, what scruples he may entertain will wither to
ashes in the fiercer flame. And how after all does he really differ from the others?

"Euan, I am sick of dread and worry, what with you out in the West with your
painted scouts, and Mr. Boyd telling me that he has his doubts concerning the reli-
ability of one o' them! And what with Lana so white and unhappy, and coming into
my bed to cry against my breast at night----"

Here the letter ended abruptly, and underneath in hurried writing:

"Major Parr calls to say that an Oneida runner is ordered to try to find you with
despatches from headquarters. I had expected to send this letter by some one in
your own regiment when it marched. But now I shall intrust it to the runner.

"I know not how to close my letter--how to say farewell--how to let you know
how truly my heart is yours. And becomes more so every hour. Nor can you understand how humbly I thank God for you--that you are what you are--and not like Sir

John and--other men.

"Women are of a multitude of kinds--until they love. Then they are of but two kinds. Of one of these kinds shall I be when I love. Not that I doubt myself, yet, who can say what I shall be? Only three, Euan--God, the man who loves me, and myself."

"I sit here waiting for a rifleman to take my letter to the General who has promised to commit it to the runner.

"A regiment is trying its muskets at the lake. I hear the firing.

"I have a tallow dip and wax and sand, ready to close my letter instantly. No one comes."

"Lana comes, very tired and pale. Her eyes frighten me, they seem so tragic. I learn that the army marches on the 9th. Yet, you went earlier, and I do not think my eyes resembled hers."

"Soldiers passing, drums beating. A Pennsylvania regiment. Lana lies on my bed, her face to the wall, scarce breathing at all, as far as I can see. Conch-horns blowing--the strange and melancholy music of your regiment. It seems to fill my heart with dread unutterable."

"The runner is here! Euan--Euan! Come back to me!

"Lois de Contrecoeur."

My eyes fell from the letter to the sleeping runner stretched out at my feet, then shifted vaguely toward the river.

After a while I drew my tablets, quill, and ink-horn from my pouch, and setting it on my knees wrote to her with a heart on fire, yet perfectly controlled.

And after I had ended, I sealed the sheet with balsam, pricking the globule from the tree behind me, and setting over it a leaf of partridge-berry. Also I wrote letters to General Clinton and to Major Parr, sealed them as I had sealed the other, and set a tiny, shining leaf on each.

Then, very gently I bent forward and aroused the Oneida runner. He sat up, rubbed his eyes, then got to his feet smiling. And I consigned to him my letters.

The Mohican, on guard by the Susquehanna, was watching me; and as soon as the Red Wings had started on his return, and was well across the Ouleout, I signalled the Sagamore to come to me, leaving the Mole and Tahoontowhee by the Susquehanna.

"Blood-brother of mine," I said as he came up, "I ask counsel of a wiser head and a broader experience than my own. What is to be done with this Wyandotte?"

"Must that be decided now, Loskiel?"

"Now. Because the Unadilla lies below not far away, and beyond that the Tioga. And I am charged to get myself thither in company with you as soon us may be. Now, what is a Sagamore's opinion of this Wyandotte?"

"Erie," he said quietly.

"You believe it?"

"I know it, Loskiel."

"And the others--the Oneidas and the Stockbridge?"

"They are as certain as I am."

"Good God! Then why have you not told me this before, Mayaro?"

"Is there haste?"

"Haste? Have I not said that we march immediately? And you would have let me give my order and include that villain in it!"

"Why not? It is an easier and safer way to take a prisoner to Tioga Point than to drag him thither tied."

"But he may escape----"

The Sagamore gave me an ironic glance.

"Is it likely," he said softly, "when we are watching?"

"But he may manage to do us a harm. You saw how cunningly he has kept up communication with our enemies, to leave a trail for them to follow."

"He has done us what harm he is able," said the Sagamore coolly.

I hesitated, then asked him what he meant.

"Why," he said, "their scouts have followed us. There are two of them now across the Susquehanna."

Thunderstruck, I stared at the river, where its sunlit surface glittered level through the trees.

"Do the others know this?" I asked.

"Surely, Loskiel."

I looked at my Indians where they lay flat behind their trees, rifles poised, eyes intent on the territory in front of them.

"If my brother does not desire to bring the Wyandotte to General Sullivan, I will go to him now and kill him," said the Mohican carelessly.

"He ought to hang," I said between my teeth.

"Yes. It is the most dreadful death a Seneca can die. He would prefer the stake and two days' torture. Loskiel is right. The Erie has been a priest of Amochol. Let him die by the rope he dreads more than the stake. For all Indians fear the rope, Loskiel, which chokes them so that they can not sing their death-song. There is not one of us who has not courage to sing his death-song at the stake; but who can sing when he is being choked to death by a rope?"

I nodded, looking uneasily toward the river where the two Seneca spies lurked unseen as yet by me.

"Let the men sling their packs," I said.

"They have done so, Loskiel."

"Very well. Our order of march will be the same as yesterday. We keep the Wyandotte between us."

"That is wisdom."

"Is it to be a running fight, Mayaro?"

"Perhaps, if their main body comes up."

"Then we had best start across the Ouleout, unless you mean to ford the Susquehanna."

The Sagamore shook his head with a grimace, saying that it would be easier to swim the Susquehanna at Tioga than to ford it here.

Very quietly we drew in or picked up our pickets, including the ruffianly Wyandotte, or Erie, as he was now judged to be, and, filing as we had filed the night before we crossed the Ouleout and entered the forest.

Two hours later the Oneida in the rear, Tahoontowhee, reported that the Seneca scouts were on our heels, and asked permission to try for a scalp.

By noon he had taken his second scalp, and had received his first wound, a mere scratch from a half-ounce ball, below the knee. But he wore it and the scalp with a dignity unequalled by any monarch loaded with jewelled orders.

"Some day," said the Sagamore in my ear, "Tahoontowhee will accept the antlers and the quiver."

"He would be greater yet if he accepted Christ," said the Stockbridge quietly.

We had halted to breathe, and were resting on our rifles as the Mohican said this; and I was looking at the Stockbridge who so quietly had confessed his Master, when of a sudden the Wyandotte, who had been leaning against a tree, straightened up, turned his head over his shoulder, stared intently at something which we could not see, and then pointed in silence.

So naturally was it done that we all turned also. Then, like a thunder-bolt, his hatchet flew, shearing the raccoon's tail from my cap, and struck the Stockbridge Indian full between the eyes, dashing his soul into eternity.

CHAPTER XIII
THE HIDDEN CHILDREN

So silently, suddenly, and with such incredible swiftness had this happened, and so utterly unprepared were we for this devilish audacity, that the Erie had shoved his trade-rifle against my ribs and fired before anybody comprehended what he was about.

But he had driven the muzzle so violently against me that the blow knocked me breathless and flat on my face, and his rifle, slipping along with the running swivel of my pouch buckle, was discharged, blowing the pouch-flap to fragments, and setting fire to my thrums without even scorching my body.

As, partly stunned, I lay on the moss, choking in the powder smoke, my head still ringing with the crash of the old smooth-bore, man after man leaped over me like frantic deer, racing at full speed toward the river. And I swayed to my knees, to my feet, and staggered after them, beating out the fire on my smoking fringes as I ran.

The Erie took the bank at one bound, struck the river sand like a ball, and bounded on. Both Oneidas shot at him, and I tried to wing him in mid-stream, but my hands were unsteady from the shock, and he went under like a diver-duck, drifted to the surface under the willows far below, and was out and among them before we could fire again.

The sight of him tore a yell of fury from the Oneidas' throats; but the Mohican, rifle a-trail, was speeding low and swiftly, and we sprang forward in his tracks.

A few moments later the Sagamore gave tongue to the fierce, hysterical view-halloo of his Wolf Clan; the Oneidas answered till the forest rang with the dreadful tumult of the pack-cry. Then, as I ran up breathless to where they were crouching, a more terrible whoop burst from them. The quarry was at bay.

It was where the river turned south, making a vast and glassy bay. A smooth cliff hung over it, wet and shining with the water from hidden springs, and sheering down into profound and limpid depths.

High on the face of the cliff, squatted on a narrow shelf, and hidden by the rocky formation, our quarry had taken cover. The twisted strands of a wild grapevine, severed by his knife, hung dangling below his eyrie, betraying his mode of ascent. He had gone up hand over hand, aided by his powerful shoulder muscles and by his feet, which must have stuck like the feet of flies to the perpendicular wall of rock.

To follow him, even with the aid of the vine he had severed, had been hopeless in the face of his rifle fire. A thousand men could not have taken him that way, while his powder and lead held out, for they would have been obliged to ascend one by one in slow and painful file, and he had but to shove his gun-muzzle in their faces as they appeared.

The war-yelps of the Oneidas had subtly changed their timbre so that ever amid the shrill yelling I marked the guttural snarls of baffled rage. The Mohican lay on his belly behind a tree, silent, but his eyes were like coals in their red intensity.

Presently the Oneidas, lying prone at our side, ceased their tumult and became silent. And for a long while we lay waiting for a shot.

All this time the Erie had given no sign of life, and I had begun to hope that he had been hit and would ultimately perish there, as wild things perish in solitude and silence.

Then the Mohican said in my ear:

"Unless we can stir him to move and expose himself, we must lose him. For his fellows will surely track us to this place."

"Good God! By what unfortunate accident should such a hiding place exist so near!" I said miserably.

The Sagamore's stern visage slightly relaxed.

"It is no accident, Loskiel. Do you not suppose he knew it was here? Else he had never dared attempt what he did."

"The vile Witch-cat has been here many a time," said the Grey-Feather, his ferocious gaze fixed on the cliff.

"Is the Mole dead?" I asked.

"He is with his God--Tharon or Christ, whichever it may be, Loskiel."

"The Mole must not be scalped," said Tahoontowhee softly. "If the Senecas pass that way they will have at last one thing to boast of."

I said to the Mohican:

"Hold the Erie. The Night-Hawk and I will go back and bury our dead against Seneca profanation."

"Let the Grey-Feather go, Loskiel."

"No. The Mole was Christian. Does a Christian fail his own kind at the last?"

"Loskiel has spoken," said the Mohican gravely. "The Grey-Feather and I will hold the filthy cat."

So we went back together across the river, the young Oneida and I; and we hid the Mole deep in the bed of a rotting log, and laid his Testament on his breast over the painted cross, and his weapons beside him. Then, working cautiously, we rolled back the log, replaced the dead leaves, brushed up the deep green pile of the moss, and smoothed all as craftily us we might, so that no Seneca prowling might suspect that a grave was here, and disinter the dead to take his scalp.

Over the blood-wet leaves where he had fallen, we made a fire of dry twigs, letting it burn enough to deceive. Then we covered it as hunters cover their ashes; the Oneida took the Erie's hatchet; and we hastened back to the others.

They were still lying exactly where we left them. Neither the Erie nor they had stirred or spoken. And, as I settled down in my ambush beside the Mohican, I asked him again whether there was any possible way to provoke the Erie so that he might stir and expose some portion of his limbs or body.

The Night-Hawk, who carried strapped to his back the quiver of an Oneida adolescent containing a boy's short bow and a dozen game arrows, consulted with the Grey-Feather in a low voice.

Presently he wriggled off to where some sun-dried birch-bark fluttered in the river breeze, returned with it, shredded it with care, strung his bow, tipped an arrow with the bark, and held it out to me.

I struck flint to steel, lighted my tinder, and set the shred of bark afire.

Then the Night-Hawk knelt, bent his bow, and the blazing arrow soared whistling with flame, and fell behind the rock on the shelf.

Arrow after arrow followed, whizzing upward and dropping accurately; but the wet mosses of the cliff extinguished the flashes.

As the last arrow fell, flared a moment, then merely smoked, an insulting laugh came from aloft, and my Indians uttered fierce exclamations and cuddled their rifle-stocks close to their cheeks, fairly trembling for a shot.

"Dogs of Oneidas!" called the Erie. "Go howl for your dead pig of a Stockbridge slave."

"The Mole wears his scalp with Tharon!" retorted the Grey-Feather, choking with fury. "But Tahoontowhee's hatchet is still sticking in the Senecas' heads!"

"For which the Night-Hawk shall burn at the Seneca stake, sobbing his death-song!" shouted the Erie, so fiercely that for a moment we lay silent, hoping that by some ungovernable movement he might expose himself.

"Taunt him!" I whispered; and the Mohican said with a derisive laugh:

"Four scalp-tufts from the mangy Cats of Amochol trim my hatchet-sheath. When the young men ask me what this sparse and sickly fur may be, I shall strip it off and cast it at their feet, saying it is but Erie filth to spit upon."

"Liar of a conquered nation!" roared the Erie, "for every priest of Amochol who fell by Otsego under your cowardly butcher's knife, a Siwanois Sagamore shall burn three days, and yet live to die the fourth! The day that August dies, so shall the Sagamore die at the Festival of Dreams in Catharines-town!"

"I shall remember," said I in a low voice to the Sagamore, "that the Onon-hou-aroria is to be celebrated in Catharines-town on the last day of August."

He nodded, then:

"A Mohican Sagamore insults a dirty priest of Amochol! I do you honour by offering you battle, with knife, with hatchet, with rifle, with naked hands! Choose, spawn of Atensi--still-born kitten of Iuskeha, choose! Not one soul except myself will raise hand against you. By Tharon, I swear it! Choose! And the victor passes freely and whither he wills!"

The Erie mocked him from his high perch:

"Squirrels talk! Long since has your Tharon been hurled headlong into Biskoo-nah by Atensi and her flaming grandson!"

At this awful blasphemy, the Mohican fairly blanched so that under his paint his skin grew ashy for a moment.

The Grey-Feather shouted:

"Lying and degraded priest! Mowawak Cannibal of a Sinako Cat! It is Atensi herself who burns with Iuskeha in Biskoonah; and the sacrilegious fires lick your altars!"

The Erie laughed horribly:

"Where is your fool of a stripling called Loskiel? Is he there with you? Or did my hatchet fetch him such a clip that he died of fright and a bullet in his belly?"

"He is unharmed," replied the Mohican, tauntingly. "A squaw shoots better than a Cat!"

"A lie! I saw my rifle blow a hole in his body!"

"Hatchet and rifle failed. The Ensign, Loskiel, laughed, asking what forest-flies were buzzing at his ear. Loskiel spits on Cats, and brushes their flying hatchets from his ears as others brush mosquitos!"

"Let him speak, then, to prove it!" shouted the Erie, incredulously.

But I remained silent.

Then the Erie's ferocious laugh rang out from the cliff.

"Now, you Mohican slave and you Oneida dogs, you shall know the power of Amochol. For what was done to Loskiel and to the Praying Mole, will be done to you all on the last day of this month, when the Dream Feast is held at Catharines-town! You shall die. And others shall die--not as you, but on the red altar of the Great Sachem Amochol! Strangled, disemboweled, sacrificed to clothe Atensi!"

The Grey-Feather, unable any longer to retain his self-control, was getting to his feet, staring wildly up at the cliff; but the Mohican drew him back into his form and held him there with powerful grip.

"Listen," he hissed, "to what this warlock blabbs."

The Erie laughed, evidently awaiting a retort. None came, and he laughed again triumphantly.

"Amochol's arm is long, O you Oneida dogs who howl outside the Long House gates! Amochol's eyes are like the white-crested eagle's eyes, seeing everything, and his ears are like the red buck's ears, so that nothing stirs unheard by him.

"Phantoms arise and walk at night; Amochol sees. Under earth and water, demons are breathing; Amochol hears. Then we Eries listen, too, and make the altar fires burn hotter. For the ghosts of the night and the demons that stir must be fed."

He waited again, doubtless expecting some exclamation of protest against his monstrous profession. After a moment he went on:

"Spectres and demons must be fed--but not on the foul flesh of dogs like you! We cut your throats to feed the Flying Heads."

He paused; and as no reply was forthcoming, the sorcerer laughed scornfully.

"Your blood becomes water! You cringe at the power of Amochol. But the red altar is not for you. Listen, dogs! Had I not found it necessary to slay your stripling, Loskiel, he had been burned and strangled an that altar!... And there is another at Otsego who shall die strangled on the altar of Amochol--the maiden called Lois! Long have we followed her. Long is the arm of the Red Priest--when his White Sorceress dreams for him!

"And now you know, you Mohican mongrel, why Amochol was at Otsego. His arm reaches even into the barracks of Clinton! Because to Atensi the sacrifice of these two would be grateful--the maiden Lois and your Loskiel. Only the pure and guarded pleasure her. And these two are Hidden Children. One has died. The other shall not escape us. She shall die strangled by Amochol upon his own altar!"

I sat up, sick with horror and surprise, and stared at the Mohican for an explanation. He and the Oneidas were now looking at me very gravely and in silence. And after a moment my head dropped.

I knew well enough what the brutal Erie meant by "Hidden Children." But that I was one I never dreamed, nor had it occurred to me that Lois was one, in spite of her strange history. For among the Iroquois and their adopted captives there are both girls and boys who are spoken of as "Hidden Persons" or "Hidden Children." They are called Ta-neh-u-weh-too, which means, "hidden in the husks," like ears of corn.

And the reason is this: a mother, for one cause or another, or perhaps for none at all, decides to make of her unborn baby a Hidden Child. And so, when born, the child is instantly given to distant foster-parents, and by them hidden; and remains so concealed until adolescence. And, being considered from birth pure and unpolluted, a girl and a boy thus hidden are expected to marry, return to their people when informed by their foster-parents of the truth, and bring a fresh, innocent, and uncontaminated strain into their clan and tribe.

What the Erie said seemed to stun me. What did this foul creature know of me? What knowledge had this murdering beast of Lois? And Amochol--what in God's name did the Red Sorcerer know of us, or of our history?

Even the horrid threat against Lois seemed so fantastic, so unreal, so meaningless, that at the moment, it did not impress me even with its unspeakable wickedness.

The Sagamore touched my arm as though with awe and pity, and I lifted my head.

"Is this true, brother?" he asked gently.

"I do not know if it is," I said, dazed.

"Then--it is the truth."

"Why do you say that, Mayaro?"

"I know it, now. I suspected it when your eyes first fell on the Ghost-bear rearing on my breast. I thought I knew you, there at Major Lockwood's house in Poundridge. It was your name, Loskiel, and your knowledge of your red brothers, that stirred my suspicions. And when I learned that Guy Johnson had sheltered you, then I was surer still."

"Who, then, am I?" I asked, bewildered.

The three Indians were staring at me as though that murderer aloft on his eyrie did not exist. I, too, had forgotten him for the moment; and it was only the loud explosion of his smooth-bore that shocked us to the instant necessity of the situation.

The bullet screamed through the leaves above us; we clapped our rifles to our cheeks, striving to glimpse him. Nothing moved on the rocky shelf.

"He fired to signal his friends," whispered the Mohican. "He must believe them to be within hearing distance."

I set my teeth and stared savagely at the cliff.

"If that is so," said I, "we must leave him here and pull foot."

There was a tense silence, then, as we rose, an infuriated yell burst from the Oneidas, and in their impotence they fired blindly at the cliff, awaking a very hell of echo.

Through the clattering confusion of the double discharge, the demoniac laughter of the Erie rang, and my Oneidas, retreating, hurled back insult and anathema, promising to return and annihilate every living sorcerer in the Dark Empire, including Amochol himself.

"Ha-e!" he shouted after us, giving the evil spirits' cry. "Ha-e! Ha-ee!" From his shelf he cast a painted stick after us, which came hurtling down and landed in the water. And he screamed as he heard us threshing over the shallows: "Koue! Askennon eskatoniot!"

The thing he had cast after us was floating, slowly turning round and round in the water; and it seemed to be a stick something thicker than an arrow and as long, and painted in concentric rings of black, vermillion, and yellow.

Then, as we gave it wide berth, to our astonishment it suddenly crinkled up and was alive, and lifted a tiny, evil head from the water, running out at us a snake's tongue that flickered.

That this was magic my Indians never doubted. They gave the thing one horrified glance, turned, and fairly leaped through the water till the shallow flood roared as though a herd of deer were passing over.

As for me, I ran, too, and felt curiously weak and shaken; though I suspected that this wriggling thing now swimming back to shore was the poison snake of the Ksaurora, and no Antouhonoran witchcraft at all, as I had seen skins of the brilliant and oddly marked little serpent at Guy Park, whither some wandering Southern Tuscaroras had brought them.

But the bestial creature of the cliff had now so inspired us all with loathing that it was as though our very breath was poisoned; and in swift and silent file we pushed forward, as if the very region--land, water, the air itself--had become impure, and we must rid ourselves of the place itself to breathe.

No war-party burning to distinguish itself ever travelled more swiftly. Sooner than I expected, we crossed the small creek which joins the river from the east, opposite the Old England District, and saw the ruins of Unadilla across the water.

Here was a known ford; and we crossed to Old Unadilla, where that pretty river and the Butternut run south into the broadening Susquehanna.

At this place we halted to eat; and I was of two minds whether to go by the West Branch of the Delaware, by Owaga and Ingaren across the Stanwix Treaty

Line to Wyalusing, and from thence up the river to the Chemung and Tioga Point; or to risk the Chenango country and travel southwest by Owego, and so cutting off that great southern loop that the Susquehanna makes through the country of the Esaurora.

But when I asked the opinion of my Indians, they were of one mind against my two, saying that to follow the river was the easiest, swiftest, and safest course to Tioga Point.

They knew better than did I. This side of Tioga the Oneidas knew the ground as well as the Siwanois; but beyond, toward Catharines-town, only my Siwanois knew. Indeed, if my Oneidas remained with me at all beyond Tioga I might deem myself lucky, in such dread and detestation did they hold that gloomy region where the Wyoming Witch brooded her deadly crew, and where the Toad Woman, her horrible sister, fed the secret and midnight fires of hell with the Red Priest, Amochol.

A grey hawk was circling above us mewing. Truly, our nerves had been somewhat shattered, for as we rose and resumed pack and sack, a distant partridge drumming on his log startled us all; and it was as though we had thought to hear the witch-drums rolling at the Onon-hou-aroria, and the hawk mewing seemed like the Sorcerers calling "Hiou! Hiou! Hiou!" And the Unadilla made a clatter over its stones like the False-Faces rattling their wooden masks.

"Eheu!" sighed the pines above us as we sped on; and ever I thought of Okwencha and the Dead Hunter. And the upward roar of a partridge covey bursting in thunder through the river willows was like the flight of the hideous Flying Heads.

On we went, every sound and movement of the forest seeming to spur us forward and add flight-feathers to our speeding feet. For in my Indians, ascendant now, was the dull horror of the supernatural; and as for me my hatred of the Sorcerers was tightening every nerve to the point of breaking.

As I travelled that trail through the strange, eternal twilight of the great trees, I vowed to myself that Amochol should die; that the Sagamore and I would guide a thousand rifles to his pagan altar and lay this foul priesthood prone upon it as the last sacrifice.

Then I recalled the Black-Snake's threat against Lois; and shuddered; then the astounding reason he had given for the Red Priest's design upon us both set me dully wondering again.

Fear that his emissaries might penetrate our lines stirred me; and I remembered the moccasins she had received, and the messages sewed within them. If a red messenger had found her every year and had left at her door, unseen, a pair of moccasins, why might not an invisible assassin find her, too? Already, within our very encampment, she had received another pair of moccasins and a message entirely different from the customary one.

Whoever had brought it had come and gone unseen.

Distressed, perplexed, half sick with fear for her, I plodded on behind the Mohican, striving to drive from me the sombre thoughts assailing me, trying to reassure myself with the knowledge that she was safe at Otsego with her new friends, and that very shortly now she would be still safer in Albany, and under the shrewd and kindly eye of Mr. Hake.

The sun had set; the pallid daylight lingering along the forest edges by the river grew sickly and died. And after a little the Mohican halted on a hillock, and we cart our packs from us and peered around.

The forms of rocks took dim shape all about us, huge slabs and benches of stone, from which great bushes of laurel and rhododendron spread, forming beyond us an entangled and impenetrable jungle.

And under these we crawled and lay, listening for snakes. But there seemed to be none there, though our rocky fastness was a very likely place. And after we had eaten and emptied our canteens, the two Oneidas went out on guard to the eastern limit of the rocks; and the Sagamore and I lay on our sides, facing each other in the dark. And for a while we lay there, neither of us speaking. Finally I said under my breath:

"Then I am one of the Hidden People."

"Yes, brother," he replied very gently.

"Tell me why you believe this to be true. Tell me all you know."

For a little while the Mohican lay there very silent, and I did not stir. And presently he said:

"It was in '57, Loskiel, when I first laid eyes on you."

"What!"

"I am more than twice your age. You were then three years old."

In my astonishment it occurred to me that instead of twenty-two I was now twenty-five years of age, if what the Mohican said were true.

"Listen, Loskiel, blood-brother of mine, for you shall hear the truth now--the truth which Guy Johnson never told you.

"It was in '57; Munro lay at Fort William Henry; Webb at Fort Edward; and Montcalm came down from the lakes with his white-coats and Hurons and shook his sword at Munro and spat upon Webb.

"Then came Sir William Johnson to Webb with half a thousand Iroquois. And because Sir William was the only white man we Delawares trusted, and in spite of his Iroquois, three Mohicans offered their services--the Great Serpent, young Uncas, and I, Mayaro, Sagamore of the Siwanois."

He paused, then with infinite contempt:

"Webb was a coward. Nor could Sir William kick him forward. He lay shivering behind the guns at Edward; and Fort William Henry fell. And the white-coats could do nothing with their Hurons; the prisoners fell under their knives and hatchets--soldiers, women, little children.

"When Montcalm had gone, Webb let us loose. And, following the trail of murder, in a thicket among the rocks we came upon a young woman with a child, very weak from privation. Guy Johnson and I discovered them--he a mere youth at that time.

"And the young woman told him how it had been with her--that her husband and herself had been taken by the St. Regis three years before--that they had slain her husband but had offered her no violence; that her child had been born a few weeks later and that the St. Regis chief who took her had permitted her to make of it a Hidden Person.

"For three years the fierce St. Regis chief wooed her, offering her the first place in his lodge. For three years she refused him, living in a bush-hut alone with her child, outside the St. Regis village, fed by them, and her solitude respected. Then Munro came and his soldiers scattered the St. Regis and took her and her baby to the fort. And the St. Regis chief sent word that he would kill her if she ever married."

So painfully intent was I on his every low-spoken word that I scarce dared breathe as the story of my mother slowly unfolded.

"Guy Johnson and I took the young woman and her child to Edward," he said. "Her name was Marie Loskiel, and she told us that she was the widow of a Scotch fur trader, one Ian Loskiel, of Saint Sacrament."

There was another silence, as though he were not willing to continue. Then in a quiet voice I bade him speak; and he spoke, very gravely:

"Your mother's religion and Guy Johnson's were different. If that were the reason she would not marry him I do not know. Only that when he went away, leaving her at Edward, they both wept. I was standing by his stirrup; I saw him--and her.

"And--he rode away, Loskiel.... Why she tried to follow him the next spring, I do not know.... Perhaps she found that love was stronger than religion.... And after all the only difference seemed to be that she prayed to the mother of the God he prayed to.... We spoke of it together, the Great Serpent, young Uncas, and I. And Uncas told us this. But the Serpent and I could make nothing of it.

"And while Guy Johnson was at Edward, only he and I and your mother ever saw or touched you.... And ever you were tracing with your baby fingers the great Ghost Bear rearing on my breast----"

"Ah!" I exclaimed sharply. "That is what I have struggled to remember!"

He drew a deep, unsteady breath:

"Do you better understand our blood-brotherhood now, Loskiel?"

"I understand--profoundly."

"That is well. That is as it should be, O my blood-brother, pure from birth, and at adolescence undefiled. Of such Hidden Ones were the White-Plumed Sagamores. Of such was Tamanund, the Silver-Plumed; and the great Uncas, with his snowy-winged and feathered head--Hidden People, Loskiel--without stain, without reproach.

"And as it was to be recorded on the eternal wampum, you were found at Guy Johnson's landing place asleep beside a stranded St. Regis canoe; and your dead mother lay beside you with a half ounce ball through her heart. The St. Regis chief had spoken."

"Why do you think he slew her?" I whispered.

"Strike flint. It is safe here."

I drew myself to my elbow, struck fire and blew the tinder to a glow.

"This is yours," he said. And laid in my hand a tiny, lacquered folder striped with the pattern of a Scotch tartan.

Wondering, I opened it. Within was a bit of wool in which still remained three rusted needles. And across the inside cover was written in faded ink:

"Marie Loskiel."

"How came you by this?" I stammered, the quick tears blinding me.

"I took it from the St. Regis hunter whom Tahoontowhee slew."

"Was he my mother's murderer!"

"Who knows?" said the Sagamore softly. "Yet, this needle-book is a poor thing for an Indian to treasure--and carry in a pouch around his neck for twenty years."

The glow-worm spark in my tinder grew dull and went out. For a long while I lay there, thinking, awed by the ways of God--so certain, so inscrutable. And understood how at the last all things must be revealed--even the momentary and lightest impulse, and every deepest and most secret thought.

Lying there, I asked of the Master of Life His compassion on us all, and said my tremulous and silent thanks to Him for the dear, sad secret that His mercy had revealed.

And, my lips resting on my mother's needle-book, I thought of Lois, and how like mine in a measure was her strange history, not yet fully revealed.

"Sagamore, my elder brother?" I said at last.

"Mayaro listens."

"How is it then with Lois de Contrecoeur that you already knew she was of the Hidden Children?"

"I knew it when I first laid eyes on her, Loskiel."

"By what sign?"

"The moccasins. She lay under a cow-shed asleep in her red cloak, her head on her arms. Beside her the kerchief tied around her bundle lay unknotted, revealing the moccasins that lay within. I saw, and knew. And for that reason have I been her friend."

"You told her this?"

"Why should I tell her?"

There was no answer to this. An Indian is an Indian.

I said after a moment:

"What mark is there on the moccasins that you knew them?"

"The wings, worked in white wampum. A mother makes a pair with wings each year for her Hidden One, so that they will bring her little child to her one day, swiftly and surely as the swallow that returns with spring."

"Has she told you of these moccasins--how every year a pair of them is left for her, no matter where she may be lodged?"

"She has told me. She has shown me the letter on bark which was found with her; the relics of her father; this last pair of moccasins, and the new message written within. And she asked me to guide her to Catharines-town. And I have refused.

"No, Loskiel, I have never doubted that she was of the Hidden People. And for that reason have I been patient and kind when she has beset me with her pleading that I show to her the trail to Catharines-town.

"But I will not. For although in rifle dress she might go with us--nay, nor do I even doubt that she might endure the war-path as well as any stripling eager for honour and his first scalp taken--I will not have her blood upon my hands.

"For if she stir thither--if she venture within the Great Shadow--the ghouls of Amochol will know it. And they will take her and slay her on their altar, spite of us all--spite of you and me and your generals and colonels, and all your troops and riflemen--spite of your whole army and its mighty armament, I say it--I, a Siwanois Mohican of the Enchanted Clan. A Sagamore has spoken."

Chill after chill crept over me so that I shook as I lay there in the darkness "Who is this maiden, Lois?" I asked.

"Do you not guess, Loskiel?"

"Vaguely."

"Then listen, brother. Her grandfather was the great Jean Coeur who married the white daughter of the Chevalier de Clauzun. Her mother was Mlle. Jeanne Coeur; her father the young Vicomte de Contrecoeur, of the Regiment de la Reine--not that stupid Captain Contrecoeur of the regiment of Languedoc, who, had it depended on him, would never have ventured to attack Braddock at all.

"This is true, because I knew them both--both of these Contrecoeur captains. And the picture she showed to me was that of the officer in the Regiment de la Reine.

"I saw that regiment die almost to a man. I saw Dieskau fall; I saw that gay young officer, de Contrecoeur, who had nicknamed himself Jean Coeur, laugh at our Iroquois as he stood almost alone--almost the last man living, among his fallen white-coats.

"And I saw him dead, Loskiel--the smile still on his dead lips, and his eyes still open and clear and seeming to laugh up at the white clouds sailing, which he could not see.

"That was the man she showed me painted on polished bone."

"And--her mother?" I asked.

"I can only guess, Loskiel, for I never saw her. But I believe she must have been with the army. Somehow, Sir William's Senecas got hold of her and took her to Catharines-town. And if the little Lois was born there or at Yndaia, or perhaps among the Lakes before the mother was made prisoner, I do not know. Only this I gather, that when the Cats of Amochol heard there was a child, they demanded it for a sacrifice. And there must have been some Seneca there--doubtless some adopted Seneca of a birth more civilized--who told the mother, and who was persuaded by her to make of it a Hidden One.

"How long it lay concealed, and in whose care, how can I know? But it is certain that Amochol learned that it had been hidden, and sent his Cat-People out to prowl and watch. Then, doubtless did the mother send it from her by the faithful one whose bark letter was found by the new foster-parents when they found the little Lois.

"And this is how it has happened, brother. And that the Cat-People now know she is alive, and who she is, does not amaze me. For they are sorcerers, and if one of them did not steal after the messenger when he left Yndaia with the poor mother's yearly gift of moccasins, then it was discovered by witchcraft."

"For Amochol never forgets. And whom the Red Priest chooses for his altar sooner or later will surely die there, unless the Sorcerer dies first and his Cat-People are slain and skinned, and the vile altar is destroyed among the ashes of its accursed fire!"

"Then, with the help of an outraged God, these righteous things shall come to pass!" I said between clenched teeth.

The Sagamore sat with his crested head bowed. And if he were in ghostly communication with the Mighty Dead I do not know, for I heard him breathe the name of Tamanund, and then remain silent as though listening for an answer.

I had been asleep but a few moments, it seemed to me, when the Grey-Feather awoke me for my turn at guard duty; and the Mohican and I rose from our blankets, reprimed our rifles, crept out from under the laurel and across the shadowy rock-strewn knoll to our posts.

The rocky slope below us was almost clear to the river, save for a bush or two.

Nothing stirred, no animals, not a leaf. And after a while the profound stillness began to affect me, partly because the day had been one to try my nerves, partly because the silence was uncanny, even to me. And I knew how dread of the super-natural had already tampered with the steadiness of my red comrades--men who were otherwise utterly fearless; and I dreaded the effect on the Mohican, whose mind now was surcharged with hideous and goblin superstitions.

In the night silence of a forest, always there are faint sounds to be heard which, if emphasizing the stillness, somehow soften it too. Leaves fall, unseen, whispering downward from high trees, and settling among their dead fellows with a faintly comfortable rustle. Small animals move in the dark, passing and repassing warily; one hears the high feathered ruffling and the plaint of sleepy birds; breezes play with the young leaves; water murmurs.

But here there was no single sound to mitigate the stillness; and, had I dared in my mossy nest behind the rocks, I would have contrived same slight stirring sound, merely to make the silence more endurable.

I could see the river, but could not hear it. From where I lay, close to the ground, the trees stood out in shadowy clusters against the vague and hazy mist that spread low over the water.

And, as I lay watching it, without the slightest warning, a head was lifted from behind a bush. It was the head of a wolf in silhouette against the water.

Curiously I watched it; and as I looked, from another bush another head was lifted--the round, flattened head and tasselled ears of the great grey lynx. And be-fore I could realize the strangeness of their proximity to each other, these two heads were joined by a third--the snarling features of a wolverine.

Then a startling and incredible thing happened; the head of the big timber-wolf rose still higher, little by little, slowly, stealthily, above the bush. And I saw to my horror that it had the body of a man. And, already overstrained as I was, it was a mercy that I did not faint where I lay behind my rock, so ghastly did this monstrous vision seem to me.

CHAPTER XIV
NAI TIOGA!

How my proper senses resisted the swoon that threatened them I do not know; but when the lynx, too, lifted a menacing and flattened head on human shoulders; and when the wolverine also stood out in human-like shadow against the foggy water, I knew that these ghostly things that stirred my hair were no hobgoblins at all, but living men. And the clogged current of my blood flowed free again, and the sweat on my skin cooled.

The furry ears of the wolf-man, pricked up against the vaguely lustrous background of the river, fascinated me. For all the world those pointed ears seemed to be listening. But I knew they were dead and dried; that a man's eyes were gazing through the sightless sockets of the beast.

From somewhere in the darkness the Mohican came gliding on his belly over the velvet carpet of the moss.

"Andastes," he whispered scornfully; "they wear the heads of the beasts whose courage they lack. Fling a stone among them and they will scatter."

As I felt around me in the darkness for a fragment of loose rock, the Mohican arrested my arm.

"Wait, Loskiel. The Andastes hang on the heels of fiercer prowlers, smelling about dead bones like foxes after a battle. Real men can not be far away."

We lay watching the strange and grotesque creatures in the starlight; and truly they seemed to smell their way as beasts smell; and they were as light-footed and as noiseless, slinking from bush to bush, lurking motionless in shadows, nosing, listening, prowling on velvet pads to the very edges of our rock escarpment.

"They have the noses of wild things," whispered the Mohican uneasily. "Somewhere they have found something that belongs to one of us, and, having once smelled it, have followed."

I thought for a moment.

"Do you believe they found the charred fragments of my pouch-flap? Could they scent my scorched thrums from where I now lie? Only a hound could do that! It is not given to men to scent a trail as beasts scent it running perdu."

The Mohican said softly:

"Men of the settlement detect no odour where those of the open perceive a multitude of pungent smells."

"That is true," I said.

"It is true, Loskiel. As a dog scents water in a wilderness and comes to it from afar, so can I also. Like a dog, too, can I wind the hidden partridge brood--though never the nesting hen--nor can a mink do that much either. But keen as the perfume of a bee-tree, and certain as the rank smell of a dog-fox in March--which even a white man can detect--are the odours of the wilderness to him whose only home it is. And even as a lad, and for the sport of it, have I followed and found by its scent alone the great night-butterfly, marked brown and crimson, and larger than a little bat, whose head bears tiny ferns, and whose wings are painted with the four quarters of the moon. Like crushed sumac is the odour of it, and in winter it hides in a bag of silk."

I nodded, my eyes following the cautious movements of the Andastes below; and again and again I saw their heads thrown buck, noses to the stars, as though sniffing and endeavouring to wind us. And to me it was horrid and unhuman.

For an hour they were around the river edge and the foot of the hillock, trotting silently and uneasily hither and thither, always seemingly at fault. Then, apparently made bold by finding no trace of what they hunted, they ranged this way and that at a sort of gallop, and we could even hear their fierce and whining speech as they huddled a moment to take counsel.

Suddenly their movements ceased, and I clutched the Mohican's arm, as a swift file of shadows passed in silhouette along the river's brink, one after another moving west--fifteen ghostly figures dimly seem but unmistakable.

"Senecas," breathed the Mohican.

The war party defiled at a trot, disappearing against the fringing gloom. And after them loped the Andastes pack, scurrying, hurrying, running into thickets and out again, but ever hastening along the flanks of their silent and murderous masters, who seemed to notice them not at all.

When they had gone, the Mohican aroused the Oneidas, and all night long we lay there behind the rocks, rifles in rest, watching the river.

What we awaited came with the dawn, and, in the first grey pallour of the breaking day, we saw their advanced guard; Cayugas and Senecas of the fierce war-chief Hiokatoo, every Indian stripped, oiled, head shaved, and body painted for war; first a single Cayuga, scouting swiftly; then three furtive Senecas, then six, then a dozen, followed by their main body.

Doubtless they had depended on the Andastes and advanced guard of Senecas for flankers, for the main body passed without even a glance up at the hilly ground where we lay watching them.

Then there was a break in the line, an interval of many minutes before their pack horses appeared, escorted by green-coated soldiers.

And in the ghostly light of dawn, I saw Sir John Johnson riding at the head of his men, his pale hair unpowdered, his heavy, colourless face sunk on his breast. After him, in double file, marched his regiment of Greens; then came more Indians--Owagas, I think--then that shameless villain, McDonald, in bonnet and tartan, and the heavy claymore a-swing on his saddle-bow, and his blue-eyed Indians swarming in the rear.

Lord, what a crew! And as though that were not enough to affront the rising sun, comes riding young Walter Butler, in his funereal cloak, white as a corpse under the black disorder of his hair, and staring at nothing like a damned man. On his horse's heels his ruffianly Rangers marched in careless disorder but with powerful, swinging strides that set their slanting muskets gleaming like ripples glinting athwart a windy pond, and their canteens all a-bobbing.

Then, hunched on his horse, rode old John Butler--squat, swarthy, weather-roughened, balancing on his saddle with the grace of a chopping block; and after him more Rangers crowding close behind.

Behind these, quite alone, stalked an Indian swathed in a scarlet blanket edged with gold, on which a silver gorget glittered. He seemed scarce darker than I in colour; and if he wore paint I saw none. There was only a scarlet band of cloth around his temples, and the flight-feather of the white-crested eagle set there low above the left ear and slanting backward.

"Brant!" I whispered to the Sagamore; and I saw him stiffen to very stone beside me; and heard his teeth grate in his jaws.

Then, last of all, came the Keepers of the Eastern Gate, the flower of the warriors of the Long House--the Mohawks.

They passed in the barbaric magnificence of paint and feather and shining steel, a hundred lithe, light-stepping warriors, rifles swinging a-trail, and gorgeous beaded sporrans tossing at every stride.

An interval, then the first wary figure of the lurking rear-guard, another, half a dozen, smooth-bore rifles at a ready, scanning river and thicket. Every one of them looked up at our craggy knoll as they glided along its base; two hesitated, ran half way up over the rock escarpment, loitered for a few moments, then slunk off, hastening to join their fellows.

After a long while a single Seneca came speeding, and disappeared in the wake of the others.

The motley Army of the West had passed.

And it was a terrible and an infamous sight to me, who had known these men under other circumstances to see the remnant of the landed gentry of Tryon County now riding the wilderness like very vagabonds, squired by a grotesque horde of bloody renegades.

To what a doleful pass had these gentlemen come, who lately had so lorded it among us--these proud and testy autocrats of County Tryon, with their vast estates, their baronial halls, their servants, henchmen, tenantry, armed retainers, slaves?

Where were all these people now? Where were their ladies in their London silks and powder? Where were their mistresses, their distinguished guests? Where was my Lord Dunmore now--the great Murray, Earl of Dunmore and Brent Meester to unhappy Norfolk! And, alas, where was the great and good Sir William--and where was Sir William's friend, Lady Grant, and the fearless Duchess of Gordon, and the dark and lovely Lady Johnson, and the pretty ladies of Guy Johnson, of Colonel Butler, of Colonel Claus? Where was Sir John's pitifully youthful and unfortunate lady, and her handsome brother, crippled at Oriskany, and the gentle, dark-eyed sister of Walter Butler, and his haughty mother? All either dead or prisoners, or homeless refugees, or exiles living on the scant bounty of the Government they had suffered for so loyally.

The merciless Committee of Sequestration had seized Johnson Hall, Fort Johnson, Guy Park, Butlersbury; Fish House was burned; Summer House Point lay in ashes, and the charming town built by Sir William was now a rebel garrison, and the jail he erected was their citadel, flying a flag that he had never heard of when he died.

All was gone--gone the kilted Highlanders from the guard house at the Hall; gone the Royal Americans with all their bugle-horns and clarions and scarlet pageantry; gone the many feathered chieftains who had gathered so often at Guy Park, or the Fort, or the Hall. Mansions, lands, families, servants, all were scattered and vanished; and of all that Tryon County glory only these harassed and haggard horsemen remained, haunting the forest purlieus of their former kingdoms with hatred in their hearts, and their hands red with murder. Truly, the Red Beast we hunted these three years through was a most poisonous thing, that it should belch forth such pests as Lord George Germaine, and Loring, and Cunningham, and turn the baronets and gentry of County Tryon into murdering and misshapen ghouls!

When the sun rose we slung pack and pulled foot. And all that day we travelled without mischance; and the next day it was the same, encountering nothing more menacing than peeled and painted trees, where some scouting war-party of the enemy had written threats and boasts, warning the "Boston people" away from the grizzly fastnesses of the dread Long House, and promising a horrid vengeance for every mile of the Dark Empire we profaned.

And so, toward sundown, the first picket of General Sullivan's army challenged us; and my Indians shouted: "Nai Tioga!" And presently we heard the evening gun very near.

Signs of their occupation became more frequent every minute now; there were batteaux and rafts being unloaded at landing places, heavily guarded by Continental soldiery; canoes at carrying places, brush huts erected along the trail, felled trees, bushes cut and lying in piles, roads being widened and cleared, and men everywhere going cheerily about their various affairs.

We encountered the cattle-guard near to a natural meadow along a tiny binikill, and they gave us an account of how Brant had fallen upon Minisink and had slain more than a hundred of our people along the Delaware and Neversink. And I saw my Indians listening with grim countenances while their eyes glowed like coals. As soon as we forded the river, we passed a part of Colonel Proctor's artillery, parleyed in a clearing, where a fine block-fort was being erected; and there were many regimental wagons and officers' horses and batt-horses and cattle to be seen there, and great piles of stores in barrels, sacks, skins, and willow baskets.

As we passed the tents of a foot regiment, the 3rd New Hampshire Line, one of their six Ensigns, Bradbury Richards, recognized me and came across the road to shake my hand, and to inform me that a small scout was to go out to reconnoitre the Indian town of Chemung; and that we would doubtless march thither on the morrow.

With Richards came also my old friend Ezra Buell, lately lieutenant in my own regiment, but now a captain in the 3rd New York Continentals, and a nephew of that Ezra Buell who ran the Stanwix survey in '69 and married a pretty Esaurora girl while marking the Treaty Line.

"Well!" says Ezra, shaking my hand, and: "How are you lazy people up the river, and what are you doing there?"

"Damming the lake," said I, "whilst you damn us for making you wait."

Bradbury Richards laughed, saying that they themselves had but just come up, admitting, however, that there had been some little cursing concerning our delay.

"It has been that way with us, too," said I, "but it is the rebel 'Grants' we curse, and the Ethan Allens and John Starks, and treacherous Green Mountain Boy's, who would shoot us in the backs or make a dicker with Sir Henry sooner than lift a finger to obey the laws of the State they are betraying."

"So hot and yet so young!" said Buell, laughing, "and after a long trail, too--" glancing at my Indians, "and another in view already! But you were ever an uncompromising youngster, Loskiel."

"Your regiment has marched for Canajoharie," I said. "When do you go a-tagging after it?"

"This evening with the headquarter's guide, Heoikim, and the express rider, James Cooke. Lord, what a dreary business!"

"Better learn the news we have concerning your back trail before you start. Ask Captain Franklin to mention it to the General."

"Certainly," said Buell. "I would to God my regiment were ordered here with the rest of them, I'm that sick of the three forts and the scalping-party fighting on the Schoharie."

"It's what you are likely to get for a long while yet," said I. "And now will you or Richards guide me and my party to headquarters?"

"Will you mess with us?" said Richards. "I'll speak to Colonel Dearborn."

I said I would with pleasure, if free to do so, and we walked on through the glorious sunset light, past camp after camp, very smoky with green fires. And I saw three more block-houses being builded, and armed with cannon.

The music of Colonel Proctor's Artillery Regiment was playing "Yankee Doodle" near headquarters as we sighted the General's marquee, and the martial sounds enthralled me.

One of the General's aides-de-camp, a certain Captain Dayton, met us most politely, detained my Indians with tobacco and pipes, and conducted me straight to the General, who, he assured me, happened to be alone. Having seen our General on various occasions, I recognized him at once, although he was in his banyan, having, I judged, been bathing himself in a small, wooden bowl full of warm water, which stood on the puncheon flooring near, very sloppy.

He received me most civilly and listened to my report with interest and politeness, whilst I gave him what news I had of Clinton and how it was with us at the Lake, and all that had happened to my scout of six--the death of the St. Regis and the two Iroquois, the treachery of the Erie and his escape, the murder of the Stockbridge--and how we witnessed the defile of Indian Butler's motley but sinister array headed northwest on the Great Warrior Trail. Also, I gave him as true and just an account as I could give of the number of soldiers, renegades, Indians, and batt-horses in that fantastic and infamous command.

"Where are your Indians?" he asked bluntly.

I informed him, and he sent his aide to fetch them.

General Sullivan understood Indians; and I am not at all sure that my services as interpreter were necessary; but as he said nothing to the contrary, I played my part, presenting to him the stately Sagamore, then the Grey-Feather, then the young warrior, Tahoontowhee, who fairly quivered with pride as I mentioned the scalps he had taken on his first war-path.

With each of my Indians the General shook hands, and on each was pleased to bestow a word of praise and a promise of reward. For a while, through medium of me, he conversed with them, and particularly with the Sagamore, concerning the trail to Catharines-town; and, seeming convinced and satisfied, dismissed us very graciously, telling an aide to place two bush-huts at our disposal, and otherwise see that we lacked nothing that could be obtained for our comfort and good cheer.

As I saluted, he said in a low voice that he preferred I should remain with the Mohican and Oneidas until the evening meal was over. Which I took to indicate that any rum served to my Indians must be measured out by me.

So that night I supped with my red comrades in front of our bush-huts, instead of joining Colonel Dearborn's mess. And I was glad I did so; and I allowed them only a gill of rum. After penning my report by the light of a very vile torch, and filing it at headquarters, I was so tired that I could scarce muster courage to write in my diary. But I did, setting down the day's events without shirking, though I yawned like a volcano at every pen-stroke.

Captains Franklin and Buell, in high spirits, came just as I finished, desiring to learn what I had to say of the road to Otsego; but when I informed them they went away looking far more serious than when they arrived.

A few minutes later I saw the scout march out, bound for Chemung--a small detachment of the 2nd Jersey, one Stockbridge Indian, and a Coureur-de-Bois in very elegant deerskin shirt and gorgeous leggins. Captain Cummins led them.

As they left, Captain Dayton arrived to take me again to the General. There was a throng of officers in the marquee when I was announced, but evidently by some preconcerted understanding all retired as soon as I entered.

When we were alone, the General very kindly pointed to a camp stool at his elbow and requested me to be seated; and for a little while he said nothing, but remained leaning with both elbows on his camp table, seeming to study space as though it were peopled with unpleasant pictures.

However, presently his symmetrical features recovered pleasantly from abstraction, and he said:

"Mr. Loskiel, it is said of you that, except for the Oneida Sachem, Spenser, you are perhaps the most accomplished interpreter Guy Johnson employed."

"No," I said, "there are many better interpreters, my General, but few, perhaps, who understand the most intimate and social conditions of the Long House better than do I."

"You are modest in your great knowledge, Mr. Loskiel."

"No, General, only, knowing as much as I do, I also perceive how much more there is that I do not know. Which makes me wary of committing myself too confidently, and has taught me that to vaunt one's knowledge is a dangerous folly."

General Sullivan laughed that frank, manly, and very winning laugh of his. Then his features gradually became sombre again.

"Colonel Broadhead, at Fortress Pitt, sent you a supposed Wyandotte who might have been your undoing," he said abruptly. "He is a cautious officer, too, yet see how he was deceived! Are you also likely to be deceived in any of your Indians?"

"No, sir."

"Oh! You are confident, then, in this matter!"

"As far as concerns the Indians now under my command."

"You vouch for them?"

"With my honour, General."

"Very well, sir.... And your Mohican Loup--he can perform what he has promised? Guide us straight to Catharines-town, I mean?"

"He has said it."

"Aye--but what is your opinion of that promise?"

"A Siwanois Sagamore never lies."

"You trust him?"

"Perfectly. We are blood-brothers, he and I."

"Oho!" said the General, nodding. "That was cunningly done, sir."

"No, sir. The idea was his own."

General Sullivan laughed again, playing with the polished gorget at his throat.

"Do you never take any credit for your accomplishments, Mr. Loskiel?" he inquired.

"How can I claim credit for that which was not of my own and proper plotting, sir?"

"Oh, it can be done," said the General, laughing more heartily. "Ask some of our brigadiers and colonels, Mr. Loskiel, who desire advancement every time that heaven interposes to save them from their own stupidities! Well, well, let it go, sir! It is on a different matter that I have summoned you here--a very different business, Mr. Loskiel--one which I do not thoroughly comprehend.

"All I know is this: that we Continentals are warring with Britain and her allies of the Long House, that our few Oneida and Stockbridge Indians are fighting with us. But it seems that between the Indians of King George and those who espouse our cause there is a deeper and bloodier and more mysterious feud."

"Yes, General."

"What is it?" he asked bluntly.

"A religious feud--terrible, implacable. But this is only between the degraded and perverted priesthood of the Senecas and our Oneidas and Mohicans, whose Sachems and Sagamores have been outraged and affronted by the blasphemous mockeries of Amochol."

"I have heard something of this."

"No doubt, sir. And it is true. The Senecas are different. They belong not in the Long House. They are an alien people at heart, and seem more nearly akin to the Western Indians, save that they share with the Confederacy its common Huron-Iroquois speech. For although their ensigns sit at the most sacred rite of the Confederacy, perhaps not daring in Federal Council to reveal what they truly are, I am convinced, sir, that of the Seneca Sachems the majority are at heart pagans. I do not mean non-Christians, of course; they are that anyway; but I mean they are degenerated from the more noble faith of the Iroquois, who, after all, acknowledge one God as we do, and have become the brutally superstitious slaves of their vile and perverted priests.

"It is the spawn of Frontenac that has done this. What the Wyoming Witch did at Wyoming her demons will do hereafter. Witchcraft, the frenzied worship of goblins, ghouls, and devils, the sacrifice to Biskoonah, all these have little by little taken the place of the grotesque but harmless rites practiced at the Onon-hou-aroria. Amochol has made it sinister and terrible beyond words; and it is making of the Senecas a swarm of fiends from hell itself.

"This, sir, is the truth. The orthodox priesthood of the Long House shudders and looks askance, but dares not interfere. As for Sir John, and Butler, and McDonald, what do they care as long as their Senecas are inflamed to fury, and fight the more ruthlessly? No, sir, only the priesthood of our own allies has dared to accept the challenge from Amochol and his People of the Cat. Between these it is now a war of utter extermination. And must be so until not one Erie survives, and until Amochol lies dead upon his proper altar!"

The General said in a low voice:

"I had not supposed that this business were so vital."

"Yes, sir, it is vital to the existence of the Iroquois as a federated people who shall remain harmless after we have subdued them, that Amochol and his acolytes die in the very ashes they have so horribly profaned. Amherst hung two of them. The nation lay stunned until he left this country. Had he remained and executed a dozen more Sachems with the rope, the world, I think, had never heard of Amochol."

The General looked hard at me:

"Can you reach Amochol, Mr. Loskiel?"

"That is what I would say to you, sir. I think I can reach him at Catharines-town with my Indians and a detachment from my own regiment, and crush him before he is alarmed by the advance of this army. I have spoken with my Indians, and they believe this can be accomplished, because we have learned that on the last day of this month the secret and debased rites of the Onon-hou-aroria will be practiced at Catharines-town; and every Sorcerer will be there."

"Do you propose to go out in advance on this business?"

"It must be done that way, sir, if we can hope to destroy this Sorcerer. The Seneca scouts most certainly watch this encampment from every hilltop. And the day this army stirs on its march to Catharines-town and Kendaia, the news will run into the North like lightning. You, sir, can hope to encounter no armed resistance as you march northward burning town after town, save only if Butler makes a stand or attempts an ambuscade in force.

"Otherwise, no Seneca will await your coming--I mean there will be no considerable force of Senecas to oppose you in their towns, only the usual scalping parties hanging just outside the smoke veil. All will retire before you. And how is Amochol to be destroyed at Catharines-town unless he be struck at secretly before your advance is near enough to frighten him?"

"What people would you take with you?"

"My Indians, Lieutenant Boyd, and thirty riflemen."

"Is that not too few?"

"In all swift and secret marches, sir, a few do better service than many--as you have taught your own people many a time."

"That is quite true. But they never seem to learn the lesson. I am somewhat astonished that you have seemed to learn it, and lay it practically to heart." He smiled, drummed on the table with a Faber pencil, then, knitting his brows, drew to him a sheet of paper and wrote on it slowly, pausing from time to time in troubled reflection. Once he glanced up at me coldly, and:

"Who is to lead this expedition?" he asked bluntly.

"Why, Lieutenant Boyd, sir," said I, wondering.

"Oh! You have no ambitions then?"

"Mr. Boyd ranks me," I said, smiling. "Who else should lead?"

"I see. Well, sir, you understand that a new commission lies all neatly folded for you in Catharines-town. Even such a modest man as you, Mr. Loskiel, could scarce doubt that," he added laughingly.

"No, sir, I do not doubt it."

"That is well, then. Orders will be sent you in due time--not until General Clinton's army arrives, however."

He looked at me pleasantly: "I have robbed you of the sleep most justly due you. But I think perhaps you may not regret this conference. Good-night, sir."

I saluted and went out. An orderly with a torch lighted me to my quarters. Inside the bush-hut assigned to the Mohican and myself, the red torch-light flickered over the recumbent Sagamore, swathed in his blanket, motionless. But even as I looked one of his eyes opened a little way, glimmering like a jewel in the ruddy darkness, then closed again.

So I stretched myself out in my blanket beside the Sagamore, and, thinking of Lois, fell presently into a sweet and dreamless sleep.

At six o'clock the morning gun awoke me with its startling and annoying thunder. The Sagamore sat up in his blanket, wearing that half-irritated, half-shamed expression always to be seen on an Indian's countenance when cannon are fired. An Indian has no stomach for artillery, and hates sight and sound of the metal monsters.

For a few moments I bantered him sleepily, then dropped back into my blanket. What cared I for their insolent morning gun! I snapped my fingers at it.

And so I lolled on my back, half asleep, yet not wholly, and soon tired of this, and, wrapping me in my blanket and drawing on ankle moccasins, went down to the Chemung where its crystal current clattered over the stones, and found me a clear, deep pool to flounder in.

Before I plunged, noticing several fine trout lying there, I played a scurvy trick on them, tickling three big ones; and had a fourth out of water, but was careless, and he slipped back.

Some Continental soldiers who had been watching me, mouths agape, went to another pool to try their skill; but while I would not boast, it is not everybody who can tickle a speckled trout; and after my bath the soldiers were still at it, and damning their eyes, their luck, and the pretty fish which so saucily flouted them.

So I flung 'em a big trout and went back to camp whistling, and there found that my Indians had fed and were now gravely renewing their paint.

Tahoontowhee dressed and cooked my fish for me, each in a bass-wood leaf, and when they were done and smelling most fragrant, we all made a delicious feast, with corn bread from the ovens and salt pork and a great jug of milk from the army's herd.

At eight o'clock another gun was fired. This was the daily signal, I learned, to stack tents and load pack-horses. And another gun fired at ten o'clock meant "March." With all these guns, and a fourth at sundown, I saw an unhappy time ahead for my Indians. Truly, I think the sound makes them sick. They all pulled wry faces now, and I had my jest at their expense, ours being a most happy little family, so amiably did the Mohican and Oneidas foregather; and also, there being among them a Sagamore and a Chief of the noble Oneida clan, I could meet them on an equality of footing which infringed nothing on military etiquette. There were doubtless many interpreters in camp, but few, if any, I suppose, who had had the advantage of such training as I under Guy Johnson, who himself, after Sir William's death, was appointed Indian Superintendent under the Crown for all North America, Guy Johnson knew the Iroquois. And if he lacked the character, personal charm, and knowledge that Sir William possessed, yet in the politics and diplomacy of Indian affairs his knowledge and practice were vast, and his services most valuable to his King.

Under him I had been schooled, and also under the veteran deputies, Colonel Croghan, Colonel Butler, and Colonel Claus; and had learned much from old Cadwallader Colden, too, who came often to Guy Park, as did our good General Philip

Schuyler in these peaceful days.

So I knew how to treat any Indian I had ever seen, save only the outlandish creatures of the Senecas. Else, perhaps, I had sooner penetrated the villainy of the Erie. Yet, even my own Indians had not been altogether certain of the traitor's identity until almost at the very end.

At ten another gun was fired, but only a small detachment of infantry marched, the other regiments unpacking and pitching tents again, and the usual routine of camp life, with its multitudinous duties and details, was resumed.

I reported at headquarters, to which my guides were now attached, and there were orders for me to hold myself and Indians in readiness for a night march to Chemung.

All that day I spent in acquainting myself with the camp which had been pitched, as I say, on the neck of land bounded by the Susquehanna and the Chemung, with a small creek, called Cayuga by some, Seneca Creek by others, intersecting it and flowing south into the Susquehanna. It was but a trout brook.

This site of the old Indian town of Tioga seemed to me very lovely. The waters were silvery and sweet, the flats composed of rich, dark soil, the forests beautiful with a great variety of noble and gigantic trees--white pines on the hills; on the level country enormous black-walnuts, oaks, button-woods, and nut trees of many species, growing wide apart, yet so roofing the forest with foliage that very little sunlight penetrated, and only the flats were open and bright with waving Indian grass, now so ripe that our sheep, cattle, and horses found in it a nourishment scarcely sufficient for beasts so exercised and driven.

That day, as I say, I walked about the camp and adjacent river-country, seeking out my friends in the various regiments to gossip with them. And was invited to a Rum Punch given by all the officers at the Artillery Lines to celebrate the victory of General Wayne at Stony Point.

Colonel Proctor's artillery band discoursed most noble music for us; and there was much hilarity and cheering, and many very boisterous.

These social parties in our army, where rum-punch was the favourite beverage, were gay and lively; but there was a headache in every cup of it, they say. I, being an interpreter, held aloof because I must ever set an example to my red comrades. And this day had all I could do to confine them to proper rations. For all spirit is a very poison to any Indian. And of all the crimes of which men of my colour stand attainted, the offering of this death-cup to our red brothers is, I think, the wickedest and the most contemptible.

For when we white men become merely exhilarated in the performance of such social usages as politeness requires of us, the Indian becomes murderous. And I remember at this Artillery Punch many officers danced a Shawanese dance, and General Hand, of the Light Troops, did lead this war-dance, which caused me discomfiture, I not at all pleased to see officers who ranked me cut school-boy capers 'round a midday fire.

And it was like very school-lads that many of us behaved, making of this serious and hazardous expedition a silly pleasure jaunt. I have since thought that perhaps the sombre and majestic menace of a sunless and unknown forest reacted a little on us all, and that many found a nervous relief in brief relaxations and harmless folly, and in antics performed on its grim and dusky edges.

For no one, I think, doubted there was trouble waiting for us within these silent shades. And the tension had never lessened for this army, what with waiting for the Right Wing, which had not yet apparently stirred from Otsego; and the inadequacy of provisions, not known to the men but whispered among the officers; and the shots already exchanged this very morning along the river between our outposts and prowling scouts of the enemy; and the daily loss of pack-animals and cattle, strayed or stolen; and of men, too, scalped since they left Wyoming, sometimes within gunshot of headquarters.

But work on the four block-forts, just begun, progressed rapidly; and, alas, the corps of invalids destined to garrison them had, since the army left Easton, increased too fast to please anybody, what with wounds, accidents in camp from careless handling of firearms, kicks from animals, and the various diseases certain to appear where many people congregate.

There were a number of regiments under tents or awaiting the unfinished log barracks at Tioga Point; in the First Brigade there were four from New Jersey; in the Second Brigade three from New Hampshire; in the Third two from Pennsylvania, and an artillery regiment; and what with other corps and the train, boatmen, guides, workmen, servants, etc., it made a great and curious spectacle even before our Right Wing joined.

Every regiment carried its colours and its music, fifes, drums, and bugle-horns; and sometimes these played on the march when a light detachment went forward for a day's scout, or to forage or to destroy. But best of all music I ever heard, I loved now to hear the band of Colonel Proctor's artillery regiment, filling me as it did with solemn, yet pleasurable, emotions, and seemingly teaching me how dear had Lois become to me.

The scout, sent out the day before, returned in the afternoon with an account that Chemung was held by the enemy, which caused a bustle in camp, particularly among the light troop.

Headquarters was very busy all day long, and sometimes even gay, for the gentlemen of General Sullivan's family were not only sufficient, but amiable and delightful. And there I had the honour of being made known to his aides-de-camp, Mr. Pierce, Mr. Van Cortlandt, and Major Hoops. I already knew Captain Dayton. Also, of the staff I met there Captain Topham, our Commissary of Militia Stores, Captain Lodge, our surveyor, Colonels Antis and Bond, Conductors of Boats, Dr. Hogan, Chief Surgeon, Lieutenant R. Pemberton, Judge Advocate, Lieutenant Colonel Frasier, Colonel Hooper, Lieutenant Colonel Barber, Adjutant General, the Reverend S. Kirkland, Chaplain, and others most agreeable but too numerous to mention. Still, I have writ them all down in my diary, as I try always to do, so that if God gives me wife and children some day they may find, perhaps, an hour of leisure, when to peruse a blotted page of what husband and father saw in the great war might not prove too tedious or disagreeable.

In this manner, then, the afternoon of that August day passed, and what with these occupations, and the catching of several trouts, which I love to do with hook and line and alder pole, and what with sending to Lois a letter by an express who went to Clinton toward evening, the time did not seem irksome.

Yet, it had passed more happily had I heard from Lois. But no runners came; and if any were sent out from Otsego and taken by the enemy I know not, only that none came through that day, Thursday, August the 12th.

One thing in camp had disagreeably surprised me, that there were women and children here, and like to remain in the block forts after the army had departed from its base for the long march through the Seneca country.

This I could not understand or reconcile with any proper measure of safety, as the cannon in the block-houses were not to be many or of any great calibre, and only the corps of invalids were to remain to defend them.

I had told Lois that no women would be permitted at Tioga Point. That these were the orders that had been generally understood at Otsego.

And now, lo and behold, here were women arrived from Easton, Bethlehem, Wyalusing, and Wyoming, including the wives and children of several non-commissioned officers and soldiers from the district; widows of murdered settlers, washerwomen, and several tailoresses--in all a very considerable number.

And I hoped to heaven that Lois might not hear of this mischievous business and discover in it an excuse for coming as the guest of any lady at Otsego, or, in fact, make any further attempt to stir until the Right Wing marched and the batteaux took the ladies of Captain Bleecker, Ensign Lansing, and Lana, and herself to Albany.

After sundown an officer came to me and said that the entire army was ordered to march at eight that evening, excepting troops sufficient to guard our camp; that there would be no alarm sounded, and that we were to observe secrecy and silence.

Also, it appeared that a gill of rum per man had been authorized, but I refused for myself and my Indians, thinking to myself that the General might have made it less difficult for me if he had confined his indulgence to the troops.

About eight o'clock a Stockbridge Indian--the one who had been with the scout to Chemung--came to me with a note from Dominie Kirkland.

I gave him my hand, and he told me that his name was Yellow Moth, and that he was a Christian. Also, he inquired about the Mole, and I was obliged to relate the circumstances of that poor convert's murder.

"God's will," said the Yellow Moth very quietly. "You, my brother, and I may see a thousand fall, and ten thousand on our right hand, and it shall not come nigh us."

"Amen," said I, much moved by this simple fellow's tranquil faith.

I made him known to the Sagamore and to the two Oneidas, who received him with a grave sincerity which expressed very plainly their respect for a people of which the Mole had been for them a respectable example.

Like the Mole, the Yellow Moth wore no paint except a white cross limned on his breast over a clan sign indecipherable. And if, in truth, there had ever really been a totem under the white paint I do not know, for like the Algonquins, these peoples had but a loose political, social, religious, and tribal organization, which never approached the perfection of the Iroquois system in any manner or detail.

About eight o'clock came Captain Carbury, of the 11th Pennsylvania, to us, and we immediately set out, marching swiftly up the Chemung River, the Sagamore and the Yellow Moth leading, then Captain Carbury and myself, then the Oneidas.

Behind us in the dusk we saw the Light Troops falling in, who always lead the army. All marched without packs, blankets, horses, or any impedimenta. And, though the distance was not very great, so hilly, rocky, and rough was the path through the hot, dark night, and so narrow and difficult were the mountain passes, that we were often obliged to rest the men. Also there were many swamps to pass, and as the men carried the cohorn by hand, our progress was slow. Besides these difficulties and trials, a fog came up, thickening toward dawn, which added to the hazards of our march.

So the dawn came and found us still marching through the mist, and it was not until six o'clock that we of the guides heard a Seneca dog barking far ahead, and so knew that Chemung was near.

Back sped Tahoontowhee to hasten the troops; I ran forward with Captain Carbury and the Sagamore, passing several outlying huts, then some barns and houses which loomed huge as medieval castles in the fog, but were really very small.

"Look out!" cried Carbury. "There is their town right ahead!"

It lay straight ahead of us, a fine town of over a hundred houses built on both sides of the pretty river. The casements of some of these houses were glazed and the roofs shingled; smoke drifted lazily from the chimneys; and all around were great open fields of grain, maize, and hay, orchards and gardens, in which were ripening peas, beans, squashes, pumpkins, watermelons, muskmelons.

"Good God!" said I. "This is a fine place, Carbury!"

"It's like a dozen others we have laid in ashes," said he, "and like scores more that we shall treat in a like manner. Look sharp! Here some our light troops."

The light infantry of Hand arrived on a smart run--a torrent of red-faced, sweating, excited fellows, pouring headlong into the town, cheering as they ran.

General Hand, catching sight of me, signalled with his sword and shouted to know what had become of the enemy.

"They're gone off!" I shouted back. "My Indians are on their heels and we'll soon have news of their whereabouts."

Then the soldiery began smashing in doors and windows right and left, laughing and swearing, and dragging out of the houses everything they contained.

So precipitate had been the enemy's flight that they had left everything--food still cooking, all their household and personal utensils; and I saw in the road great piles of kettles, plates, knives, deerskins, beaver-pelts, bearhides, packs of furs, and bolts of striped linen, to which heaps our soldiers were adding every minute.

Others came to fire the town; and it was sad to see these humble homes puff up in a cloud of smoke and sparks, then burst into vivid flame. In the orchards our men were plying their axes or girdling the heavily-fruited trees; field after field of grain was fired, and the flames swept like tides across them.

The corn was in the milk, and what our men could not burn, using the houses for kilns, they trampled and cut with their hangers--whole regiments marching through these fields, destroying the most noble corn I ever saw, for it was so high that it topped the head of a man on horseback.

So high, also, stood the hay, and it was sad to see it burn.

And now, all around in this forest paradise, our army was gathered, destroying, raging, devastating the fairest land that I had seen in many a day. All the country was aflame; smoke rolled up, fouling the blue sky, burying woodlands, blotting out the fields and streams.

From the knoll to which I had moved to watch the progress of my scouts, I could see an entire New Jersey regiment chasing horses and cattle; another regiment piling up canoes, fish-weirs, and the hewn logs of bridges, to make a mighty fire; still other regiments trampling out the last vestige of green stuff in the pretty gardens.

Not a shot had yet been fired; there was no sound save the excited and terrifying roar of a vast armed mob obliterating in its fury the very well-springs that enabled its enemies to exist.

Cattle, sheep, horses were being driven off down the trail by which we had come; men everywhere were stuffing their empty sacks with green vegetables and household plunder; the town fairly whistled with flame, and the smoke rose in a great cloud-shape very high, and hung above us, tenting us from the sun.

In the midst of this uproar the Grey-Feather came speeding to me with news that the enemy was a little way upstream and seemed inclined to make a stand. I immediately informed the General; and soon the bugle-horns of the light infantry sounded, and away we raced ahead of them.

I remember seeing an entire company marching with muskmelons pinned on their bayonets, all laughing and excited; and I heard General Sullivan bawl at them:

"You damned unmilitary rascals, do you mean to open fire on 'em with vegetables?"

Everybody was laughing, and the General grinned as Hand's bugle-horns played us in.

But it was another matter when the Seneca rifles cracked, and a sergeant and a drummer lad of the 11th Pennsylvania fell. The smooth-bores cracked again, and four more soldiers tumbled forward sprawling, the melons on their bayonets rolling off into the bushes.

Carbury, marching forward beside me, dropped across my path; and as I stooped over him gave me a ghastly look.

"Don't let them scalp me," he said--but his own men came running and picked him up, and I ran forward with the others toward a wooded hill where puffs of smoke spotted the bushes.

Then the long, rippling volleys of Hand's men crashed out, one after another, and after a little of this their bugle-horns sounded the charge.

But the Senecas did not wait; and it was like chasing weasels in a stone wall, for even my Indians could not come up with them.

However, about two o'clock, returning to that part of the town across the river, which Colonel Dearborn's men were now setting afire, we received a smart volley from some ambushed Senecas, and Adjutant Huston and a guide fell.

It was here that the Sagamore made his kill--just beyond the first house, in some alders; and he came back with a Seneca scalp at his girdle, as did the Grey-Feather also.

"Hiokatoo's warriors," remarked the Oneida briefly, wringing out his scalp and tying it to his belt.

I looked up at the hills in sickened silence. Doubtless Butler's men were watching us in our work of destruction, not daring to interfere until the regulars arrived from Fort Niagara. But when they did arrive, it meant a battle. We all knew that. And knew, too, that a battle lost in the heart of that dark wilderness meant the destruction of every living soul among us.

About two o'clock, having eaten nothing except what green and uncooked stuff we had picked up in field and garden, our marching signal sounded and we moved off; driving our captured stock, every soldier laden with green food and other plunder, and taking with us our dead and wounded.

Chemung had been, but was no longer. And if, like Thendara, it was ever again to be I do not know, only that such a horrid and pitiful desolation I had never witnessed in all my life before. For it was not the enemy, but the innocent earth we had mutilated, stamping an armed heel into its smiling and upturned face. And what we had done sickened me.

Yet, this was scarcely the beginning of that terrible punishment which was to pass through the Long House in flame and smoke, from the Eastern Door to the Door of the West, scouring it fiercely from one end to the other, and leaving no living thing within--only a few dead men prone among its blood-soaked ashes.

*Etho ni-ya-wenonh![1]

By six that evening the army was back in its camp at Tioga Point. All the fever and excitement of the swift foray had passed, and the inevitable reaction had set in. The men were haggard, weary, sombre, and harassed. There was no elation after success either among officers or privates; only a sullen grimness, the sullenness of repletion after an orgy--the grimness of disgust for an unwelcome duty only yet begun.

Because this sturdy soldiery was largely composed of tillers of the soil, of pioneer farmers who understood good land, good husbandry, good crops, and the stern privations necessary to wrest a single rod of land from the iron jaws of the wilderness.

To stamp upon, burn, girdle, destroy, annihilate, give back to the forest what human courage and self-denial had wrested from it, was to them in their souls abhorrent.

---

1   Thus it befell!

Save for the excitement of the chase, the peril ever present, the certainty that failure meant death in its most dreadful forms, it might have been impossible for these men to destroy the fruits of the earth, even though produced by their mortal enemies, and designed, ultimately, to nourish them.

Even my Indians sat silent and morose, stretching, braiding, and hooping their Seneca scalps. And I heard them conversing among themselves, mentioning frequently the Three Sisters[2] they had destroyed; and they spoke ever with a hint of tenderness and regret in their tones which left me silent and unhappy.

To slay in the heat and fury of combat is one matter; to scar and cripple the tender features of humanity's common mother is a different affair. And I make no doubt that every blow that bit into the laden fruit trees of Chemung stabbed more deeply the men who so mercilessly swung the axes.

Well might the great Cayuga chieftain repeat the terrible prophecy of Toga-na-etah the Beautiful:

"When the White Throats shall come, then, if ye be divided, ye will pull down the Long House, fell the tall Tree of Peace, and quench the Onondaga Fire forever."

As I stood by the rushing current of the Thiohero[3], on the profaned and desolate threshold of the Dark Empire, I thought of O-cau-nee, the Enchantress, and of Na-wenu the Blessed, and of Hiawatha floating in his white canoe into the far haven where the Master of Life stood waiting.

And now, for these doomed people of the Kannonsi, but one rite remained to be accomplished. And the solemn thunder of the last drum-roll must summon them to the great Festival of the Dead.

CHAPTER XV
BLOCK-HOUSE NO. 2

On the 14th the army lay supine. There was no news from Otsego. One man

2 Corn, squash, and bean were so spoken of affectionately, as they always were planted together by the Iroquois.

3 Seneca River.

fell dead in camp of heart disease. The cattle-guard was fired on. On the 15th a corporal and four privates, while herding our cattle, were fired on, the Senecas killing and scalping one and wounding another. On the 16th came a runner from Clinton with news that the Otsego army was on the march and not very far distant from the Ouleout; and a detachment of eight hundred men, under Brigadier General Poor, was sent forward to meet our Right Wing and escort it back to this camp.

By one of the escort, a drummer lad, I sent a letter directed to Lois, hoping it might be relayed to Otsego and from thence by batteau to Albany. The Oneida runner had brought no letters, much to the disgust of the army, and no despatches except the brief line to our General commanding. The Brigadiers were furious. So also was I that no letters came for me.

On the 17th our soldier-herdsmen were again fired on, and, as before, one poor fellow was killed and partly scalped, and one wounded. The Yellow Moth, Tahoontowhee, and the Grey-Feather went out at night on retaliation bent, but returned with neither trophies nor news, save what we all knew, that the Seneca scouts were now swarming like hornets all around us ready to sting to death anyone who strayed out of bounds.

On the 18th the entire camp lay dull, patiently expectant of Clinton. He did not come. It rained all night.

On Thursday, the 19th, it still rained steadily, but with no violence--a fine, sweet, refreshing summer shower, made golden and beautiful at intervals by the momentary prophecy of the sun; yet he did not wholly reveal himself, though he smiled through the mist at us in friendly fashion.

I had been out fishing for trouts very early, the rain making it favourable for such pleasant sport, and my Indians and I had finished a breakfast of corn porridge and the sweet-fleshed fishes that I took from the brook where it falls into the Susquehanna.

It was still very early--near to five o'clock, I think--for the morning gun had not yet bellowed, and the camp lay very still in the gentle and fragrant rain.

A few moments before five I saw a company of Jersey troops march silently down to the river, hang their cartouche-boxes on their bayonets, and ford the stream, one holding to another, and belly deep in the swollen flood.

Thinks I to myself, they are going to protect our cattle-guards; and I turned and walked down to the ford to watch the crossing.

Then I saw why they had crossed: there were some people come down to the landing place on the other bank in two batteaux and an Oneida canoe--soldiers, boatmen, and two women; and our men were fording the river to protect the crossing of this small flotilla.

I seated myself, wondering what foolhardy people these might be, and trying to see more plainly the women in the two batteaux. As the boatmen poled nearer, it seemed to me that some of the people looked marvelously like the riflemen of my own corps; and a few moments later I sprang to my feet astounded, for of the two women in the nearest batteau one was Lois de Contrecoeur and the other Lana Helmer.

Suddenly the Oneida canoe shot out from the farther shore, passed both batteaux, paddles flashing, and came darting toward the landing where I stood. Two riflemen were in it; one rose as the canoe's nose grated on the gravel, cast aside the bow-paddle, balanced himself toward the bow with both hands, and leaped ashore, waving at me a gay greeting.

"My God!" said I excitedly, as Boyd ran lightly up the slope. "Are you stark mad to bring ladies into this damnable place?"

"There are other women, too. Why, even that pretty jade, Dolly Glenn, is coming! What could I do? The General himself permitted it. Miss de Contrecoeur and Lana heard that a number of women were already here, and so come for a frolic they must."

"Who accompanies them? I see no older woman yonder."

"Mrs. Sabin, the lady of Captain Sabin, Staff Commissary of Issues."

"Where is she, then?"

"We left her with the army at the Ouleout."

"Where do you propose to quarter these ladies?"

"We understand that you have four block-forts mounting cannon. That would argue barracks. Therefore, I don't think the danger is very considerable. Do you?"

"There is danger, of course," I said. "The entire Seneca nation is here with Indian Butler and Brant."

"Well, then, we'll turn your Butler into a turn-spit, and make of your wild Brant a domestic gander!"

He spoke coolly, a slight smile on his eager, handsome features. And I wondered how he could make a jest of this business, and how he could have permitted so mad a prank if he truly entertained any very deep regard for Lana Helmer.

"Danger," I repeated coldly. "Yes, there is a-plenty of that hereabouts, what with the Seneca scalping parties combing the woods around us, and the cattle-guard fired upon in plain sight of headquarters."

"Well, there were and still are some few scalping parties hanging around Otsego. I myself see no real reason why the ladies should not pay us a visit here, have their frolic, and later return with the heavier artillery down the river to Easton. Or, if they choose, they shall await our return from Catharines-town."

"And if we do not return? Have you thought of that, Boyd?"

"You shall not conjure me with any such forebodings!" he laughed. "This raid of ours will be no very great or fearsome affair. They'll run--your Brants and Butlers--I warrant you. And we'll follow and burn their towns. Then, like the French king of old, down hill we'll all go strutting, you and I and the army, Loskiel; and no great harm done to anybody or anything, save to the Senecas' squash harvest, and the sensitive feelings of Walter Butler!"

While he was speaking, I kept my eye on the slow batteau which led. Three boatmen poled it; Lois and Lana sat in the middle; behind them crouched two riflemen, long weapons ready, the ringed coon-tail floating in the breeze.

Neither of the ladies had yet recognized me; Lana leaned lightly against Lois, her cheek resting on her companion's shoulder.

A black rage against Boyd rose suddenly in my breast; and so savage and abrupt was the emotion that I could scarce stifle and subdue it.

"It is wrong for them to come," I said with an effort to speak calmly, "----utterly and wickedly wrong. Our block-forts are not finished. And when they are they will be more or less vulnerable. I can not understand why you did not make every effort to prevent their coming here."

"I made every proper effort," he said carelessly. "What man is vain enough to believe he can influence a determined woman?"

I did not like what he said, and so made him no answer.

"Is your camp still asleep?" he asked, yawning.

"Yes. The morning gun is usually fired at six."

"Can you lodge us and bait us until I make my report?"

"I can lodge the ladies and give breakfast to you all. How near is our main army?"

"Between twenty and thirty miles above--one can scarce tell the way this accursed river winds about. Our men are exhausted. They'll not arrive tonight. General Poor's men from this camp met us last night. Clinton desired me to take a few riflemen and push forward; and the ladies--except the fat one--begged so prettily to go with us that he consented. So we took two empty batteaux and a canoe and came on in advance, with no effort whatever."

"That was a rash business!" I said, controlling my anger. "The river woods along the Ouleout swarm with Seneca scouts. Didn't you understand that?"

"So I told 'em," he said, laughing, "but do you know, Loskiel, between you and me I believe that your pretty inamorata really loves the thrill of danger. And I know damned well that Lana Helmer loves it. For when we came through without so much as sighting a muskrat, 'What!' says she, 'Not a savage to be seen and not a shot fired! Lord,' says she, 'I had as lief take the air on Bowling Green--there being some real peril of beaux and macaronis!'"

Everything this man said now conspired to enrage me; and it was a struggle for me to restrain the bitter affront ever twitching at my lips for utterance. Perhaps I might not have restrained it any longer had I not seen Lois lean suddenly forward in her seat, shade her eyes with her hands, then stand up beside one of the boatmen. And I knew she recognized me.

Instantly within me all anger, rancour, and even dread melted in the warmer and more generous emotion which nigh overwhelmed me, so that for an instant I could scarce see her for the glimmering of my eyes.

But that passed; I went down to the shore and stood there while the clumsy boat swung inshore, the misty waves slapping at the bow and side. The landing planks lay on the gravel. Boyd and I laid them. Lana, wrapped in her camblet, crossed them first, giving me her hand with a pale smile. I laid my lips to it; she passed, Boyd moving forward beside her.

Then came Lois in her scarlet capuchin, eager and shy at the same time, smiling, yet with fearfulness and tenderness so strangely blended that ever her laughing eyes seemed close to tears and the lips that smiled were tremulous.

"I came--you see.... Are you angry?" she asked as I bent low over her little hand. "You will not chide me--will you, Euan?"

"No. What is done is done. Are you well, Lois?"

"Perfect in health, my friend. And if you truly are glad to see me, then I am content. But I am also very wet, Euan, spite of my capuchin. Lana and I have a common box. It belongs to her. May our boatmen carry it ashore?"

I gave brief directions to the men, returned the smiling salute of my wet riflemen from the other boat now drawing heavily inshore, and climbed the grassy bank with Lois to where Lana and Boyd stood under the trees awaiting us.

"I have but one bush-hut to offer you at present," I said. "Proper provision in barracks will be made, no doubt, as soon as the General learns who it is who has honoured him so unexpectedly with a visit."

"That's why we came, Euan--to honour General Sullivan," said Lois demurely. "Did we not, Lanette?"

Then again I noticed that the old fire, the old gaiety in Lana Helmer had been almost quenched. For instead of a saucy reply she only smiled; and even her eyes seemed spiritless as they rested on me a moment, then turned wearily elsewhere.

"You are much fatigued," I said to Lois.

"I? No. But my poor Lana slept very badly in the boat. Before dawn we went ashore for an hour's rest. That seemed sufficient for me, but Lana, poor dove, did not profit, I fear. Did you, dearest?"

"Very little," said Lana, forcing a gaiety she surely did not inspire in others with her haunted eyes that looked at everything, yet saw nothing--or so it seemed to me.

As we came to our bush-huts, Lois caught sight of the Sagamore for the first time, and held out both hands with a pretty cry of recognition:

"Nai, Mayaro!"

The Sagamore turned in silent astonishment; though when he saw Boyd there also his features became smooth and blank again. But he came forward with stately grace to welcome her; and, bending his crested head, took her hands and laid them lightly over his heart.

"Nai, Lois!" he exclaimed emphatically.

"Itoh, Mayaro!" she replied gaily, pressing his hands in hers. "I am that contented to see you! Are you not amazed to see me here?" she insisted, mischievously amused at his unaltered features.

The Sagamore said smilingly:

"When she wills it, who can follow the Rosy-throated Pigeon in her swift flight? Not the Enchantress in the moon. Tharon alone, O Rosy-throated One!"

"The wild pigeon has outwitted you all, has she not, Mayaro, my friend?"

"Nakwah! Let my brother Loskiel deny it, then. I, a Sagamore, know better than to deny a fire its ashes, or a wild pigeon its magic flight."

Boyd now spoke to the Mohican, who returned his greeting courteously, but very gravely. I then made the Mohican known to Lana, who gave him a lifeless hand from the green folds of her camblet. My Oneidas, who had finished their somewhat ominous painting, came from the other hut in company with the Yellow Moth, the latter now painted for the first time in a brilliant and poisonous yellow. All these people I made acquainted one with another. Lois was very gracious to them all, using what Indian words she knew in her winning greetings--and using them quite wrongly--God bless her!

Then the Yellow Moth hung my new blue blanket, which I had lately drawn from our Commissary of Issues, across the door of my hut; two huge boatmen came up with Lana's box, swung between them, and deposited it within the hut.

"By the time you are ready," said I, "we will have a breakfast for you such as only the streams of this country can afford."

The six o'clock gun awoke the camp and found me already at the General's tent, awaiting permission to see him.

He seemed surprised that Clinton had allowed any ladies to accompany the Otsego army, but it was evident that the happiness and relief he experienced at learning that Clinton was on the Ouleout had put him into a most excellent humour. And he straightway sent an officer with orders to remove Lana's box to Block-Fort No. 2 in the new fort, where were already domiciled the wives of two sergeants and a corporal, and gave me an order assigning to Lois and Lana a rough loft there.

But the General's chief concern and curiosity was for Boyd and the eight riflemen who had come through from the Ouleout as the first advanced guard of that impatiently awaited Otsego army; and I heard Boyd telling him very gaily that they were bringing more than two hundred batteaux, loaded with provisions. And, this,

I think, was the best news any man could have brought to our Commander at that moment. One thing I do know; from that time Boyd was an indulged favourite of our General, who admired his many admirable qualities, his gay spirits, his dashing enterprise, his utter fearlessness; and who overlooked his military failings, which were rashness to the point of folly, and a tendency to obey orders in a manner which best suited his own ideas. Captain Cummings was a far safer man.

I say this with nothing in my heart but kindness for Boyd. God knows I desire to do him justice--would wish it for him even more than for myself. And I not only was not envious of his good fortune in so pleasing our General, but was glad of it, hoping that this honour might carry with it a new and graver responsibility sufficiently heavy to curb in him what was least admirable and bring out in him those nobler qualities so desirable in officer and man.

When I returned to my hut there were any fish smoking hot on their bark plates, and Lana and Lois in dry woollen dresses, worsted stockings, and stout, buckled shoon, already at porridge.

So I sat down with them and ate, and it was, or seemed to be, a happy company there before our little hut, with officers and troops passing to and fro and glancing curiously at us, and our Indians squatted behind us all a-row, and shining up knife and hatchet and rifle; and the bugle-horns of the various regiments sounding prettily at intervals, and the fifers and drummers down by the river at distant morning practice.

"You love best the bellowing conch-horn of the rifles," observed Lana to Lois, with a touch of her old-time impudence.

"I?" exclaimed Lois.

"You once told me that every blast of it sets you a-trembling," insisted Lana. "Naturally I take it that you quiver with delight--having some friend in that corps----"

"Lana! Have done, you little baggage!"

"Lord!" said Lana. "'Twas Major Parr I meant. What does an infant Ensign concern such aged dames as you and I?"

Lois, lovely under her mounting colour, continued busy with her porridge. Lana said in my ear:

"She is a wild thing, Euan, and endures neither plaguing nor wooing easily.

How I have gained her I do not know.... Perhaps because I am aging very fast these days, and she hath a heart as tender as a forest dove's."

Lois looked up, seeing us whispering together.

"Uncouth manners!" said she. "I am greatly ashamed of you both."

I thought to myself, wondering, how utter a change had come over the characters of these two in twice as many weeks! Lois had now something of that quick and mischievous gaiety that once was Lana's; and the troubled eyes that once belonged to Lois now were hers no longer, but Lana's. It seemed very strange and sad to me.

"Had I a dozen beaux," quoth Lois airily, "I might ask of one o' them another bit of trout." And, "Oh!" she exclaimed, in affected surprise, as I aided her. "It would seem that I have at least one young man who aspires to that ridiculous title. Do you covet it, Euan? And humbly?"

"Do I merit it?" I asked, laughing.

"Upon my honour," she exclaimed, turning to Lana, "I believe the poor young gentleman thinks he does merit the title. Did you ever hear of such insufferable conceit? And merely because he offers me a bit of trout."

"I caught them, too," said I. "That should secure me in my title."

"Oh! You caught them too, did you! And so you deem yourself entitled to be a beau of mine? Lana, do you very kindly explain to the unfortunate Ensign that you and I were accustomed at Otsego to a popularity and an adulation of which he has no conception. Colonels and majors were at our feet. Inform him very gently, Lana."

"Yes," said Lana, "you behaved very indiscreetly at Otsego Camp, dear one-- sitting alone for hours and hours over this young gentleman's letters----"

"Traitor!" exclaimed Lois, blushing. "It was a letter from his solicitor, Mr. Hake, that you found me doting on!"

"Did you then hear from Mr. Hake?" I asked, laughing and very happy.

"Indeed I did, by every post! That respectable Albany gentleman seemed to feel it his duty to write me by every batteau and inquire concerning my health, happiness, and pleasure, and if I lacked anything on earth to please me. Was it not most extraordinary behaviour, Euan?"

She was laughing when she spoke, and for a moment her eyes grew strangely tender, but they brightened immediately and she tossed her head.

"Oh, Lana!" said she. "I think I may seriously consider Mr. Hake and his very evident intentions. So I shall require no more beaux, Euan, and thank you kindly for volunteering. Besides, if I want 'em, this camp seems moderately furnished with handsome and gallant young officers," she added airily, glancing around her. "Lana! Do you please observe that tall captain with the red facings! And the other staff-major yonder in blue and buff! Is he not beautiful as Apollo? And I make no doubt that this agreeable young Ensign of ours will presently make them known to us for our proper diversion."

Somehow, now, with the prospect of all these officers besetting her with their civilities and polite assiduities, nothing of the old and silly jealousy seemed to stir within me. Perhaps because, although for days I had not seen her, I knew her better. And also I had begun to know myself. Even though she loved not me in the manner I desired, yet the lesser, cruder, and more unworthy solicitude which at first seemed to have possessed me in her regard was now gone. And if inexperience and youth had inspired me with unworthy jealousies I do not know; but I do know that I now felt myself older--years older than when first I knew Lois; and perhaps my being so honestly in love with her wrought the respectable change in me. For real love ages the mind, even when it makes more youthful the body, and so controls both body and mind. And I think it was something that way with me.

Presently, as we sat chattering there, came men to take away Lana's box to Block-House No. 2 on the peninsula. So Lana went into the bush-hut and refilled and locked the box, and then we all walked together to the military works which were being erected on a cleared knoll overlooking both rivers, and upon which artillerymen were now mounting the three-pounder and the cohorn, or "grasshopper," as our men had named it, because our artillery officers had taken it from its wooden carriage and had mounted it on a tripod. And at every discharge it jumped into the air and kicked over backward.

This miniature fortress, now called Fort Sullivan, was about three hundred feet square, with strong block-forts at the four corners, so situated as to command both rivers; and these fortifications were now so nearly completed that the men of the invalid corps who were to garrison the place had already marched into their barracks, and were now paraded for inspection.

The forts had been very solidly constructed of great logs, the serrated palisade, deeply and solidly embedded, rose twelve feet high. A rifle platform ran inside this, connecting the rough barracks and stables, which also were built of logs, the crevices stuffed with moss and smeared and plastered with blue clay from the creek.

These, with the curtain, block-forts, and a deep ditch over which was a log bridge, composed the military works at Tioga; and this was the place into which we now walked, a sentry directing us to Block-House No. 2, which overlooked the Chemung.

And no sooner had we entered and climbed the ladder to the women's quarters overhead, than:

"What luxury!" exclaimed Lois, looking down at her bed of fresh-cut balsam, over which their blankets had been cast. "Could any reasonable woman demand more? With a full view of the pretty river in the rain, and a real puncheon floor, and a bed of perfume to dream on, and a brave loop to shoot from! What more could a vain maid ask?" She glanced at me with sweet and humorous eyes, saying: "Fort Orange is no safer than this log bastion, so scowl on me no more, Euan, but presently take Lanette and me to the parapet where other and lovelier wonders are doubtless to be seen."

"What further wonders?" asked Lana indifferently.

"Why, sky and earth and river, dear, and the little dicky birds all a-preening under this sweet, sunny veil of rain. Is not all this mystery of nature wonderful enough to lure us to the rifle-platform?"

Said Lana listlessly: "I had liefer court a deeper mystery."

"Which, dear one?"

"Sleep," said Lana briefly; and I saw how pale she was, kneeling there beside the opened box and sorting out the simple clothing they had brought with them.

For a few minutes longer we conversed, talking of Otsego and of our friends there; and I learned how Colonel Gansevoort had left with his regiment and Lieutenant-Colonel Willet, and was marching hither with Clinton after all.

A soldier brought a wooden bowl, an iron sap-kettle full of sweet water, a hewn bench, and nailed up a blanket cutting the room in two. Their quarters were now furnished.

I pushed aside the blanket, walked to the inner loop, and gazed down on the miniature parade where the invalids were now being inspected by Colonel Shreve.

When I returned, Lana had changed to a levete and was lying on her balsam couch, cheek on hand, looking up at Lois, who knelt beside her on the puncheon floor, smoothing back her thick, bright hair. And in the eyes of these two was an expression the like of which I had never before seen, and I stepped back instinctively, like a man who intrudes on privacy unawares.

"Come in, Euan!" cried Lois, with a gaiety which seemed slightly forced; and I came, awkwardly, not meeting their eyes, and made for the ladder to get myself below.

Whereat both laughed. Lois rose and went behind the blanket to the loop, and Lana said, with a trace of her former levity:

"Broad-brim! Do you fly blushing from my levete? The Queen of France receives in scanter attire, I hear. Sit you on yonder bench and play courtier amiably for once."

She seemed so frail and white and young, lying there, her fair hair unpowdered and tumbled about her face--so childlike and helpless--that a strange and inexplicable apprehension filled me; and, scarce thinking what I did, I went over to her and knelt down beside her, putting one arm around her shoulders.

Her expression, which had been smiling and vaguely audacious, changed subtly. She lay looking up at me very wistfully for a moment, then lifted her hands a little way. I laid them to my lips, looking over them down into her altered eyes.

"Always," she said under her breath, "always you have been kind and true, Euan, even when I have used you with scant courtesy."

"You have never used me ill."

"No--only to plague you as a girl torments what she truly loves.... Lois and I have spoken much of you together----" She turned her head. "Where are you, sweeting?"

Lois came from behind the blanket and knelt down so close to me that the fragrance of her freshened the air; and once again, as it happened at the first day's meeting in Westchester, the same thrill invaded me. And I thought of the wild rose that starlight night, and how fitly was it her symbol and her flower.

Lana looked at us both, unsmiling; then drew her hands from mine and crook'd her arms behind her neck, cradling her head on them, looking at us both all the while. Presently her lids drooped on her white cheeks.

When we rose on tiptoe, I thought she was asleep, but Lois was not certain; and as we crept out onto the rifle-platform and seated ourselves in a sheltered corner under the parapet, she said uneasily:

"Lanette is a strange maid, Euan. At first I knew she disliked me. Then, of a sudden, one day she came to me and clung like a child afraid. And we loved from that minute.... It is strange."

"Is she ill?"

"In mind, I think."

"Why?"

"I do not know, Euan."

"Is it love, think you--her disorder?"

"I do not know, I tell you. Once I thought it was--that. But knew not how to be certain."

"Does Boyd still court her?"

"No--I do not know," she said with a troubled look.

"Is it that affair which makes her unhappy?"

"I thought so once. They were ever together. Then she avoided him--or seemed to. It was Betty Bleecker who interfered between them. For Mrs. Bleecker was very wrathful, Euan, and Lana's indiscretions madded her.... There was a scene.... So Boyd came no more, save when other officers came, which was every day. Some-how I have never been certain that he and Lana did not meet in secret when none suspected."

"Have you proof?" I asked, cold with rage.

She shook her head, and her gaze grew vague and remote. After a while she seemed to put away her apprehensions, and, smiling, she turned to me, challenging me with her clear, sunny eyes:

"Come, Euan, you shall do me reason, now that my curly pate is innocent of powder, no French red to tint my lips and hide my freckles, and but a linsey-wool-sey gown instead of chintz and silk to cover me! So tell me honestly, does not the enchantment break that for a little while seemed to hold you near me?"

"Do you forget," said I, "that I first saw my enchantress in rags and tattered shoon?"

"Oh!" she said, tossing her pretty head. "Extremes attract all men. But now in this sober and common guise of every day, I am neither Cinderella nor yet the Princess--merely a frowsy, rustic, freckled maid with a mouth somewhat too large for beauty, and the clipped and curly poll of a careless boy. And I desire to know, once for all, how I now suit you, Euan."

"You are perfection--once for all."

"I? What obstinate foolishness you utter! In all seriousness--"

"You are--more beautiful than ever--in all seriousness!"

"What folly!" She began to laugh nervously, then shrugged her shoulders, adding: "This young man is plainly partizan and deaf to reason."

"Being in love."

"You! In love! What nonsense!"

"Do you doubt it?"

"Oh!" she said carelessly. "You are in love with love--as all men are--and not particularly in love with me. Men, my dear Euan, are gamblers. When first you saw me in tatters, you laid a wager with yourself that I'd please you in silks. A gay hazard! A sporting wager! And straight you dressed me up to suit you; and being a man, and therefore conceited, you could scarcely admit that you had lost your wager to your better senses. Could you? But now you shall admit that in this frowsy, woollen gown the magic of both Cinderella and the Princess vanishes with yesterday's enchantment, and, instead of Chloe, pink and simpering, only a sturdy comrade stands revealed who now, as guerdon for the future, strikes hands with you--like this! Koue!" And with the clear and joyous cry on her lips she struck my palm violently with hers, nor winced under my quick-closing grip.

"Is all now clear and plain between us, Euan?" she inquired. And it seemed to me that her eagerness and fervour rang false.

"You can not love me, then?" I asked in a low voice.

"I? What has love to do with us--here in the woods--and I without knowledge and experience----"

"You do not love me, then?"

"I can not."

"Why?"

She made no answer, but bit her lip.

"You need not reply," said I. "Yet--that night I left Otsego--and when I passed you in the dark--I thought----"

"My heart was full that night! What comrade could feel less and still possess a human heart?" she said almost sullenly.

"Your letter--and mine--encouraged me to believe----"

"I know," she said, with the curt and almost breathless impatience of haste, "but have I ever denied our bond of intimacy, Euan? Closer bond have I with no man. But it must be a comrade's bond between us.... I meant to make that plain to you--and doubtless, my heart being full--and I but a girl--conveyed to you--by what I said--and did----"

"Lois! Is it not in you to love me as a woman loves a man?"

"I told you that when the time arrived I would doubtless be what you wish me to be----"

"You can love me, then?"

"How do I know? You perplex and vex me. Who else would I love but you? Who else is there in the world--except my mother?"

There was a silence; then I said:

"Has this passionate quest of her so wholly absorbed and controlled you that all else counts as nothing?"

"Yes, yes! You know it. You knew it at Otsego! Nothing else matters. I will not permit anything else to matter! And, lest you deem me cold, thankless, inhuman, ask of yourself, Euan, why such a lonely girl as I should close her eyes and stop her ears and lock her heart and--and turn her face away when the man--to whom she owes all--to whom she is--utterly devoted--urges her toward emotions--toward matters strange to her--and too profound as yet. So I ask you, for a time, to let what sleeps within us both lie sleeping, undisturbed. There is a love more natural, more imperious, more passionate still; and--it has led me here! And I will not confuse it with any other sentiment; nor share it with any man--not even with you--dear as you have become to me--lonely as I am,--no, not even with you will I share it! For I have vowed that I shall never slake my thirst with love save first in her dear embrace.... After these wistful, stark, and barren years--loveless, weary, naked, and unkind----" Suddenly she covered her face with her hands, bowing her head to her knees.

"Yet you bid me hope, Lois?" I asked under my breath.

She nodded.

"You make me happy beyond words," I whispered.

She looked up from her hands:

"Is that all you required to make you happy?"

"Can I ask more?"

"I--I thought men were more ruthless--more imperious and hotly impatient with the mistress of their hearts--if truly I am mistress of yours, as you tell me."

"I am impatient only for your happiness; ruthless only to secure it."

"For my happiness? Not for your own?"

"How can that come to me save when yours comes to you?"

"Oh!... I did not understand. I had not thought it mattered very greatly to men, so that they found their happiness--so that they found contentment in their sweethearts' yielding.... Then my surrender would mean nothing to you unless I yielded happily?"

"Nothing. Good God! In what school have you learned of love!"

She nodded thoughtfully, looking me in the eyes.

"What you tell me, Euan, is pleasant to think on. It reassures and comforts; nay, it is the sweetest thing you ever said to me--that you could find no happiness in my yielding unless I yield happily.... Why, Euan, that alone would win me--were it time. It clears up much that I have never understood concerning you.... Men have not used me gently.... And then you came.... And I thought you must be like the others, being a man, except that you are the only one to whom I was at all inclined--perhaps because you were from the beginning gentler and more honest with me.... What a way to win a woman's heart! To seek her happiness first of all!... Could you give me to another--if my happiness required it?"

"What else could I do, Lois?"

"Would you do that!" she demanded hotly.

"Have I any choice?"

"Not if your strange creed be sincere. Is it sincere?"

"There is no other creed for those who really love."

"You are wrong," she said angrily, looking at me with tightened lips.

"How wrong?"

"Because--I would not give you to another woman, though you cried out for her till the heavens fell!"

I began to laugh, but her eyes still harboured lightning.

"You should not go to her, whether or not you loved her!" she repeated. "I would not have it. I would not endure it!"

"Yet--if I loved another----"

"No! That is treason! Your happiness should be in me. And if you wavered I would hold you prisoner against your treacherous and very self!"

"How could you hold me?"

"What? Why--why--I----" She sat biting her scarlet lips and thinking, with straight brows deeply knitted, her greyish-purple eyes fixed hard on me. Then a slight colour stained her cheeks, and she looked elsewhere, murmuring: "I do not know how I would hold you prisoner. But I know I should do it, somehow."

"I know it, too," said I, looking at my ring she wore.

She blushed hotly: "It is well that you do, Euan. Death is the dire penalty if my prisoner escapes!" She hesitated, bit her lip, then added faintly: "Death for me, I mean." After a moment she slowly lifted her eyes to mine, and so still and clear were they that it seemed my regard plunged to the very depths of her.

"You do love me then," I said, taking her hand in mine.

Her face paled, and she caught her breath.

"Will you not wait--a little while--before you court me?" she faltered. "Will you not wait because I ask it of you?"

"Yes, I will wait."

"Nor speak of love--until----"

"Nor speak of love until you bid me speak."

"Nor--caress me--nor touch me--nor look in my eyes--this way----" Her hand had melted somehow closely into mine. We both were trembling now; and she withdrew her hand and slowly pressed it close against her heart, gazing at me in a white and childish wonder, as though dumb and reproachful of some wound that I had dealt her. And as I saw her there, so hurt and white and sweet, all quivering under the first swift consciousness of love, I trembled, too, with the fierce desire to take her in my arms and whisper what was raging in my heart of passionate assurance and devotion.

And I said nothing, nor did she. But presently the wild-rose tint crept back into her pale cheeks, and her head dropped, and she sat with eyes remote and vaguely sweet, her hands listless in her lap.

And I, my heart in furious protest, condemned to batter at its walls in a vain summons to the silent lips that should have voiced its every beat, remained mute in futile and impotent adoration of the miracle love had wrought under my very eyes.

Consigned to silence, condemned to patience super-human, I scarce knew how to conduct. And so cruelly the restraint cut and checked me that what with my perplexity, my happiness, and my wretchedness, I was in a plight.

No doubt the spectacle that my features presented--a very playground for my varying emotions--was somewhat startling to a maid so new at love. For, glancing with veiled eyes at me, presently her own eyes flew open wide. And:

"Euan!" she faltered. "Is aught amiss with you? Are you ill, dear lad? And have not told me?"

Whereat I was confused and hot and vexed; and I told her very plainly what it was that ailed me. And now mark! In place of an understanding and sympathy and a nice appreciation of my honourable discomfort, she laughed; and as her cheeks cooled she laughed the more, tossing back her pretty head while her mirth, now uncontrolled, rippled forth till the wild birds, excited, joined in with restless chirping, and a squirrel sprung his elfin rattle overhead.

"And that," said I, furious, "is what I get for deferring to your wishes! I've a mind to kiss you now!"

Breathless, her hands pressed to her breast, she looked at me, and made as though to speak, but laughter seized her and she surrendered to it helplessly.

Whereat I sprang to my feet and marched to the parapet, and she after me, laying her hand on my arm.

"Dear lad--I do not mean unkindness.... But it is all so new to me--and you are so tall a man to pull such funny faces--as though love was a stomach pain----" She swayed, helpless again with laughter, still clinging to my arm.

"If you truly find my features ridiculous----" I began, but her hand instantly closed my lips. I kissed it, however, with angry satisfaction, and she took it away hurriedly.

"Are you ashamed--you great, sulky and hulking boy--to take my harmless pleasantry so uncouthly? And how is this?" says she, stamping her foot. "May I not laugh a little at my lover if I choose? I will have you know, Euan, that I do what pleases me with mine own, and am not to sit in dread of your displeasure if I have a mind to laugh."

"It hurt me that you should make a mockery----"

"I made no mockery! I laughed. And you shall know that one day, please God, I shall laugh at you, plague you, torment you, and----" She looked at me smilingly, hesitating; then in a low voice: "All my caprices you shall endure as in duty bound.... Because your reward shall be--the adoration of one who is at heart--your slave already.... And your desires will ever be her own--are hers already, Euan.... Have I made amends?"

"More fully than----"

"Then be content," she said hastily, "and pull me no more lugubrious faces to fright me. Lord! What a vexing paradox is this young man who sits and glowers and gnaws his lips in the very moment of his victory, while I, his victim, tranquil and happy in defeat, sit calmly telling my thoughts like holy beads to salve my new-born soul. Ai-me! There are many things yet to be learned in this mad world of men."

We leaned over the parapet, shoulder to shoulder, looking down upon the river. The rain had ceased, but the sun gleamed only at intervals, and briefly.

After a moment she turned and looked at me with her beautiful and candid eyes--the most honest eyes I ever looked upon.

"Euan," she said in a quiet voice, "I know how hard it is for us to remain silent in the first flush of what has so sweetly happened to us both. I know how natural it is for you to speak of it and for me to listen. But if I were to listen, now, and when one dear word of yours had followed another, and the next another still; and when our hands had met, and then our lips--alas, dear lad, I had become so wholly yours, and you had so wholly filled my mind and heart that--I do not know, but I deeply fear--something of my virgin resolution might relax. The inflexible will--the undeviating obstinacy with which I have pursued my quest as far as this forest place, might falter, be swerved, perhaps, by this new and other passion--for I am as yet ignorant of its force and possibilities. I would not have it master me until I am free to yield. And that freedom can come happily and honourably to me only when I set my foot in Catharines-town. Do you understand me, Euan?"

"Yes."

"Then--we will not speak of love. Or even let the language of our eyes trouble each other with all we may not say and venture.... You will not kiss me, will you? Before I ask it of you?"

"No."

"Under no provocation? Will you--even if I should ask it?"

"No."

"I will tell you why, Euan. I have promised myself--it is odd, too, for I first thought of it the day I first laid eyes on you. I said to myself that, as God had kept me pure in spite of all--I should wish that the first one ever to touch my lips should be my mother. And I made that vow--having no doubt of keeping it--until I saw you again----"

"When?"

"When you came to me in Westchester before the storm."

"Then!" I exclaimed, amazed.

"Is it not strange, Euan? I know not how it was with me or why, all suddenly, I seemed to know--seemed to catch a sudden glimmer of my destiny--a brief, confusing gleam. And only seemed to fear and hate you--yet, it was not hate or fear, either.... And when I came to you in the rain--there at the stable shed--and when you followed, and gave your ring--such hell and heaven as awakened in my heart you could not fathom--nor could I--nor can I yet understand.... Do you think I loved you even then? Not knowing that I loved you?"

"How could you love me then?"

"God knows.... And afterward, on the rock in the moonlight--as you lay there asleep--oh, I knew not what so moved me to leave you my message and a wild-rose lying there.... It was my destiny--my destiny! I seemed to fathom it.... For when you spoke to me on the parade at the Middle Fort, such a thrill of happiness possessed me----"

"You rebuked and rebuked me, sweeting!"

"Because all my solicitude was for you, and how it might disgrace you."

"I could have knelt there at your ragged feet, in sight of all the fort!"

"Could you truly, Euan?"

"As willingly as I kneel at prayer!"

"How dear and gallant and sweet you are to me----" She broke off in dismay. "Ai-me! Heaven pity us both, for we are saying what should wait to be said, and have talked of love only while vowing not to do so!... Let loose my hand, Euan--that somehow has stolen into yours. Ai-me! This is a very maze I seem to travel in, with every pitfall hiding all I would avoid, and everywhere ambush laid for me.... Listen, dear lad, I am more pitifully at your mercy than I dreamed of. Be faithful to my faithless self that falters. Point out the path from your own strength and compassion.... I--I must find my way to Catharines-town before I can give myself to thoughts of you--to dreams of all that you inspire in me."

"Listen, Lois. This fort is as far as you may go."

"What!"

"Truly, dear maid. It is not alone the perils of an unknown country that must check you here. There is a danger that you know not of--that you never even heard of."

"A danger?"

"Worse. A threat of terrors hellish, inconceivable, terrible beyond words."

"What do you mean? The hatchet? The stake? Dear lad, may I not then venture what you soldiers brave so lightly?"

"It is not what we brave that threatens you!"

"What then?" she asked, startled.

"Dear did you ever learn that you are a 'Hidden Child'?"

"What is that, Euan?"

"Then you do not know?"

She shook her head.

And so I told her; told her also all that we had guessed concerning her; how that her captive mother, terrified by Amochol and his red acolytes, had concealed her, consecrated her, and, somehow, had found a runner to carry her beyond the doors of the Long House to safety.

This runner must have written the Iroquois message which I had read amid the corn-husks of her garret. It was all utterly plain and horrible now, to her and to myself.

As for the moccasins, the same faithful runner must have carried them to her, year after year, and taken back with him to the desolate mother the assurance that her child was living and still undiscovered and unharmed by Amochol.

All this I made plain to her; and I also told her that I, too, was of the Hidden Ones; and made it most clear to her who I really was. And I told her of the Cat-People, and of the Erie, and how the Sorcerer had defied us and boasted that the Hidden Child should yet die strangled upon the altar of Red Amochol.

She was quiet and very pale while I was speaking, and at moments her grey eyes widened with the unearthly horror of the thing; but never a tremour touched her, nor did lid or lips quiver or her gaze falter.

And when I had done she remained silent, looking out over the river at our feet, which was now all crinkling with the sun's bright network through the tracery of leaves.

"There is a danger to you," I said, "which will not cease until this army has left the Red Priest dead amid the sacrilegious ashes of his own vile altar. My Indians have made a vow to leave no Erie, no blasphemous and perverted priest alive. Amochol, the Wyoming Witch, the Toad-Woman--all that accursed spawn of Frontenac must die.

"Major Parr is of the same opinion; Clinton sees the importance of this, having had the sense to learn of Amherst how to stop the Seneca demons with a stout hempen rope. Two Sachems he hung, and the whole nation cowed down in terror of him while his authority remained.

"But Amherst left us; and the yelps of the Toad-Woman aroused the Sorcerers from their torpor. But I swear to you by St. Catharine, who is the saint of the Iroquois also, that the sway of Amochol shall end, and that he shall lie on his own bloody altar, nor die there before he sees the flames of Catharines-town touch the very heaven of an affronted God!"

"Can you do this?"

"With God's help and General Sullivan's," I said cheerfully. "For I daily pray to the One, and I have the promise of the other that before our marching army alarms Catharines-town, I and my Indians and Boyd and his riflemen shall strike the Red Priest there at the Onon-hou-aroria."

"What is that, Euan?"

"Their devil-rites--an honest feast which they have perverted. It was the Dream

Feast, Lois, but Amochol has made of it an orgy unspeakable, where human sacrifices are offered to the Moon Witch, Atensi, and to Leshi and the Stone-Throwers, and the Little People--many of which were not goblins and ghouls until Amochol so decreed them."

"When is this feast to be held in Catharines-town?"

"On the last day of this month. Until then you must not leave this camp; and after the army marches you must not go outside this fort. Amochol's arm is long. His acolytes are watching. And now I think you understand at last."

She nodded. Presently she rested her pale cheek on her arms and looked at the reddening edges of the woods. Northwest lay Catharines-town, so Mayaro said. And into the northwest her grey eyes now gazed, calmly and steadily, while the sun went out behind the forest and the high heavens were plumed with fire.

Under us the river ran, all pink and primrose, save where deep, glassy shadows bounded it under either bank. The tips of the trees glowed with rosy flame, faded to ashes, then, burnt out, stood once more dark and serrated against the evening sky.

Suddenly an unearthly cry rang out from somewhere close to the river bank up stream. Instantly a sentry on the parapet near us fired his piece.

"Oh, God! What is it!" faltered Lois, grasping my arm. But I sprang for the ladder and ran down it; and the scattered soldiers and officers below on the parade were already running some grasping their muskets, others drawing pistols and hangers.

We could hear musketry firing ahead, and drums beating to arms in our camp behind us.

"The cattle-guard!" panted an officer at my elbow as we ran up stream along the river-bank. "The Senecas have made their kill again, God curse them!"

It was so. Out of the woods came running our frightened cattle, with the guard plodding heavily on their flanks; and in the rear two of our soldiers urged them on with kicks and blow; two more retreated backward, facing the dusky forest with levelled muskets, and a third staggered beside them, half carrying, half trailing a man whose head hung down crimsoning the leaves as it dragged over them.

He had been smoking a cob pipe when the silent assassin's hatchet struck him, and the pipe now remained clenched between his set teeth. At first, for the dead leaves stuck to him, we could not see that he had been scalped, but when we turned him over the loose and horrible features, all wrinkled where the severed brow-muscles had released the skin, left us in no doubt.

"This man never uttered that abominable cry," I said, shuddering. "Is there yet another missing from the guard?"

"Oh, no, sir," said the soldier who had dragged him. "That there was a heifer bawling when them devils cut her throat."

He stood scratching his head and gazing blankly down at his dead comrade.

"Jesus," he drawled. "What be I a-goin' for to tell his woman now?"

CHAPTER XVI
LANA HELMER

Our Sunday morning gun had scarce been fired when from up the river came the answering thunder of artillery. Thirteen times did the distant cannon bellow their salute, announcing Clinton's advance, our camp swarmed like an excited hive, mounted officers galloping, foot officers running, troops tumbling out as the drums rattled the "general" in every regimental bivouac.

Colonel Proctor's artillery band marched out toward the landing place as I entered No. 2 Block-House and ran up the ladder, and I heard the ford-guard hurrahing and the garrison troops on the unfinished parapets answering them with cheer after cheer.

At my loud rapping on the flooring, Lois opened the trap for me, her lovely, youthful features flushed with excitement; Lana, behind her, beckoned me; and I sprang up into the loft and paid my duty to them both.

"What a noble earthquake of artillery up the river!" said Lois. "Butler has no cannon, has he?"

"Not even a grasshopper!" said I gaily. "Those cannon shot are Clinton's how d'ye do!"

"Poor's guns, were they not?" asked Lana, striving to smile. "And that means you march away and leave us with 'The World Turned Upside Down!'" And she shrugged her shoulders and whistled a bar of the old-time British air.

"Come to the parapet!" said Lois impatiently. "For the last few minutes there has been a sound in the woods--very far away, Euan--yet, if one could hear so far I would swear that I heard the conch-horn of your rifles!"

"Did I not tell you she knew it well?" said Lana with her pallid smile, as we opened the massive guard-door, squeezed through the covered way, and came out along the rifle-platform among our noisy soldiers.

"Listen!" murmured Lois, close at my elbow. "There! It comes again! Do you not hear it, Euan! That low, long, sustained and heart-thrilling undertone droning in the air through all this tumult!"

And presently I heard the sound--the wondrous melancholy, yet seductive music of our conch-horn. Its magic call set my every pulse a-throbbing. All the alluring mystery and solitude, all the sorrow of the wilderness were in those long-drawn blasts; all the enchantment of the woodland, too, calling, calling to the sons of the forest, riflemen, hunter, Coureur-de-Bois.

For its elfin monotone was the very voice of the forest itself--the deep, sweet whisper of virgin wilds, sacred, impenetrable, undefiled, tempting forever the sons of men.

And now, across the misty river, there was a great tumult of shouting as the first Otsego batteaux came into view; louder boomed our jolly cohorn, leaping high in its sulphurous powder-cloud; and the artillery band at the landing began to play "Iunadilla," which so deeply pleasured me that I forgot and caught Lois's hands between my own and pressed them there while her shoulder trembled against mine, and her breath came faster as the music swung into "The Huron" with a barbaric clash of cymbals.

It was a wondrous spectacle to see the navy of our Right Wing coming on, the waves slapping on bow and quarter--two hundred and ten loaded batteaux in line falling grandly down with the smooth and sunlit current, three men to every boat. Then, opposite, a wild flurry of bugle-horns announced our light infantry; and on they came, our merry General Hand riding ahead. And we saw him dismount, fling his bridle to an orderly, and lifting his sword and belt above his head, wade straight into the ford. And Asa Chapman and Justus Gaylord guided him.

After these came the light troops in their cocked hats, guided by Frederick Eveland; then a dun-coloured and dusty column emerged from the brilliant green of the woods, a mass of tossing fringes and ringed coon-tails and flashing rifle-barrels.

"The Rifles! hurrah for Morgan's men! Ha-i! The Eleventh Virginia!" roared the soldiery all about us, while Lois tightened her arm around mine and almost crushed my fingers with her own.

"There is Major Parr--and Captain Simpson--oh, and yonder minces my macaroni Ensign!" cried Lois, as the brown column swung straight into the ford, every rifle lifted, powder-horn and cartouche-box high swinging and glittering in the sun.

I turned to look for Lana; and first caught sight of the handsome wench, Dolly Glenn. And, following her restless gaze, I saw that Boyd had come up to the rifle-platform to join Lana, and that they stood together at a little distance from us. Also, I noticed that Lana's hand was resting an his arm. In sharp contrast to the excited, cheering soldiery thronging the platform, the attitude of these two seemed dull and spiritless; and Boyd looked more frequently at her than on the stirring pageant below; and once, under cover of the movement and tumult, I saw her pale cheek press for a moment against his green fringed shoulder cape--lightly--only for one brief moment. Yonder was no coquetry, no caprice of audacity. There was a heart there as heavy as the cheek was pale. It was love and nothing less--the pitiful devotion of a lass in love whose lover marches on the morrow. Lord--Lord! Had we but known!

As I stood beside Lois, I could not refrain from glancing toward them at moments, not meaning to spy, yet somehow held fascinated and troubled by what I had seen; for it seemed plain to me that if there was love there, little of happiness flavored it. Also, whenever I looked at them always I saw Dolly Glenn watching Boyd out of her darkly beautiful and hostile eyes.

And afterward, when our big riflemen marched on to the parade below, and we all hastened down, and the whole fort was a hubbub of cries and cheers and the jolly voices of friends greeting friends--even then I could scarce keep my eyes from these two and from the Glenn girl. And I was glad when a large, fat dame came a-waddling, who proved to be Mrs. Sabin; and she had a cold and baleful eye for Boyd, which his gay spirits and airy blandishments neither softened nor abated.

Lois made me known to her very innocently and discreetly, and I made her my best manners; but to my mortification, the disdain in her gaze increased, as did her stiffness with Boyd and her chilling hauteur. Lord! Here was no friend to men--at least, no friend to young men! That I comprehended in a trice; and my chagrin was nothing mended as I caught a sly glance from the merry and slightly malicious eyes of Boyd.

"Her husband is a fussy fat-head and she's a basalisk," he whispered. "I thought she'd bite my head of when the ladies came on under my protection."

She was more square and heavily solid than fat, like a squat block-house; and as I stole another glance at her I wondered how she was to mount the ladder and get her through the trap above. And by heaven! When the moment came to try it, she could not. She attempted it thrice; and the third effort hung her there, wedged in, squeaking like a fat doe-rabbit--and Boyd and I, stifling with laughter, now pushing, now tugging at her fat ankles. And finally got her out upon the ladder platform, crimson and speechless in her fury; and we lingered not, but fled together, not daring to face the lady at whose pudgy and nether limbs we had pulled so heartily.

"Lord!" said Boyd. "If she complains of us to her Commissary husband, there'll be a new issue not included in his department!"

And it doubled us with laughter to think on't, so that for lack o' breath I sat down upon a log to hold my aching sides.

"Now, she'll be ever on their heels," muttered Boyd, "hen-like, malevolent, and unaccountable. No man dare face and flout that lady, whose husband also is utterly subjected. It was Betty Bleecker who set her on me. Well, so no more of yonder ladies save in her bristling presence."

Yet, as it happened, one thing barred Mistress Sabin from a perpetual domination and sleepless supervision of her charges, and that was the trap-door. Through it she could not force herself, nor could she come around by the guard-door, for the covered way would not admit her ample proportions. She could but mount her guard at the ladder's foot. And there were two exits to that garret room.

That day I would have messed with my own people, Major Parr inviting me, but that our General had all the Otsego officers to dine with him at headquarters, and a huge punch afterward, from which I begged to be excused, as it was best that I look to my Indians when any rum was served in camp.

Boyd came later to the bush-hut, overflushed with punch, saying that he had drawn sixty pair of shoes for his men, to spite old Sabin, and meant to distribute them with music playing; and that afterward I was to join him at the fort as he had orders for himself and for me from the General, and desired to confer with me concerning them.

Later came word from him that he had a headache and would confer with me on the morrow. Neither did I see Lois again that evening, a gill of rum having been issued to every man, and I sticking close as a wood-tick to my red comrades-- indeed, I had them out after sunset to watch the cattle-guard, who were in a sorry pickle, sixty head having strayed and two soldiers missing. And the manoeuvres of that same guard did ever sicken me.

It proved another bloody story, too, for first we found an ox with throat cut; and, it being good meat, we ordered it taken in. And then, in the bushes ahead, a soldier begins a-bawling that the devil is in his horses, and that they have run back into the woods.

I heard him chasing them, and shouted for him to wait, but the poor fool pays no heed, but runs on after his three horses; and soon he screams out:

"God a'mighty!" And, "Christ have mercy!"

With that I blow my ranger's whistle, and my Indians pass me like phantoms in the dusk, and I hot-foot after them; but it was too late to save young Elliott, who lay there dead and already scalped, doubled up in the bed of a little brook, his clenched hand across his eyes and a Seneca knife in his smooth, boyish throat.

Late that night the Sagamore started, chased, and quickly cornered something in a clump of laurel close to the river bank; and my Indians gathered around like fiercely-whining hounds. It was starlight, but too dark to see, except what was shadowed against the river; so we all lay flat, waiting, listening for whatever it was, deer or bear or man.

Then the Night Hawk, who stood guard at the river, uttered the shrill Oneida view-halloo; and into the thicket we all sprang crashing, and strove to catch the creature alive; but the Sagamore had to strike to save his own skull; and out of the bushes we dragged one of Amochol's greasy-skinned assassins, still writhing, twisting, and clawing as we flung him heavily and like a scotched snake upon the river sand, where the Mohican struck him lifeless and ripped the scalp from his oiled and shaven head.

The Erie's lifeless fist still clutched the painted casse-tete with which he had aimed a silently murderous blow at the Sagamore. Grey-Feather drew the death-maul from the dead warrior's grasp, and handed it to the Siwanois.

Then Tahoontowhee, straightening his slim, naked figure to its full and graceful height, raised himself on tiptoe and, placing his hollowed hands to his cheeks, raised the shuddering echoes with the most terrific note an Indian can utter.

As the forest rang with the fierce Oneida scalp-yell, very far away along the low-browed mountain flank we could hear the far tinkle of hoof and pebble, where the stolen horses moved; and out of the intense blackness of the hills came faintly the answering defiance of the Senecas, and the hideous miauling of the Eries, quavering, shuddering, dying into the tremendous stillness of the Dark Empire which we had insulted, challenged, and which we were now about to brave.

Once more Tahoontowhee's piercing defiance split the quivering silence; once more the whining panther cry of the Cat-People floated back through the far darkness.

Then we turned away toward our pickets; and, as we filed into our lines, I could smell the paint and oil on the scalp that the Siwanois had taken. And it smelled rank enough, God wot!

About nine on Monday morning the entire camp was alarmed by irregular and heavy firing along the river; but it proved to be my riflemen clearing their pieces; which did mortify General Clinton, and was the subject of a blunt order from headquarters, and a blunter rebuke from Major Parr to Boyd, who, I am inclined to think, did do this out of sheer deviltry. For that schoolboy delight of mischief which never, while he lived, was entirely quenched, was ever sparkling in those handsome and roving eyes of his. For which our riflemen adored him, being by every instinct reckless and irresponsible themselves, and only held to discipline by their worship of Daniel Morgan, and the upright character and the iron rigour of Major Parr.

Not that the 11th Virginia ever shrank from duty. No regiment in the Continental army had a prouder record. But the men of that corps were drawn mostly from those free-limbed, free-thinking, powerful, headlong, and sometimes ruthless backwoodsmen who carried law into regions where none but Nature's had ever before existed. And the law they carried was their own.

It was a reproach to us that we scalped our red enemies. No officer in the corps could prevent these men from answering an Indian's insult with another of the same kind. And there remained always men in that command who took their scalps as carelessly as they clipped a catamount of ears and pads.

As for my special detail, I understood perfectly that I could no more prevent my Indians from scalping enemies of their own race than I could whistle a wolf-pack up wind. But I could stop their lifting the hair from a dead man of my own race, and had made them understand very plainly that any such attempt would be instantly punished as a personal insult to myself. Which every warrior understood. And I have often wondered why other officers commanding Indians, and who were ever complaining that they could not prevent scalping of white enemies, did not employ this argument, and enforce it, too. For had one of my men, no matter which one, disobeyed, I would have had him triced up in a twinkling and given a hundred lashes.

Which meant, also, that I would have had to kill him sooner or later.

There was a stink of rum in camp that morning and it is a quaffing beverage which while I like to drink it in punch, the smell of it abhors me. And ever and anon my Indians lifted their noses, sniffling the tainted air; so that I was glad when a note was handed me from Boyd saying that we were to take a forest stroll with my Indians around the herd-guard, during which time he would unfold to me his plans.

So I started for the fort, my little party carrying rifles and sidearms but no packs; and there waited across the ditch in the sunshine my Indians, cross-legged in a row on the grass, and gravely cracking and munching the sweet, green hazelnuts with which these woods abound.

On the parade inside the fort, and out o' the tail of my eye, I saw Mistress Sabin knitting on a rustic settle at the base of Block-house No. 2, and Captain Sabin beside her writing fussily in a large, leather-bound book.

She did not know that the dovecote overhead was now empty, and that the pigeons had flown; nor did I myself suspect such a business, even when from the woods behind me came the low sound of a ranger's whistle blown very softly. I turned my head and saw Boyd beckoning; and arose and went thither, my Indians trotting at my heels.

Then, as I came up and stood to offer the officer's salute, Lois stepped from behind a tree, laughing and laying her finger across her lips, but extending her other hand to me.

And there was Lana, too, paler it seemed to me than ever, yet sweet and simple in her greeting.

"The ladies desire to see our cattle," said Boyd, "The herd-guard is doubled, our pickets trebled, and the rounds pass every half hour. So it is safe enough, I think."

"Yet, scarce the country for a picnic," I said, looking uneasily at Lois.

"Oh, Broad-brim, Broad-brim!" quoth she. "Is there any spice in life to compare to a little dash o' danger?"

Whereat I smiled at her heartily, and said to Boyd:

"We pass not outside our lines, of course."

"Oh, no!" he answered carelessly. Which left me still reluctant and unconvinced. But he walked forward with Lana through the open forest, and I followed beside Lois; and, without any signal from me my Indians quietly glided out ahead, silently extending as flankers on either side.

"Do you notice what they are about?" said I sourly. "Even here within whisper of the fort?"

"Are you not happy to see me, Euan?" she cooed close to my ear.

"Not here; inside that log curtain yonder."

"But there is a dragon yonder," she whispered, with mischief adorable in her sparkling eyes; then slipped hastily beyond my reach, saying: "Oh, Euan! Forget not our vows, but let our conduct remain seemly still, else I return."

I had no choice, for we were now passing our inner pickets, where a line of bush-huts, widely set, circled the main camp. There were some few people wandering along this line--officers, servants, boatmen, soldiers off duty, one or two women.

Just within the lines there was a group of people from which a fiddle sounded; and I saw Boyd and Lana turn thither; and we followed them.

Coming up to see who was making such scare-crow music, Lana said in a low voice to us:

"It's an old, old man--more than a hundred years old, he tells us--who has lived on the Ouleout undisturbed among the Indians until yesterday, when we burnt the village. And now he has come to us for food and protection. Is it not pitiful?"

I had a hard dollar in my pouch, and went to him and offered it. Boyd had Continental money, and gave him a handful.

He was not very feeble, this ancient creature, yet, except among Indians who live sometimes for more than a hundred years, I think I never before saw such an aged visage, all cracked into a thousand wrinkles, and his little, bluish eyes peering out at us through a sort of film.

To smile, he displayed his shrivelled gums, then picked up his fiddle with an agility somewhat surprising, and drew the bow harshly, saying in his cracked voice that he would, to oblige us, sing for us a ballad made in 1690; and that he himself had ridden in the company of horse therein described, being at that time thirteen years of age.

And Lord! But it was a doleful ballad, yet our soldiers listened, fascinated, to his squeaking voice and fiddle; and I saw the tears standing in Lois's eyes, and Lana's lips a-quiver. As for Boyd, he yawned, and I most devoutly wished us all elsewhere, yet lost no word of his distressing tale:

> "God prosper long our King and Queen,
> Our lives and safeties all;
> A sad misfortune once there did
> Schenectady befall.
>   "From forth the woods of Canady
> The Frenchmen tooke their way,
> The people of Schenectady
> To captivate and slay.
>   "They march for two and twenty daies,
> All thro' ye deepest snow;
> And on a dismal winter night
> They strucke ye cruel blow.
>   "The lightsome sunne that rules the day
> Had gone down in the West;
> And eke the drowsie villagers
> Had sought and found their reste.
>   "They thought they were in safetie all,
> Nor dreamt not of the foe;
> But att midnight they all swoke

In wonderment and woe.
  "For they were in their pleasant beddes,
And soundlie sleeping, when
Each door was sudden open broke
By six or seven menne!
  "The menne and women, younge and olde,
And eke the girls and boys,
All started up in great affright
Att the alarming noise.
  "They then were murthered in their beddes
Without shame or remorse;
And soon the floors and streets were strew'd
With many a bleeding corse.
  "The village soon began to blaze,
Which shew'd the horrid sight;
But, O, I scarce can beare to tell
The mis'ries of that night.
  "They threw the infants in the fire,
The menne they did not spare;
But killed all which they could find,
Tho' aged or tho' fair.

  "But some run off to Albany
And told the doleful tale;
Yett, tho' we gave our chearful aid,
It did not much avail.
  "And we were horribly afraid,
And shook with terror, when
They gave account the Frenchmen were
More than a thousand menne.
  "The news came on a Sabbath morn,
Just att ye break o' day;
And with my companie of horse

I galloped away.
  "Our soldiers fell upon their reare,
And killed twenty-five;
Our young menne were so much enrag'd
They took scarce one alive.
  "D'Aillebout them did command,
Which were but thievish rogues,
Else why did they consent to goe
With bloodye Indian dogges?
  "And here I end my long ballad,
The which you just heard said;
And wish that it may stay on earth
Long after I be dead."

The old man bowed his palsied head over his fiddle, struck with his wrinkled thumb a string or two; and I saw tears falling from his almost sightless eyes.

Around him, under the giant trees, his homely audience stood silent and spellbound. Many of his hearers had seen with their own eyes horrors that compared with the infamous butchery at Schenectady almost a hundred years ago. Doubtless that was what fascinated us all.

But Boyd, on whom nothing doleful made anything except an irritable impression, drew us away, saying that it was tiresome enough to fight battles without being forced to listen to the account of 'em afterward; at which, it being true enough, I laughed. And Lois looked up winking away her tears with a quick smile. As for Lana, her face was tragic and colourless as death itself. Seeing which, Boyd said cheerfully:

"What is there in all the world to sigh about, Lanette? Death is far away and the woods are green."

"The woods are green," repeated Lana under her breath, "yet, there are many within call who shall not live to see one leaf fall."

"Why, what a very dirge you sing this sunny morning!" he protested, still laughing; and I, too, was surprised and disturbed, for never had I heard Lana Helmer speak in such a manner.

"'Twas that dreary old fiddler," he added with a shrug. "Now, God save us all, from croaking birds of every plumage, and give us to live for the golden moment."

"And for the future," said Lois.

"The devil take the future," said Boyd, his quick, careless laugh ringing out again. "Today I am lieutenant, and Loskiel, here, is ensign. Tomorrow we may be captains or corpses. But is that a reason for pulling a long face and confessing every sin?"

"Have you, then, aught to confess?" asked Lois, in pretense of surprise.

"I? Not a peccadillo, my pretty maid--not a single one. What I do, I do; and ask no leniency for the doing. Therefore, I have nothing to confess."

Lana stopped, bent low over a forest blossom, and touched her face to it. Her cheeks were burning. All about us these frail, snowy blossoms grew, and Lois gathered one here and yonder while Boyd and I threw ourselves down on a vast, deep bed of moss, under which a thread of icy water trickled.

Ahead of us, in plain view, stood one of our outer picket guards, and below in a wide and bowl-shaped hollow, running south to the river, we could see cattle moving amid the trees, and the rifle-barrel of a herd guard shining here and there.

My Indians on either flank advanced to the picket line, and squatted there, paying no heed to the challenge of the sentinels, until Boyd was obliged to go forward and satisfy the sullen Pennsylvania soldiery on duty there.

He came back in his graceful, swinging stride, chewing a twig of black-birch, his thumbs hooked in his belt, damning all Pennsylvanians for surly dogs.

I pointed out that many of them were as loyal as any man among us; and he said he meant the Quakers only, and cursed them for rascals, every one. Again I reminded him that Alsop Hunt was a Quaker; and he said that he meant not the Westchester folk, but John Penn's people, Tories, every one, who would have hired ruffians to do to the Connecticut people in Forty Fort what later was done to them by Indians and Tory rangers.

Lana protested in behalf of the Shippens in Philadelphia, but Boyd said they were all tarred with the same brush, and all were selfish and murderous, lacking only the courage to bite--yes, every Quaker in Penn's Proprietary--the Shippens, Griscoms, Pembertons, Norrises, Whartons, Baileys, Barkers, Storys--'"Every damned one o' them!" he said, "devised that scheme for the wanton and cruel massacre of the Wyoming settlers, and meant to turn it to their own pecuniary profit!"

He was more than partly right; yet, knowing many of these to be friends and kinsmen to Lana Helmer, he might have more gracefully remained silent. But Boyd had not that instinctive dread of hurting others with ill-considered facts; he blurted out all truths, whether timely or untimely, wherever and whenever it suited him.

For the Tory Quakers he mentioned I had no more respect than had he, they being neither fish, flesh, nor fowl, but a smooth, sanctimonious and treacherous lot, more calculated to work us mischief because of their superior education and financial means. Indeed, they generally remained undisturbed by the ferocious Iroquois allies of our late and gentle King; secure in their property and lives while all around them men, women, and little children fell under the dripping hatchets.

"Had I my say," remarked Boyd loudly, "I'd take a regiment and scour me out these rattlesnakes from the Proprietary, and pack 'em off to prison, bag and baggage!"

Lana had knelt, making a cup of her hand, and was drinking from the silvery thread of water at our feet. Now, as Boyd spoke, she straightened up and cast a shower of sparkling drops in his face, saying calmly that she prayed God he might have the like done for him when next he needed a cooling off.

"Lanette," said he, disconcerted but laughing, "do you mean in hell or at the Iroquois stake?"

Whereupon Lana flushed and said somewhat violently that he should not make a jest of either hell or stake; and that she for one marvelled at his ill-timed pleasantries and unbecoming jests.

So here was a pretty quarrel already sur le tapis; but neither I nor Lois interposed, and Lana, pink and angry, seated herself on the moss and gazed steadily at our watchful Indians. But in her fixed gaze I saw the faint glimmer of tears.

After a moment Boyd got up, went down to her, and asked her pardon. She made no answer; they remained looking at each other for another second, then both smiled, and Boyd lay down at her feet, resting his elbow on the moss and his cheek on his hand, so that he could converse with me across her shoulder.

And first he cautioned both Lana and Lois to keep secret whatever was to be said between us two, then, nodding gaily at me:

"You were quite right, Loskiel, in speaking to the General about the proper trap for this Wizard-Sachem Amochol, who is inflaming the entire Seneca nation to such a fury."

"I know no other way to take and destroy him," said I.

"There is no other way. It must be done secretly, and by a small party manoeuvring ahead and independently of our main force."

"Are you to command?" I asked.

"I am to have that honour," he said eagerly, "and I take you, your savages, and twenty riflemen----"

"What is this?" said Lana sharply; but he lifted an impatient hand and went on in his quick, interested manner, to detail to me the plan he had conceived for striking Amochol at Catharines-town, in the very midst of the Onon-hou-aroria.

"Last night," he said, "I sent out Hanierri and Iaowania, the headquarters scouts; and I'm sorry I did, for they came in this morning with their tails between their legs, saying the forest swarmed with the Seneca scouts, and it was death to stir.

"And I was that disgusted--what with their cowardice and the aftermath of that headquarters punch--that I bade them go paint and sing their death-songs----"

"Oh, Lord! You should not lose your temper with an Indian!" I said, vexed at his indiscretion.

"I know it. I'll not interfere with your tame wolves, Loskiel. But Hanierri madded me; and now he's told Dominie Kirkland's praying Indians, and not one o' them will stir from Tioga--the chicken-hearted knaves! What do you think of that, Loskiel?"

"I am sorry. But we really need no other Indians than my Sagamore, the two Oneidas, and the Stockbridge, Yellow Moth, to do Amochol's business for him, if you and your twenty riflemen are going."

"I think as you do; and so I told the General, who wanted Major Parr to command and the entire battalion to march. 'Oh, Lord!' says I. 'Best bring Colonel Proctor's artillery band, also!' And was frightened afterward at what I said, with so little reflection and respect; but the General, who had turned red as a pippin, burst out laughing and says he: 'You are a damnably disrespectful young man, sir, but you and your friend Loskiel may suit yourselves concerning the taking of this same Amochol. Only have a care to take or destroy him, for if you do not, by God, you shall be detailed to the batteaux and cool your heels in Fort Sullivan until we return!'"

We both laughed heartily, and Boyd added:

"He said it to fright me for my impudence. Trust that man to know a man when he sees one!"

"Meaning yourself?" said I, convulsed.

"And you, too, Loskiel," he said so naively that Lois, too, laughed, exclaiming:

"What modest opinions of themselves have these two boys! Do you hear them, Lana, dubbing each other men?"

"I hear," said Lana listlessly.

Boyd plucked a long, feathery stalk, and with its tip caressed Lana's cheeks.

"Spiders!" said he. "Spinning a goblin veil for you!"

"I wish the veil of Fate were as transparent," said she.

"Would you see behind it if you could?"

She said under her breath:

"I sometimes dream I see behind it now."

"What do you see?" he asked.

She shook her head; but we all begged her to disclose her dreams, saying laughingly that as dreams were the most important things in the lives of all Indians, our close association with them had rendered us credulous.

"Come, Lanette," urged Boyd, "tell us what it is you see in dreams behind the veil."

She hesitated, shuddered:

"Flames--always flames. And a man in black with leaden buttons, whose face is always hidden in his cloak. But, oh! I know--I seem to know that he has no face at all, but is like a skull under his black cloak."

"A merry dream," said Boyd, laughing.

"Is there more to it?" asked Lois seriously.

"Yes.... Lieutenant Boyd is there, and he makes a sign--like this----"

"What!" exclaimed Boyd, sitting up, astounded. "Where did you learn that sign?"

"In my dream. What does it mean?"

"Make it no more, Lana," he said, in a curiously disturbed voice. "For wherever you have learned it--if truly from a dream, or from some careless fellow--of my own----" He hesitated, glanced at me. "You are not a Mason, Loskiel. And Lana has just given the Masonic signal of distress--having seen me give it in a dream. It is odd." He sat very silent for a moment, then lay down again at Lana's feet; and for a little while they conversed in whispers, as though forgetting that we were there at all, his handsome head resting against her knees, and her hand touching the hair on his forehead lightly at intervals.

After a few moments I rose and, with Lois, walked forward toward our picket line, from where we could see very plainly the great cattle herd among the trees along the river.

She said in a low and troubled voice:

"It has come so far, then, that Lana makes no longer a disguise of her sentiments before you and me. It seems as though they had bewitched each other--and find scant happiness in the mutual infatuation."

I said nothing.

"Is he not free to marry her?" asked Lois.

"Why, yes--I suppose he is--if she will have him," I said, startled by the direct question. "Why not?"

"I don't know. Once, at Otsego Camp I overheard bitter words between them--not from him, for he only laughed at what she said. It was in the dusk, close to our tent; and either they were careless or thought I slept.... And I heard her say that he was neither free nor fit to speak of marriage. And he laughed and vowed that he was as free and fit as was any man. 'No,' says she, 'there are other men like Euan Loskiel in the world.' 'Exceptions prove the case,' says he, laughing; and there was a great sob in her voice as she answered that such men as he were born to damn women. And he retorted coolly that it was such women as she who ever furnished the provocation, but that only women could lose their own souls, and that it was the same with men; but neither of 'em could or ever had contributed one iota toward the destruction of any soul except their own.... Then Lana came into our tent and stood looking down at me where I lay; and dimly through my lashes I could perceive the shadow of Boyd behind her on the tent wall, wavering, gigantic, towering to the ridge-pole as he set the camp-torch in its socket on the flooring." She passed her slim hand across her eyes. "It was like an unreal scene--a fevered vision of two phantoms in the smoky, lurid lustre of the torch. Boyd stood there dark against the light, edged with flickering flame as with a mantle, figure and visage scintilant with

Lucifer's own beauty--and Lana, her proud head drooping, and her sad, young eyes fixed on me--Oh, Euan!" She stood pressing down both eyelids with her fingers, motionless; then, with a quick-drawn breath and a brusque gesture, flung her arms wide and let them drop to her sides. "How can men follow what they call their 'fortune,' headlong, unheeding, ranging through the world as a hot-jowled hound ranges for rabbits? Are they never satiated? Are they never done with the ruthless madness? Does the endless chase with its intervals of killing never pall?"

"Hounds are hounds," I said slowly. "And the hound will chase his thousandth hare with all the unslaked eagerness that thrilled him when his first quarry fled before him."

"Why?"

But I shook my head in silence.

"Are you that way?"

"I have not been."

"The instinct then is not within you?"

"Yes, the instinct is.... But some hounds are trained to range only as far as their mistress, Old Dame Reason, permits. Others slip leash and take to the runways to range uncontrolled and mastered only by a dark and second self, urging them ever forward.... There are but two kinds of men, Lois--the self-disciplined, and the unbroken. But the raw nature of the two differed nothing at their birth."

She stood looking down at the distant cattle along the river for a while without speaking; then her hand, which hung beside her, sought mine and softly rested within my clasp.

"It is wonderful," she murmured, "that it has been God's pleasure I should come to you unblemished--after all that I have lived to learn and see. But more wonderful and blessed still it is to me to find you what you are amid this restless, lawless, ruthless world of soldiery--upright and pure in heart.... It seems almost, with us, as though our mothers had truly made of us two Hidden Children, white and mysterious within the enchanted husks, which only our own hands may strip from us, and reveal ourselves unsullied as God made us, each to the other--on our wedding morn."

I lifted her little hand and laid my lips to it, touching the ring. Then she bent timidly and kissed the rough gold circlet where my lips had rested. Somehow, a shaft of sunlight had penetrated the green roof above, and slanted across her hair, so that the lovely contour of her head was delicately edged with light.

* "Nene-nea-wen-ne, Lois!" I whispered passionately.[4]

* "Nen-ya-wen-ne, O Loskiel! Teni-non-wes."[5]

We stood yet a while together there, and I saw her lift her eyes and gaze straight ahead of us beyond our picket line, and remain so, gazing as though her regard could penetrate those dim and silent forest aisles to the red altar far beyond in unseen Catharines-town.

"When must you go?" she asked under her breath.

"The army is making ready today."

"To march into the Indian country?"

I nodded.

"When does it march?"

"On Friday. But that is not to be known at present."

"I understand. By what route do you go?"

"By Chemung."

"And then?"

"At Chemung we leave the army, Boyd and I. You heard."

"Yes, Euan."

I said, forcing myself to speak lightly:

"You are not to be afraid for us, Little Rosy Pigeon of the Forest. Follow me with your swift-winged thoughts and no harm shall come to me."

"Must you go?"

I laughed: * "Ka-teri-oseres, Lois."[6]

* "Wa-ka-ton-te-tsihon," she said calmly. "Wa-ka-ta-tiats-kon."[7]

Then I gave way to my increasing surprise:

"Wonder-child!" I exclaimed. "When and where have you learned to understand and answer me in the tongue of the Long House?"

---

4 "This thing shall happen, Lois!"

5 "It shall happen, O Loskiel! We love, thou and I."

6 "I am going to this war, Lois."

7 "I understand perfectly. I am resigned."

* "Kio-ten-se," she said with a faint smile.[8]

"For whom?"

"For my mother, Euan. Did you suppose I could neglect anything that might be useful in my life's quest? Who knows when I might need the tongue I am slowly learning to speak?... Oh, and I know so little, yet. Something of Algonquin the Mohican taught me; and with it a little of the Huron tongue. And now for nearly a month every day I have learned a little from the Oneidas at Otsego--from the Oneida girl whose bridal dress you bought to give to me. Do you remember her? The maid called Drooping Wings?"

"Yes--but--I do not understand. To what end is all this? When and where is your knowledge of the Iroquois tongue likely to aid you?"

She gave me a curious, veiled look--then turned her face away.

"You do not dream of following our army, do you?" I demanded. "Not one woman would be permitted to go. It is utterly useless for you to expect it, folly to dream of such a thing.... You and Lana are to go to Easton as soon as the heavier artillery is sent down the river, which will be the day we start--Friday. This frontier gypsying is ended--all this coquetting with danger is over now. The fort here is no place for you and Lana. Your visit, brief as it has been, is rash and unwarranted. And I tell you very plainly, Lois, that I shall never rest until you are at Easton, which is a stone town and within the borders of civilization. The artillery will be sent down by boat, and all the women and children are to go also. Neither Boyd nor I have told this to you and Lana, but----" I glanced over my shoulder. "I think he is telling her now."

Lois slowly turned and looked toward them. Evidently they no longer cared what others saw or thought, for Lana's cheek lay pressed against his shoulder, and his arm encircled her body.

We walked back, all together, to the fort, and left Lois and Lana at the postern; then Boyd and I continued on to my bush-hut, the Indians following.

Muffled drums of a regiment were passing, and an escort with reversed arms, to bury poor Kimball, Captain in Colonel Cilly's command, shot this morning through the heart by the accidental discharge of a musket in the careless hands of one of his own men.

---

8   "I am working for somebody."

We stood at salute while the slow cortege passed.

Said Boyd thoughtfully:

"Well, Kimball's done with all earthly worries. There are those who might envy him."

"You are not one," I said bluntly.

"I? No. I have not yet played hard enough in the jolly blind man's buff--which others call the game of life. I wear the bandage still, and still my hands clutch at the empty air, and in my ears the world's sweet laughter rings----" He smiled, then shrugged. "The charm of Fortune's bag is not what you pull from it, but what remains within."

"Boyd," I said abruptly. "Who is that handsome wench that followed us from Otsego?"

"Dolly Glenn?"

"That is her name."

"Lord, how she pesters me!" he said fretfully. "I chanced upon her at the Middle Fort one evening--down by the river. And what are our wenches coming to," he exclaimed impatiently, "that a kiss on a summer's night should mean to them more than a kiss on a night in summer!"

"She is a laundress, is she not?"

"How do I know? A tailoress, too, I believe, for she has patched and mended for me; and she madded me because she would take no pay. There are times," he added, "when sentiment is inconvenient----"

"Poor thing," I said.

"My God, why? When I slipped my arm around her she put up her face to be kissed. It was give and take, and no harm done--and the moon a-laughing at us both. And why the devil she should look at me reproachfully is more than I can comprehend."

"It seems a cruel business," said I.

"Cruel!"

"Aye--to awake a heart and pass your way a-whistling."

"Now, Loskiel," he began, plainly vexed, "I am not cruel by nature, and you know it well enough. Men kiss and go their way----"

"But women linger still."

"Not those I've known."

"Yet, here is one----"

"A silly fancy that will pass with her. Lord! Do you think a gentleman accountable to every pretty chit of a girl he notices on his way through life?"

"Some dare believe so."

He stared at me, then laughed.

"You are different to other men, of course," he said gaily. "We all understand that. So let it go----"

"One moment, Boyd. There is a matter I must speak of--because friendship and loyalty to a childhood friend both warrant it. Can you tell me why Lana Helmer is unhappy?"

A dark red flush surged up to the roots of his hair, and the muscles in his jaw tightened. He remained a moment mute and motionless, staring at me. But if my question, for the first moment, had enraged him, that quickly died out; and into his eyes there came a haggard look such as I had never seen there.

He said slowly:

"Were you not the man you are, Loskiel, I had answered in a manner you might scarcely relish. Now, I answer you that if Lana is unhappy I am more so. And that our unhappiness is totally unnecessary--if she would but listen to what I say to her."

"And what is it that you say to her?" I inquired as coolly as though his answer might not very easily be a slap with his fringed sleeve across my face.

"I have asked her to marry me," he said. "Do you understand why I tell you this?"

I shook my head.

"To avoid killing you at twenty paces across the river.... I had rather tell you than do that."

"So that you have told me," said I, "the reason for your telling matters nothing. And my business with you ends with your answer.... Only--she is my friend, Boyd--a playmate of pleasant days. And if you can efface that wretchedness from her face--brighten the quenched sparkle of her eyes, paint her cheeks with rose again--do it, in God's name, and make of me a friend for life."

"Shall I tell you what has gone amiss--from the very first there at Otsego?"

"No--that concerns not me----"

"Yes, I shall tell you! It's that she knew about--the wench here--Dolly Glenn."

"Is that why she refuses you and elects to remain unhappy?" I said incredulously.

"Yes--I can say no more.... You are right, Loskiel, and such men as I are wrong--utterly and wretchedly wrong. Sooner or later comes the bolt of lightning. Hell! To think that wench should hurl it!"

"But what bolt had she to hurl?" said I, astonished.

He reddened, bit his lip savagely, made as though to speak, then, with a violent gesture, turned away.

A few moments later a cannon shot sounded. It was the signal for striking tents and packing up; and in every regiment hurry and confusion reigned and the whole camp swarmed with busy soldiery.

But toward evening orders came to unpack and pitch tents again; and whether it had been an exercise to test the quickness of our army for marching, or whether some accident postponed the advance, I do not know.

All that evening, being on duty with my Indians to watch the cattle-guard, I did not see Lois.

The next day I was ordered to take the Indians a mile or two toward Chemung and lie there till relieved; so we went very early and remained near the creek on observation, seeing nothing, until evening, when the relief came with Hanierri and three Stockbridges. These gave us an account that another soldier had been shot in camp by the accidental discharge of a musket, and that the Light Troops had marched out of their old encampment and had pitched tents one hundred rods in advance.

Also, they informed us that the flying hospital and stores had been removed to the fort, and that Colonel Shreve had taken over the command of that place.

By reason of the darkness, we were late in getting into camp, so again that day I saw nothing of Lois.

On Wednesday it rained heavily about eleven o'clock, and the troops made no movement. Some Oneidas came in and went to headquarters. My Indians did not seem to know them.

I was on duty all day at headquarters, translating into Iroquois for the General a speech which he meant to deliver to the Tuscaroras on his return through Easton. The rain ceased late in the afternoon. Later, an express came through from Fort Pitt; and before evening orders had gone out that the entire army was to march at eight o'clock in the morning.

Morning came with a booming of cannon. We did not stir.

Toward eleven, however, the army began to march out as though departing in earnest; but as Major Parr remained with the Rifles, I knew something had gone amiss.

Yet, the other regiments, including my own, marched away gaily enough, with music sounding and colours displayed; and the garrison, boatmen, artillerymen, and all the civil servants and women and children waved them adieu from the parapets of the fort.

But high water at Tioga ford, a mile or two above, soon checked them, and there they remained that night. As I was again on duty with Hanierri and the Dominie, I saw not Lois that day.

Friday was fair and sunny, and the ground dried out. And all the morning I was with Dominie Kirkland and Hanierri, translating, transcribing, and writing out the various speeches and addresses left for me by General Sullivan.

Runners came in toward noon with news that our main forces had encamped at the pass before Chemung, and were there awaiting us.

Murphy, the rifleman, came saying that our detail was packing up at the fort, that Major Parr had sent word for Lieutenant Boyd to strike tents and pull foot, and that the boats were now making ready to drop down the river with the non-combatants.

My pack, and those of my Indians, had been prepared for days, and there was little for me to do to make ready. Some batt-men carried my military chest to the fort, where it was bestowed with the officers' baggage until we returned.

Then I hastened away to the fort and discovered our twenty riflemen paraded there, and Boyd inspecting them and their packs. His face seemed very haggard under its dark coat of sunburn, but he returned my salute with a smile, and presently came over to where I stood, saying coolly enough:

"I have made my adieux to the ladies. They are at the landing place expecting you. Best not linger. We should reach Chemung by dusk."

"My Indians are ready," said I.

"Very well," he said absently, and returned to his men, continuing his careful inspection.

As I passed the log bridge, I saw Dolly Glenn standing there with a frightened look on her face, but she paid no heed to me, and I went on still haunted by the girl's expression.

A throng of people--civilians and soldiers--were at the landing. The redoubtable Mrs. Sabin was bustling about a batteau, terrorizing its crew and bullying the servants, who were stowing away her property. Looking about me, I finally discovered Lois and Lana standing on the shore a little way down stream, and hastened to them.

Lana was as white as a ghost, but to my surprise Lois seemed cheerful and in gayest spirits, and laughed when I saluted her hand. And it relieved me greatly to find her so animated and full of confidence that all would be well with us, and the parting but a brief one.

"I know in my heart it will be brief," she said smilingly, and permitting both her hands to remain in mine. "Soon, very soon, we shall be again together, Euan, and this interrupted fairy tale, so prettily begun by you and me, shall be once more resumed."

"To no fairy finish," I said, "but in sober reality."

She looked at Lana, laughing:

"What a lad is this, dear! How can a fairy tale be ever real? Yet, he is a magician like Okwencha, this tall young Ensign of mine, and I make no doubt that his wizardry can change fancy to fact in the twinkling of an eye. Indeed, I think I, too, am something of a witch. Shall I make magic for you, Euan? What most of anything on earth would you care to see tonight?"

"You, Lois."

"Hai-e! That is easy. I will some night send to you my spirit, and it shall be so like me and so vivid nay, so warm and breathing--that you shall think to even touch it.... Shall I do this with a spell?"

"I only have to close my eyes and see you. Make it that I can also touch you."

"It shall be done."

We both were smiling, and I for one was forcing my gay spirits, for now that the moment had arrived, I knew that chance might well make of our gay adieux an endless separation.

Lana had wandered a little way apart; I glanced at Lois, then turned and joined her. She laid her hand on my arm, as though her knees could scarcely prop her, and turned to me a deathly face.

"Euan," she breathed, "I have said adieu to him. Somehow, I know that he and I shall never meet again.... Tell him I pray for him--for his soul.... And mine.... And that before he goes he shall do the thing I bid him do.... And if he will not--tell him I ask God's mercy on him.... Tell him that, Euan."

"Yes," I said, awed.

She stood resting her arm on mine to support her, closed her eyes for a moment, then opened them and looked at me. And in her eyes I saw her heart was breaking as she stood there.

"Lana! Lanette! Little comrade! What is this dreadful thing that crushes you? Could you not tell me?" I whispered.

"Ask him, Euan."

"Lana, why will you not marry him, if you love him so?"

She shuddered and closed her eyes.

Neither of us spoke again. Lois, watching us, came slowly toward us, and linked her arm in Lana's.

"Our batteau is waiting," she said quietly.

I continued to preserve my spirits as we walked together down to the shore where Mrs. Sabin stood glaring at me, then turned her broad back and waddled across the planks.

Lana followed; Lois clung a second to my hands, smiling still; then I released her and she sprang lightly aboard.

And now batteau after batteau swung out into the stream, and all in line dropped slowly down the river, pole and paddle flashing, kerchiefs fluttering.

For a long way I could see the boat that carried Lois gliding in the channel close along shore, and the escort following along the bank above, with the sunshine glancing on their slanting rifles. Then a bend in the river hid them; and I turned away and walked slowly toward the fort.

By the gate my Indians were waiting. The Sagamore had my pack and rifle for me. On the rifle-platform above, the soldiers of the garrison stood looking down at us.

And now I heard the short, ringing word of command, and out of the gate marched our twenty riflemen, Boyd striding lightly ahead.

Then, as he set foot on the log bridge, I saw Dolly Glenn standing there, confronting him, blocking his way, her arms extended and her eyes fixed on him.

"Are you mad?" he said curtly.

"If you go," she retorted unsteadily, "leaving me behind you here--unwedded--God will punish you."

The column had came to a halt. There was a dead silence on parapet and parade while three hundred pair of eyes watched those two there on the bridge of logs.

"Dolly, you are mad!" he said, with the angry colour flashing in his face and staining throat and brow.

"Will you do me justice before you go?"

"Will you stand aside?" he said between his teeth.

"Yes--I will stand aside.... And may you remember me when you burn at the last reckoning with God!"

"'Tention! Trail arms! By the left flank--march!" he cried, his voice trembling with rage.

The shuffling velvet tread of his riflemen fell on the bridge; and they passed, rifles at a trail, and fringes blowing in the freshening breeze.

Without a word I fell in behind. After me loped my Indians in perfect silence.

CHAPTER XVII
THE BATTLE OF CHEMUNG

Toward sundown we hailed our bullock guard below the ruins of Old Chemung, and passed forward through the army to the throat of the pass, where the Rifles lay.

The artillery was already in a sorry mess, nine guns stalled and an ammunition wagon overturned in the ford. And I heard the infantry cursing the drivers and saying that we had lost thousands of cartridges. Stewart's bullock-guard was in a plight, too, forty head having strayed.

At the outlet to the pass Major Parr met us, cautioning silence. No fires burned and the woods were very still, so that we could hear in front of us the distant movement of men; and supposed that the enemy had come down to Chemung in force. But Major Parr told us that our scouts could make nothing of these incessant noises, reporting only a boatload of Sir John Johnson's green-coated soldiers on the river, and a few Indians in two canoes; and that he had no knowledge whether Sir John, the two Butlers, McDonald, and Brant lay truly in front of us, or whether these people were only a mixed scalping party of blue-eyed Indians, Senecas, and other ragamuffin marauders bent on a more distant foray, and now merely lingering along our front over night to spy out what we might be about.

Also, he informed us that a little way ahead, on the Great Warrior trail, lay an Indian town which our scouts reported to be abandoned; and said that he had desired to post our pickets there, but that orders from General Hand had prevented that precaution until the General commanding arrived at the front.

Some few minutes after our appearance in camp, and while we were eating supper, there came a ruddy glimmer of torches from behind us, lighting up the leaves overhead; and Generals Sullivan, Clinton, Hand, and Poor rode up and drew bridle beside Major Parr, listening intently to the ominous sounds in front of us.

And, "What the devil do you make of it, Major?" says Sullivan, in a low voice. "It sounds like a log-rolling in March."

"My scouts give me no explanation," says Parr grimly. "I think the rascals are terrified."

"Send Boyd and that young interpreter," said Sullivan curtly.

So, as nobody could understand exactly what these noises indicated, and as headquarters' scouts could obtain no information, Lieutenant Boyd and I, with my Indians, left our supper of fresh roast corn and beans and went forward at once. We moved out of the defile with every precaution, passing the throat of the rocky pass and wading the little trout-brook over which our trail led, the Chemung River now lying almost south of us. Low mountains rose to the north and west, very dark and clear against the stars; and directly ahead of us we saw the small Indian town surrounded by corn fields; and found it utterly deserted, save for bats and owls; and not even an Indian dog a-prowling there.

A little way beyond it we crossed another brook close to where it entered the river, opposite an island. Here the Chemung makes a great bend, flowing in more than half a circle; and there are little hills to the north, around which we crept, hearing always the stirring and movements of men ahead of us, and utterly unable to comprehend what they were so busily about.

Just beyond the island another and larger creek enters the river; and here, no longer daring to follow the Seneca trail, we turned southwest, slinking across the river flats, through the high Indian grass, until we came to a hardwood ridge, from whence some of these sounds proceeded.

We heard voices very plainly, the splintering of saplings, and a heavier, thumping sound, which the Mohican whispered to us was like hewn logs being dragged over the ground and then piled up. A few moments later, Tahoontowhee, who had crept on ahead, glided up to us and whispered that there was a high breastwork of logs on the ridge, and that many men were cutting bushes, sharpening the stems, and planting them to screen this breastwork so that it could not be seen from the Seneca trail north of us, along which lay our army's line of march. A pretty ambuscade, in truth! But Braddock's breed had passed.

Silently, stealthily, scarcely breathing, we got out of that dangerous place, re-crossed the grassy flats, and took to the river willows the entire way back. At the mouth of the pass, where my battalion lay asleep, we found Major Parr anxiously awaiting us. He sent Captain Simpson back with the information.

Before I could unlace my shirt, drag my pack under my head, and compose myself to sleep, Boyd, who had stretched himself out beside me, touched my arm.

"Are you minded to sleep, Loskiel?"

"I own that I am somewhat inclined that way," said I.

"As you please."

"Why? Are you unwell?"

He lay silent for a few moments, then:

"What a mortifying business was that at the Tioga fort," he said under his breath. "The entire garrison saw it, did they not, Loskiel? Colonel Shreve and all?"

"Yes, I fear so,"

"It will be common gossip tomorrow," he said bitterly. "What a miserable affair to happen to an officer of Morgan's!"

"A sad affair," I said.

"It will come to her ears, no doubt. Shreve's batt-men will carry it down the river."

I was silent.

"Rumour runs the woods like lightning," he said. "She will surely hear of this disgraceful scene. She will hear of it at Easton.... Strange," he muttered, "strange how the old truths hold!... Our sins shall find us out.... I never before believed that, Loskiel--not in a wilderness, anyway.... I had rather be here dead and scalped than have had that happen and know that she must hear of it one day."

He lay motionless for a while, then turned heavily on his side, facing me across the heap of dead leaves.

"Somehow or other," he said, "she heard of that miserable business--heard of it even at Otsego.... That is why she would not marry me, Loskiel. Did you ever hear the like! That a man must be so utterly and hopelessly damned for a moment's careless folly--lose everything in the world for a thoughtless moonlight frolic! Where lies the justice in such a judgment?"

"It is not the world that judges you severely. The world cares little what a man's way may be with a maid."

"But--Lana cares. It has ended everything for her."

I said in a low voice:

"You ended everything for Dolly Glenn."

"How was I to know she was no light o' love--this camp tailoress--this silly little wench who--but let it go! Had she but whimpered, and seemed abashed and unfamiliar with a kiss---- Well, let it go.... But I could cut my tongue out that I ever spoke to her. God! How lightly steps a man into a trap of his own contriving!... And here I lie tonight, caring not whether I live or die in tomorrow's battle already dawning on the Chemung. And yonder, south of us, in the black starlight, drift the batteaux, dropping down to Easton under the very sky that shines above us here.... If Lana be asleep at this moment I do not know.... She tells me I have broke her heart--but yet will have none of me.... Tells me my duty lies elsewhere; that I shall make amends. How can a man make amends when his heart lies not in the deed?... Am I then to be fettered to a passing whim for all eternity? Does an instant's idle folly entail endless responsibility? Do I merit punishment everlasting for a silly amourette that lasted no longer than the July moon? Tell me, Loskiel, you who are called among us blameless and unstained, is there no hope for a guilty man to shrive himself and walk henceforward upright?"

"I can not answer you," I said dully. "Nor do I know how, of such a business, a man may be shriven, or what should be his amends.... It all seems pitiful and sad to me--a matter perplexing, unhappy, and far beyond my solving.... I know it is the fashion of the times to regard such affairs lightly, making of them nothing.... Much I have heard, little learned, save that the old lessons seem to be the truest; the old laws the best. And that our cynical and modern disregard of them make one's salvation none the surer, one's happiness none the safer."

I heard Boyd sigh heavily, where he lay; but he said nothing more that I heard; for I slept soon afterward, and was awakened only at dawn.

Everywhere in the rocky pass the yawning riflemen were falling in and calling off; a detail of surly Jersey men, carrying ropes, passed us, cursing the artillery which, it appeared, was in a sorry plight again, the nine guns all stalled behind us, and an entire New Jersey brigade detailed to pull them out o' the mud and over the rocks of the narrowing defile.

Boyd shared my breakfast, seeming to have recovered something of his old-time spirits. And if the camp that night had gossiped concerning what took place at Tioga Fort, it seemed to make no difference to his friends, who one and all greeted him with the same fellowship and affection that he had ever inspired among fighting men. No man, I think, was more beloved and admired in this Western army, by officers and men alike; for in him were naturally combined all those brilliant qualities of daring, fearlessness, and gaiety in the face of peril, which endear, and which men strive to emulate. In no enterprise had he ever failed to perform the part allotted him; never had he faltered in the hundred battles fought by Morgan's veteran corps; never had he seemed dismayed. And if sometimes he did a little more than he was asked to do, his superior officers forgave this handsome, impetuous young man--the more readily, perhaps, because, so far, no disaster had befallen when he exceeded the orders given him.

My Indians had eaten, and were touching up their paint when Major Parr came up, wearing a magnificent new suit of fringed buckskins, and ordered us to guide the rifle battalion. A moment later our conch-horn boomed out its thrilling and melodious warning. Far in the rear I heard the drums and bugle-horns of the light infantry sounding the general.

As we went forward in the early daylight, the nature of the ambuscade prepared for us became very plain to me; and I pointed out to Major Parr where the unseen enemy rested, his right flank protected by the river, his left extending north along the hog-bank, so that his lines enveloped the trail on which we marched, threatening our entire army in a most cunning and evil manner. Truly there was no fox like Butler in the Northland!

All was very still about us as we marched; the river mist hung along the woods; a few birds sang; the tops of the Indian corn rustled.

Toward eight o'clock the conch-horn blew; our riflemen halted and deployed in perfect silence, facing the unseen works on the wooded ridge ahead. Another division of troops swung to the left, continuing the movement to the river in splendid order, where they also halted and formed a line of battle, facing north. And still the unseen enemy gave no sign; birds sang; the mist drifted up through the trees.

From where we lay we could see our artillery horses straining, plunging, stumbling up a high knoll in the centre of our line, while Maxwell's division halted and extended behind our riflemen to support the artillery, and Clinton's four splendid New York regiments hurried forward on a double, regiment after regiment dropping their packs behind our lines and running north through the open woods, their officers all finely mounted and cantering ahead, swords drawn.

A few moments later, General Sullivan passed along our front on horseback, and drew bridle for a moment where Boyd and I were standing at salute.

"Now is your opportunity, young gentlemen," he said in a low voice. "If you would gain Catharines-town and destroy Amochol before we drive this motley Tory army headlong through it, you should start immediately. And have a care; Butler's entire army and Brant's Mohawks are now intrenched in front of us; and it is a pitched battle we're facing--God be thanked!"

He spurred forward with a friendly gesture toward us, as we saluted; and his staff officers followed him at a canter while our riflemen turned their heads curiously to watch the brilliant cavalcade.

"Where the devil are their log works?" demanded Major Parr, using his field glasses. "I can see naught but green on that ridge ahead."

Boyd painted at the crest; but our Major could see nothing; and I called to Timothy Murphy and Dave Elerson to climb trees and spy out if the works were still occupied.

Murphy came down presently from the dizzy top of a huge black-walnut tree, reporting that he had been able to see into the river angle of their works; had for a while distinguished nothing, but presently discovered Indians, crouched motionless, the brilliancy of their paint, which at first he had mistaken for patches of autumn leaves, betraying them when they moved.

"Now, God be praised!" said Major Parr grimly. "For we shall this day furnish these Western-Gate Keepers with material for a Condolence Feast such as no Seneca ever dreamed of. And if you gentlemen can surprise and destroy Amochol, it will be a most blessed day for our unhappy country."

General Hand, in his patched and faded uniform of blue and buff, drew his long, heavy sword and walked his horse over to Major Parr.

"Well, sir," he said, "we must amuse them, I suppose, until the New Yorkers gain their left. Push your men forward and draw their fire, Major."

There came a low order; the soft shuffle of many mocassined feet; silence. Presently, ahead of us, a single rifle-shot shattered the stillness.

Instantly a mighty roar of Tory musketry filled the forest; and their Indians, realizing that the ambuscade had been discovered, came leaping down the wooded ridge, yelling and firing all along our front; and our rifles began to speak quicker and quicker from every rock and tuft and fallen log.

"Are we to miss this?" said Boyd, restlessly. "Listen to that firing! The devil take this fellow Amochol and his Eries! I wish we were yonder with our own people. I wish at least that I could see what our New Yorkers are about!"

Behind us, Boyd's twenty riflemen stood craning their sunburnt necks; and my Indians, terribly excited, fairly quivered where they crouched beside us. But all we could see was the rifle smoke sifting through the trees, and early sunshine slanting on the misty river.

The fierce yelling of the unseen Mohawks and Senecas on the wooded ridge above us had become one continuous and hideous scream, shrill and piercing above the racket of musketry and rifle fire; sometimes the dreadful volume of sound surged nearer as though they were charging, or showing themselves in order to draw us into a frontal attack on their pits and log breastworks; but always after a little while the yelping tumult receded, and our rifle fire slackened while the musketry from the breastworks grew more furious, crashing out volley on volley, while the entire ridge steamed like a volcano in action. Further to the north we heard more musketry break out, as our New York regiments passed rapidly toward Butler's left flank. And by the running fire we could follow their hurried progress.

"Hell!" said Boyd, furiously, flinging his rifle to his shoulder. "Come on, Loskiel, or we'll miss this accursed Amochol also." And he gave the signal to march.

As we skirted the high knoll where our artillery was planted, the first howitzer shot shook the forest, and my Indians cringed as they ran beside me. High towering rose the shell, screaming like a living thing, and plunged with a shriek into the woods on the ridge, exploding there with a most infernal bang.

Up through the trees gushed a very fountain of smoke, through which we could dimly see dark objects falling; but whether these were the limbs of trees or of men we could not tell.

Crash! A howitzer hurled its five and a half inch shell high into the sunshine. Boom! Another shot from a three-pounder. Bang! The little cohorn added its miniature bellow to the bigger guns, which now began to thunder regularly, one after another, shaking the ground we trod. The ridge was ruddy with the red lightning of exploding shells. Very far away in the forest we could hear entire regiments, as they climbed the slopes, cheering above the continuous racket of musketry; the yelling of the Senecas and Mohawks grew wavering, becoming ragged and thinner.

It was hard for us all, I think, to turn our backs on the first real battle we had seen in months--hard for Boyd, for me, and for our twenty riflemen; harder, perhaps, for our Indians, who could hear the yells of their most deadly enemies, and who knew that they were within striking distance at last.

As we marched in single file, I leading with my Indians, I said aloud, in the Iroquois tongue:

"If in this Battle of the Chemung the Mountain Snake be left writhing, yet unless we crush his head at Catharines-town, the serpent will live to strike again. For though a hundred arrows stick in the Western Serpent's body, his poison lies in his fangs; his fangs are rooted in his head; and the head still hisses at God and man from the shaggy depths of Catharines-town. It is for us of the elect to slay him there--for us few and chosen ones honoured by this mandate from our commander. Why, then, should the thunder of Proctor's guns arouse in us envy for those who join in battle? Let the iron guns do their part; let the men of New York, of Jersey, of Virginia, of New Hampshire, of Pennsylvania, do the great part allotted them. Let us in our hearts pray God to speed them. For if we do our part as worthily, only then shall their labour be not in vain. Their true title to glory is in our keeping, locked inevitably with our own. If we fail, they have failed. Judge, therefore, O Sagamore, judge, you Yellow Moth, and you Oneidas--Grey-Feather, with your war-chief's feather and your Sachem's ensign, Tahoontowhee, chieftain to be--judge, all of you, where the real glory lies--whether behind us in the rifle smoke or before us in the red glare of Amochol's accursed altar!"

They had been listening to every word as I walked beside them. The Mohican made answer first:

"It was hard for us to leave the Chemung, O Loskiel, my brother--with the dog-yelps at the Sinako and Mowawaks insulting our ears. But it was wiser. I, a Sagamore, say it!"

"It is God's will," said the Yellow Moth. But his eyes were still red with his fierce excitement; and the distant cannonade steadily continued as we marched.

"I am Roya-neh!" said the Grey-Feather. "What wisdom counsels I understand, He who would wear the scaly girdle must first know where the fangs lie buried.... But to hear the Antouhonoran scalp-yelp, and to turn one's back, is very hard, O my friend, Loskiel."

The Night-Hawk controlled his youthful features, forcing a merry smile as my eye fell on him.

"Koue!" he exclaimed softly. "I have made promise to my thirsty hatchet, O Loskiel! Else it might have leaped from its sheath and bitten some one."

"A good hatchet and a good dog bite only under orders," I said. "My younger brother's hatchet has acquired glory; now it is acquiring wisdom."

Boyd came up along the line, his deerskin shirt open to the breastbone, the green fringe blowing in the hill wind.

Far below us in the river valley sounded the uproar of the battle--a dull, confused, and distant thunder--for now we could no longer hear the musketry and rifle fire, only the boom-booming of the guns and the endless roar of echoes.

Here on a high hill's spur, with a brisk wind blowing in our faces, the heavy rumble of forest warfare became deadened; and we looked out over the naked ridge of rock, across the forests of this broken country, into a sea of green which stretched from horizon to horizon, accented only by the silver glimmer of lakes and the low mountain peaks east, west, and south of us.

Below us lay a creek, its glittering thread visible here and there. The Great Warrior trail crossed it somewhere in that ravine.

I drew the Mohican aside.

"Sagamore," said I, "now is your time come. Now we depend on you. If it lay with us, not one white man here, not one Indian, could take us straight to Catharines-town; for the Great Warrior trail runs not thither. Are you, then, confident that you know the way?"

"I know the way, Loskiel."

"Is there then a trail that leads from the Great Warrior trail below?"

"There are many."

"And you know the right one?"

"I have spoken, brother."

"I am satisfied. But we must clearly mark the trail for our surveyors and for the army."

"We will mark it," he said meaningly, "so that no Seneca dog can ever mistake which way we passed."

I did not exactly understand him, but I nodded to Boyd and he gave the signal, and we began the descent through the warm twilight of an open forest that sloped to the creek a thousand feet below us.

Down and down we went, partly sliding, and plowing up the moss and leaves knee-deep, careless how we left our trail, as there was none to follow, save the debris of a flying army or the flanking scouts of a victorious one.

Below us the foaming rifles of the creek showed white in the woodland gloom, and presently we heard its windy voice amid rocks and fallen trees, soughing all alone through leafy solitudes; and its cool, damp breath mounted to us as we descended.

The Indians dropped prone to slake their thirst; the riflemen squatted and used their cups of bark or leather, pouring the sweet, icy water over their cropped heads and wrists.

"Off packs!" said Boyd quietly, and drew a bit of bread and meat from his beaded wallet. And so the Mohican and I left them all eating by the stream, and crossed to the western bank. Here the Sagamore pointed to the opposite slope; I gave a low whistle, and Boyd looked across the water at me.

Then I drew my hatchet and notched a tree so that he saw what I did; he nodded comprehension; we went on, notching trees at intervals, and so ascended the slope ahead until we arrived at the top.

Here the forest lay flat beyond, and the Great Warrior trail ran through it--a narrow path fifteen inches wide, perhaps, and worn nearly a foot deep, and patted as hard as rock by the light feet of generations--men and wild beasts--which had traversed it for centuries.

North and south the deeply graven war trail ran straight through the wilderness. The Mohican bent low above it, scrutinizing it in the subdued light, then stepped lightly into it, and I behind him.

For a little way we followed it, seeing other and narrower trails branching from it right and left, running I knew not whither--the narrow, delicate lanes made by game--deer and bear, fox and hare--all spreading out into the dusk of the unknown forest.

Presently we came to a trail which seemed wet, as though swampy land were not far away; and into this the Mohican turned, slashing a great scar on the nearest tree as he entered it.

There was a mossy stream ahead, and the banks of it were dark and soft. Here we rested high and dry on the huge roots of an oak, and ate our midday meal.

In a little while the remainder of our party came gliding through the trees, Boyd ahead.

"Is this the Catharines-town trail?" he asked. "By God, they'll never get their artillery through here. Mark it, all the same," he added indifferently, and seated himself beside me, dropping his rifle across his knees with a gesture of weariness.

"Are you tired?" I asked.

He looked up at me with a wan smile.

"Weary of myself, Loskiel, and of a life lived too lightly and now nigh ended."

"Nigh ended!" I repeated.

"I go not back again," he said, sombrely.

I glanced sharply at him, where he sat brooding over his rifle; and there was in his face an expression such as I had never before seen there--something unnatural that altered him altogether, as death alters the features, leaving them strangely unfamiliar. And even as I looked, the expression passed. He lifted his eyes to mine, and even smiled.

"There is," he said, "a viewless farm which companions even the swiftest on the last long trail, a phantom-pilot which leads only toward that Shadowed Valley of endless rest. In my ears all day--close, close to my ear, I have heard the whisper of this unseen ghost--everywhere I have heard it, amid the din of the artillery, on windy hill-tops, in the long silence of the forest, through the noise of torrents in lost ravines, by flowing rivers sparkling in the sun--everywhere my pilot whispers to me. I can not escape, Loskiel; whatever trail I take, that is the trail; whichever way I turn, that is the way. And ever my phantom pilots me--forward or back, aside or around--it is all one to him and to me, for at the end of every trail I take, nearer and nearer draw I to mine end."

I had heard of premonitions before a battle; had known officers and soldiers to utter them--brave men, too, yet obsessed by the conviction of their approaching death. Sometimes they die; sometimes escape, and the premonition ends forever. But until the moment of peril is passed, or they fall as they had foretold, no argument will move them, no assurance cheer them. But our corps had been in many battles during the last three years, and I had never before seen Boyd this way.

He said, brooding on his rifle:

"The one true passion of my life has been Lana Helmer. It began ignobly; it continues through all this pain and bewilderment, a pure, clean current, running to the deep, still sea of dreams.... There it is lost; I follow it no further.... And were I here today as upright and as stainless as are you, Loskiel, still I could follow it no further than that sea of dreams. Nor would my viewless pilot lead me elsewhere than to the destiny of silence that awaits me; and none the less would I hear his whisper in my ears.... My race is run."

I said: "Is it vain to appeal to your reason when your heart is heavy?"

"Had I another chance," he said, "I would lighten the load of sin I bear--the heavy load I bear with me into the unknown."

"God gives us all our chance."

"He gave me my last chance at Tioga Fort. And I cursed it in my heart and put it aside."

"One day you will return,"

"Never again, Loskiel.... I am no coward. I dare face the wrath to come. It is not that; but--I am sorry I did not spare when I might have been more generous.... The little thing was ignorant.... Doves mate like that.... And somewhere--somehow--I shall be required to answer for it all--shall be condemned to make amends.... I wonder how the dead make their amends?... For me to burn in hell avails her nothing.... If she thought it she would weep uncomforted.... No; there is a justice. But how it operates I shall never understand until it summons me to hear my sentence."

"You will return and do what a contrite heart bids you to do," I said.

"If that might be," he said gently, "that would I do--for the child's sake and for hers."

"Good God!" I said under my breath.

"Did you not surmise it?"

"No."

"Well, then, now you know how deeply I am damned.... God gave me a last chance. There was a chaplain at the fort."

"Kirkland."

"Yes, Gann went forward.... But--God's grace was not within me.... And to see her angered me--that and the blinding hurt I had when Lana left--heart-broken, wretched, still loving me, but consigning me to my duty.... So I denied her at the bridge.... And from that moment has my unseen pilot walked beside me, and I know he leads me swiftly to my end."

I raised my troubled eyes and glanced toward my Indians. They had stripped great squares of bark from half a dozen trees, and were busily painting upon them, in red and blue, insulting signs and symbols--a dead tree-cat, scalped, and full of arrows; a snake severed into sections; a Seneca tied to a post and a broken wampum belt at his feet. And on every tree they had also painted the symbol of their own clans and nation--pointed stones and the stars of the Pleiades; a witch-wolf and an enchanted bear; a yellow moth alighted on a white cross; a night-hawk, perfectly recognizable, soaring high above a sun, setting, bisecting the line of the horizon.

Every scalp taken was duly enumerated and painted there, together with every captured weapon. Such a gallery of art in the wilderness I had never before beheld.

Boyd's riflemen sat around, cross-legged on the moss, watching the Indians at their labour--all except Murphy and Elerson, who, true to their habits, had each selected a tree to decorate, and were hard at work with their hunting knives on the bark.

On Murphy's tree I read: "To hell with Walter Butler."

Elerson, who no doubt had scraped the outlines of this legend with his knife-point before Murphy carved it, had produced another message on his own tree, not a whit more complimentary: "Dam Butler, Brant, Hiakotoo, and McDonald for bloody rogues and murtherin' rascals all!"

They were ever like this, these two great overgrown boys, already celebrated so terribly in song and legend. And the rank and file of Morgan's resembled them--brave to a fault, innately lawless, of scant education save what the forest had taught them, headstrong, quick to anger, quick to forgive, violent in every emotion through the entire gamut from love to hatred.

Boyd rose, glanced quietly at me, then made his signal. And in a few moments the riflemen were on the trail again, spotting it wherever a new path led away, trotting steadily forward in single file, my Indians ranging wide on either flank.

Late in the afternoon we came to the height of land, where the little watercourses all ran north; and here we halted, dropped packs, and the men sat down while the Sagamore and I once more went forward to the headwaters of a stream, beside which the narrow and swampy trail ran due north. And here the nature of the country changed entirely, for beyond it was all one vast swamp, as still and dark as death.

A little way along this blackish stream Mayaro halted, and for a while stood motionless, his powerful arms folded, gazing straight in front of him with the half-closed eyes of a dreaming wolf.

Never had I looked upon so sinister a country or a swamp so vast and desolate. It seemed more black than dusky, and the gloom lay not in the obscure light of thick-set spruce, pine, and hemlock, but in the shaggy, monstrous, and forbidding growth which appeared to be soiled with some common dye, water, earth, tree-trunks, foliage--all wore the same inky livery, and seemed wrought of rusty iron, so still the huge trees stood, with every melancholy branch a-droop.

Sign of life there was none; the current of the narrow stream ran like smooth oil; nor was its motion visible where it wound between soft, black banks of depthless swamp through immemorial shadows.

The Mohican's voice came to me, low in the silence, sounding dull and remote; nor did his dreaming eyes move in their vague intensity.

"This is the land of Amochol," he said. "Here, through these viewless shades, his sway begins, as this stream begins, whose source is darkness and whose current moves slowly like thick blood. Here is the haunt of witch and sorcerer--of the hag Catrine, of the Wyoming Fiend, of Amochol--of Amochol! Here run the Andastes, hunting through the dusk like wolves and foxes--running, smelling, listening, ever hunting. Here slink the Cat-People under a moon which is hidden forever by this matted forest roof. This is the Dark Empire, O Loskiel! Behold!"

A slight shudder chilled me, but I said calmly enough:

"Where lies Catharines-town, O Sagamore?"

"This thick, dark stream runs through it."

"Through Catharines-town?"

"Aye."

"And then?"

"Along the vast chain of inland seas--first into the Lake of the Senecas, then to that of the Cayugas, fed by Owasco, by Onondaga, by Oneida, until it is called Oswego, and flows north by the great fort into the sea Ontario."

"And where lies Catharines-town?"

"Nine miles beyond us, northward."

"And the trail?"

"None, Loskiel, save for the maze of game trails where long leaps are made from tussock to swale, from root to rotting log across black pools of mud, and quivering quicksands whose depths are white as snow under the skin of mud, set with tarnished rainbow bubbles."

"But--those who come after us, Mayaro! The army--the wagons, horses, artillery, cattle--nay, the men themselves! How are they to pass?"

He pointed east, then west: "For six miles, flanking this swamp, run ridges of high hills northward. By these must the army march to Catharines-town, the pioneers opening a road for the artillery. This you shall make plain to Boyd presently, for he must march that way, marking plain the trail north on the eastern ridge of hills, then west. Thus shall Boyd move to cut off Amochol from the lake, while you and I and the Oneidas and the Yellow Moth must thread this swamp and comb it clean to head him from the rivers south of us."

"Is there a path along the ridge?"

"No path, Loskiel. So Boyd shall march by compass, slowly, seeking over the level way, and open woods, with the artillery and wagons ever in his thoughts. Six miles due north shall he march; then, where the hills end a swamp begins--thick, miry, set with maple, brier, and tamarack. But through this he must blaze his trail, and the pioneers who are to follow shall lay their wagon-path across felled trees, northward still, across the forests that border the flats of Catharines-town; and then, still northward for a mile; and so swing west, severing the lake trail. Thus we shall trap Amochol between us."

Slowly we walked back together to the height of land, where our little party lay looking down at the dark country below. I sat down beside Boyd, cleared from the soil the leaves for a little space, drew my knife, and with its point traced out the map.

He listened in silence, while I went over all that the Sagamore had taught me; and around us squatted our Indians, motionless, fiercely intent upon my every word and gesture.

"Today is Sunday," I said. "By this hour, Butler's people should be in headlong flight. Our army will not follow them at once, because it will take all day tomorrow for our men to destroy the corn along the Chemung. But on Tuesday our army will surely march, laying waste the Indian towns and fields. Therefore, giving them ample time for this, they should arrive at this spot on Wednesday."

"I have so calculated," said Boyd, listlessly.

"But Wednesday is the first day of September; and if we are to strike Amochol at all it must be done during the Onon-hou-aroria. And that ends on Tuesday. Therefore, must you move within the hour. And by tomorrow evening you shall have blazed your hill-trail and shall be lying with your men beside the stream and across the lake trail, north of Catharines-town."

He nodded.

"Tonight," said I, "I and my Indians lie here on this height of land, watching the swamp below, that nothing creep out of it. On Monday morning, we move through it, straight northward, following the stream, and by Monday night we scout to Catharines-town."

"That is clear," he said, lifting his handsome head from his hands. "And the signal should come from me. Listen, Loskiel; you shall expect that signal between midnight of Monday and dawn."

He rose, and I stood up; and for a moment we looked each other steadily in the eye. Then he smiled faintly, shaking his head:

"Not this time, Loskiel," he said in a low voice. "My spectral pilot gives no sign. Death lies beyond the fires of Catharines-town. I know, Loskiel--I know."

"I also," said I in a low voice, taking his outstretched hand, "for you shall live to make material amends as you have made them spiritually. Only the act of deep contrition lies between you and God's swift pardon. It were a sin to doubt it."

But he slowly shook his head, the faint smile lingering still. Then his grip closed suddenly on my hand, released it, and he swung on his heel.

"Attention!" he said crisply. "Sling packs! Fall in! Tr-r-rail arms! March!"

CHAPTER XVIII
THE RITE OF THE HIDDEN CHILDREN

My Indians and I stood watching our riflemen as they swung to the east and trotted out of sight among the trees. Then, at a curt nod from me, the Indians lengthened their line, extending it westward along the height of land, and so spreading out that they entirely commanded the only outlet to the swamp below, by encircling both the trail and the headwaters of the evil-looking little stream.

Through the unbroken thatch of matted foliage overhead no faintest ray of sunlight filtered--not even where the stream coiled its slimy way among the tamaracks and spruces. But south of us, along the ascending trail by which we had come, the westering sun glowed red across a ledge of rock, from which the hill fell sheer away, plunging into profound green depths, where unseen waters flowed south-ward to the Susquehanna.

Around the massive elbow of this ledge, our back-trail, ascending into view, curved under shouldering boulders. Blueberry scrub, already turning gold and crimson, grew sparsely on the crag--cover enough for any watcher of the trail. And thither I crept and stretched me out flat in the bushes, where I could see the trail we had lately traversed, and look along it far to our rear as clearly as one sees through a dim and pillared corridor.

West of me, a purplish ridge ran north, the sun shining low through a pine-clad notch. Southwest of me, little blue peaks pricked the primrose sky; south-east lay endless forests, their green already veiled in an ashy blue bloom. Far down, under me, wound the narrow back-trail through the gulf below.

Presently, beside me came creeping the lithe Mohican, and lay down prone, smooth and golden, and shining like a sleek panther in the sun.

"Is all well guarded, brother?" I whispered.

"Not even a wood-mouse could creep from the swamp unless our warriors see it."

"And when dark comes?"

"Our ears must be our eyes, Loskiel.... But neither the Cat-People nor the An-dastes will venture out of that morass, save only by the trail. And we shall have two watchers on it through the night."

"There is no other outlet?"

"None, except by the ridge Boyd travels. He blocks that pass with his twenty men."

"Then we should have their egress blocked, except only in the north?"

"Yes--unless they learn of this by magic," muttered the Mohican.

It was utterly useless for me to decry or ridicule his superstitions; and there was but one way to combat them.

"If witchcraft there truly be in Catharines-town," said I, "it is bad magic, and therefore weak; and can avail nothing against true priesthood. What could the de-graded acolytes of this Red Priest do against a consecrated Sagamore of the Lenape--against an ensign of the Enchanted Clan? Else why do you wear your crest--or the great Ghost Bear there rearing upon your breast?"

"It is true," he murmured uneasily. "What spell can Amochol lay upon us? What magic can he make to escape us? For the trail from Catharines-town is stopped by a Siwanois Sagamore and a Mohican warrior! It is closed by an Oneida Sachem who stand watching. When the Ghost Bear and the Were-Wolf watch, then the whole forest watches with them--Loup, Blue Wolf, and Bear. Where, then, can the Forest Cats slink out? Where can the filthy Carcajou escape?"

"Mayaro has spoken. It is a holy barrier that locks and bolts this door of secret evils. Under Tharon shall this trap remain inviolate till the last sorcerer be taken in it, the last demon be dead!"

* "Yo-ya-ne-re!" he said, deliberately employing the Canienga expression with a fierce scorn that, for a moment, made his noble features terrible. Then he spat as though to wash from his mouth the taste of the hated language that had soiled it, even when used in contempt and derision; and he said in the suave tongue of his own people: "Pray to your white God, Holder of Heaven, Master of Life and Death, that into our hands be delivered these scoffers who mock at Him and at Tharon-- these Cat-murderers of little children, these pollutors of the Three Fires. And in the morning I shall arise and look into the rising sun, and ask the same of the far god who made of me a Mohican, a Siwanois, and a Sagamore. Let these things be done, brother, ere our hatchets redden in the flames of Catharines-town. For," he added, naively, "it is well that God should know what we are about, lest He misunderstand our purpose."

[* "It is well!"]

I assented gravely.

The sun hung level, now, sending its blinding light straight into our eyes; and for precaution's sake we edged away under the blue shadows of the shrubbery, in case some far prowler note the light spots where our faces showed against the wall of green behind us.

"How far from Catharines-town," I asked, "lies the Vale Yndaia, of which our little Lois has spoken?"

"It is the next valley to the westward. A pass runs through and a little brook. Pleasant it is, Loskiel, with grassy glades and half a hundred little springs which we call 'Eyes of the Inland Seas.'"

"You know," I said, "that in this valley all the hopes of Lois de Contrecoeur are centred."

"I know, Loskiel," he answered gravely.

"Do you believe her mother lives there still?"

"How shall I know, brother? If it were with these depraved and perverted Senecas as it is with other nations, the mother of a Hidden Child had lived there unmolested. Her lodge would have remained her sanctuary; her person had been respected; her Hidden One undisturbed down to this very hour. But see how the accursed Senecas have dealt with her, so that to save her child from Amochol she sent it far beyond the borders of the Long House itself! What shame upon the Iroquois that the Senecas have defiled their purest law! May Leshi seize them all! So how, then, shall I know whether this white captive mother lives in the Vale Yndaia still--or if she lives at all? Or if they have not made of her a priestess--a sorceress--perhaps The Dreaming Prophetess of the Onon-hou-aroria!--by reason of her throat being white!"

"What!" I exclaimed, startled.

"Did not the Erie boast a Prophetess to confound us all?"

"I did not comprehend."

"Did he not squat, squalling at us from his cave, deriding every secret plan we entertained, and boasting that the Senecas had now a prophetess who could reveal to them everything their white enemies were plotting--because her own throat was white?"

I looked at him in silent horror.

"Hai-ee!" he said grimly. "If she still lives at all it is because she dreams for Amochol. And this, Loskiel, has long remained my opinion. Else they had slain her on their altars long ago--strangled her as soon as ever she sent her child beyond their reach. For what she did broke sanctuary. According to the code of the Long House, the child belonged to the nation in which the mother was a captive. And by the mother's act this child was dedicated to a stainless marriage with some other child who also had been hidden. But the Red Sorcerer has perverted this ancient law; and when he would have taken the child to sacrifice it, then did the mother break the law of sanctuary and send her child away, knowing, perhaps, that the punishment for this is death.

"So you ask me whether or not she still lives. And I say to you that I do not know; only I judge by the boasting of that vile Erie Cat that she has bought her life of them by dreaming for their Red Priest. And if she has done this thing, and has deceived them until this day, then it is very plain to me that they believe her to be a witch. For it is true, Loskiel, that those who dream wield heavy influences among all Indians--and among the Iroquois in particular. Yet, with all this, I doubt not that, if she truly be alive, her life hangs by a single thread, ever menaced by the bloody knife of Amochol."

"I can not understand," said I, "why she sent out no appeal during her long captivity. Before this war broke, had her messengers to Lois gone to Sir William Johnson, or to Guy Johnson, with word that the Senecas held in their country a white woman captive, she had been released within a fortnight, I warrant you!"

"Loskiel, had that appeal gone out, and a belt been sent to Catharines-town from Johnstown or Guy Park, the Senecas would have killed her instantly and endured the consequences--even though Amherst himself was thundering on their Western Gate."

"Are you sure, Mayaro?"

"Certain, Loskiel. She could not have lived a single moment after the Senecas learned that she had sent out word of her captivity. That is their law, which even Amochol could not break."

"It was a mercy that our little Lois appealed not to His Excellency, so that the word ran through Canada by flag to Haldimand."

"She might have done this," said the Sagamore quietly. "She asked me at Poundridge how this might be accomplished. But when I made it clear to her that it meant her mother's death, she said no more about it."

"But pushed on blindly by herself," I exclaimed, "braving the sombre Northland forests with her little ragged feet--half naked, hungry, friendless, and alone, facing each terror calmly, possessed only of her single purpose! O Sagamore of a warrior clan that makes a history of brave deeds done, can you read in the records of your most ancient wampum a braver history than this?"

He said: "Let what this maid has done be written in the archives of the white men, where are gathered the records of brave but unwise deeds. So shall those who come after you know how to praise and where to pity our little rosy pigeon of the forest. No rash young warrior of my own people, bound to the stake itself can boast of greater bravery than this. And you, blood-brother to a Siwanois, shall witness what I say."

After a silence I said: "They must have passed Wyoming already. At this hour our little Lois may be secure under the guns of Easton. Do you not think so, Mayaro?"

As he made no answer, I glanced around at him and found him staring fixedly at the trail below us.

"What do you see on our back-trail?" I whispered.

"A man, Loskiel--if it be not a deer."

A moment and I also saw something moving far below us among the trees. As yet it was only a mere spot in the dim light of the trail, slowly ascending the height of land. Nearer, nearer it came, until at length we could see that it was a man. But no rifle slanted across his shoulder.

"He must be one of our own people," I said, puzzled. "Somebody sends us a messenger. Is he white or Indian?"

"White," said the Sagamore briefly, his eyes still riveted on the approaching figure, which now I could see was clothed in deerskin shirt and leggins.

"He carries neither pack nor rifle; only a knife and pouch. He is a wood-running fool!" I said, disgusted. "Why do they send us such a forest-running battman, when they have Oneidas at headquarters, and Coureurs-de-Bois to spare who understand their business?"

"I make nothing of him," murmured the Mohican, his eyes fairly glittering with excitement and perplexity.

"Is he, perhaps, some fugitive from Butler's rangers?" I whispered, utterly at a loss to account for such a silly spectacle. "The pitiful idiot! Did you ever gaze upon the like, Mayaro--unless he be some French mission priest. Otherwise, yonder walks the greatest of God's fools!"

"Then he is easily taken," muttered Mayaro. "Fix thy flint, Loskiel, and prime. Here is a business I do not understand."

Once the man halted and looked up at our ledge of rock, where the last sun rays still lingered, then lightly continued the ascent. And I, turning to the Mohican for some possible explanation of this amazing sight, ere we crept out to closer ambush, found Mayaro staring through the trees with a glassy and singular expression which changed swiftly to astonishment, and then to utter blankness.

"Etho!" he exclaimed, bluntly, springing to his feet behind the nearer trees, regardless whether or not the stranger saw him. "Go forward now, Loskiel. This is a fool's business--and badly begun. Now, let a white man's wisdom finish it."

I, too, had risen in surprise, stepping backward also, in order that the trees might screen me. And at the same moment the stranger rounded the jutting shoulder of our crag, and came suddenly face to face with me in midtrail.

"Euan!"

So astounded was I that my rifle fell clattering from my nerveless hand as she sprang forward and caught my shoulders with both her hands. And I saw her grey eyes filling and her lips quivering with words she could not utter.

"Lois!" I repeated, as though stupefied. "Lois!"

"Oh, Euan! Euan! I thought I would never, never come up with you!" she whimpered. "I left the batteau where it touched at Towanda Creek, and hid in the woods and dressed me in the Oneida dress you gave me. Then, by the first batt-man who passed, I sent a message to Lana saying that I was going back to--to join you. Are you displeased?"

Her trembling hands clasped my shoulders tighter, and her face drew closer, so that her sweet, excited breath fell on my cheek.

"Listen!" she stammered. "I desire to tell you everything! I will tell you all, Euan! I ran back along the trail, meeting the boat-guard, batt-men, and the sick horses all along the way to Tioga, where they took me over on a raft of logs.... I paid them three hard shillings. Then Colonel Shreve heard of what I had been about, and sent a soldier after me, but I avoided the fort, Euan, and went boldly up through the deserted camps until I came to where the army had crossed. Some teamsters mending transport wagons gave me bread and meat enough to fill my pouch; and one of them, a kindly giant, took me over the Chemung dry shod, I clinging to his broad back like a very cat--and all o' them a-laughing fit to burst!... Are you displeased, dear lad?... Then, just at night, I came up with the rear-guard, where they were searching for strayed cattle; and I stowed myself away in a broken-down wagon, full of powder--quietly, like a mouse, no one dreaming that I was not the slender youth I looked. So none molested me where I lay amid the powder casks and sacking."

She smiled wistfully, and stood caressing my arms with her eager little hands, as though to calm the wrath to come.

"I heard your regiment's pretty conch-horn in the morning," she said, "and slipped out of my wagon and edged forward amid all that swearing, sweating confusion, noticed not at all by anybody, save when a red-head Jersey sergeant bawled at me to man a rope and haul at the mired cannon with the others. But I was deaf just then, Euan, and got free o' them with nothing worse than a sound cursing from the sergeant; and away across the creek I legged it, where I hid in the bush until the firing began and the horrid shouting on the ridge. Then it was that, badly scared, I crept through the Indian grass like a hunted hare, and saw Lieutenant Boyd there, and his men, halted across the trail. And very soon our cannon began, and then it was that I saw you and your Indians filing out to the right. So I followed you. Oh, Euan, are you very angry? Because, dear lad, I have had so lonely a trail, what with keeping clear of your party so that you might not catch me and send me back, and what with losing you after you had left the main, trodden trail! Save for the marks you left on trees, I had been utterly lost--and must have perished, no doubt----" She looked at me with melting eyes.

"Think on that, Euan, ere you grow too angry and are cruel with me."

"Cruel? Lois, you have been more heartless than I ever----"

"There! I knew it! Your anger is about to burst its dreadful bounds----"

"Child! What is there to say or do now? What is there left for me, save to offer you what scant protection I may--good God!--and take you forward with us in the morning? This is a cruel, unmerited perplexity you have caused me, Lois. What unkind inspiration prompted you to do this rash, mad, foolish thing! How could you so conduct? What can you hope to accomplish in all this wicked and bloody business that now confronts us? How can I do my duty--how perform it to the letter--with you beside me--with my very heart chilling to water at thought of your peril----"

"Hush, dearest lad," she whispered, tightening her fingers on my sleeve. "All in the world I care for lies in this place where we now stand--or near it. Have I not told you that I must go to Catharines-town? How could I remain behind when every tie I have in all the world was tugging at my heart to draw me hither? You ask me what I can do--what I can hope to accomplish. God knows--but my mother and my lover are here--and how could I stay away if there was a humble chance that I might do some little thing to aid her--to aid you, Euan?

"Why do you scowl at me? Try me, Test me. I am tough as an Indian youth, strong and straight and supple--and as tireless. See--I am not wearied with the trail! I am not afraid. I can do what you do. If you fast I can fast, too; when you go thirsty I can endure it also; and you may not even hope to out-travel me, Euan, for I am inured to sleeplessness, to hunger, to fatigue, by two years' vagabondage--hardened of limb and firm of body, self-taught in self-denial, in quiet endurance, in stealth, and patience. Oh, Euan! Make me your comrade, as you would take a younger brother, to school him in the hardy ways of life you know so well! I will be no burden to you; I will serve you humbly and faithfully; prove docile, obedient, and grateful to the end. And if the end comes in the guise of death--Euan--Euan! Why may I not share that also with you? For the world's joy dies when you die, and my body might as well die with it!"

So eager and earnest her argument, so tightly she clung to my arms, so pleading and sweet her ardent face, upturned, with the tears scarcely dry under her lashes, that I found nought to answer her, and could only look into her eyes--deep, deep into those grey-blue wells of truth--troubled to silence by her present plight and mine.

I could not take her back now, and also keep my tryst with Boyd at Catharinestown. I could not leave her here by this trail, even guarded--had I the guards to spare--for soon in our wake would come thundering the maddened debris of the Chemung battle, pell-mell, headlong through the forests, desperate, with terror leading and fury lashing at their heels.

I laid my hands heavily upon her firm, young shoulders, and strove to think the while I studied her; but the enchantment of her confused my mind, and I saw only the crisp and clustering curls, and clear, young eyes looking into mine, and the lips scarce parted, hanging breathless on my words.

"O boy-girl comrade!" I said in a low, unsteady voice. "Little boy-girl born to do endless mischief in this wide and wind-swept forest world of men! What am I to say to you, who have your will of everyone beneath the sun? Who am I to halt the Starry Dancers, or bar your wayward trail when Tharon himself has hidden you, and the Little People carry to you 'winged moccasins for flying feet as light and swift!' For truly I begin to think it has been long since woven in the silvery and eternal wampum--belt after belt, string twisted around string--that you shall go to Catharines-town unscathed.

"Where she was born returns the rosy Forest Pigeon to her native tree for mating. White-Throat--White-Throat--your course is flown! For this is Amochol's frontier; and by tomorrow night we enter Catharines-town--thou and I, little Lois- -two Hidden Children--one hidden by the Western Gate, one by the Eastern Gate's dark threshold, 'hidden in the husks.'....How shall it be with us now, O little rosy spirit of the home-wood? My Indians will ask. What shall I say to them concerning you?"

"All laws break of themselves before us twain, who, having been hidden, are prepared for mating--where we will--and when.... And if the long flight be truly ended--and the home forests guard our secret--and if Tharon be God also--and His stars the altar lights--and his river-mist my veil----" She faltered, and her clear gaze became confused. "Why should your Indians question you?" she asked.

The last ray of the sun reddened the forest, lingered, faded, and went out in ashes. I said:

"God and Tharon are one. Priest and Sagamore, clergyman and Sachem, min- ister, ensign, Roya-neh--red men or white, all are consecrated before the Master of Life. If in these Indians' eyes you are still to remain sacred, then must you promise yourself to me, little Lois. And let the Sagamore perform the rite at once."

"Betroth myself, Euan?"

"Yes, under the Rite of the Hidden Children. Will you do this--so that my Indians can lay your hands upon their hearts? Else they may turn from you now-- perhaps prove hostile."

"I had desired to have you take me from my mother's arms."

"And so I will, in marriage--if she be alive to give you."

"Then--what is this we do?"

"It is our White Bridal."

"Summon the Sagamore," she said faintly.

And so it was done there, I prompting her with her responses, and the mys- terious rite witnessed by the priesthood of two nations--Sachem and Sagamore, Iroquois and Algonquin, with the tall lodge-poles of the pines confirming it, and the pale ghost-flowers on the moss fulfilling it, and the stars coming one by one to nail our lodge door with silver nails, and the night winds, enchanted, chanting the Karenna of the Uncut Corn.

And now the final and most sacred symbol of betrothal was at hand; and the Oneida Sachem drew away, and the Yellow Moth and the Night Hawk stood aside, with heads quietly averted, leaving the Sagamore alone before us. For only a Sagamore of the Enchanted Clan might stand as witness to the mystery, where now the awful, viewless form of Tharon was supposed to stand, white winged and plumed, and robed like the Eight Thunders in snowy white.

"Listen, Loskiel," he said, "my younger brother, blood-brother to a Siwanois. Listen, also, O Rosy-Throated Pigeon of the Woods--home from the unseen flight to mate at last!"

He plucked four ghost-flowers, and cast the pale blossoms one by one to the four great winds.

"O untainted winds that blow the Indian corn," he said, "winds of the wilderness, winds of the sounding skies--clean and pure as ye are, not one of you has blown the green and silken blankets loose from these, our Hidden Children, nestling unseen, untouched, unstained, close cradled in a green embrace. Nor wind, nor rain, nor hail, not the fierce heat of many summers have revealed these Hidden Ones, stripped them of the folded verdure that conceals them still, each wrapped within the green leaves of the corn.

"Continue to listen, winds of the sounding skies. Let the Eight White-plumed Thunders listen. An ensign of the Magic Clan bears witness under Tharon. A Sagamore veils his face. Let Tharon hear these children when they speak. Let Tamenund listen!"

Standing straight and tall there in the starlight, he drew his blanket across his eyes. The Oneidas and the Stockbridge did the same.

Slowly, timidly, in compliance with my whispered bidding, the slender, trembling hands of Lois unlaced my throat-points to the shoulder, baring my chest. Then she said aloud, but in a voice scarce audible, I prompting every word:

"It is true! Under the folded leaves a Hidden Youth is sleeping. I bid him sleep awhile. I promise to disturb no leaf. This is the White Bridal. I close what I have scarcely parted. I bid him sleep this night. When--when----"

I whispered, prompting her, and she found her voice, continuing:

"When at his lodge door they shall come softly and lay shadows to bar it, a moon to seal it, and many stars to nail it fast, then, in the dark within, I shall hear the painted quiver rattle as he puts it off; and the antlers fall clashing to the ground. Only the green and tender cloak of innocence shall endure--a little while--then, falling, enfold us twain embraced where only one had slept before. A promised bride has spoken."

She bowed her head, took my hands in hers, laid them lightly on her heart; then straightened up, with a long-drawn, quivering breath, and stood, eyes closed, as I unlaced her throat-points, parting the fawn-skin cape till the soft thrums lay on her snowy shoulders.

"It is true," I whispered. "Under the folded leaves a Hidden Maid lies sleeping. I bid her sleep awhile; I bid her dream in innocence through this White Bridal night. I promise to disturb no leaf that sheathes her. I now refold and close again what I have scarcely touched and opened. I bid her sleep.

"When on my lodge door they nail the Oneida stars, and seal my door with the moon of Tharon, and lay long shadows there to bar it; then I, within the darkness there, shall hear the tender rustle of her clinging husks, parting to cradle two where one alone had slept since she was born."

Gently I drew the points, closing the cape around her slender throat, knotted the laces, smoothed out the thrums, took her small hands and laid them on my breast.

One by one the stately Indians came to make their homage, bending their war-crests proudly and placing her hands upon their painted breasts. Then they went away in silence, each to his proper post, no doubt. Yet, to be certain, I desired to make my rounds, and bade Lois await me there. But I had not proceeded three paces when lo! Of a sudden she was at my side, laughing her soft defiance at me in the darkness.

"No orders do I take save what I give myself," she said. "Which is no mutiny, Euan, and no insubordination either, seeing that you and I are one--or are like to be when the brigade chaplain passes--if the Tories meddle not with his honest scalp! Come! Honest Euan, shall we make our rounds together? Or must I go alone?"

And she linked her arm in mine and put one foot forward, looking up at me with all the light mischief of the very boy she seemed in her soft rifle-dress and leggins, and the bright hair crisply curling 'round her moleskin cap.

"Have a care of the trees, then, little minx," I said.

"Pooh! Can you not see in the dark?"

"Can you?"

"Surely. When you and I went to the Spring Waiontha, I needed not your lantern light to guide me."

"I see not well by night," I admitted.

"You do see well by night--through my two eyes! Are we not one? How often must I repeat it that you and I are one! One! One! O Loskiel--stealer of hearts, if you could only know how often on my knees I am before you--how truly I adore, how humbly, scarcely daring to believe my heart that tells me such a tale of magic and enchantment--after these barren, loveless years. Mark! Yonder stands the Grey-Feather! Is that his post?"

"Wonder-eyes, I see him not! Wait--aye, you are right. And he is at his post. Pass to the left, little minx."

And so we made the rounds, finding every Indian except the Sagamore at his post. He lay asleep. And after we had returned to our southern ledge of rock, and I had spread my blanket for her and laid my pack to pillow her, I picked up my rifle and rose from my knees.

"And you?" she asked.

"I stand guard across the trail below."

"Why? When all except the Siwanois are watching! The Night Hawk is there. Stretch yourself here beside me and try to sleep. Your watch will come too soon to suit you, or me either, for that matter."

"Do you mean to go on guard with me?"

"Do you dream that I shall let you stand your guard alone, young sir?"

"This is folly, Lois--"

"Euan, you vex me. Lie beside me. Here is sufficient blanket room and pillow. And if you do not sleep presently and let me sleep too, our wits will all be sadly addled when they summon us."

So I stretched myself out beside her and looked up, open eyed, into darkness.

"Sleep well," she whispered, smothering a little laugh.

"Sleep safely, Lois."

"That is why I desired you--so I might sleep safely, knowing myself safe when you are, too. And you are safe only when you are at my side. Do you follow my philosophy?"

I said presently: "This is our White Bridal, Lois. The ceremony completes itself by dawn."

"Save that the Sagamore is but a heathen priest, truly I feel myself already wedded to you, so solemn was our pretty rite.... Dare you kiss me, Euan? You never have. Christians betrothed may kiss each other once, I think."

"Not such as we--if the rite means anything to us."

"Why?"

"Not on the White Bridal night--if we regard this rite as sacred."

"I feel its sacredness. That is why I thought no sin if you should kiss me--on such a night."

She sat up in her blanket; and I sat up, too.

* "Tekasenthos," she said.

[* "I am weeping."]

* "Chetena, you are laughing!"

[* "Mouse."]

* "Neah. Tekasenthos!" she insisted.

[* "No, I am weeping."]

"Why?"

"You do not love me," she remarked, kicking off one ankle moccasin.

* "Kenonwea-sasita-ha-wiyo, chetenaha!" I said, laughing.

[* "I love your beautiful foot, little mouse."]

* "Akasita? Katontats. But is that all of me you love?"

[* "My foot? I consent."]

"The other one also."

"The other one also."

* "Neah-wenh-a, O Loskiel. I shall presently slay you and go to sleep."

[* "I thank you."]

There fell a silence, then:

"Do you not know in your heart how it is with me?" I said unsteadily.

She lay down, facing me.

"In my heart I know, beloved above all men! But I am like a child with you-
-desiring to please, ardent, confused, unaccustomed. And everything you say de-
lights me--and all you do--or refrain from doing--thrills me with content.... It was
so true and sweet of you to leave my lips untouched. I adore you for it--but then I
had adored you if you had kissed me, also. Always, your decision pleasures me."

After a long while I spoke cautiously. She lay asleep, her lips scarce parted;
but in her sleep she seemed to hear my voice, for one arm stole out in the dark and
closed around my neck.

And so we lay until the dark forms gliding from the forest summoned me to
mount my guard, and Lois awoke with a little sigh, sat upright, then sprang to her
feet to face the coming dawn alone with me.

CHAPTER XIX
AMOCHOL

By daybreak we had salted our parched corn, soaked, and eaten it, and my Indians were already freshening their paint. The Sagamore, stripped for battle, barring
clout and sporran, stood tall and powerfully magnificent in his white and vermilion
hue of war. On his broad chest the scarlet Ghost Bear reared; on his crest the scarlet
feathers slanted low. The Yellow Moth was unbelievably hideous in the poisonous hue of a toad-stool; his crest and all his skin glistened yellow, shining like the
sulphurous belly of a snake. But the Grey-Feather was ghastly; his bony features
were painted like a skull, spine, ribs, and limb-bones traced out heavily in yellowish
white so that he seemed a stalking and articulated skeleton as he moved in the dim
twilight of the trees. And I could see that he was very proud of the effect.

As for the young and ambitious Night Hawk, he had simply made one murderous symbol of himself--a single and terrific emblem of his entire body, for he was
painted black from head to foot like an Iroquois executioner, and his skin glistened
as the plumage of a sleek crow shines in the sunlight of a field. Every scalp-lock
was neatly braided and oiled; every crown shaven; every knife and war-axe and
rifle-barrel glimmered silver bright under the industrious rubbing; flints had been
renewed; with finest priming powder pans reprimed; and now all my Indians squat-

ted amiably together in perfect accord, very loquacious in their guarded voices, Iroquois, Mohican, and Stockbridge, foregathering as though there had never been a feud in all the world.

Through the early dusk of morning, Lois had stolen away, having discovered a spring pool to bathe in, the creek water being dark and bitter; and I had freshened myself, too, when she returned, her soft cheeks abloom, and the crisp curls still wet with spray.

When we had eaten, the Sagamore rose and moved noiselessly down the height of land to the trail level, where our path entered the ghostly gloom of the evergreens. I followed; Lois followed me, springing lightly from tussock to rotting log, from root to bunchy swale, swift, silent footed, dainty as a lithe and graceful panther crossing a morass dry-footed.

Behind her trotted in order the Yellow Moth, Tohoontowhee, and lastly the Grey-Feather--"Like Father Death herding us all to destruction," whispered Lois in my ear, as I halted while the Sagamore surveyed the trail ahead with cautious eyes.

As we moved forward once more, I glanced around at Lois and thought I never had seen such fresh and splendid vigor in any woman. Nor had I ever seen her in such a bright and happy spirit, as though the nearness to the long sought goal was changing her every moment, under my very eyes, into a lovelier and more radiant being than ever had trod this war-scarred world.

While we had eaten our hasty morning meal, I had told her what I had learned of the Vale Yndaia; and this had excited her more than anything I ever saw to happen to her, so that her grey eyes sparkled with brilliant azure lights, and the soft colour flew from throat to brow, waxing and waning with every quick-drawn breath.

She wore also, and for the first time, the "moccasins for flying feet"--and ere she put them on she showed them to me with eager and tender pride, kissing each soft and beaded shoe before she drew it over her slender foot. Around her throat, lying against her heart, nestled her father's faded picture. And as we sped I could hear her murmuring to herself:

"Jean Coeur! Jean Coeur! Enfin! Me voici en chemin!"

North, always north we journeyed, moving swiftly on a level runway, or, at fault, checked until the Sagamore found the path, sometimes picking our dangerous ways over the glistening bog, from swale to log, now leaping for some solid root or bunch of weed, now swinging across quicksands, hanging to tested branches by our hands.

Duller grew the light as the foliage overhead became denser, until we could scarce see the warning glimmer of the bog. Closer, taller, more unkempt grew the hemlocks on every hand. In the ghostly twilight we could not distinguish their separate spectral trunks, so close they grew together. And it seemed like two solid walls through which wound a dusky corridor of mud and bitter tasting water.

Then, far ahead a level gleam caught my eye. Nearer it grew and brighter; and presently out of the grewsome darkness of the swamp we stepped into a lovely oval intervale of green ferns and grasses, set with oak trees, and a clear, sweet thread of water dashing through it, and spraying the tall ferns along its banks so that they quivered and glistened with the sparkling drops. And here we saw a little bird flitting--the first we had seen that day.

At the western end of the oval glade a path ran straight away as far as we could see, seeming to pierce the western wall of the hills. The little brook followed at.

As Lois knelt to drink, the Sagamore whispered to me:

"This is the pass to the Vale Yndaia! You shall not tell her yet--not till we have dealt with Amochol."

"Not till we have dealt with Amochol," I repeated, staring at the narrow opening which crossed this black and desolate region like a streak of sunshine across burnt land.

Tahoontowhee examined the trail; nothing had passed since the last rain, save deer and fox.

So I went over to where Lois was bathing her flushed face in the tiny stream, and lay down to drink beside her.

"The water is cold and sweet," she said, "not like that bitter water in the swamp." She held her cupped hands for me to drink from. And I kissed the fragrant cup.

As we rose and I shouldered my rifle, the Grey-Feather began to sing in a low, musical, chanting voice; and all the Indians turned merry faces toward Lois and me as they nodded time to the refrain:

"Continue to listen and hear the truth,
Maiden Hidden and Hidden Youth.
The song of those who are 'more than men'!
*Thi-ya-en-sa-y-e-ken!"
    [* "They will (live to) see it again!"]
"It is the chant of the Stone Throwers--the Little People!" said Mayaro, laughing. "Ye two are fit to hear it."

"They are singing the Song of the Hidden Children," I whispered to Lois. "Is it not strangely pretty?"

"It is wild music, but sweet," she murmured, "--the music of the Little People--che-kah-a-hen-wah."

"Can you catch the words?"

"Aye, but do not understand them every one."

"Some day I will make them into an English song for you. Listen! 'The Voices' are beginning! Listen attentively to the Chant of *Ta-neh-u-weh-too!"

    [* "Hidden in the Husks."]

The Night Hawk was singing now, as he walked through the sunlit glade, hip-deep in scented ferns and jewel-weed. Two brilliant humming-birds whirled around him as he strode.

A VOICE

"Who shall find my Hidden Maid
Where the tasselled corn is growing?
Let them seek her in Kandaia,
Let them seek her in Oswaya,
Where the giant pines are growing,
Let them seek and be afraid!
Where the Adriutha flowing
Splashes through the forest glade,
Where the Kennyetto flowing
Thunders through the hemlock shade,

Let them seek and be afraid,
From Oswaya To Yndaia,
All the way to Carenay!"

ANOTHER VOICE

"Who shall find my Hidden Son
Where the tasselled corn is growing?
Let them seek my Hidden One
From the Silver Horicon
North along the Saguenay,
Where the Huron cocks are crowing,
Where the Huron maids are mowing
Hay along the Saguenay;
Where the Mohawk maids are hoeing
Corn along the Carenay,
Let them seek my Hidden Son,
West across the inland seas,
South to where the cypress trees
Quench the flaming scarlet flora
Of the painted Esaurora,
Drenched in rivers to their knees!
*Honowehto! Like Thendara!
[* "They have vanished."]
Let them hunt to Danascara
Back along the Saguenay,
On the trail to Carenay,
Through the Silver Horicon
Till the night and day are one!
Where the Adriutha flowing
Sings below Oswaya glowing.
Where the sunset of Kandaia
Paints the meadows of Yndaia,

Let them seek my Hidden Son
'Till the sun and moon are one!"
  *TE-KI-E-HO-KEN
[* "Two Voices (together)."]
  * "Nai Shehawa! She lies sleeping,
[* "Behold thy children!"]
Where the green leaves closely fold her!
He shall wake first and behold her
Who is given to his keeping;
He shall strip her of her leaves
Where she sleeps amid the sheaves,
Snowy white, without a stain,
Nothing marred of wind or rain.
So from slumber she shall waken,
And behold the green robe shaken
From his shoulders to her own!
*Ye-ji-se-way-ad-kerone!"
[* "So ye two are laid together."]

The pretty song of the Hidden Children softened to a murmur and died out as our trail entered the swamp once more, north of the oval glade. And into its sombre twilight we passed out of the brief gleam of sunshine. Once more the dark and bitter water coiled its tortuous channel through the slime; huge, gray evergreens, shaggy and forbidding, towered above, closing in closer and closer on every side, crowding us into an ever-narrowing trail.

But this trail, since we had left the sunny glade, had become harder under foot, and far more easy to travel; and we made fast time along it, so that early in the afternoon we suddenly came out into that vast belt of firm ground and rocky, set with tremendous oaks and pines and hemlocks, on the northern edge of which lies Catharines-town, on both banks of the stream.

And here the stream rushed out through this country as though frightened, running with a mournful sound into the northern forest; and the pines were never still, sighing and moaning high above us, so that the never ceasing plaint of wind and water filled the place.

And here, on a low, bushy ridge, we lay all day, seeing in the forest not one living thing, nor any movement in that dim solitude, save where the grey and wraith-like water tossed a flat crest against some fallen tree, or its dull and sullen surface gleamed like lead athwart the valley far ahead.

My Indians squatted, or sprawled prone along the ridge; Lois lay flat on her stomach beside me, her chin resting on her clasped hands. We talked of many things that afternoon--of life as we had found it, and what it promised us--of death, if we must find it here in these woods before I made her mine. And of how long was the spirit's trail to God--if truly it were but a swift, upward flight like to the rushing of an arrow already flashing out of sight ere the twanging buzz of the bow-string died on the air. Or if it were perhaps a long, slow, painful journey through thick night, toilsome, blindly groping, wings adroop trailing against bruised heels. Or if we two must pass by hell, within sight and hearing of the thunderous darkness, and feel the rushing wind of the pit hot on one's face.

Sometimes, like a very child, she prattled of happiness, which she had never experienced, but meant to savour, wedded or not--talked to me there of all she had never known and would now know and realize within her mother's tender arms.

"And sometimes, Euan, dreaming of her I scarce see how, within my heart, I can find room for you also. Yet, I know well there is room for both of you, and that one without the other would leave my happiness but half complete.... I wonder if I resemble her? Will she know me--and I her? How shall we meet, Euan--after more than a score of years? She will see my moccasins, and cry out! She will see my face and know me, calling me by name! Oh, happiness! Oh, miracle! Will the night never come!"

"Dear maid and tender! You should not build your hopes too high, so that they crush you utterly if they must fall to earth again."

"I know. Amochol may have slain her. We will learn all when you take Amochol--when God delivers him into your hands this night.... How will you do it, Euan?"

"Take him, you mean?"

"Aye."

"We lie south, just outside the fire-ring's edge. Boyd watches them from the north. His signal to us begins the business. We leap straight for the altar and take Amochol at its very foot, the while Boyd's heavy rifles deal death on every side, keeping the others busy while we are securing Amochol. Then we all start south for the army, God willing, and meet our own people on the high-ridge east of us."

"But Yndaia!"

"That we will scour the instant we have Amochol."

"You promise?"

"Dearest, I promise solemnly. Yet--I think--if your mother lives--she may be here in Catharines-town tonight. This is the Dream Feast, Lois. I and my Indians believe that she has bought her life of Amochol by dreaming for them. And if this be true, and she has indeed become their Prophetess and Interpreter of Dreams, then this night she will be surely here to read their dreams for them."

"Will we see her before you begin the attack?"

"Little Lois, how can I tell you such things? We are to creep up close to the central fire--as close as we dare."

"Will there be crowds of people there?"

"Many people."

"Warriors?"

"Not many. They are with Hiokatoo and Brant. There will be hunters and Sachems, and the Cat-People, and the Andastes pack, and many women. The False Faces will not be there, nor the Wyoming Witch, nor the Toad Woman, because all these are now with Hiokatoo and Walter Butler. For which I thank God and am very grateful."

"How shall I know her in this fire-lit throng?" murmured Lois, staring ahead of her where the evening dusk had now veiled the nearer trees with purple.

Before I could reply, the Sagamore rose from his place on my left, and we all sprang lightly to our feet, looked to our priming, covered our pans, and trailed arms.

"Now!" he muttered, passing in front of me and taking the lead; and we all filed after him through the open forest, moving rapidly, almost on a run, for half a mile, then swung sharply out to the right, where the trees grew slimmer and thinner, and plunged into a thicket of hazel and osier.

"I smell smoke," whispered Lois, keeping close to me.

I nodded. Presently we halted and stood in silence, minute after minute, while the purple dusk deepened swiftly around us, and overhead a few stars came out palely, as though frightened.

Then Mayaro dropped noiselessly to the ground and began to crawl forward over the velvet moss; and we followed his example, feeling our way with our right hands to avoid dry branches and rocks. From time to time we paused to regain our strength and breathe; and the last time we did so the aromatic smell of birch-smoke blew strong in our nostrils, and there came to our ears a subdued murmur like the stirring of pine-tops in a steady breeze. But there were no pines around us now, only osier, hazel, and grey-birch, and the deep moss under foot.

"A house!" whispered the Yellow Moth, pointing.

There it stood, dark and shadowy against the north. Another loomed dimly beyond it; a haystack rose to the left.

We were in Catharines-town.

And now, as we crawled forward, we could see open country on our left, and many unlighted houses and fields of corn, dim and level against the encircling forest. The murmur on our right had become a sustained and distinct sound, now swelling in the volume of many voices, now subsiding, then waxing to a dull tumult. And against the borders of the woods, like a shining crimson curtain shifting, we could see the red reflection of a fire sweeping across the solid foliage.

With infinite precautions, we moved through the thicket toward it, the glare growing yellower and more brilliant as we advanced. And now we remained motionless and very still.

Massed against the flare of light were crowded many people in a vast, uneven circle ringing a great central fire, except at the southern end. And here, where the ring was open so that we could see the huge fire itself, stood a great, stone slab on end, between two round mounds of earth. It was the altar of Amochol, and we knew it instantly, where it stood between the ancient mounds raised by the Alligewi.

The drums had not yet begun while we were still creeping up, but they began now, muttering like summer thunder, the painted drummers marching into the circle and around it twice before they took their places to the left of the altar, squatting there and ceaselessly beating their hollow sounding drums. Then, in file, the eight Sachems of the dishonoured Senecas filed into the fiery circle, chanting and timing their slow steps to the mournful measure of their chant. All wore the Sachem's crest painted white; their bodies were most barbarously striped with black and white, and their blankets were pure white, crossed by a single blood-red band.

What they chanted I could not make out, but that it was some blasphemy which silently enraged my Indians was plain enough; and I laid a quieting hand on the Sagamore's shaking arm, cautioning him; and he touched the Oneidas and the Stockbridge, one by one, in warning.

Opposite us, the ruddy firelight played over the massed savages, women, children, and old men mostly, gleaming on glistening eyes, sparkling on wampum and metal ornaments. To the right and left of us a few knives and hatchets caught the firelight, and many multi-coloured plumes and blankets glowed in its shifting brilliancy.

The eight Sachems stood, tall and motionless, behind the altar; the drumming never ceased, and from around the massed circle rose a low sing-song chant, keeping time to the hollow rhythm of the drums:

* "Onenh are oya
Egh-des-ho-ti-ya-do-re-don Nene ronenh 'Ken-ki-ne ne-nya-wenne!"

[* "Now again they decided and said: 'This shall be done!'"]

Above this rumbling undertone sounded the distant howling of dogs in Catharines-town; and presently the great forest owls woke up, yelping like goblins across the misty intervale. Strangely enough, the dulled pandemonium, joined in by dog and owl and drum and chanting savages, made but a single wild and melancholy monotone seeming to suit the time and place as though it were the voice of this fierce wilderness itself.

Now into the circle, one by one, came those who had dreamed and must be answered--not as in the old-time and merry Feast of Dreams, where the rites were harmless and the mirth and jollity innocent, if rough--for Amochol had perverted the ancient and innocent ceremony, making of a fourteen-day feast a sinister rite which ended in a single night.

I understood this more clearly now, as I lay watching the proceedings, for I had seen this feast in company with Guy Johnson on the Kennyetto, and found in it nothing offensive and no revolting license or blasphemy, though others may say this is not true.

Yet, how can a rite which begins with three days religious services, including confession of sins on wampum, be otherwise than decent? As for the rest of the feast, the horse-play, skylarking, dancing, guessing contests--the little children's dance on the tenth day, the Dance for Four on the eleventh, the Dance for the Eight Thunders on the thirteenth--the noisy, violent, but innocent romping of the False Faces--all this I had seen in the East, and found no evil in it and no debauchery.

But what was now already going on I had never seen at any Iroquois feast or rite, and what Amochol had made of this festival I dared not conjecture as I gazed at the Dreamers now advancing into the circle with an abandon and an effrontery scarcely decent.

Six young girls came first, naked except for a breadth of fawn-skin falling from waist to instep. Their bodies were painted vermilion from brow to ankle; they carried in their hands red harvest apples, which they tossed one to another as they move lightly across the open space in a slow, springy, yet not ungraceful dance.

Behind them came a slim maid, wearing only a black fox-head, and the soft pelt dangling from her belt, and the tail behind. She was painted a ruddy yellow everywhere except a broad line of white in front, like a fox's belly; and, like a fox, too, her feet and hands were painted black.

Following her came eight girls plumed in spotless white and clothed only in white feathers--aping the Thunders, doubtless; but even to me, a white man and a Christian, it was a sinister and evil sight to see this mockery as they danced forward, arms entwined, and the snowy plumes floating out in the firelight, disclosing the white painted bodies which the firelight tinted with rose and amber lights.

Then came dancing other girls, dressed in most offensive mockery of the harmless and ancient rite--first the Fire Keeper, crowned with oak leaves instead of wild cherry, and wearing a sewed garment made of oak twigs and tufted leaves, from which the acorns hung. Followed two girls in cloaks of shimmering pine-needles, and wearing wooden masks, dragging after them the carcasses of two white dogs, to "Clothe the Moon Witch!" they cried to the burly Erie acolyte who followed them, his heavy knife shining in his hand.

Then the Erie disemboweled the strangled dogs, cast their entrails into the fire, and kicked aside the carcasses, shouting:

"Atensi stands naked upon the Moon! What shall she wear to cover her?"

"The soft hide of a Hidden Child!" answered a Sachem from behind the altar. "We have so dreamed it."

"It shall be done!" cried the Erie; and, lifting himself on tip toe, he threw back his brutal head and gave the Panther Cry so that his voice rang hideously through the night.

Instantly into the circle came scurrying the Andastes, some wearing the heads of bulls, some of wolves, foxes, bears, their bodies painted horribly in raw reds and yellows, and running about like a pack of loosened hounds. All their movements were wild and aimless, and like animals, and they seemed to smell their way as they ran about hither and thither, sniffing, listening, but seldom looking long or directly at any one thing.

I was sorely afraid that some among them might come roving and muzzling into the bushes where we lay; but they did not, gradually gathering into an uneasy pack and settling on their haunches near the dancing girls, who played with them, and tormented them with branches of hazel, samphire and green osier.

Suddenly a young girl, jewelled with multi-coloured diamonds of paint, and jingling all over with little bells, came dancing into the ring, beating a tiny, painted drum as she advanced. She wore only a narrow sporran of blue-birds' feathers to her knees, glistening blue moccasins of the same plumage, and a feathered head dress of the scarlet fire-bird. Behind her filed the Cat-People, Amochol's hideous acolytes, each wearing the Nez Perce ridge of porcupine-like hair, the lynx-skin cloak and necklace of claws; and all howling to the measure of the little painted drum. I could feel Mayaro beside me, quivering with eagerness and fury; but the time was not yet, and he knew it, as did his enraged comrades.

For behind the Eries, moving slowly, came a slender shape, shrouded in white. Her head was bent in the shadow of her cowl; her white wool vestments trailed behind her. Both hands were clasped together under her loose robe. On her cowl was a wreath of nightshade, with its dull purple fruit and blossoms clustering around her shadowed brow.

"Who is that?" whispered Lois, beginning to tremble, "God knows," I said.

"Wait!"

The shrouded shape moved straight to the great stone altar and stood there a moment facing it; then, veiling her face with her robe, she turned, mounted the left hand mound, and seated herself, head bowed.

Toward her, advancing all alone, was now approaching a figure, painted, clothed, and plumed in scarlet. Everything was scarlet about him, his moccasins, his naked skin, the fantastic cloak and blanket, girdle, knife-hilt, axe shaft, and the rattling quiver on his back--nay, the very arrows in it were set with scarlet feathers, and the looped bowstring was whipped with crimson sinew.

The Andastes came moaning, cringing, fawning, and leaping about his knees; he noticed them not at all; the Cat-People, seated in a semicircle, looked up humbly as he passed; he ignored them.

Slowly he moved to the altar and laid first his hand upon it, then unslung his bow and quiver and laid them there. A great silence fell upon the throng. And we knew we were looking at last upon the Scarlet Priest.

Yes, this was Amochol, the Red Sachem, the vile, blaspheming, murderous, and degraded chief who had made of a pure religion a horror, and of a whole people a nation of unspeakable assassins.

As the firelight flashed full in his face, I saw that his features were not painted; that they were delicate and regular, and that the skin was pale, betraying his French ancestry.

And good God! What a brood of demons had that madman, Frontenac, begot to turn loose upon this Western World! For there appeared to be a Montour in every bit of devil's work we ever heard of--and it seemed as though there was no end to their number. One, praise God, had been slain before Wyoming--which some said enraged the Witch, his mother, to the fearsome deeds she did there--and one was this man's sister, Lyn Montour--a sleek, lithe girl of the forest, beautiful and depraved. But the Toad Woman, mother of Amochol, was absent, and of all the Montours only this strange priest had remained at Catharines-town. And him we were now about to take or slay.

"Amochol!" whispered the Sagamore in my ear.

"I know," I said. "It is strange. He is not like a monster, after all."

"He is beautiful," whispered Lois.

I stared at the pale, calm face over which the firelight played. The features seemed almost perfect, scarcely cruel, yet there was in the eyes a haunting beauty that was almost terrible when they became fixed.

To his scarlet moccasins crept the Andastes, one by one, and squatted there in silence.

Then a single warrior entered the ring. He was clad in the ancient arrow-proof armour of the Iroquois, woven of sinew and wood. His face was painted jet black, and he wore black plumes. He mounted the eastern mound, strung his bow, set an arrow to the string, and seated himself.

The red acolytes came forward, and the slim Prophetess bent her head till the long, dark hair uncoiled and fell down, clouding her to the waist in shadow.

"Hereckenes!" cried Amochol in a clear voice; and at the sound of their ancient name the Cat-People began a miauling chant.

"Antauhonorans!" cried Amochol.

Every Seneca took up the chant, and the drums timed it softly and steadily.

"Prophetess!" said Amochol in a ringing voice. "I have dreamed that the Moon Witch and her grandson Iuskeha shall be clothed. With what, then, shall they be clothed, O Woman of the Night Sky? Explain to my people this dream that I have dreamed."

The slim, white-cowled figure answered slowly, with bowed head, brooding motionless in the shadow of her hair:

"Two dogs lie yonder for Atensi and her grandson. Let them be painted with the sun and moon. So shall the dream of Amochol come true!"

"Sorceress!" he retorted fiercely. "Shall I not offer to Atensi and Iuskeha two Hidden Children, that white robes may be made of their unblemished skins to clothe the Sun and Moon?"

"Into the eternal wampum it is woven that the soft, white skins shall clothe their bodies till the husks fall from the silken corn."

"And then, Witch of the East? Shall I not offer them when the husks are stripped?"

"I see no further than you dream, O Amochol!"

He stretched out his arm toward her, menacingly:

"Yet they shall both be strangled here upon this stone!" he said. "Look, Witch!

Can you not see them lying there together? I have dreamed it."

She silently pointed at the two dead dogs.

"Look again!" he cried in a loud voice. "What do you see?"

She made no reply.

"Answer!" he said sharply.

"I have looked. And I see only the eternal wampum lying at my feet--lacking a single belt."

With a furious gesture the Red Priest turned and stared at the dancing girls who raised their bare arms, crying:

"We have dreamed, O Amochol! Let your Sorceress explain our dreams to us!"

And one after another, as their turns came, they leaped up from the ground and sprang forward. The first, a tawny, slender, mocking thing, flung wide her arms.

"Look, Sorceress! I dreamed of a felled sapling and a wolverine! What means my dream?"

And the slim, white figure, head bowed in her dark hair, answered quietly:

"O dancer of the Na-usin, who wears okwencha at the Onon-hou-aroria, yet is no Seneca, the felled sapling is thou thyself. Heed lest the wolverine shall scent a human touch upon thy breast!" And she pointed at the Andastes.

A dead silence followed, then the girl, horror struck, shrank back, her hands covering her face.

Another sprang forward and cried:

"Sorceress! I dreamed of falling water and a red cloud at sunset hanging like a plume!"

"Water falls, daughter of Mountain Snakes. Every drop you saw was a dead man falling. And the red cloud was red by reason of blood; and the plume was the crest of a war chief."

"What chief!" said Amochol, turning his deadly eyes on her.

"A Gate-Keeper of the West."

The shuddering silence was broken by the eager voice of another girl, bounding from her place--a flash of azure and jewelled paint.

"And I, O Sorceress! I dreamed of night, and a love song under the million stars. And of a great stag standing in the water."

"Had the stag no antlers, little daughter?"

"None, for it was spring time."

"You dreamed of night. It shall be night for a long while--for ages and ages, ere the stag's wide antlers crown his head again. For the antlers were lying upon a new made grave. And the million stars were the lights of camp-fires. And the love-song was the Karenna. And the water you beheld was the river culled Chemung."

The girl seemed stunned, standing there plucking at her fingers, scarlet lips parted, and her startled eyes fixed upon the white-draped sibyl.

"Executioner! Bend your bow!" cried Amochol, with a terrible stare at the Sorceress.

The man in woven armour raised his bow, bent it, drawing the arrow to the tip. At the same instant the Prophetess rose to her feet, flung back her cowl, and looked Amochol steadily in the eyes from the shadow of her hair.

So, for a full minute in utter silence, they stared at each other; then Amochol said between his teeth:

"Have a care that you read truly what my people dream!"

"Shall I lie?" she asked in even tones. And, quivering with impotent rage and superstition, the Red Priest found no word to answer.

"O Amochol," she said, "let the armoured executioner loose his shaft. It is poisoned. Never since the Cat-People were overthrown has a poisoned arrow been used within the Long House. Never since the Atotarho covered his face from Hiawatha--never since the snakes were combed from his hair--has a Priest of the Long House dared to doubt the Prophetess of the Seneca nation. Doubt--and die!"

Amochol's face was like pale brown marble; twice he half turned toward the executioner, but gave no signal. Finally, he laid his hand flat on the altar; the executioner unbent his bow and the arrow drooped from the painted haft and dangled there, its hammered iron war-head glinting in the firelight.

Then the Prophetess turned and stood looking out over the throng through the thick, aromatic smoke from the birch-fire, and presently her clear voice rang through the deathly silence:

"O People of the Evening Sky! Far on the Chemung lie many dead men. I see them lying there in green coats and in red, in feathers and in paint! Through forests, through mountains, through darkness, have my eyes beheld this thing. There is a new thunder in the hills, and red fire flowers high in the pines, and a hail falls, driving earthward in iron drops that slay all living things.

"New clouds hang low along the river; and they are not of the water mist that comes at twilight and ascends with the sun. Nor is this new thunder in the hills the voice of the Eight White Plumed Ones; nor is the boiling of the waters the stirring of the Serpent Bride.

"Red run the riffles, yet the sun is high; and those who would cross at the ford have laid them down to dam the waters with their bodies.

"And I see fires along the flats; I see flames everywhere, towns on fire, corn burning, hay kindling to ashes under a white ocean of smoke--the Three Sisters scorched, trampled, and defiled!" She lifted one arm; her spellbound audience never stirred.

"Listen!" she cried, "I hear the crashing of many feet in northward flight! I hear horses galloping, and the rattle of swords. Many who run are stumbling, falling, lying still and crushed and wet with blood. I, Sorceress of the Senecas, see and hear these things; and as I see and hear, so must I speak my warning to you all!"

She whirled on Amochol, flinging back her hair. Her skin was as white us my own!

With a stifled cry Lois sprang to her feet; but I caught her and held her fast.

"Good God!" I whispered to the Sagamore. "Where is Boyd?"

The executioner had risen, and was bending his bow; the Sorceress turned deathly pale but her blue eyes flashed, never swerving from the cruel stare of Amochol.

"Where is Boyd?" I whispered helplessly. "They mean to murder her!"

"Kill that executioner!" panted Lois, struggling in my arms. "In God's name, slay him where he stands!"

"It means our death," said the Sagamore.

The Night Hawk came crouching close to my shoulder. He had unslung and strung his little painted bow of an adolescent, and was fitting the nock of a slim arrow to the string.

He looked up at me; I nodded; and as the executioner clapped his heels together, straightened himself, and drew the arrow to his ear, we heard a low twang! And saw the black hand of the Seneca pinned to his own bow by the Night Hawk's shaft.

So noiselessly was it done that the fascinated throng could not at first understand what had happened to the executioner, who sprang into the air, screamed, and stood clawing and plucking at the arrow while his bow hung dripping with blood, yet nailed to his shrinking palm.

Amochol, frozen to a scarlet statue, stared at the contortions of the executioner for a moment, then, livid, wheeled on the Prophetess, shaking from head to foot.

"Is this your accursed magic?" he shouted. "Is this your witchcraft, Sorceress of Biskoonah? Is it thus you strike when threatened? Then you shall burn! Take her, Andastes!"

But the Andastes, astounded and terrified, only cowered together in a swaying pack.

Restraining Lois with all my strength, I said to the Mohican:

"If Boyd comes not before they take her, concentrate your fire on Amochol, for we can not hope to make him prisoner----"

"Hark!" motioned the Sagamore, grasping my arm. I heard also, and so did the others. The woods on our left were full of noises, the trample of people running, the noise of crackling underbrush.

We all thought the same thing, and stood waiting to see Boyd's onset break from the forest. The Red Priest also heard it, for he had turned where he stood, his rigid arm still menacing the White Sorceress.

Suddenly, into the firelit circle staggered a British soldier, hatless, dishevelled, his scarlet uniform in rags.

For a moment he stood staring about him, swaying where he stood, then with a hopeless gesture he flung his musket from him and passed a shaking hand across his eyes.

"O Amochol!" cried the Sorceress, pointing a slim and steady finger at the bloody soldier. "Have I dreamed lies or have I dreamed the truth? Hearken! The woods are full of people running! Do you hear? And have I lied to you, O Amochol?"

"From whence do you come?" cried Amochol, striding toward the soldier.

"From the Chemung. Except for the dead we all are coming--Butler and Brant and all. Bring out your corn, Seneca! The army starves."

Amochol stared at the soldier, at the executioner still writhing and struggling to loose his hand from the bloody arrow, at the Sorceress who had veiled her face.

"Witch!" he cried, "get you to Yndaia. If you stir elsewhere you shall burn!"

He had meant to say more, I think, but at that moment, from the southern woods men came reeling out into the fire-circle--ghastly, bloody, ragged creatures in shreds of uniforms, green, red, and brown--men and officers of Sir John's regiment, men of Butler's Rangers, British regulars. On their heels glided the Seneca warriors, warriors of the Cayugas, Onondagas, Caniengas, Esauroras, and here and there a traitorous Oneida, and even a few Hurons.

Pell-mell this mob of fighting men came surging through the fire-circle, and straight into Catharines-town, while I and my Indians crouched there, appalled and astounded.

I saw Sir John Johnson come up with the officers of his two battalions and a captain, a sergeant, a corporal, and fifteen British regulars.

"Clear me out this ring of mummers!" he said in his cold, penetrating voice. "And thou, Amochol, if this damned town of thine be stocked, bring out the provisions and set these Eries a-roasting corn!"

I saw McDonald storming and cursing at his irregulars, where the poor brutes had gathered into a wavering rank; I saw young Walter Butler haranguing his Rangers and Senecas; I saw Brant, calm, noble, stately, standing supported by two Caniengas while a third examined his wounded leg.

The whole place was a tumult of swarming savages and white men; already the Seneca women, crowding among the men, were raising the death wail. The dancing girls huddled together in a frightened and half-naked group; the Andastes cowered apart; the servile Eries were staggering out of the corn fields laden with ripe ears; and the famished soldiers were shouting and cursing at them and tearing the corn from their arms to gnaw the raw and milky grains.

How we were to withdraw and escape destruction I did not clearly see, for our path must cross the eastern belt of forest, and it was still swarming with fugitives arriving, limping, dragging themselves in from the disaster of the Chemung.

Hopeless to dream of taking or slaying Amochol now; hopeless to think of warning Boyd or even of finding him. Somewhere in the North he had met with obstacles which delayed him. He must scout for himself, now, for the entire Tory army was between him and us.

"There is but one way now," whispered the Mohican.

"By Yndaia," I said.

My Indians were of the same opinion.

"I should have gone there anyway," said Lois, still all a-quiver, and shivering close to my shoulder. I put my arm around her; every muscle of her body was rigid, taut, yet trembling, as a smooth and finely turned pointer trembles with eagerness and powerful self-control.

"Amochol has driven her thither," she whispered. "Shall we not be on our way?"

"Can you lead, Mayaro?" I whispered.

The Mohican turned and crawled southward on his hands and knees, moving slowly.

"For God's sake let them hear no sound in this belt of bush," I whispered to Lois.

"I am calm, Euan. I am not afraid."

"Then fallow the Sagamore."

One by one we turned and crept away southward; and I was ever fearful that some gleam from the fire, catching our rifle-barrels or axe-heads, might betray us. But we gained the denser growth undiscovered, then rose to our feet in the open forest and hurried forward in file, crowding close to keep in touch.

Once Lois turned and called back in a low, breathless voice;

"I thank Tahoontowhee from my heart for his true eye and his avenging arrow."

The young warrior laughed; but I knew he was the proudest youth in all the West that night.

The great cat-owls were shrieking and yelping through the forest as we sped southward. My Indians, silent and morose, their vengeance unslaked and now indefinitely deferred, moved at a dog trot through the forest, led by the Sagamore, whose eyes saw as clearly in the dark as my own by day.

And after a little while we noticed the stars above us, and felt ferns and grass under our feet, and came out into that same glade from whence runs the trail to Yndaia through the western hill cleft.

"People ahead!" whispered the Sagamore. "Their Sorceress and six Eries!"

"Are you certain?" I breathed, loosening my hatchet.

"Certain, Loskiel. Yonder they are halted within the ferns. They are at the stream, drinking."

I caught Lois by the wrist.

"Come with me--hurry!" I said, as the Indians darted away and began to creep out and around the vague and moving group of shadows. And as we sped forward I whispered brokenly my instructions, conjuring her to obey.

We were right among them before they dreamed of our coming; not a war-cry was uttered; there was no sound save the crashing blows of hatchets, the heavy, panting breathing of those locked in a death struggle, the deep groan and coughing as a knife slipped home.

I flung a clawing Erie from me ere his blood drenched me, and he fell floundering, knifed through and through, and tearing a hole in my rifle-cape with his teeth as he fell. Two others lay under foot; my Oneidas were slaying another in the ferns, and the Sagamore's hatchet, swinging like lightning, dashed another into eternity.

The last one ran, but stumbled, with three arrows in his burly neck and spine; and the Night Hawk's hatchet flew, severing the thread of life far him and hurling him on his face. Instantly the young Oneida leaped upon the dead man's shoulders, pulled back his heavy head, and tore the scalp off with a stifled cry of triumph.

"The Black-Snake!" said the Sagamore at my side, breathing heavily from his bloody combat, and dashing the red drops from the scalp he swung. "Look yonder, Loskiel! Our little Rosy Pigeon has returned at last!"

I had seen it already, but I turned to look. And I saw the White Sorceress and my sweetheart close locked in each other's arms--so close and motionless that they seemed but a single snowy shape there under the lustre of the stars.

CHAPTER XX
YNDAIA

At the mouth of the pass which led to the Vale Yndaia I lay with my Indians that night, two mounting guard, then one, then two more, and the sentinels changed every three hours throughout the night. But all were excited and all slept lightly.

Within the Vale Yndaia, perhaps a hundred yards from the mouth of the pass, stood the lonely little house of bark in which Madame de Contrecoeur had lived alone for twenty years.

And here, that night, Lois lay with her mother; and no living thing nearer the dim house than we who mounted guard--except for the little birds asleep that Madame de Contrecoeur had tamed, and the small forest creatures which had learned to come fearlessly at this lonely woman's low-voiced call. And these things I learned not then, but afterwards.

Never had I seen such utter loneliness--for it had been less a solitude, it seemed to me, had the little house not stood there under the pale lustre of the stars.

On every side lofty hills enclosed the valley, heavily timbered to their crests; and through the intervale the rill ran, dashing out of the pass and away into that level, wooded strip to the fern-glade which lay midway between the height of land and Catharines-town; and there joined the large stream which flowed north. I could see in the darkness little of the secret and hidden valley called Yndaia, only the heights silhouetted against the stars, a vague foreground sheeted with mist, and the dark little house standing there all alone under the stars.

All night long the great tiger-owls yelped and hallooed across the valley; all night the spectral whip-poor-will whispered its husky, frightened warning. And long after midnight a tiny bird awoke and sang monotonously for an hour or more.

Awaiting an attack from Catharines-town at any moment, we dared not make a fire or even light a torch. Rotten trunks which had fallen across the stream we dragged out and piled up across the mouth of the pass to make a defence; but we could do no more than that; and, our efforts ended, my Indians sat in a circle cross-legged, quietly hooping and stretching their freshly taken scalps by the dim light of the stars, and humming their various airs of triumph in low, contented, and purring voices. All laboured under subdued excitement, the brief and almost silent slaughter in the ferns having thoroughly aroused them. But the tension showed only in moments of abrupt gaiety, as when Mayaro challenged them to pronounce his name, and they could not, there being no letter "M" in the Iroquois language--neither "P" nor "B" either, for that matter--so they failed at "Butler" too, and Philip Schuyler, which aroused all to nervous merriment.

The Yellow Moth finished braiding his trophy first, went to the stream, and washed the blood from his weapons and his hands, polished up knife and hatchet, freshened his priming and covered it, and then, being a Christian, said his prayers on his knees, rolled over on his blanket, and instantly fell asleep.

One by one the others followed his example, excepting the Sagamore, who yawning with repressed excitement, picked up his rifle, mounted the abattis, and squatted there, his chin on a log, motionless and intent as a hunting cat in long grass. I joined him; and there we sat unstirring, listening, peering ahead into the mist-shot darkness, until our three hours' vigil ended.

Then we noiselessly summoned the Grey-Feather, and he crept up to the log defence, rifle in hand, to sit there alone until his three hours' duty was finished, when the Yellow Moth and Tahoontowhee should take his place.

It was already after sunrise when I was awakened by the tinkle of a cow-bell. A broad, pinkish shaft of sunshine slanted through the pass into the hidden valley; and for the first time in my life I now beheld the Vale Yndaia in all the dewy loveliness of dawn. A milch cow fed along the brook, flank-deep in fern. Chickens wandered in its wake, snapping at gnats and tiny, unseen creatures under the leaves.

Dainty shreds of fog rose along the stream, films of mist floated among sun-tipped ferns and bramble sprays. The little valley, cup-shaped and green, rang with the loud singing of birds. The pleasant noises of the brook filled my ears. All the western hills were now rosy where the rising sun struck their crests; north and south a purplish plum-bloom still tinted velvet slopes, which stretched away against a saffron sky untroubled by a cloud.

But the pretty valley and its green grass and ferns and hills held my attention only at moments, for my eyes ever reverted to the low bark house, with its single chimney of clay, now stained orange by the sun.

All the impatience and tenderness and not ignoble curiosity so long restrained assailed me now, as I gazed upon that solitary dwelling, where the unhappy mother of Lois de Contrecoeur had endured captivity for more than twenty years.

Vines of the flowering scarlet bean ran up the bark sides of the house, and over the low doorway; and everywhere around grew wild flowers and thickets of laurel and rhododendron, as in a cultivated park. And I saw that she had bordered a walk of brook-pebbles with azaleas and marsh-honeysuckles, making a little path to the brook over which was a log bridge with hand rails.

But laurel, azalea, and rhododendron bloomed no longer; the flowers that now blossomed in a riot of azure, purple, and gold on every side were the lovely wild asters and golden-rod; and no pretty garden set with formal beds and garnished artfully seemed to compare with this wild garden in the Vale Yndaia.

As the sun warmed the ground, the sappy perfume of tree and fern and grass mounted, scenting the pure, cool air with warm and balm-like odours. Gauzy winged creatures awoke, flitted, or hung glittering to some frail stem. The birds' brief autumn music died away; only the dry chirring of a distant squirrel broke the silence, and the faint tinkle of the cow-bell.

My Indians, now all awake, were either industriously painting their features or washing their wounds and scratches and filling them with balsam and bruised witch-hazel, or were eating the last of our parched corn and stringy shreds of leathery venison. All seemed as complacent as a party of cats licking their rumpled fur; and examining their bites, scratches, bruises, and knife wounds, I found no serious injury among them, and nothing to stiffen for very long the limbs of men in such a hardy condition.

The youthful Night Hawk was particularly proud of an ugly knife-slash, with which the Black Snake had decorated his chest--nay, I suspected him of introducing sumac juice to make it larger and more showy--but said nothing, as these people knew well enough how to care for their bodies.

Doubtless they were full as curious as was I concerning Madame de Contrecoeur--perhaps more so, because not one of them but believed her the Sorceress which unhappy circumstances had obliged her to pretend to be. Pagan or Christian, no Indian is ever rid of superstition.

Yet, devoured by curiosity, not one of them betrayed it, forbearing, at least in my presence, even to mention the White Prophetess of the Senecas, though they voiced their disappointment freely enough concerning the escape of Amochol.

So we ate our corn and dried meat, and drank at the pretty rill, and cleansed us of mud and blood, each after his own fashion--discussing the scalping of the Eries the while, the righteous death of the Black-Snake, the rout of Butler's army, and how its unexpected arrival had saved Amochol. For none among us doubted that, another half hour at most, and we had heard the cracking signal of Boyd's rifles across the hideous and fiery space.

We were not a whit alarmed concerning Boyd and his party. Reconnoitring Catharines-town from the north, they must have very quickly discovered the swarm of partly crippled hornets, so unexpectedly infesting the nest; and we felt sure that they had returned in safety to watch and keep in touch with the beaten army.

Yet, beaten at Chemung, exhausted after a rapid and disorderly retreat, this same defeated Tory army was still formidable and dangerous. We had seen enough of them to understand that. Fewer men than these at Catharines-town had ambuscaded Braddock; fewer still had destroyed another British expedition; while in the north Abercrombie had been whipped by an enemy less than a quarter as strong as his own force.

No, we veteran riflemen knew that this motley army of Butler and McDonald, if it had indeed lost a few rattles, had however parted with none of its poison fangs. Also, Amochol still lived. And it had been still another Montour of the wily and accursed Frontenac breed--"Anasthose the Huron"--who had encompassed the destruction of Braddock.

That the night had passed without a sign of an enemy, and the dawn had heralded no yelling onset, we could account for either because no scouts from Catharines-town had as yet discovered the scalped bodies of the Eries in the glade, or because our own pursuing army was so close that no time could be taken by the Senecas to attack a narrow pass held by five resolute men.

Now that the sun had risen I worried not at all over our future prospects, believing that we would hear from our advancing army by afternoon; and the Sagamore was of my opinion.

And even while we were discussing these chances, leaning against our log abattis in the sunshine, far away across the sunlit flat-woods we saw a man come out among the ferns from the southward, and lie down. And then another man came creeping from the south, and another, and yet another, the sunlight running red along their rifle barrels.

After them went both Oneidas, gliding swiftly out and speeding forward just within the encircling cover, taking every precaution, although we were almost certain that the distant scouts were ours.

And they proved to be my own men--a handful of Morgan's--pushing far in advance to reconnoitre Catharines-town from the south, although our main army was marching by the western ridges, where Boyd had marked a path for them.

A corporal in my corps, named Baily, came back with the Oneidas, climbed with them over the logs, sprang down inside, and saluted me coolly enough.

His scout of four, he admitted, had made a bad job of the swamp trail--and his muddy and disordered dress corroborated this. But the news he brought was interesting.

He had not seen Boyd. The Battle of the Chemung had ended in a disorderly rout of Butler's army, partly because we had outflanked their works, partly because Butler's Indians could not be held to face our artillery fire, though Brant displayed great bravery in rallying them. We had lost few men and fewer officers; grain-fields, hay-stacks, and Indian towns were afire everywhere along our line of march.

Detachments followed every water-course, to wipe out the lesser towns, gardens, orchards, and harvest fields on either flank, and gather up the last stray head of the enemy's cattle. The whole Iroquois Empire was now kindling into flames and the track our army left behind it was a blackened desolation, as horrible to those who wrought it as to the wretched and homeless fugitives who had once inhabited it.

He added to me in a lower voice, glancing at my Indians with the ineradicable distrust of the average woodsman, that our advanced guard had discovered white captives in several of the Indian towns--in one a young mother with a child at her breast. She, her husband, and five children had been taken at Wyoming. The Indians and Tories had murdered all save her and her baby. Her name was Mrs. Lester.

In one town, he said, they found a pretty little white child, terribly emaciated, sitting on the grass and playing with a chicken. It could speak only the Iroquois language. Doubtless its mother had been murdered long since. So starved was the little thing that had our officers not restrained it the child might have killed itself by too much eating.

Also, they found a white prisoner--a man taken at Wyoming, one Luke Sweatland; and it was said in the army that another young white girl had been found in company with her little brother, both painted like Indians, and that still another white child was discovered, which Captain Machin had instantly adopted for his own.

The Corporal further said that our army was proceeding slowly, much time be-ing consumed in laying the axe to the plum, peach, and apple orchards; and that it was a sad sight to see the heavily fruited trees fall over, crushing the ripe fruit into the mud.

He thought that the advanced guard of our army might be up by evening to burn Catharines-town, but was not certain. Then he asked permission to go back and rejoin the scout which he commanded; which permission I gave, though it was not necessary; and away he went, running like a young deer that has lagged from the herd--a tall, fine, wholesome young fellow, and as sturdy and active as any I ever saw in rifle-dress and ruffles.

My Indians lay down on their bellies, stretching themselves out in the sun across the logs, and, save for the subdued but fierce glimmer under their lazy lids, they seemed as pleasant and harmless as four tawny pumas a-sunning on the rocks.

As for me, I wandered restlessly along the brook, as far as the bridge, and, seat-ing myself here, fished out writing materials and my journal from my pouch, and filled in the events of the preceding days as briefly and exactly as I knew how. Also I made a map of Catharines-town and of Yndaia from memory, resolving to correct it later when Mr. Lodge and his surveyors came up, if opportunity permitted.

As I sat there musing and watching the chickens loitering around the dooryard, I chanced to remember the milch cow.

Casting about for a receptacle, I discovered several earthen jars of Seneca make set in willow baskets and standing by the stream. These I washed in the icy water, then slinging two of them on my shoulder I went in quest of the cow.

She proved tame enough and glad, apparently, to be relieved of her milk, I kneeling to accomplish the business, having had experience with the grass-guard of our army on more than one occasion.

Lord! How sweet the fragrance of the milk to a man who had seen none in many days. And so I carried back my jars and set them by the door of the bark house, covering each with a flat stone. And as I turned away, I saw smoke coming from the chimney; and heard the shutters on the southern window being gently opened.

Lord! What a sudden leap my heart gave as the door before me moved with the soft sliding of the great oak bolt, and was slowly opened wide to the morning sunshine.

For a moment I thought it was Lois who stood there so white and still, looking at me with grey, unfathomable eyes; then I stepped forward uncertainly, bending in silence over the narrow, sun-tanned hand that lay inert under the respectful but trembling salute I offered.

"Euan Loskiel," she murmured in the French tongue, laying her other hand over mine and looking me deep in the eyes. "Euan Loskiel, a soldier of the United States! May God ever mount guard beside you for all your goodness to my little daughter."

Tears filled her eyes; her pale, smooth cheeks were wet.

"Lois is still asleep," she said. "Come quietly with her mother and you shall see her where she sleeps."

Cap in hand, coon-tail dragging, I entered the single room on silent, moccasined feet, set my rifle in a corner, and went over to the couch of tumbled fawn-skin and silky pelts.

As I stood looking down at the sweetly flushed face, her mother lifted my brier-scarred hand and pressed her lips to it; and I, hot and crimson with happiness and embarrassment, found not a word to utter.

"My little daughter's champion!" she murmured. "Brave, and pure of heart! Ah, Monsieur, chivalry indeed is of no nation! It is a broader nobility which knows neither race nor creed nor ancestry nor birth.... How the child adores you!"

"And you, Madame. Has ever history preserved another such example of dauntless resolution and filial piety as Lois de Contrecoeur has shown us all?"

Her mother's beautiful head lifted a little:

"The blood of France runs in her veins, Monsieur." Then, for the first time, a pale smile touched her pallour. "Quand meme! No de Contrecoeur tires of endeavour while life endures.... Twenty-two years, Monsieur. Look upon her!... And for one and twenty years I have forced myself to live in hope of this moment! Do you understand?" She made a vague gesture and shook her head. "Nobody can understand--not even I, though I have lived the history of many ages."

Still keeping my hand in hers, she stood there silent, looking down at her daughter. Then, silently, she knelt beside her on the soft fawnskin, drawing me gently to my knees beside her.

"And you are to take her from me," she murmured.

"Madame----"

"Hush, soldier! It must be. I give her to you in gratitude--and tears.... My task is ended; yours at last begins. Out of my arms you shall take her as she promised. What has been said shall be done this day in the Vale Yndaia.... May God be with us all."

"Madame--when I take her--one arm of mine must remain empty--as half her heart would be--if neither may hold you also to the end."

She bent her head; her grey eyes closed, and I saw the tears steal out along the long, soft lashes.

"Son, if you should come to love me----"

"Madame, I love you now."

She covered her face with her slim hands; I drew it against my shoulder. A moment later Lois unclosed her eyes, looked up at us; then rose to her knees in her white shift and put both bare arms around her mother's neck. And, kneeling so, turned her head, offering her untouched lips to me. Thus, for the first time in our lives, we kissed each other.

There was milk, ash-bread, corn, and fresh laid eggs for all our party when Lois went to the door and called, in a clear, sweet voice:

* "Nai! Mayaro! Yon-kwa-ken-nison!"

[* "Oh, Mayaro! We are all assembled!"]

Never have I seen any Indian eat as did my four warriors--the Yellow Moth cleaning his bark platter, where he sat on guard upon the logs at the pass, the others in a circle at our threshold.

Had we a siege to endure in this place, there was a store of plenty here, not only in apple-pit and corn-pit, but in the good, dry cellar with which the house was provided.

Truly, the Senecas had kept their Prophetess well provided; and now, before the snow of a not distant winter choked this pass, the place had been provisioned from the harvest against November's wants and stress.

And it secretly amused me to note the ever latent fear born of respect which my Indians endeavoured not to betray when in the presence of Madame de Contre-coeur; nor could her gentle dignity and sweetness toward them completely reassure them. To them a sorceress was a sorceress, and must ever remain a fearsome and an awesome personage, even though it were plain that she was disposed toward them most agreeably.

So they replied to her cautiously, briefly, but very respectfully, nor could her graciousness to the youthful Night Hawk for his unerring arrow, nor her quiet kindness toward the others, completely reassure them. They were not accustomed to converse, much less to take their breakfast, with a Sorceress of Amochol, and though this dread fact did nothing alter their appetites, it discouraged any freedom of conversation.

Lois and her mother and I understood this; Lois and I dared not laugh or rally them; Madame de Contrecoeur, well versed, God knows, in Indian manners and customs, calmly and pleasantly accepted the situation; and I think perhaps quietly enjoyed it.

But neither mother nor daughter could keep their eyes from each other for any length of time, nor did their soft hand-clasp loosen save for a moment now and then.

Later, Lois came to me, laid both hands over mine, looked at me a moment in silence too eloquent to misunderstand, then drew her mother with her into the little house. And I went back on guard to join my awed red brethren.

So the soft September day wore away with nothing untoward to alarm us, until late in the afternoon we saw smoke rising above the hills to the southwest. This meant that our devastating army was well on its way, and, as usual, laying waste the Indian towns and hamlets which its flanking riflemen discovered; and we all jumped up on our breastworks to see better.

For an hour we watched the smoke staining the pure blue sky; saw where new clouds of smoke were rising, always a little further northward. At evening it rolled, glowing with sombre tints, in the red beams of the setting sun; then dusk came and we could see the reflection on it of great fires raging underneath.

And where we were watching it came a far, dull sound which shook the ground, growing louder and nearer, increasing to a rushing, thundering gallop; and presently we heard our riflemen running through the flat-woods after the frightened herds of horses which were bred in Catharines-town for the British service, and which had now been discovered and frightened by our advance.

Leaving the Mohican and the Oneidas on guard, I went out with the Stockbridge, and soon came in touch with our light troops, stealing westward through the flat-woods to surround Catharines-town.

When I returned to our breastworks, Lois and her mother were standing there, looking at the fiery smoke in the sky, listening to the noise of the unseen soldiery. But on my explaining the situation, they went back to the little house together, after bidding us all good night.

So I set the first watch for the coming night, rolled myself in my blanket, and went to sleep with the lightest heart I had carried in my breast for many a day.

At dawn I was awakened by the noise of horses and cattle and the shouting of the grass-guard, where they were rounding to the half-wild stock from Catharines-town, and our own hoofed creatures which had strayed in the flat-woods.

A great cloud of smoke was belching up above the trees to the northward; and we knew that Catharines-town was on fire, and the last lurking enemy gone.

Long before Lois was astir, I had made my way through our swarming soldiery to Catharines-town, where there was the usual orderly confusion of details pulling down houses or firing them, troops cutting the standing corn, hacking apple-trees, kindling the stacked hay into roaring columns of flame.

Regiment after regiment paraded along the stream, discharged its muskets, filling the forests with crashing echoes and frightening our cattle into flight again; but they were firing only to clean out their pieces, for the last of our enemies had pulled foot before sunset, and the last howling Indian dog had whipped his tail between his legs and trotted after them.

Suddenly in the smoke I saw General Sullivan, mounted, and talking with Boyd; and I hastened to them and reported, standing at salute.

"So that damned Red Sachem escaped you?" said the General, biting his lip and looking now at me, now at Boyd.

Boyd said, glancing curiously at me:

"When we came up we found the entire Tory army here. I must admit, sir, that we were an hour late, having been blocked by the passage of two hundred Hurons and Iroquois who crossed our trail, cutting us from the north."

"What became of them?"

"They joined Butler, Brant, and Hiokatoo at this place, General."

Then the General asked for my report; and I gave it as exactly as I could, the General listening most attentively to my narrative, and Boyd deeply and sombrely interested.

When I ended he said:

"We have taken also a half-breed, one Madame Sacho. You say that Madame de Contrecoeur is at the Vale Yndaia with her daughter?"

"Guarded by my Indians, General."

"Very well, sir. Today we send back ten wagons, our wounded, and four guns of the heavier artillery, all under proper escort. You will notify Madame de Contre-coeur that there will be a wagon for her and her daughter."

"Yes, General."

He gathered his bridle, leaned from his saddle, and looked coldly at Boyd and me.

"Gentlemen," he said, "I shall expect you to take Amochol, dead or alive, before this command marches into the Chinisee Castle. How you are to accomplish this business is your own affair. I leave you full liberty, except," turning to Boyd, "you, sir, are not to encumber yourself again with any such force as you now have with you. Twenty men are too many for a swift and secret affair. Four is the limit--and four of Mr. Loskiel's Indians."

He sat still, gnawing at his lip for a moment, then:

"I am sorry that, through no fault apparently of your own, this Sorcerer, Amo-chol, escaped. But, gentlemen, the service recognizes only success. I am always ready to listen to how nearly you failed, when you have succeeded; I have no inter-est in hearing how nearly you succeeded when you have failed. That is all, gentle-men."

We stood at salute while he wheeled, and, followed by his considerable staff, walked his fine horse away toward the train of artillery which stood near by, the gun-teams harnessed and saddled, the guns limbered up, drivers and cannoneers in their saddles and seats.

"Well," said Boyd heavily, "shall we be about this matter of Amochol?"

"Yes.... Will you aid me in placing Madame de Contrecoeur and her daughter in the wagon assigned them?"

He nodded, and together we started back toward the Vale Yndaia in silence.

After a long while he looked up at me and said:

"I know her now."

"What?"

"I recognize your pretty Lois de Contrecoeur. For weeks I have been troubled, thinking of her and how I should have known her face. And last night, lying north of Catharines-town, it came to me suddenly."

I was silent.

"She is the ragged maid of the Westchester hills," he said.

"She is the noblest maid that ever breathed in North America," I said.

"Yes, Loskiel.... And, that being true, you are the fittest match for her the world could offer."

I looked up, surprised, and flushed; and saw how colourless and wasted his face had grown, and how in his eyes all light seemed quenched. Never have I gazed upon so hopeless and haunted a visage as he turned to me.

"I walk the forests like a damned man," he said, "already conscious of the first hot breath of hell.... Well--I had my chance, Loskiel."

"You have it still."

But he said no more, walking beside me with downcast countenance and brooding eyes fixed on our long shadows that led us slowly west.

CHAPTER XXI
CHINISEE CASTLE

For twelve days our army, marching west by north, tore its terrible way straight through the smoking vitals of the Iroquois Empire, leaving behind it nearly forty towns and villages and more than two hundred cabins on fire; thousands and thousands of bushels of grain burning, thousands of apple, peach, pear, and plum trees destroyed, thousands of acres of pumpkins, beans, peas, corn, potatoes, beets, turnips, carrots, watermelons, muskmelons, strawberry, black-berry, raspberry shrubs crushed and rotting in the trampled gardens under the hot September sun.

In the Susquehanna and Chinisee Valleys, not a roof survived unburnt, not a fruit tree or an ear of corn remained standing, not a domestic animal, not a fowl, was left. And, save for the aged squaw we left at Chiquaha in a new hut of bark, with provisions sufficient for her needs, not one living soul now inhabited the charred ruins of the Long House behind us, except our fierce soldiery. And they, tramping doggedly forward, voluntarily and cheerfully placing themselves on half rations, were now terribly resolved to make an end for all time of the secret and fruitful Empire which had nourished so long the merciless marauders, red and white, who had made of our frontiers but one vast slaughter-house and bloody desolation.

Town after town fell in ashes as our torches flared; Kendaia, Kanadesaga, Goth-sunquin, Skoi-yase, Kanandaigua, Haniai, Kanasa; acre after acre was annihilated. So vast was one field of corn that it took two thousand men more than six hours to destroy it. And the end was not yet, nor our stern business with our enemies ended.

As always on the march, the division of light troops led; the advance was pilot-ed by my guides, reinforced by Boyd with four riflemen of Morgan's--Tim Murphy, David Elerson, and Garrett Putnam, privates, and Michael Parker, sergeant.

Close behind us, and pretty well ahead of the rifle battalion, under Major Parr, and the pioneers, followed Mr. Lodge, the surveyor, and his party--Thomas Grant with the Jacob-staff, four chain-carriers, and Corporal Calhawn. Usually we re-mained in touch with them while they ran their lines through the wilderness, but sometimes we were stealing forward, far ahead and in touch with the retreating Tory army, patiently and persistently contriving plans to get at Amochol. But the painted hordes of Senecas enveloped the Sorcerer and his acolytes as with a living blanket; and, prowling outside their picket fires at night, not one ridged-crest did we see during those twelve days of swift pursuit.

Boyd, during the last few days, had become very silent and morose; and his men and my Indians believed that he was brooding over his failure to take the Red Priest at Catharines-town. But my own heavy heart told me a different story; and the burden of depression which this young officer bore so silently seemed to weight me also with vague and sinister apprehensions.

I remember, just before sunset, that our small scout of ten were halted by a burnt log bridge over a sluggish inlet to a lake. The miry trail to the Chinisee Castle led over it, swung westward along the lake, rising to a steep bluff which was gashed with a number of deep and rocky ravines.

It was plain that the retreating Tory army had passed over this bridge, and that their rearguard had set it afire.

I said to Boyd, pointing across the southern end of the lake:

"From what I have read of Braddock's Field, yonder terrain most astonishingly resembles it. What an ambuscade could Butler lay for our army yonder, within shot of this crossing!"

"Pray God he lays it," said Boyd between his teeth.

"Yet, we could get at him better beyond those rocky gashes," I muttered, using my spyglass.

"Butler is there," said the Mohican, calmly.

Both Boyd and I searched the wooded bluffs in vain for any sign of life, but the Sagamore and the other Indians quietly maintained their opinion, because, they explained, though patches of wild rice grew along the shore, the wild ducks and geese had left their feeding coves and were lying half a mile out in open water. Also, the blue-jays had set up a screaming in the yellowing woods along the western shore, and the tall, blue herons had left their shoreward sentry posts, and now mounted guard far to the northward among the reeds, where solitary black ducks dropped in at intervals, quacking loudly.

Boyd nodded; the Oneidas drew their hatchets and blazed the trees; and we all sat down in the woods to await the coming of our advanced guard.

After a little while, our pioneers appeared, rifles slung, axes glittering on their shoulders, and immediately began to fell trees and rebuild the log bridge. Hard on their heels came my rifle battalion; and in the red sunshine we watched the setting of the string of outposts.

Far back along the trail behind us we could hear the halted army making camp; flurries of cheery music from the light infantry bugle-horns, the distant rolling of drums, the rangers penetrating whistle, lashes of wagoners cracking, the melancholy bellow of the beef herd.

Major Parr came and talked with us for a few minutes, and went away convinced that Butler's people lay watching us across the creek. Ensign Chambers came a-mincing through the woods, a-whisking the snuff from his nose with the only laced hanker in the army; and:

"Dear me!" says he. "Do you really think we shall have a battle, Loskiel? How very interesting and enjoyable it will be."

"Who drilled your pretty hide, Benjamin?" said I bluntly, noting that he wore his left arm in a splint.

"Lord!" says he. "'Twas a scratch from a half-ounce ball at the Chemung. Dear, dear, how very disappointing was that affair, Loskiel! Most annoying of them not to stand our charge!" And, "Dear, dear, dear," he murmured, mincing off again with all the air of a Wall Street beau ogling the pretty dames on Hanover Square.

"Where is this damned Castle?" growled Boyd. "Chinisee, Chenussio, Genesee--whatever it is called? The name keeps buzzing in my head--nay, for the last three days I have dreamed of it and awakened to hear it sounding in my ears, as though beside me some one stooped and whispered it."

I pulled out our small map, which we had long since learned to distrust, yet even our General had no better one.

Here was marked the Chinisee Castle, near the confluence of Canaseraga Creek and the Chinisee River; and I showed the place to Boyd, who looked at it curiously.

Mayaro, however, shook his crested head:

"No, Loskiel," he said. "The Chinisee Castle stands now on the western shore. The Great Town should stand here!"--placing his finger on an empty spot on the map. "And here, two miles above, is another town."

"And you had better tell that to the General when he comes," remarked Boyd. And to me he said: "If we are to take Amochol at all, it will be this night or at dawn at the Chinisee Castle."

"I am also of that opinion," said I.

"I shall want twenty riflemen," he said.

"If it can not be done with four, and my Indians, we need not attempt it."

"Why?" he asked sullenly.

"The General has so ordered."

"Yes, but if I am to catch Amochol I must do it in my own way. I know how to do it. And if I risk taking my twenty riflemen, and am successful, the General will not care how it was accomplished."

I said nothing, because Boyd ranked me, but what he proposed made me very uneasy. More than once he had interpreted orders after his own fashion, and, being always successful in his enterprises, nothing was said to him in reproof.

My Indians had made a fire, I desiring to let the enemy suppose that we suspected nothing of his ambuscade so close at hand; and around this we lay, munching our meagre meal of green corn roasted on the coals, and ripe apples to finish.

As we ended, the sun set behind the western bluffs, and our evening gun boomed good-night in the forest south of us. And presently came, picking their way through the trail-mire, our General, handsomely horsed as usual, attended by Major Adam Hoops, of his staff, and several others.

We instantly waited on him and told him what we knew and suspected; and I showed him my map and warned him of the discrepancy between its marked places and the report of the Mohican Sagamore.

"Damnation!" he said. "Every map I have had lies in detail, misleading and delaying me when every hour empties our wagons of provisions. Were it not for your Indians, Mr. Loskiel, and that Sagamore in particular, we had missed half the game as it lies."

He sat his saddle in silence for a while, looking at the unfinished log bridge and up at the bluffs opposite.

"I feel confident that Butler is there," he said bluntly. "But what I wish to know is where this accursed Chinisee Castle stands. Boyd, take four men, move rapidly just before midnight, find out where this castle stands, and report to me at sunrise."

Boyd saluted, hesitated, then asked permission to speak. And when the General accorded it, he explained his plan to take Amochol at the Chinisee Castle, and that this matter would neither delay nor interfere with a prompt execution of his present orders.

"Very well," nodded the General, "but take no more than four men, and Mr. Loskiel and his Indians with you; and report to me at sunrise."

I heard him say this; Major Hoops heard him also. So I supposed that Boyd would obey these orders to the letter.

When the mounted party had moved away, Boyd and I went back to the fire and lay down on our blankets. We were on the edge of the trees; it was still daylight; the pioneers were still at work; and my Indians were freshening their paint, rebraiding their scalp-locks, and shining up hatchet, rifle, and knife.

"Look at those bloodhounds," muttered Boyd. "They did not hear what we were talking about, but they know by premonition."

"I do not have any faith in premonitions," said I.

"Why?"

"I have dreamed I was scalped, and my hair still grows."

"You are not out of the woods yet," he said, sombrely.

"That does not worry me."

"Nor me. Yet, I do believe in premonition."

"That is old wives' babble."

"Maybe, Loskiel. Yet, I know I shall not leave this wilderness alive."

"Lord!" said I, attempting to jest. "You should set up as a rival to Amochol and tell us all our fortunes."

He smiled--and the effort distorted his pale, handsome face.

"I think it will happen at Chinisee," he said quietly.

"What will happen?"

"The end of the world for me, Loskiel."

"It is not like you, Boyd, to speak in such a manner. Only lately have I ever heard from you a single note of such foreboding."

"Only lately have I been dowered with the ominous clairvoyance. I am changed, Loskiel."

"Not in courage."

"No," he said with a shrug of his broad shoulders that set ruffles and thrums a-dancing on his rifle-dress.

We were silent for a while, watching the Indians at their polishing. Then he said in a low but pleasant voice:

"How proud and happy must you be with your affianced. What a splendour of happiness lies before you both! An unblemished past, an innocent passion, a future stretching out unstained before you--what more can God bestow on man and maid?... May bright angels guard you both, Loskiel."

I made to thank him for the wish, but suddenly found I could not control my voice, so lay there in silence and with throat contracted, looking at this man whose marred young life lay all behind him, and whose future, even to me, lowered strangely and ominously veiled.

And as we lay there, into our fire-circle came a dusty, mud-splashed, and naked runner, plucking from his light skin-pouch two letters, one for Boyd and one for me.

I read mine by the flickering fire; it was dated from Tioga Point:

"Euan Loskiel, my honoured and affianced husband, and my lover, worshipped and adored, I send you by this runner my dearest affections, my duties, and my most sacred sentiments.

"You must know that this day we have arrived at the Fort at Tioga Point without any accident or mischance of any description, and, indeed, not encountering one living creature between Catharines-town and this post.

"My beloved mother desires her particular and tender remembrances to be conveyed to you, her honoured son-in-law to be, and further commands that I express to you, as befittingly as I know how, her deep and ever-living gratitude and thanks for your past conduct in regard to me, and your present and noble-minded generosity concerning the dispositions you have made for us to remain under the amiable protection of Mr. Hake in Albany.

"Dear lad, what can I say for myself? You are so glorious, so wonderful--and in you it does seem that all the virtues, graces, and accomplishments are so perfectly embodied, that at moments, thinking of you, I become afraid, wondering what it is in me that you can accept in exchange for the so perfect love you give me.

"I fear that you may smile on perusing this epistle, deeming it, perhaps, a trifle flowery in expression--but, Euan, I am so torn between the wild passion I entertain for you, and a desire to address you modestly and politely in terms of correspondence, as taught in the best schools, that I know not entirely how to conduct. I would not have you think me cold, or too stiffly laced in the formalities of polite usage, so that you might not divine my heart a-beating under the dress that covers me, be it rifle-frock or silken caushet. I would not have you consider me over-bold, light-minded, or insensible to the deep and sacred tie that already binds me to you evermore--which even, I think, the other and tender tie which priest and church shall one day impose, could not make more perfect or more secure.

"So I must strive to please you by writing with elegance befitting, yet permitting you to perceive the ardent heart of her who thinks of you through every blessed moment of the day.

"I pray, as my dear mother prays, that God, all armoured, and with His bright sword drawn, stand sentinel on your right hand throughout the dangers and the trials of this most just and bloody war. For your return I pray and wait.

"Your humble and dutiful and obedient and adoring wife to be,

     "Lois de Contrecoeur.

"Post scriptum: The memory of our kiss fades not from my lips. I will be content when circumstances permit us the liberty to repeat it."

When I had read the letter again and again, I folded it and laid it in the bosom of my rifle-shirt. Boyd still brooded over his letter, the red firelight bathing his face to the temples.

After a long while he raised his eyes, saw me looking at him, stared at me for a moment, then quietly extended the letter toward me.

"You wish me to read it?" I asked.

"Yes, read it, Loskiel, before I burn it," he said drearily. "I do not desire to have it discovered on my body after death."

I took the single sheet of paper and read:

   "Lieutenant Thomas Boyd,
"Rifle Corps,
"Sir:
   "For the last time, I venture to importune you in behalf of one for whose present despair you are entirely responsible. Pitying her unhappy condition, I have taken her as companion to me since we are arrived at Easton, and shall do what lies within my power to make her young life as endurable as may be.
   "You, sir, on your return from the present campaign, have it in your power to make the only reparation possible. I trust that your heart and your sense of honour will so incline you.
   "As for me, Mr. Boyd, I make no complaint, desire no sympathy, expect none. What I did was my fault alone. Knowing that I was falling in love with you, and at the same time aware what kind of man you had been and must still be, I permitted myself to drift into deeper waters, too weak of will to make an end, too miserable

to put myself beyond the persuasion of your voice and manner. And perhaps I might never have found courage to give you up entirely had I not been startled into comprehension by what I learned concerning the poor child in whose behalf I now am writing.

"That instantly sobered me, ending any slightest spark of hope that I might have in my secret heart still guarded. For, with my new and terrible knowledge, I understood that I must pass instantly and completely out of your life; and you out of mine. Only your duty remained--not to me, but to this other and more unhappy one. And that path I pray that you will follow when a convenient opportunity arises.

"I am, sir y' ob't, etc., etc.

"Magdalene Helmer.
"P. S. If you love me, Tom, do your full duty in the name of God!
"Lana."

I handed the letter back to him in silence. He stared at it, not seeing the written lines, I think, save as a blurr; and after a long while he leaned forward and laid it on the coals.

"If I am not already foredoomed," he said to me, "what Lana bids me do that I shall do. It is best, is it not, Loskiel?"

"A clergyman is fitter to reply to you than I."

"Do you not think it best that I marry Dolly Glenn?"

"God knows. It is all too melancholy and too terrible for me to comprehend the right and wrong of it, or how a penitence is best made. Yet, as you ask me, it seems to me that what she will one day become should claim your duty and your future. The weakest ever has the strongest claim."

"Yes, it-is true. I stand tonight so fettered to an unborn soul that nothing can unloose me.... I wish that I might live."

"You will live! You must live!"

"Aye, 'must' and 'will' are twins of different complexions, Loskiel.... Yet, if I live, I shall live decently and honestly hereafter in the sight of God and--Lana Helmer."

402   *The Hidden Children*

We said nothing more. About ten o'clock Boyd rose and went away all alone. Half an hour later he came back, followed by some score and more of men, a dozen of our own battalion, half a dozen musket-men of the 4th Pennsylvania Regiment, three others, two Indians, Hanierri, the headquarters Oneida guide, and Yoiakim, a Stockbridge.

"Volunteers," he said, looking sideways at me. "I know how to take Amochol; but I must take him in my own manner."

I ventured to remind him of the General's instructions that we find the Chinisee Castle and report at sunrise.

"Damn it, I know it," he retorted impatiently, "but I have my own plans; and the General will bear me out when I fling Amochol's scalp at his feet."

The Grey-Feather drew me aside and said in a low, earnest voice:

"We are too many to surprise Amochol. Before Wyoming, with only three others I went to Thenondiago, the Castle of the Three Clans--The Bear, The Wolf, and The Turtle--and there we took and slew Skull-Face, brother of Amochol, and wounded Telenemut, the husband of Catrine Montour. By Waiandaia we stretched the scalp of Skull-Face; at Thaowethon we painted it with Huron and Seneca teardrops; at Yaowania we peeled three trees and wrote on each the story so that the Three Clans might read and howl their anguish. Thus should it be done tonight if we are to deal with Amochol!"

Once more I ventured to protest to Boyd.

"Leave it to me, Loskiel," he said pleasantly. And I could say no more.

At eleven our party of twenty-nine set out, Hanierri, the Oneida, from headquarters, guiding us; and I could not understand why Boyd had chosen him, for I was certain he knew less about this region than did Mayaro, However, when I spoke to Boyd, he replied that the General had so ordered, and that Hanierri had full instructions concerning the route from the commander himself.

As General Sullivan was often misinformed by his maps and his scouts, I was nothing reassured by Boyd's reply, and marched with my Indians, feeling in my heart afraid. And, without vaunting myself, nor meaning to claim any general immunity from fear, I can truly say that for the first time in my life I set forth upon an expedition with the most melancholy forebodings possible to a man of ordinary courage and self-respect.

We followed the hard-travelled war-trail in single file; and Hanierri did not lose his way, but instead of taking, as he should have done, the unused path which led to the Chinisee Castle, he passed it and continued on.

I protested most earnestly to Boyd; the Sagamore corroborated my opinion when summoned. But Hanierri remained obstinate, declaring that he had positive information that the Chinisee Castle lay in the direction we were taking.

Boyd seemed strangely indifferent and dull, making apparently no effort to sift the matter further. So strange and apathetic had his manner become, so unlike himself was he, that I could make nothing of him, and stood in uneasy wonderment while the Mohican and the Oneida, Hanierri, were gravely disputing.

"Come," he said, in his husky and altered voice, "let us have done with this difference in opinion. Let the Oneida guide us--as we cannot have two guides' opinions. March!"

In the darkness we crept past Butler's right flank, silently and undiscovered; nor could we discover any sign of the enemy, though now not one among us doubted that he lay hidden along the bluffs, waiting for our army to move at sunrise into the deadly trap that the nature of the place had so perfectly provided.

All night long we moved on the hard and trodden trail; and toward dawn we reached a town. Reconnoitering the place, we found it utterly abandoned. If the Chinisee Castle lay beyond it, we could not determine, but Hanierri insisted that it was there. So Boyd sent back four men to Sullivan to report on what we had done; and we lay in the woods on the outskirts of the village, to wait for daylight.

When dawn whitened the east, it became plain to us all that we had taken the wrong direction. The Chinisee Castle was not here. Nothing lay before us but a deserted village.

I knew not what to make of Boyd, for the discovery of our mistake seemed to produce no impression on him. He stood at the edge of the woods, gazing vacantly across the little clearing where the Indian houses straggled on either side of the trail.

"We have made a bad mistake," I said in a low voice.

"Yes, a bad one," he said listlessly.

"Shall we not start on our return?" I asked.

"There is no hurry."

"I beg your pardon, but I have to remind you that you are to report at sunrise."

"Aye--if that were possible, Loskiel."

"Possible!" I repeated, blankly. "Why not?"

"Because," he said in a dull voice, "I shall never see another sunrise save this one that is coming presently. Let me have my fill of it unvexed by Generals and orders."

"You are not well, Boyd," I said, troubled.

"As well as I shall ever be--but not as ill, Loskiel."

At that moment the Sagamore laid his hand on my shoulder and pointed. I saw nothing for a moment; then Boyd and Murphy sprang forward, rifles in hand, and Mayaro after them, and I after them, running into the village at top speed. For I had caught a glimpse of a most unusual sight; four Iroquois Indians on horseback, riding into the northern edge of the town. Never before, save on two or three occasions, had I ever seen an Iroquois mounted on a horse.

We ran hard to get a shot at them, and beyond the second house came in full view of our enemies. Murphy fired immediately, knocking the leading Indian from his horse; I fired, breaking the arm of the next rider; both my Indians fired and missed; and the Iroquois were off at full speed. Boyd had not fired.

We ran to where the dead man was lying, and the Mohican recognized him as an Erie named Sanadaya. Murphy coolly took his scalp, with an impudent wink at the Sagamore and a grin at Boyd and me.

In the meanwhile, our riflemen and Indians had rushed the town and were busy tearing open the doors of the houses and setting fire to them. In vain I urged Boyd to start back, pointing out that this was no place for us to linger in, and that our army would burn this village in due time.

But he merely shrugged his shoulders and loitered about, watching his men at their destruction; and I stood by, a witness to his strange and inexplicable delay, a prey to the most poignant anxiety because the entire Tory army lay between us and our own army, and this smoke signal must draw upon us a very swarm of savages to our inevitable destruction.

At last Boyd sounded the recall on his ranger's whistle, and ordered me to take my Indians and reconnoiter our back trail. And no sooner had I entered the woods than I saw an Indian standing about a hundred yards to the right of the trail, and looking up at the smoke which was blowing southward through the tree-tops.

His scarlet cloak was thrown back; he was a magnificent warrior, in his brilliant paint, matching the flaming autumn leaves in colour. My Indians had not noticed him where he stood against a crimson and yellow maple bush. I laid my rifle level and fired. He staggered, stood a moment, turning his crested head with a bewildered air, then swayed, sank at the knee joints, dropped to them, and very slowly laid his stately length upon the moss, extending himself like one who prepared for slumber.

We ran up to where he lay with his eyes closed; he was still breathing. A great pity for him seized me; and I seated myself on the moss beside him, staring into his pallid face.

And as I sat beside him while he was dying, he opened his eyes, and looked at me. And I knew that he knew I had killed him. After a few moments he died.

"Amochol!" I said under my breath. "God alone knows why I am sorry for this dead priest." And as I rose and stared about me, I caught sight of two pointed ears behind a bush; then two more pricked up sharply; then the head of a wolf popped up over a fallen log. But as I began to reload my rifle, there came a great scurrying and scattering in the thickets, and I heard the Andastes running off, leaving their dead master to me and to my people, who were now arriving.

I do not know who took his scalp; but it was taken by some Indian or Ranger who came crowding around to look down upon this painted dead man in his scarlet cloak.

"Amochol is dead," I said to Boyd.

He looked at me with lack-lustre eyes, nodding. We marched on along the trail by which we had arrived.

For five miles we proceeded in silence, my Indians flanking the file of riflemen. Then Boyd gave the signal to halt, and sent forward the Sagamore, the Grey-Feather, and Tahoontowhee to inform the General that we would await the army in this place.

The Indians, so coolly taken from my command, had gone ere I came up from the rear to find what Boyd had done.

"Are you mad?" I exclaimed, losing my temper, "Do you propose to halt here at the very mouth of the hornet's nest?"

He did not rebuke me for such gross lack of discipline and respect--in fact, he seemed scarcely to heed at all what I said, but seated himself at the foot of a pine tree and lit his pipe. As I stood biting my lip and looking around at the woods encircling us, he beckoned two of his men, gave them some orders in a low voice, crossed one leg over the other, and continued to smoke the carved and painted Oneida pipe he carried in his shot-pouch.

I saw the two riflemen shoulder their long weapons and go forward in obedience to his orders; and when again I approached him he said:

"They will make plain to Sullivan what your Indians may garble in repeating--that I mean to await the army in this place and save my party these useless miles of travelling. Do you object?"

"Our men are not tired," I said, astonished, "and our advanced guard can not be very far away. Do you not think it more prudent for us to continue the movement toward our own people?"

"Very well--if you like," he said indifferently.

After a few minutes' inaction, he rose, sounded his whistle; the men got to their feet, fell in, and started, rifles a-trail. But we had proceeded scarcely a dozen rods into the big timber when we discovered our two riflemen, who had so recently left us, running back toward us and looking over their shoulders as they ran. When they saw us, they halted and shouted for us to hasten, as there were several Seneca Indians standing beside the trail ahead.

In a flash of intuition it came to me that here was a cleared runway to some trap.

"Don't leave the trail!" I said to Boyd. "Don't be drawn out of it now. For God's sake hold your men and don't give chase to those Indians."

"Press on!" said Boyd curtly; and our little column trotted forward.

Something crashed in a near thicket and went off like a deer. The men, greatly excited, strove to catch a glimpse of the running creature, but the bush was too dense.

Suddenly a rifleman, who was leading our rapid advance, caught sight of the same Senecas who had alarmed him and his companion; and he started toward them with a savage shout, followed by a dozen others.

Hanierri turned to Boyd and begged him earnestly not to permit any pursuit. But Boyd pushed him aside impatiently, and blew the view-halloo on his ranger's whistle; and in a moment we all were scattering in full pursuit of five lithe and agile Senecas, all in full war-paint, who appeared to be in a panic, for they ran through the thickets like terrified sheep, huddling and crowding on one another's heels.

"Boyd!" I panted, catching up with him. "This whole business looks like a trap to me. Whistle your men back to the trail, for I am certain that these Senecas are drawing us toward their main body."

"We'll catch one of them first," he said; and shouted to Murphy to fire and cripple the nearest. But the flying Senecas had now vanished into a heavily-wooded gully, and there was nothing for Murphy to fire at.

I swung in my tracks, confronting Boyd.

"Will you halt your people before it is too late?" I demanded. "Where are your proper senses? You behave like a man who has lost his mental balance!"

He gave me a dazed look, where he had been within his rights had he cut me down with his hatchet.

"What did you say?" he stammered, passing his hand over his eyes as though something had obscured his sight.

"I asked you to sound the recall. Those Indians we chase are leading us whither they will. What in God's name ails you, Boyd? Have you never before seen an ambush?"

He stood motionless, as though stupefied, staring straight ahead of him. Then he said, hesitatingly, that he desired Tim Murphy to cripple one of the Senecas and fetch him in so that we might interrogate him.

Such infant's babble astounded and sickened me, and I was about to retort when a shout from one of our men drew our attention to the gully below. And there were our terrified Indians peering out cunningly at us like so many foxes playing tag with an unbroken puppy pack.

"Come, sir," said I in deepest anxiety, "the game is too plain for anybody but a fool to follow. Sound your recall!"

He set his whistle to his lips, and as I stood there, thunderstruck and helpless, the shrill call rang out: "Forward! Hark-away!"

Instantly our entire party leaped forward; the Indians vanished; and we ran on headlong, pell-mell, hellward into the trap prepared for our destruction.

The explosion of a heavy rifle on our right was what first halted us, I think. One of the soldiers from the 4th Pennsylvania was down in the dead leaves kicking and scuffling about all over blood. Before he had rolled over twice, a ragged but loud volley on our left went through our disordered files, knocking over two more soldiers. The screaming of one poor fellow seemed to bring Boyd to his senses. He blew the recall, and our men fell back, and, carrying the dead and wounded, began to ascend the wooded knoll down which we had been running when so abruptly checked.

There was no more firing for the moment; we reached the top of the knoll, laid our dead and wounded behind trees, loaded, freshened our priming, and stood awaiting orders.

Then, all around us, completely encircling the foot of our knoll, woods, thickets, scattered bushes, seemed to be literally moving in the vague forest light.

"My God!" exclaimed Elerson to Murphy. "The woods are crawling with savages!"

A dreadful and utter silence fell among us; Boyd, pale as a corpse, motioned his men to take posts, forming a small circle with our dead and wounded in the centre.

I saw Hanierri, the Oneida guide, fling aside his blanket, strip his painted body to the beaded clout, draw himself up to his full and superb height, muttering, his eyes fixed on the hundreds of dark shapes stealing quietly among the thickets below our little hill.

The two Stockbridge Indians, the Yellow Moth and Yoiakim, pressed lightly against me on either side, like two great, noble dogs, afraid, yet trusting their master, and still dauntless in the threatening face of duty.

Through the terrible stillness which had fallen upon us all, I could hear the Oneida guide muttering his death-song; and presently my two Christian Indians commenced in low voices to recite the prayers for the dying.

The next moment, Murphy and Elerson began to fire, slowly and deliberately; and for a little while these two deadly and unerring rifles were the only pieces that spoke from our knoll. Then my distant target showed for a moment; I fired, reloaded, waited; fired again; and our little circle of doomed men began to cheer as a brilliantly painted warrior sprang from the thicket below, shouted defiance, and crumpled up as though smitten by lightning when Murphy's rifle roared out its fatal retort.

Then, for almost every soul that stood there, the end of the world began; for a thousand men swarmed out of the thickets below, completely surrounding us; and like a hurricane shrilling through naked woods swept the death-halloo of five hundred Iroquois in their naked paint.

On every side the knoll was black with them as they came leaping forward, hatchets glittering; while over their heads the leaden hail of Tory musketry pelted us from north and south and east and west.

Down crashed Yoiakim at my side, his rifle exploding in mid-air as he fell dead and rolled over and over down the slope toward the masses of his enemies below.

As a Seneca seized the rolling body, set his foot on the dead shoulders and jerked back the head to scalp him, the Yellow Moth leaped forward, launching his hatchet. It flew, sparkling, and struck the scalper full in the face. The next instant the Yellow Moth was among them, snarling, stabbing, raging, almost covered by Senecas who were wounding one another in their eagerness to slay him.

For a moment it seemed to me that there was a chance in this melee for us to cut our way through, and I caught Boyd by the arm and pointed. A volley into our very backs staggered and almost stupefied us; through the swirling powder gloom, our men began to fall dead all around me. I saw Sergeant Hungerman drop; privates Harvey, Conrey, Jim McElroy, Jack Miller, Benny Curtin and poor Jack Putnam.

Murphy, clubbing his rifle, was bawling to his comrade, Elerson:

"To hell wid this, Davey! Av we don't pull foot we're a pair o' dead ducks!"

"For God's sake, Boyd!" I shouted. "Break through there beside the Yellow Moth!"

Boyd, wielding his clubbed rifle, cleared a circle amid the crowding savages; Sergeant Parker ran out into the yelling crush; the two gigantic riflemen, Murphy and Elerson, swinging their terrible weapons like flails, smashed their way forward; behind them, using knife, hatchet, and stock, I led out the last men living on that knoll--Ned McDonald, Garrett Putnam, Jack Youse, and a French coureur-de-bois whose name I have never learned.

All around us raged and yelled the maddened Seneca pack, slashing each other again and again in their crazed attempts to reach us. The Yellow Moth was stabbed through and through a hundred times, yet the ghastly corpse still kept its feet, so terrible was the crushing pressure on every side.

Suddenly, tearing a path through the frenzied mob, I saw a mob of cursing, sweating, green-coated soldiers and rangers, struggling toward us--saw one of Butler's rangers seize Sergeant Parker by the collar of his hunting shirt, bawling out:

"Hurrah! Hurrah! Prisoner taken from Morgan's corps!"

Another, an officer of British regulars, I think, threw himself on Boyd, shouting:

"By heaven! It's Boyd of Derry! Are you not Tom Boyd, of Derry, Pennsylvania?"

"Yes, you bloody-backed Tory!" retorted Boyd, struggling to knife him under his gorget. "And I'm Boyd of Morgan's, too!"

I aimed a blow at the red-coated officer, but my rifle stock broke off across the skull of an Indian; and I began to beat a path toward Boyd with the steel barrel of my weapon, Murphy and Elerson raging forward beside me in such a very whirlwind of half-crazed fury that the Indians gave way and leaped aside, trying to shoot at us.

Headlong through this momentary opening rushed Garrett Putnam, his rifle-dress torn from his naked body, his heavy knife dripping in the huge fist that clutched it. After him leaped Ned McDonald, the coureur-de-bois, and Jack Youse, letting drive right and left with their hatchets. And, as the painted crowd ahead recoiled and shrank aside, Murphy, Elerson, and I went through, smashing out the way with our heavy weapons.

How we got through God only knows. I heard Murphy bellowing to Elerson:

"We're out! We're out! Pull foot, Davey, or the dirty Scutts will take your hair!"

A Pennsylvania soldier, running heavily down hill ahead of me, was shot, sprang high into the air in one agonized bound, like a stricken hare, and fell forward under my very feet, so that I leaped over him as I ran. The Canadian coureur-de-bois was hit, but the bullet stung him to a speed incredible, and he flew on, screaming with pain, his broken arm flapping.

Behind me I dared not look, but I knew the Seneca warriors were after us at full speed. Bullets whined and whizzed beside us, striking the trees on every side. A long slope of open woods now slanted away below us.

As I ran, far ahead of me, among the trees, I saw men moving, yet dared not change my course. Then, as I drew nearer, I recognized Mr. Lodge, our surveyor, and Thomas Grant with the Jacob-staff, the four chain-bearers with the chain, and Corporal Calhawn, all standing stock still and gazing up the slope toward us.

The next moment Grant dropped his Jacob-staff, turned and ran; the chain-men flung away their implements, and Mr. Lodge and the entire party, being totally unarmed, turned and fled, we on their heels, and behind us a score of yelling Senecas, now driven to frenzy by the sight of so much terrified game in flight.

I saw poor Calhawn fall; I saw Grant run into the swamp below, shouting for help. Mr. Lodge, closely chased by a young warrior, ran toward a distant sentinel, and so eager was the Seneca to slay him that he chased the fleeing surveyor past the sentinel, and was shot in the back by the amazed soldier.

And now, all along the edge of the morass where our pickets were posted, the bang! bang! bang! of musketry began. Murphy and Elerson bounded into safety; Ned McDonald, Garrett Putnam, the coureur-de-bais, and Jack Youse went staggering and reeling into the swamp. I attempted to follow them, but three Senecas cut me out, and, with bursting heart, I sheered off and ran parallel with them, striving to reach our lines, the sentinels firing at my pursuers and running forward to intercept them. Yet, so intent were these Seneca bloodhounds on my destruction that they never swerved under the running fire of musketry; and I was forced out and driven into the woods again to the northwest of our lines.

Farther and farther away sounded the musketry in my ears, until the pounding pulses deadened and finally obliterated the sound. I could no longer carry the shattered and bloody fragment of my rifle, and dropped it. Bullet-pouch, shot-pouch, powder-horn, water-bottle, hatchet I let fall, keeping only my knife, belt, and the thin, flat wallet which contained my letters from Lois and my journal. Even my cap I flung away, moving always forward on a dog-trot, and ever twisting my sweat-drenched head to look behind.

Several times I caught distant glimpses of my pursuers, and saw that they walked sometimes, as though exhausted. Yet, I dared not bear to the South, not knowing how many of them had continued on westward to cut me off from a return; so I jogged on northward, my heart nigh broken with misery and foreboding, sickened to the very soul with the memory of our slaughtered men upon the knoll. For of some thirty-odd riflemen, Indians, line soldiers, and scouts that Boyd had led out the night before, only Elerson, Murphy, McDonald, Youse, the coureur-de-bois, and I remained alive or untaken. Boyd was a prisoner, together with Sergeant Parker; all the others were dead to a man, excepting possibly my three Indians, Mayaro, Grey-Feather, and Tahoontowhee, who Boyd had sent in to report us before we had sighted the Senecas, and who might possibly have escaped the ambuscade.

As I plodded on, I dared not let my imagination dwell on Boyd and Parker, for a dreadful instinct told me that the dead men on the knoll were better off. Yet, I tried to remember that a red-coated officer had taken Boyd, and one of Sir John's soldiers had captured Michael Parker. But I could find no comfort, no hope in this thought, because Walter Butler was there, and Hiokatoo, and McDonald, and all that bloody band. The Senecas would surely demand the prisoners. There was not one soul to speak a word for them, unless Brant were near. That noble and humane warrior alone could save them from the Seneca stake. And I feared he was at the burnt bridge with his Mohawks, facing our army as he always faced it, dauntless, adroit, resourceful, and terrible.

A little stony stream ran down beside the trackless course I travelled and I seized the chance of confusing the tireless men who tracked me, and took to the stones, springing from one step to the next, taking care not to wet my moccasins, dislodge moss or lichen, or in any manner mark the stones I trod on or break or disturb the branches and leaves above me.

The stream ran almost north as did all the little water-courses hereabouts, and for a long while I followed it, until at last, to my great relief, it divided; and I followed the branch that ran northeast. Again this branch forked; I took the eastern course until, on the right bank, I saw long, naked beds of rock stretching into low crags and curving eastward.

Over this rock no Seneca could hope to track a cautious and hunted man. I walked sometimes, sometimes trotted; and so jogged on, bearing ever to the east and south, meaning to cross the Chinisee River north of the confluence, and pass clear around the head of the lake.

Here I made my mistake by assuming that, as our pioneers must still be working on the burnt bridge, the enemy that had merely enveloped our party by curling around us his right flank, would again swing back to their bluffs along the lake, and, though hope of ambuscade was over, dispute the passage of the stream and the morass with our own people.

But as I came out among the trees along the river bank, to my astonishment and alarm I saw an Indian house, and smoke curling from the chimney. So taken aback was I that I ran south to a great oak tree and stood behind it, striving to collect my thoughts and make out my proper bearings. But off again scattered every idea I had in my head, and I looked about me in a very panic, for I heard close at hand the barking of Indian dogs and a vast murmur of voices; and, peering out again from behind my tree I could see other houses close to the strip of forest where I hid, and the narrow lane between them was crowded with people.

Where I was, what this town might be, I could not surmise; nor did I perceive any way out of this wasp's nest where I was now landed, except to retrace my trail. And that I dared not do.

There was now a great shouting in the village as though some person had just made a speech and his audience remained in two nods concerning its import.

Truly, this seemed to be no place for me; the woods were very open--a sugar bush in all the gorgeous glory of scarlet, yellow, and purple foliage, heavily fringed with thickets of bushes and young hardwood growth, which for the moment had hid the town from me, and no doubt concealed me from the people close at hand. To retreat through such a strip of woodland was impossible without discovery. Besides, somewhere on my back trail were enemies, though just where I could not know. For a moment's despair, it seemed to me that only the wings of a bird could save me now; then, as I involuntarily cast my gaze aloft, the thought to climb followed; and up I went into the branches, where the blaze of foliage concealed me; and lay close to a great limb looking down over the top of the thicket to the open river bank. And what I saw astounded me; the enemy's baggage wagons were fording the river; his cattle-drove had just been herded across, and the open space was already full of his gaunt cows and oxen.

Rangers and Greens pricked them forward with their bayonets, forcing them out of the opening and driving them northwest through the outskirts of the village. The wagons, horses, and vehicles, in a dreadful plight, followed the herd-guard. After them marched Butler's rear-guard, rangers, Greens, renegades, Indians sullenly turning their heads to listen and to gaze as the uproar from the village increased and burst into a very frenzy of diabolical yelling.

Suddenly, out through the narrow lane or street surged hundreds of Seneca warriors, all clustering and crowding around something in the centre of the mass; and as the throng, now lurching this way, now driving that way, spread out over the cleared land up to the edges of the very thicket which I overlooked, my blood froze in my veins.

For in the centre of that mass of painted, capering demons, walked Boyd and Parker, their bloodless faces set and grim, their heads carried high.

Into this confusion drove the baggage wagons; the herd-guards began to shout angrily and drive back the Indians; the wagons drove slowly through the lane, the drivers looking down curiously at Boyd and his pallid companion, but not insulting them.

One by one the battered and rickety wagons jolted by; then came the bloody and dishevelled soldiery plodding with shouldered muskets through the lanes of excited warriors, scarcely letting their haggard eyes rest on the two prisoners who stood, unpinioned in the front rank.

A mounted officer, leaning from his saddle, asked the Senecas what they meant to do with these prisoners; and the ferocious response seemed to shock him, for he drew bridle and stared at Boyd as though fascinated.

So near to where I lay was Boyd standing that I could see the checked quiver of his lips as he bit them to control his nerves before he spoke. Then he said to the mounted officer, in a perfectly even and distinct voice:

"Can you not secure for us, sir, the civilized treatment of prisoners of war?"

"I dare not interfere," faltered the officer, staring around at the sea of devilish faces.

"And you, a white man, return me such a cowardly answer?"

Another motley company came marching up from the river, led by a superb Mohawk Indian in full war-paint and feathers; and, blocked by the mounted officer in front, halted.

I saw Boyd's despairing glance sweep their files; then suddenly his eyes brightened.

"Brant!" he cried.

And then I saw that the splendid Mohawk leader was the great Thayendanegea himself.

"Boyd," he said calmly, "I am sorry for you. I would help you if I could. But," he added, with a bitter smile, "there are those in authority among us who are more savage than those you white men call savages. One of these--gentlemen--has overruled me, denying my more humane counsel.... I am sorry, Boyd."

"Brant!" he said in a ringing voice. "Look at me attentively!"

"I look upon you, Boyd."

Then something extraordinary happened; I saw Boyd make a quick sign; saw poor Parker imitate him; realized vaguely that it was the Masonic signal of distress.

Brant remained absolutely motionless for a full minute; suddenly he sprang forward, pushed away the Senecas who immediately surrounded the prisoners, shoving them aside right and left so fiercely that in a moment the whole throng was wavering and shrinking back.

Then Brant, facing the astonished warriors, laid his hand on Boyd's head and then on Parker's.

"Senecas!" he said in a cold and ringing voice. "These men are mine; Let no man dare interfere with these two prisoners. They belong to me. I now give them my promise of safety. I take them under my protection--I, Thayendanegea! I do not ask them of you; I take them. I do not explain why. I do not permit you--not one among you to--to question me. What I have done is done. It is Joseph Brant who has spoken!"

He turned calmly to Boyd, said something in a low voice, turned sharply on his heel, and marched forward at the head of his company of Mohawks and half-breeds.

Then I saw Hiokatoo come up and stand glaring at Boyd, showing his teeth at him like a baffled wolf; and Boyd laughed in his face and seated himself on a log beside the path, coolly and insolently turning his back on the Seneca warriors, and leisurely lighting his pipe.

Parker came and seated himself beside him; and they conversed in voices so low that I could not hear what they said, but Boyd smiled at intervals, and Parker's bruised visage relaxed.

The Senecas had fallen back in a sullen line, their ferocious eyes never shifting from the two prisoners. Hiokatoo set four warriors to guard them, then, passing slowly in front of Boyd, spat on the ground.

"Dog of a Seneca!" said Boyd fiercely. "What you touch you defile, stinking wolverine that you are!"

"Dog of a white man!" retorted Hiokatoo. "You are not yet in your own kennel! Remember that!"

"But you are!" said Boyd. "The stench betrays the wolverine! Go tell your filthy cubs that my young men are counting the scalps of your Cat-People and your Andastes, and that the mangy lock of Amochol shall be thrown to our swine!"

Struck entirely speechless by such rash effrontery and by his own fury, the dreaded Seneca war-chief groped for his hatchet with trembling hands; but a warning hiss from one of his own Mountain Snakes on guard brought him to his senses.

Such an embodiment of devilish fury I had never seen on any human countenance; only could it be matched in the lightning snarl of a surprised lynx or in the deadly stare of a rattlesnake. He uttered no sound; after a moment the thin lips, which had receded, sheathed the teeth again; and he walked to a tree and stood leaning against it as another company of Sir John's Royal Greens marched up from the river bank and continued northwest, passing between the tree where I lay concealed, and the log where Boyd and Parker sat.

McDonald, mounted, naked claymore in his hand, came by, leading a company of his renegades. He grinned at Boyd, and passed his basket-hilt around his throat with a significant gesture, then grinned again.

"Not yet, you Scotch loon!" said Boyd gently. "I'll live to pepper your kilted tatterdemalions so they'll beg for the mercies of Glencoe!"

After that, for a long while only stragglers came limping by--lank, bloody, starved creatures, who never even turned their sick eyes on the people they passed among.

Then, after nearly half an hour, a full battalion of Johnson's Greens forded the river, and behind them came Butler's Rangers.

Old John Butler, squatting his saddle like a weather-beaten toad, rode by with scarcely a glance at the prisoners; and Greens and Rangers passed on through the village and out of sight to the northwest.

I had thought the defile was ended, when, looking back, I saw some Indians crossing the ford, carrying over a white officer. At first I supposed he was wounded, but soon saw that he had not desired to wet his boots.

What had become of his horse I could only guess, for he wore spurs and sword, and the sombre uniform of the Rangers.

Then, as he came up I saw that he was Walter Butler.

As he approached, his dark eyes were fixed on the prisoners; and when he came opposite to them he halted.

Boyd returned his insolent stare very coolly, continuing to smoke his pipe. Slowly the golden-brown eyes of Butler contracted, and into his pale, handsome, but sinister face crept a slight colour.

"So you are Boyd!" he said menacingly.

"Yes, I am Boyd. What next?"

"What next?" repeated Walter Butler. "Well, really I don't know, my impudent friend, but I strongly suspect the Seneca stake will come next."

Boyd laughed: "We gave Brant a sign that you also should recognize. We are now under his protection."

"What sign?" demanded Butler, his eyes becoming yellow and fixed. And, as Boyd carelessly repeated the rapid and mystical appeal, "Oh!" he said coolly. "So that is what you count on, is it?"

"Naturally."

"With me also?"

"You are a Mason."

"Also," snarled Butler, "I am an officer in his British Majesty's service. Now, answer the questions I put to you. How many cannon did your Yankee General send back to Tioga after Catharines-town was burnt, and how many has he with him?"

"Do you suppose that I am going to answer your questions?" said Boyd, amused.

"I think you will, Come, sir; what artillery is he bringing north with him?"

And as Boyd merely looked at him with contempt, he stepped nearer, bent suddenly, and jerked Boyd to his feet.

"You Yankee dog!" he said; "Stand up when your betters stand!"

Boyd reddened to his temples.

"Murderer!" he said. "Does a gentleman stand in the presence of the Cherry Valley butcher?" And he seated himself again on his log.

Butler's visage became deathly, and for a full minute he stood there in silence. Suddenly he turned, nodded to Hiokatoo, pointed at Boyd, then at Parker. Both prisoners rose as a yell of ferocious joy split the air from the Senecas. Then, wheeling on Boyd:

"Will you answer my questions?"

"No!"

"Do you refuse to answer the military questions put to you by an officer?"

"No prisoner of war is compelled to do that!"

"You are mistaken; I compel you to answer on pain of death!"

"I refuse."

Both men were deadly pale. Parker also had risen and was now standing beside Boyd.

"I claim the civilized treatment due to an officer," said Boyd quietly.

"Refused unless you answer!"

"I shall not answer. I am under Brant's protection!"

"Brant!" exclaimed Butler, his pallid visage contorted. "What do I care for Brant? Who is Brant to offer you immunity? By God, sir, I tell you that you shall answer my questions--any I think fit to ask you--every one of them--or I turn you over to my Senecas!"

"You dare not!"

"Answer me, or you shall soon learn what I dare and dare not do!"

Boyd, pale as a sheet, said slowly:

"I do believe you capable of every infamy, Mr. Butler. I do believe, now, that the murderer of little children will sacrifice me to these Senecas if I do not answer his dishonorable questions. And so, believing this, and always holding your person in the utmost loathing and contempt, I refuse to reveal to you one single item concerning the army in which I have the honour and privilege to serve."

"Take him!" said Butler to the crowding Senecas.

I have never been able to bring myself to write down how my comrade died. Many have written something of his death, judging the manner of it from the condition in which his poor body was discovered the next day by our advance. Yet, even these have shrunk from writing any but the most general details, because the horror of the truth is indescribable, and not even the most callous mind could endure it all.

God knows how I myself survived the swimming horror of that hellish scene--for the stake was hewn and planted full within my view.... And it took him many hours to die--all the long September afternoon.... And they never left him for one moment.

No, I can not write it, nor could I even tell my comrades when they came up next day, how in detail died Thomas Boyd, lieutenant in my regiment of rifles. Only from what was left of him could they draw their horrible and unthinkable conclusions.

I do not know whether I have more or less of courage than the usual man and soldier, but this I do know, that had I possessed a rifle where I lay concealed, long before they wrenched the first groan from his tortured body I would have fired at my comrade's heart and trusted to my Maker and my legs.

No torture that I ever heard of or could ever have conceived--no punishment, no agony, no Calvary ever has matched the hellish hideousness of the endless execution of this young man.... He was only twenty-two years old; only a lieutenant among the thousands who served their common motherland. No man who ever lived has died more bravely; none, perhaps, as horribly and as slowly. And it seemed as though in that powerful, symmetrical, magnificent body, even after it became scarcely recognizable as human, that the spark of life could not be extinguished even though it were cut into a million shreds and scattered to the winds like the fair body of Osiris.

And this is all I care to say how it was that my comrade died, save that he endured bravely; and that while consciousness remained, not one secret would he reveal; not one plea for mercy escaped his lips.

Parker died more swiftly and mercifully.

It was after sunset when the Senecas left the place, but the sky above was still rosy. And as they slowly marched past the corpses of the two men whom they had slain, every Seneca drew his hatchet and shouted:

"Salute! O Roya-neh!" fiercely honoring the dead bodies of the bravest men who had ever died in the Long House.

On the following afternoon I ventured from my concealment, and was striving to dig a grave for my two comrades, using my knife to do it, when the riflemen of our advance discovered me across the river.

A moment later I looked up, my eyes blinded by tears, as the arm of the Sagamore was flung round my shoulders, and the hands of the Grey-Feather and Tahoontowhee timidly sought mine.

"Brother!" they said gently.

* "Tekasenthos, O Sagamore!" I whispered, dropping my head on his broad shoulder. "Issi tye-y-ad-akeron, akwah de-ya-kon-akor-on-don!"

[* "I weep, O Sagamore! Yonder are lying bodies, yea, and of chiefs!"]

CHAPTER XXII
MES ADIEUX

For my acquaintances in and outside of the army, and for my friends and relatives, this narrative has been written; and if in these pages I have seemed to present myself, my thoughts, and behaviour as matters of undue importance, it is not done so purposely or willingly, but because I knew no better method of making from my daily journal the story of the times and of the events witnessed by me, and of which I was a small and modest part.

It is very true that no two people, even when standing shoulder to shoulder, ever see the same episode in the same manner, or draw similar conclusions concerning any event so witnessed. Yet, except from hearsay, how is an individual to describe his times except in the light of personal experience and of the emotions of the moment so derived?

In active events, self looms large, even in the crisis of supreme self-sacrifice. In the passive part, which even the most active among us play for the greater portion of our lives, self is merged in the detached and impersonal interest which we take in what passes before our eyes. Yet must we describe these things only as they are designed and coloured by our proper eyes, and therefore, with no greater hope of accuracy than to approximate to the general and composite truth.

Of any intentional injustice to our enemies, their country, and their red allies, I do not hesitate to acquit myself; yet, because I have related the history of this campaign as seen through the eyes of a soldier of the United States, so I would not deny that these same and daily episodes, as seen by a British soldier, might wear forms and colours very different, and yet be as near to the truth as any observations of my own.

Therefore, without diffidence or hesitation--because I have explained myself--and prejudiced by an unalterable belief in the cause which I have had the honour and happiness to serve, it is proper that I bring my narrative of these three months to a conclusion.

With these same three months the days of my youth also ended. No stripling could pass through those scenes and emerge still immature. The test was too terrible; the tragedy too profound; the very setting of the tremendous scene--all its monstrous and gigantic accessories--left an impression ineradicable upon the soul. Adolescence matured to manhood in those days of iron; youthful ignorance became stern experience, sobering with its enduring leaven the serious years to come.

I remember every separate event after the tragedy of Chenundana, where they found me dazed with grief and privation, digging with my broken hunting knife a grave for my dead companions.

The horror of their taking off passed from my shocked brain as the exigencies of the perilous moments increased, demanding of me constant and untiring effort, and piling upon my shoulders responsibilities that left no room for morbid brooding or even for the momentary inaction of grief.

From Tioga, Colonel Shreve sent forward to us a wagon train of provisions, even wines and delicacies for our sick and wounded; but even with this slight aid our men remained on half rations; and for all our voluntary sacrifice we could not hope now to reach Niagara and deliver the final blow to that squirming den of serpents.

True, Amochol was dead; but Walter Butler lived. And there was now no hope of reaching him. Bag and baggage, horse, foot, and Indians, he had gone clear out of sight and sound into a vast and trackless wilderness which we might not hope to penetrate because, even on half rations, we had now scarcely enough flour left to take us back to the frontiers of civilization.

Of our artillery we had only a light piece or two left, and the cohorn; of cattle we had scarcely any; of wagons and horses very few, having killed and eaten the more worn-out animals at Horseheads. Only the regimental wagons contained any flour; half our officers were without mounts; ammunition was failing us; and between us and our frontiers lay the ashes of the Dark Empire and hundreds of miles of a wilderness so dreary and so difficult that we often wondered whether it was possible for human endurance to undergo the endless marches of a safe return.

But our task was ended; and when we set our faces toward home, every man in our ragged, muddy, brier-torn columns knew in his heart that the power of the Iroquois Empire was broken forever. Senecas, Cayugas, Onondagas, might still threaten and even strike like crippled snakes; but the Long House lay in ashes, and the heart of every Indian in it was burnt out.

Swinging out our wings east and west as we set our homeward course, burning and destroying all that we had hitherto spared, purposely or by accident, we started south; and from the fifteenth of September until the thirtieth the only living human being we encountered was the aged squaw we had left at Catharines.

Never had I seen such a desolation of utter destruction, for amid the endless ocean of trees every oasis was a blackened waste, every town but a heap of sodden ashes, every garden a mass of decay, rotting under the autumn sun.

On the 30th of September, we marched into Tioga Fort, Colonel Shreve's cannon thundering their welcome, and Colonel Proctor's artillery band playing a most stirring air. But Lord! What a ragged, half-starved army it was! Though we cared nothing for that, so glad were we to see our flag flying and the batteaux lying in the river. And the music of the artillery filled me with solemn thoughts, for I thought of Lois and of Lana; and of Boyd, where he lay in his solitary grave under the frosty stars.

On the third of October, the army was in marching order once more; Colonel Shreve blew up the Tioga military works; the invalids, women and children, and some of the regiments went by batteaux; but we marched for Wyoming, passing through it on the tenth, and arriving at Easton on the fifteenth.

And I remember that, starved as we were, dusty, bloody with briers, and half naked, regiment after regiment halted, sent back for their wagons, combed out and tied their hair, and used the last precious cupfulls of flour to powder their polls, so that their heads, at least might make a military appearance as they marched through the stone-built town of Easton.

And so, with sprigs of green to cock their hats, well floured hair, and scarce a pair of breeches to a company, our rascals footed it proudly into Easton town, fifes squealing, drums rattling, and all the church bells and the artillery of the place clanging and booming out a welcome to the sorriest-clad army that ever entered a town since Falstaff hesitated to lead his naked rogues through Coventry.

Here the thanksgiving service was held; and Lord, how we did eat afterward! But for the rest or repose which any among us might have been innocent enough to suppose the army had earned, none was meted out. Nenny! For instead, marching orders awaited us, and sufficient clothing to cool our blushes; and off we marched to join His Excellency's army in the Highlands; for what with the new Spanish alliance and the arrival of the French fleet, matters were now stewing and trouble a-brewing for Sir Henry. They told us that His Excellency required pepper for the dose, therefore had he sent for us to mix us into the red-hot draught that Sir Henry and my Lord Cornwallis must presently prepare to swallow.

I had not had a letter or any word from Lois at Fort Tioga. At Easton there was a letter which, she wrote, might not reach me; but in it she said that they had taken lodgings in Albany near to the house of Lana Helmer; that Mr. Hake had been more than kind; that she and her dear mother awaited news of our army with tenderest anxiety, but that up to the moment of writing no news was to be had, not even any rumours.

Her letter told me little more, save that her mother and Mr. Hake had conferred concerning the estate of her late father; and that Mr. Hake was making preparations to substantiate her mother's claim to the small property of the family in France--a house, a tiny hamlet, and some vineyards, called by the family name of Contrecoeur, which meant her mother was her father's wedded wife.

"Also," she wrote, "my mother has told me that there are in the house some books and pictures and pretty joyeaux which were beloved by my father, and which he gave to her when she came to Contrecoeur, a bride. Also that her dot was still untouched, which, with her legal interest in my father's property, would suffice to properly endow me, and still leave sufficient to maintain her.

"So you see, Euan, that the half naked little gypsy of Poundridge camp comes not entirely shameless to her husband after all. Oh, my own soldier, hasten--hasten! Every day I hear drums in Albany streets and run out to see; every evening I sit with my mother on the stoop and watch the river redden in the sunset. Over the sandy plains of pines comes blowing the wind of the Western wilderness. I feel its breath on my cheek, faintly frosty, and wonder if the same wind had also touched your dear face ere it blew east to me."

Often I read this letter on the march to the Hudson; ever wondering at the history of this sweet mistress of my affections, marvelling at its mystery, its wonders, and eternally amazed at this young girl's courage, her loyalty and chaste devotion.

I remember one day when we were halted at a cavalry camp, not far from the Hudson, conversing with three soldiers--Van Campen, Perry, and Paul Sanborn, they being the three men who first discovered poor Boyd's body; and then noticed me a-digging in the earth with bleeding fingers and a broken blade.

And they knew the history of Lois, and how she had dressed her in rifle-dress, and how she had come to French Catharines. And they told me that in the cavalry camp there was talk of a young English girl, not yet sixteen, who had clipped her hair, tied it in a queue, powdered it, donned jack-boots, belt, and helmet, and come across the seas enlisted in a regiment of British Horse, with the vague idea of seeking her lover who had gone to America with his regiment.

Further, they told me that, until taken by our men in a skirmish, her own comrades had not suspected her sex; that she was a slim, boyish, pretty thing; that His Excellency had caused inquiry to be made; and that it had been discovered that her lover was serving in Sir John's regiment of Royal Greens.

This was a true story, it seemed; and that very morning His Excellency had sent her North to Haldimand with a flag, offering her every courtesy and civility and recommendation within his power.

Which pretty history left me very thoughtful, revealing as it did to me that my own heart's mistress was not the solitary and bright exception in a sex which, like other men, I had deemed inferior in every virile and mental virtue, and only spiritually superior to my own. And I remembered the proud position of social and political equality enjoyed by the women of the Long House; and vaguely thought it was possible that in this matter the Iroquois Confederacy was even more advanced in civilization than the white nations, who regarded its inhabitants as debased and brutal savages.

In three months I had seen an Empire crash to the ground; already in the prophetic and visionary eyes of our ragged soldiery, a mightier empire was beginning to crumble under the blasts from the blackened muzzles of our muskets. Soon kings would live only in the tales of yesterday, and the unending thunder of artillery would die away, and the clouds would break above the smoky field, revealing as our very own all we had battled for so long--the right to live our lives in freedom, self-respect, and happiness.

And I wondered whether generations not yet born would pay to us the noble tribute which the sons of the Long House so often and reverently offered to the dead who had made for them their League of Peace--alas! now shattered for all time.

And in my ears the deep responses seemed to sound, solemnly and low, as the uncorrupted priesthood chanted at Thendara:

> "Continue to listen,
> Thou who wert ruler,
> Ayonhwahtha!
> Continue to listen,
> Thou who wert ruler,
> Shatekariwate!
>   This was the roll of you,
> You who have laboured,
> You who completed
> The Great League!
>   Continue to listen,
> Thou who wert ruler,
> Sharenhaowane!
> Continue to listen,
> Thou who wert ruler--"

And the line of their noble hymn, the "Karenna": "I come again to greet and thank the women!"

Lord! A great and noble civilization died when the first cancerous contact of the lesser scratched its living Eastern Gate.

* "Hiya-thondek! Kahiaton. Kadi-kadon."

[* "Listen! It is written. Therefore, I speak."]

My commission as lieutenant in the 6th company of Morgan's Rifles afforded me only mixed emotions, but became pleasurable when I understood that staff duty as interpreter and chief of Indian guides permitted me to attach to my person not only Mayaro, the Mohican Sagamore, but also my Oneidas, Grey-Feather and Ta-hoontowhee.

Mounted service the two Oneidas abhorred, preferring to trot along on either side of me; but the Sagamore, being a Siwanois, was a horseman, and truly he presented a superb figure as the handsome General and his staff led the New York brigade into the city of Albany, our battered old drums thundering, our fifes awaking the echoes in the old Dutch city, and our pretty faded colors floating in the primrose light of early evening.

Right and left I glanced as we rode up the hilly street; and suddenly saw Lois! And so craned my head and twisted my neck and fidgeted that the General, who was sometimes humorous, and who was perfectly acquainted with my history, said to me that I had his permission to ride standing on my head if I liked, but for the sake of military decency he preferred that I dismount at once and make my manners otherwise to my affianced wife.

Which I lost no time in doing, not noticing that my Indians were following me, and drew bridle at the side-path and dismounted.

But where, in the purple evening light, Lois had been standing on her stoop, now there was nobody, though the front door was open wide. So I ran across the street between the passing ranks of Gansevoort's infantry, sprang up the steps, and entered the dusky house. Through the twilight of the polished hallway she came forward, caught me around the neck with a low cry, clung to me closer as I kissed her, holding to me in silence.

Outside, the racketting drums of a passing regiment filled the house with crashing echoes. When the noise had died away again, and the drums of the next regiment were still distant, she loosened her arms, whispering my name, and framing my face with her slim hands.

Then, out of the corner of my eye, I caught a glimpse of three tall and shadowy figures hovering in the doorway. Lois saw them, too, and stretched out one hand. One after another my three Indians came to her, bent their stately crests in silence, took her small hand, and laid it on their hearts.

"Shall I bid them to dine with us tomorrow?" she whispered.

"Bid them."

So she asked them a trifle shyly, and they thanked her gravely, turned one by one to take a silent leave of me, then went noiselessly out into the early dusk.

"Euan, my dear mother is awaiting you in our best room."

"I will instantly pay my duties and----"

"Lana is there also."

"Does she know?"

"Yes. God help her and the young thing she has taken to her heart. The news came by courier a week ago."

"How he died? Does she know?"

"Oh, Euan! Yes, we all know now!... I have scarce slept since I heard, thinking of you.... When you have paid your respects to my mother and to Lana, come quietly away with me again. Lana has been weeping--what with the distant music of the approaching regiments, and the memory of him who will come no more----"

"I understand."

She lifted her face to mine, laying her hands upon my shoulders.

"Dost thou truly love me, Lois?" I asked.

* "Sat-kah-tos," she murmured.

[* "Thou seest."]

* "Se-non-wes?" I insisted.

[* "Dost thou love?"]

* "Ke-non-wes, O Loskiel." Her arms tightened around my neck, "Ai-hai! Ae-saya-tyen-endon! Ae-sah-hah-i-yen-en-hon----"

[* "I love thee, O Loskiel... Ah, thou mightest have been destroyed! If thou hadst perished by the wayside----"]

"Hush, dearest--dearest maid. 'Twixt God and Tharon, nothing can harm us now."

And I heard the faint murmur of her lips on mine:

"Etho, ke-non-wes. Nothing can harm us now."

www.bookjungle.com *email: sales@bookjungle.com fax: 630-214-0564 mail: Book Jungle PO Box 2226 Champaign, IL 61825*

The Codes Of Hammurabi And Moses
W. W. Davies

QTY

The discovery of the Hammurabi Code is one of the greatest achievements of archaeology, and is of paramount interest, not only to the student of the Bible, but also to all those interested in ancient history...

Religion   **ISBN:** *1-59462-338-4*   **Pages:132**
MSRP $12.95

The Theory of Moral Sentiments
Adam Smith

QTY

This work from 1749. contains original theories of conscience amd moral judgment and it is the foundation for systemof morals.

Philosophy   ISBN: *1-59462-777-0*   **Pages:536**
MSRP $19.95

Jessica's First Prayer
Hesba Stretton

QTY

In a screened and secluded corner of one of the many railway-bridges which span the streets of London there could be seen a few years ago, from five o'clock every morning until half past eight, a tidily set-out coffee-stall, consisting of a trestle and board, upon which stood two large tin cans, with a small fire of charcoal burning under each so as to keep the coffee boiling during the early hours of the morning when the work-people were thronging into the city on their way to their daily toil...

Childrens   ISBN: *1-59462-373-2*   **Pages:84**
MSRP $9.95

My Life and Work
Henry Ford

QTY

Henry Ford revolutionized the world with his implementation of mass production for the Model T automobile. Gain valuable business insight into his life and work with his own auto-biography... "We have only started on our development of our country we have not as yet, with all our talk of wonderful progress, done more than scratch the surface. The progress has been wonderful enough but..."

Biographies/   ISBN: *1-59462-198-5*   **Pages:300**
MSRP $21.95

www.bookjungle.com *email: sales@bookjungle.com fax: 630-214-0564 mail: Book Jungle PO Box 2226 Champaign, IL 61825*

The Art of Cross-Examination
Francis Wellman

QTY

I presume it is the experience of every author, after his first book is published upon an important subject, to be almost overwhelmed with a wealth of ideas and illustrations which could readily have been included in his book, and which to his own mind, at least, seem to make a second edition inevitable. Such certainly was the case with me; and when the first edition had reached its sixth impression in five months, I rejoiced to learn that it seemed to my publishers that the book had met with a sufficiently favorable reception to justify a second and considerably enlarged edition. ..

Reference   **ISBN:** *1-59462-647-2*

Pages:412

MSRP $19.95

On the Duty of Civil Disobedience
Henry David Thoreau

QTY

Thoreau wrote his famous essay, On the Duty of Civil Disobedience, as a protest against an unjust but popular war and the immoral but popular institution of slave-owning. He did more than write—he declined to pay his taxes,   and was hauled off to gaol in consequence. Who can say how much this refusal of his hastened the end of the war and of slavery ?

Law   **ISBN:** *1-59462-747-9*

Pages:48

MSRP $7.45

Dream Psychology Psychoanalysis for Beginners
Sigmund Freud

QTY

Sigmund Freud, born Sigismund Schlomo Freud (May 6, 1856 - September 23, 1939), was a Jewish-Austrian neurologist and psychiatrist who co-founded the psychoanalytic school of psychology. Freud is best known for his theories of the unconscious mind, especially involving the mechanism of repression; his redefinition of sexual desire as mobile and directed towards a wide variety of objects; and his therapeutic techniques, especially his understanding of transference in the therapeutic relationship and the presumed value of dreams as sources of insight into unconscious desires.

Psychology   **ISBN:** *1-59462-905-6*

Pages:196

MSRP $15.45

The Miracle of Right Thought
Orison Swett Marden

QTY

Believe with all of your heart that you will do what you were made to do. When the mind has once formed the habit of holding cheerful, happy, prosperous pictures, it will not be easy to form the opposite habit. It does not matter how improbable or how far away this realization may see, or how dark the prospects may be, if we visualize them as best we can, as vividly as possible, hold tenaciously to them and vigorously struggle to attain them, they will gradually become actualized, realized in the life. But a desire, a longing without endeavor, a yearning abandoned or held indifferently will vanish without realization.

Pages:360

Self Help   **ISBN:** *1-59462-644-8*

MSRP $25.45

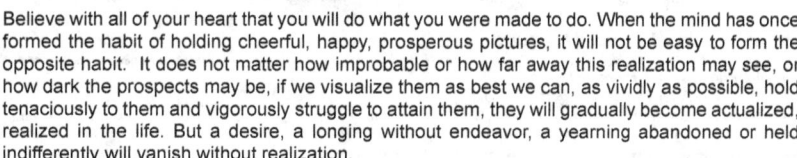

www.bookjungle.com *email: sales@bookjungle.com fax: 630-214-0564 mail: Book Jungle PO Box 2226 Champaign, IL 61825*

QTY

The Rosicrucian Cosmo-Conception Mystic Christianity *by Max Heindel*   ISBN: *1-59462-188-8* **$38.95**
The Rosicrucian Cosmo-conception is not dogmatic, neither does it appeal to any other authority than the reason of the student. It is: not controversial, but is: sent forth in the, hope that it may help to clear...   New Age/Religion Pages 646

Abandonment To Divine Providence *by Jean-Pierre de Caussade*   ISBN: *1-59462-228-0* **$25.95**
"The Rev. Jean Pierre de Caussade was one of the most remarkable spiritual writers of the Society of Jesus in France in the 18th Century. His death took place at Toulouse in 1751. His works have gone through many editions and have been republished...   Inspirational/Religion Pages 400

Mental Chemistry *by Charles Haanel*   ISBN: *1-59462-192-6* **$23.95**
Mental Chemistry allows the change of material conditions by combining and appropriately utilizing the power of the mind. Much like applied chemistry creates something new and unique out of careful combinations of chemicals the mastery of mental chemistry...   New Age Pages 354

The Letters of Robert Browning and Elizabeth Barret Barrett 1845-1846 vol II   ISBN: *1-59462-193-4* **$35.95**
by Robert Browning and Elizabeth Barrett   Biographies Pages 596

Gleanings In Genesis (volume I) *by Arthur W. Pink*   ISBN: *1-59462-130-6* **$27.45**
Appropriately has Genesis been termed "the seed plot of the Bible" for in it we have, in germ form, almost all of the great doctrines which are afterwards fully developed in the books of Scripture which follow...   Religion/Inspirational Pages 420

The Master Key *by L. W. de Laurence*   ISBN: *1-59462-001-6* **$30.95**
In no branch of human knowledge has there been a more lively increase of the spirit of research during the past few years than in the study of Psychology, Concentration and Mental Discipline. The requests for authentic lessons in Thought Control, Mental Discipline and...   New Age/Business Pages 422

The Lesser Key Of Solomon Goetia *by L. W. de Laurence*   ISBN: *1-59462-092-X* **$9.95**
This translation of the first book of the "Lernegton" which is now for the first time made accessible to students of Talismanic Magic was done, after careful collation and edition, from numerous Ancient Manuscripts in Hebrew, Latin, and French...   New Age/Occult Pages 92

Rubaiyat Of Omar Khayyam *by Edward Fitzgerald*   ISBN:*1-59462-332-5* **$13.95**
Edward Fitzgerald, whom the world has already learned, in spite of his own efforts to remain within the shadow of anonymity, to look upon as one of the rarest poets of the century, was born at Bredfield, in Suffolk, on the 31st of March, 1809. He was the third son of John Purcell...   Music Pages 172

Ancient Law *by Henry Maine*   ISBN: *1-59462-128-4* **$29.95**
The chief object of the following pages is to indicate some of the earliest ideas of mankind, as they are reflected in Ancient Law, and to point out the relation of those ideas to modern thought.   Religiom/History Pages 452

Far-Away Stories *by William J. Locke*   ISBN: *1-59462-129-2* **$19.45**
"Good wine needs no bush, but a collection of mixed vintages does. And this book is just such a collection. Some of the stories I do not want to remain buried for ever in the museum files of dead magazine-numbers an author's not unpardonable vanity..."   Fiction Pages 272

Life of David Crockett *by David Crockett*   ISBN: *1-59462-250-7* **$27.45**
"Colonel David Crockett was one of the most remarkable men of the times in which he lived. Born in humble life, but gifted with a strong will, an indomitable courage, and unremitting perseverance...   Biographies/New Age Pages 424

Lip-Reading *by Edward Nitchie*   ISBN: *1-59462-206-X* **$25.95**
Edward B. Nitchie, founder of the New York School for the Hard of Hearing, now the Nitchie School of Lip-Reading, Inc, wrote "LIP-READING Principles and Practice". The development and perfecting of this meritorious work on lip-reading was an undertaking...   How-to Pages 400

A Handbook of Suggestive Therapeutics, Applied Hypnotism, Psychic Science   ISBN: *1-59462-214-0* **$24.95**
by Henry Munro   Health/New Age/Health/Self-help Pages 376

A Doll's House: and Two Other Plays *by Henrik Ibsen*   ISBN: *1-59462-112-8* **$19.95**
Henrik Ibsen created this classic when in revolutionary 1848 Rome. Introducing some striking concepts in playwriting for the realist genre, this play has been studied the world over.   Fiction/Classics/Plays 308

The Light of Asia *by sir Edwin Arnold*   ISBN: *1-59462-204-3* **$13.95**
In this poetic masterpiece, Edwin Arnold describes the life and teachings of Buddha. The man who was to become known as Buddha to the world was born as Prince Gautama of India but he rejected the worldly riches and abandoned the reigns of power when...   Religion/History/Biographies Pages 170

The Complete Works of Guy de Maupassant *by Guy de Maupassant*   ISBN: *1-59462-157-8* **$16.95**
"For days and days, nights and nights, I had dreamed of that first kiss which was to consecrate our engagement, and I knew not on what spot I should put my lips..."   Fiction/Classics Pages 240

The Art of Cross-Examination *by Francis L. Wellman*   ISBN: *1-59462-309-0* **$26.95**
Written by a renowned trial lawyer, Wellman imparts his experience and uses case studies to explain how to use psychology to extract desired information through questioning.   How-to/Science/Reference Pages 408

Answered or Unanswered? *by Louisa Vaughan*   ISBN: *1-59462-248-5* **$10.95**
Miracles of Faith in China   Religion Pages 112

The Edinburgh Lectures on Mental Science (1909) *by Thomas*   ISBN: *1-59462-008-3* **$11.95**
This book contains the substance of a course of lectures recently given by the writer in the Queen Street Hall, Edinburgh. Its purpose is to indicate the Natural Principles governing the relation between Mental Action and Material Conditions...   New Age/Psychology Pages 148

Ayesha *by H. Rider Haggard*   ISBN: *1-59462-301-5* **$24.95**
Verily and indeed it is the unexpected that happens! Probably if there was one person upon the earth from whom the Editor of this, and of a certain previous history, did not expect to hear again...   Classics Pages 380

Ayala's Angel *by Anthony Trollope*   ISBN: *1-59462-352-X* **$29.95**
The two girls were both pretty, but Lucy who was twenty-one who supposed to be simple and comparatively unattractive, whereas Ayala was credited, as her Bombwhat romantic name might show, with poetic charm and a taste for romance. Ayala when her father died was nineteen...   Fiction Pages 484

The American Commonwealth *by James Bryce*   ISBN: *1-59462-286-8* **$34.45**
An interpretation of American democratic political theory. It examines political mechanics and society from the perspective of Scotsman James Bryce   Politics Pages 572

Stories of the Pilgrims *by Margaret P. Pumphrey*   ISBN: *1-59462-116-0* **$17.95**
This book explores pilgrims religious oppression in England as well as their escape to Holland and eventual crossing to America on the Mayflower, and their early days in New England...   History Pages 268

www.bookjungle.com *email: sales@bookjungle.com fax: 630-214-0564 mail: Book Jungle PO Box 2226 Champaign, IL 61825*

QTY

The Fasting Cure *by Sinclair Upton*   ISBN: *1-59462-222-1*   **$13.95**
In the Cosmopolitan Magazine for May, 1910, and in the Contemporary Review (London) for April, 1910, I published an article dealing with my experiences in fasting. I have written a great many magazine articles, but never one which attracted so much attention... New Age/Self Help/Health Pages 164

Hebrew Astrology *by Sepharial*   ISBN: *1-59462-308-2*   **$13.45**
In these days of advanced thinking it is a matter of common observation that we have left many of the old landmarks behind and that we are now pressing forward to greater heights and to a wider horizon than that which represented the mind-content of our progenitors... Astrology Pages 144

Thought Vibration or The Law of Attraction in the Thought World   ISBN: *1-59462-127-6*   **$12.95**
by William Walker Atkinson   Psychology/Religion Pages 144

Optimism *by Helen Keller*   ISBN: *1-59462-108-X*   **$15.95**
Helen Keller was blind, deaf, and mute since 19 months old, yet famously learned how to overcome these handicaps, communicate with the world, and spread her lectures promoting optimism. An inspiring read for everyone... Biographies/Inspirational Pages 84

Sara Crewe *by Frances Burnett*   ISBN: *1-59462-360-0*   **$9.45**
In the first place, Miss Minchin lived in London. Her home was a large, dull, tall one, in a large, dull square, where all the houses were alike, and all the sparrows were alike, and where all the door-knockers made the same heavy sound... Childrens/Classic Pages 88

The Autobiography of Benjamin Franklin *by Benjamin Franklin*   ISBN: *1-59462-135-7*   **$24.95**
The Autobiography of Benjamin Franklin has probably been more extensively read than any other American historical work, and no other book of its kind has had such ups and downs of fortune. Franklin lived for many years in England, where he was agent... Biographies/History Pages 332

Name	
Email	
Telephone	
Address	
City, State ZIP	

☐ **Credit Card**   ☐ **Check / Money Order**

Credit Card Number	
Expiration Date	
Signature	

Please Mail to: Book Jungle
PO Box 2226
Champaign, IL 61825
or Fax to: 630-214-0564

ORDERING INFORMATION

web: *www.bookjungle.com*
email: *sales@bookjungle.com*
fax: *630-214-0564*
mail: *Book Jungle PO Box 2226 Champaign, IL 61825*
or PayPal *to sales@bookjungle.com*

Please contact us for bulk discounts

DIRECT-ORDER TERMS

**20% Discount if You Order
Two or More Books**
Free Domestic Shipping!
Accepted: Master Card, Visa,
Discover, American Express

www.ingramcontent.com/pod-product-compliance
Lightning Source LLC
Chambersburg PA
CBHW081140020726
47504CB00009B/1936